MASTER PIECE

ANDY DANE NYE

ARTAVIA
PUBLISHING

Copyright © Andy Dane Nye 2019

First published in 2019 by Artavia Publishing

1 3 5 7 9 10 8 6 4 2

The right of Andy Dane Nye to be identified as the author of this work
has been asserted by him in accordance with the Copyright, Designs and
Patents Act, 1988.

A CIP catalogue record for this book is available from the British Library.

ISBN 978 1 913351 00 7

Typeset in Crimson Text by Google Fonts

Printed and bound in Great Britain by Clays Ltd, Elcograf S.p.A.

Cover design © Artavia Publishing 2019

Cover background image: The Crab Nebula, combining data from almost
the entire electromagnetic spectrum, courtesy of:
NASA, ESA, G. Dubner (IAFE, CONICET-University of Buenos Aires) et
al.; A. Loll et al.; T. Temim et al.; F. Seward et al.;
VLA/NRAO/AUI/NSF; Chandra/CXC; Spitzer/JPL-Caltech; XMM-
Newton/ESA; and Hubble/STScI

Artavia Publishing's policy is to use papers that are natural, renewable and
recyclable products and made from wood grown in sustainable forests.
The logging and manufacturing processes are expected to conform to the
environmental regulations of the country of origin.

As "we're all in this together"…
If you've enjoyed reading this book and think others might too, please would you be so kind as to shout the fact on social media. All authors need as much help… and love… as they can get. *Especially* new ones! Thank you!

Interested in finding out more about what goes on in the author's head?

Visit

www.andydanenye.com

for various "things"… including subscribing to a mailing list, so that you can be the first to know what he's up to.

Pssst…

'I mean... there must be a reason for our existence.'

'There is,' said Shepherd Two. 'It's to look after the sheep.'

'But... have you ever wondered why *they're* here?'

'To give us something to do?' suggested Shepherd Two.

Shepherd One considered the idea. 'I never thought of that,' he said.

There was half an hour of silence.

'Tumbleweed!' shouted Shepherd Three.

Four weeks later, in a dilapidated house – beneath framed pictures of ironing boards – a man in a tin hat and neck brace began writing the most amazing plays.

THE END... perhaps

Norman's face quivered.

Gabriel acknowledged the tiny vibrations with a nod of appreciation.

'Here...' Norman offered up the chequebook. 'I believe this is yours.'

'You're forgetting something,' said Gabriel. 'I don't do solids. You'll just have to hang onto it yourself. I'm sure you'll be able to put it to good use.'

Norman's jaw dropped even lower than it had when he'd first encountered the Archangel.

His hand started shaking as he absorbed the implications of the gift. 'But...'

Suddenly words were inadequate. Not that it mattered. His brain was whirling so fast, any would have simply been tripped up by his thoughts.

'It's only money,' said Gabriel. 'It can't buy you a place in Heaven.'

'Then... given I'm gonna have to find myself some new accommodation, I'll settle for a place in the country,' Norman finally managed, 'and promise to work hard on the other!' He exhaled the rush of adrenalin that had made him feel like he'd grown his *own* set of wings. 'But first... I'm gonna travel!' His eyes widened. 'There's so much I need to catch up on, now I appreciate how precious every day is! I could get to see all those fantastic works of art by people like Michelangelo and Leonardo da Vinci... those artists who were inspired *before* the sphere of knowledge ever existed! How fantastic would *that* be!'

'Then you will,' promised Gabriel. 'Remember... there is power in positive thinking.'

'I certainly hope so,' Norman smiled mischievously. 'Because, before all that... I think I'm gonna enquire about getting my teeth fixed!'

'Ever wondered why we're here?' asked Shepherd One, surveying the barren landscape.

'What do you mean?' enquired Shepherd Three, two hours later.

soon as we'd dropped you off. But I insisted on getting this chequebook back to you. So Stump took off and landed in the garden of a private residence a little further on. It was such a massive house, we didn't fink anyone would mind. But this grey haired lady in a green headscarf has threatened to set her corgis on him if he doesn't move on!'

'Thank you for your honesty,' said Norman, taking the chequebook from her outstretched hand.

'No...' said Xanthia, keeping it there. 'Thank you for *yours*. You're the first person who hasn't tried to take advantage of me... even when I was offered to them on a plate. That makes you very special, Norman Penkridge.' She lent forward and gave him a gentle kiss on the cheek.

'Stump's a lucky man,' blushed Norman, trying hard to remain standing.

'Not for long,' she pouted. 'I can't believe he did what he did with that smelly, red man. I don't fink I want to be with him now.' She fumbled awkwardly in a small, silver, sequinned handbag and handed Norman a piece of paper, looking hurriedly away. 'I've written my mobile number down for you... just in case you want to call me.'

Norman was suddenly aware of his heartbeat pounding in his ears... which was ironic, given he could no longer believe what he was hearing.

'I know the name of a good ornithologist,' she added.

'She means *orthodontist*,' whispered Gabriel.

'I thought you might like to get in touch sometime so that I can give you their details.' With that... she turned and teetered away.

'Interesting soul,' observed Gabriel.

'Interesting *angle*,' replied Norman, mouth agape.

Gabriel let out an uncharacteristic sigh. 'Well... I guess this is it, Norman. I'll never quite view mortals the same way again. It's been an experience... and you... quite a challenge!'

Norman felt as if a hand had just reached inside and pulled the rug from under his emotions. 'I won't be seeing you again?'

'Perhaps in paintings,' Gabriel smiled.

'I feel a sense of *déjà vu*,' Gabriel sighed.

'When I looked into the future... I saw *myself* becoming the new Saviour.'

'Whilst there is only one future, it has many angles from which it can be viewed,' explained Gabriel. 'That is why things are not always what they seem. But when it comes to angles... my best advice is to always view it from a positive one.'

'Well... I wish I'd understood about those angles when I was younger,' said Norman wistfully.

'You're keeping something from me,' said Gabriel, sensing a change in his vibration.

'It's nothing,' sighed Norman.

'Oh... I think she means *everything*... to you, at least.'

Norman looked sheepish. 'I took the opportunity to look at something else in my future,' he admitted.

'I assumed you might.'

'I saw myself with Xanthia. We were together... and there were children... But... I guess I must've been looking from the wrong angle.' Norman's shoulders dropped.

'It's a bit of a *pencil* moment,' said Gabriel, 'but there is no such thing as a *wrong* angle.' He acknowledged a figure teetering towards them on stiletto heels. 'It's just a question of *believing* you've found the right one.'

'Pooey!' shouted the figure... waving her hand so vigorously, her halter top was in danger of failing to do its job. 'Sorry,' she said breathlessly, as she reached him. 'I mean... *Norman*... You left this behind.' She held out his chequebook. 'It's not the sort of fing you ought to leave lying around, you know.' She looked at the smouldering remains of 66 Armageddon Terrace... and then at the firemen, fire appliances, flashing blue lights, ladders and hoses. 'Has there been a fire?' she asked.

What astute perception, drooled Norman.

'I can't stay long,' said Xanthia. 'Stump wants to get airborne as soon as possible. He's having a bit of trouble with the locals.'

'I told him they wouldn't want him landing in the park,' said Norman.

'You're right,' said Xanthia. 'The police tried to arrest us as

'What is?'

'The painting. It's been destroyed... along with our chances of resurrecting the sphere.'

'*Destroyed?*'

'Don't ask,' said Gabriel, shaking his head.

Norman looked at him incredulously. 'So... what happens now? Do we all just wait to die?'

'You're forgetting, Norman... if the Universe ceases to exist, death won't even be an option!'

'Then... *what?*'

'I suggest prayer might be the best place to start. It seems to have suddenly become extremely fashionable. We've witnessed an enormous change in attitude throughout the world in recent days. People have finally begun to realise that materialism is a false prophet... no pun intended. They've started looking inward for answers to fill the void caused by its collapse, wondering if an investment of time and effort might be better spent on their souls. Such ripples in the thinking of man can only have positive results. The cult of *self* has been dealt a serious blow. If the human race manages to realise it can *share* its faith... the danger that prompted our quest will not be so imminent and, who knows... might even disappear altogether.'

'But is that likely? Surely there are some whose attitudes are too entrenched to embrace such a change?'

'You have proved that is not the case. If a soul like Stump's can be pulled from the abyss, there is hope for us all! And we will have two powerful allies to assist us in inspiring similarly wayward souls... art and music. For there will be a welcome side-effect to the sphere of knowledge shattering into so many pieces again. Its vibrations having been dispersed into the ether... the Earth is in for a golden period of intense artistic creativity! As the Universal spirit is recaptured and displayed for new generations to behold, its glory may yet inspire and save the world. In this modern world of mass-communication, perhaps the new Saviour will be all of mankind itself!'

'Maybe,' said Norman, scratching his head. 'But there's something I don't understand.'

5

'You haven't any wings!'

'Of course not,' said Gabriel. 'That would look ridiculous.'

Norman let out a long sigh. 'We failed, didn't we?'

'Yes... we did,' confirmed Gabriel. 'As is evident from the fact you've had to ask. The sphere of knowledge shattered before it could be transferred to you.'

'We could try again,' suggested Norman, his face lighting up as a thought suddenly struck him. 'This needn't be the end of it!'

Gabriel smiled weakly. 'It would be impossible to gather all those works of art for a second time, now that our mission has been so heavily compromised.'

'But that's just it!' said Norman excitedly. 'We don't have to!'

'The data on your computers could not have withstood the explosion,' said Gabriel. 'That's the trouble with the material plane. It means it is now lost.'

'The data on *my* computers might be... But what about the copies of it I uploaded to those on the internet... my virtual super-computer? That stuff's still out there... distributed all around the world. All we have to do is build another system and reactivate it!'

Gabriel's expression changed. 'You mean... it's *all* there?'

'Yes...! Well... all except the encoding I got Spikey to bounce up and down to. But that was only one painting. I'm sure it wouldn't be too difficult to get hold of just that one again.'

'I suppose not,' said Gabriel, his face beginning to glow. 'Which painting do you require?'

'That's easy to work out,' said Norman. 'I thought it would be fitting to have Spikey end the project... so I gave him the last encoding... before we realised we needed Stump's *Sex Wench*, of course.'

'And that was?'

'The very last painting to be delivered... The Turner.'

Gabriel bowed his head. 'Fate has danced cruelly,' he said.

'No... we're alright,' insisted Norman. 'It wasn't one of those paintings in danger of being withheld. In fact... it couldn't be easier. I believe it came from a gallery here in London!'

'I know,' said Gabriel quietly. '*That's* the problem.'

this ever happened.'

'AH!' cried Donald. 'OUR FRIENDS FROM ACROSS THE WATER! Well... at least I can take comfort in knowing that you failed in whatever it was you intended doing... and – ironically – had one of you been less sceptical, you might've succeeded!'

'I'm not sure how you did it,' whispered Chad. 'But I'll eventually work it out... just like I did the lights in the temple.'

'YES... IT'S HIM!' yelled Donald. 'WHAT...? ALRIGHT... I'LL PASS IT ON!' As Donald was placed inside the ambulance, he peered across the bridge of his nose at Chad. 'Whitebait says he has a message for the one who thinks he's smart.' His singed eyebrows raised a little. 'IS *THAT* IT...? You'll have to excuse the fishing metaphor... he used to be a trawlerman. BEWARE OF RELYING ON LOGIC... BECAUSE A HERRING STILL RESEMBLES A HERRING, EVEN WHEN IT'S RED.'

'What's that supposed to mean?' asked Chad, as the ambulance doors shut.

'I don't know,' shouted Donald through them. 'But it makes a change from Shakespeare!'

'I guess that's that, then,' said the figure standing next to Norman. He'd been watching the clearing up in silence, his head covered by the hood of his coat.

'In more ways than you'll ever know,' said Norman despondently.

'Cheer up,' said the figure. 'There's always tomorrow!'

I wouldn't be so sure, thought Norman to himself.

'That's true, I suppose,' said the figure. 'But we can hope. And while there's hope, there's positive energy sending out its ripples.'

Startled... Norman turned and gazed at the figure beside him. '*Gabriel?*'

'Not so loud,' said the Archangel. 'It's been a very busy day and I couldn't face the thought of any more role-playing.'

'But... you look different!'

'Just the way you expected me to.'

around its base.'

His colleague tilted his head. 'Are you sure they're not ostriches?'

As the hose was unclipped from the fire engine, Oppenheimer came running over.

'You men are not leaving, are you?' he asked agitatedly.

'Everything's damped down, sir. We've done all we need to.'

'But what about my mother?'

'What about her?'

'She's still in the building!'

The fireman shot a concerned glance at his colleague. 'We didn't find anybody in there,' he said.

'She was upstairs. She didn't come out!'

'Get the chief on the radio,' whispered the fireman to his colleague through the side of his mouth. 'We might have missed a body.'

'She's dead!' yelled Oppenheimer.

'Whoa, sir... I was just using a figure of speech.'

'No... she really is... She's dead!'

'You don't know that for sure, now, do you, sir?'

'Yes I do!' exclaimed Oppenheimer. 'I watched her being buried in 1953!'

The fireman took a few moments to reflect on the situation. 'You wouldn't know anything about a large cock and balls... would you?' he asked suspiciously.

A large crowd of onlookers watched as Donald was carefully placed on a stretcher, his body strapped to a latticework of splints.

'WHAT DO YOU MEAN... *WE'RE* LUCKY TO BE ALIVE? *YOU'RE* DEAD!' he shouted, trying to twist his body to the left.

'He's delirious,' voiced the paramedic. 'Must be the blow to the back of his head.'

'He doesn't have a head!' objected Donald, 'He's bloody well inside *mine!*'

Someone squeezed his arm.

'Remember, Donald,' a voice whispered. 'You forget any of

8

supply switch.

'NO!' screamed Norman, rushing towards him.

Boi...

It was just as the sphere of knowledge was about to be transferred to its distracted recipient, that a change occurred in its behaviour.

Its blue, vein-like innards began pulsating wildly... violent discharges emanating from its unstable surface.

'I think it's going to blow!' exclaimed Gabriel from the room above, holding his hands to his head in horror.

A dishevelled face appeared at the window.

'Are you in there?' asked Donald, from atop the truck's roof.

As the ball of vibrations exploded, a large chunk of it sent him flying backwards into the street.

*   *   *

'It was obvious from the minute we set foot in the basement that it had been started deliberately,' said the fireman to his colleague winding up the hose. 'The accelerant had been poured on the carpet in the shape of a large cock and balls!'

'I've just seen the police cart away the young lad who lived there,' returned his colleague. 'He was telling them the Devil had instructed him to do it!'

'That old chestnut! You know what always amazes me about those pyromaniacal nutters...? Surely they'd think that if the Prince of Darkness ever bothered to appear on Earth and demand such a thing of 'em, it would be to sabotage a building of slightly more importance than a shabby collection of bedsits off the Bayswater Road!' He shook his head and stepped over the charred remains of a large wooden object that had been dragged from the hall of the building.

'What was *that* in a previous life?' asked his colleague, pointing at it.

'Dunno... But it looks like it once had baby seals carved

'We can use this truck!' shouted Donald, looking through the driver's window and seeing its keys still in the ignition. 'If we get it below your window, you'll be able to climb out onto its roof!'

'Just do it!' yelled Norman, the seat of his pants beginning to feel uncomfortably warm.

But it wasn't the flames that were responsible.

A bright, neon-blue light had materialised in the room... fingers of lightning-like static criss-crossing its pulsating interior.

'It's working!' announced Gabriel. 'The master vibration is coming together!'

As it grew stronger and larger in size, the smoke and flames in the room found themselves squeezed out and back through the door.

Seizing his chance, Norman bolted from the window and followed their retreat down the stairs.

Reaching Oppenheimer's door, he noticed it was closed... the heat in the hall having been so intense it had melted the tip of the letter *b*, causing it to bend over.

'Are you in there?' he yelled, knocking frantically.

There was no reply.

'Mister Oppenheimer! Are you alright?'

Ignoring the chaotic swirls of light that were now focusing in on him, Norman took a few paces back... then charged the door with his foot extended.

As he crashed through it, he saw Oppenheimer standing at the open cupboard housing the electricity meter... his eyes staring manically at the rotating dial.

'Nine!' he yelled.

'I didn't think you were,' said Norman, in response.

'Not *nein*... Nine!'

'What?'

'Hippopotami! I warned you, Penkridge! You stole my Lotty from me... and now you've stolen my mutter. But I'll be damned if I'll let you steal my *electricity!*'

With that... he reached up and grabbed hold of the mains

10

'But if it's you… you'll never have what you told me you most desired,' said the Devil, panic beginning to infiltrate his voice. 'If you strike that key, you'll never *belong!* You will be ridiculed… You will be ostracised… and worse… you will be targeted… forever living in danger. You will be vilified by those who think you a fraud and a blasphemer. The religious market place has become too crowded!'

'True,' smiled Norman. 'But look on the bright side… At least, for once in my life, I'll have all the answers!' He brought his hand crashing down on the keyboard.

Boing.

Spikey appeared and began to bounce.

'Hold on tight!' warned Gabriel.

'If it's all the same to you,' coughed Norman, heading for the door. 'I'm getting outta here!'

As he attempted to open the door, the heat from the metal handle burnt his hand. Removing his suit jacket, he used it as a glove and tried again.

As he succeeded, a blast of hot air shot into the room… an accompanying wall of flames forcing him backwards.

'The window!' said Gabriel. 'You must summon help!'

There was so much smoke in the room, Norman was finding it difficult to see and breathe. He dropped to the floor to inhale the less acrid air.

He could hear Spikey bouncing away to his right. Using the noise as a directional beacon, he crawled his way to where he knew the window to be.

Opening it, he stuck his head out. 'Someone get a ladder!'

'Where from?' yelled Donald, having awoken from his felling.

'I don't know!' screamed Norman. 'Try the local hardware store!'

'They've closed down,' said a passer-by, who'd stopped to observe the inferno.

'I don't believe it!' cried Norman.

'I know,' said the passer-by. 'They were doing half litres of emulsion at twenty percent discount!'

11

ways than you could ever imagine!'

'We're running out of time,' said Gabriel, pointing at the carpet of smoke now billowing under the door.

'We certainly are,' agreed the Devil. 'This Universe is coming to an end... and with it... the suffering I've had to endure for millennia!'

'What suffering?' scoffed Norman. 'You're the root of it all. You encourage the negative side of every vibration. You've admitted as much yourself!'

'Oh... I've *suffered*,' said the Devil. 'You and I have much in common, Norman. We have *both* been made outsiders... and felt the pain of it. And if you allow the sphere of knowledge to be completed, you will become the greatest outsider of all!'

'The fire, Norman!' said Gabriel. 'He's trying to distract you!'

'No!' shouted the Devil. 'It is *you* who wishes to distract him! Ask me the question you're dying to ask, Norman! Ask me how the spiritual paradox was resolved! How could your lowly soul be given such privileged information without breaking the rules of Heaven?'

'No!' cried Norman, the smoke beginning to sting his eyes. 'You've failed!'

'ASK ME!'

'I don't need to!' shouted Norman. 'I already know the answer! They're going to drop the sphere of knowledge on *me!* That way, what I have already learnt will become an irrelevance!'

Gabriel looked shocked.

'I took a peek into the future,' Norman answered his embarrassed stare. 'When I was floating in eternity. You said that everything that would ever be was also in front of me. So... when I realised I could conjure up images of whatever I thought about... I thought about my future. I was curious to see what happened. You know me... I couldn't help myself! That's when I knew I was to be the new Saviour.'

'I'm sorry,' said Gabriel. 'We could think of no other way.'

'It's alright... *someone's* got to do it.' Norman clenched his raised hand into a fist.

'It must be Lucifer's work. I can feel him near.'

'Then let's set these vibrations in motion and get ourselves outta here!' exclaimed Norman, typing a series of commands into the Ark's console so furiously, his fingers were in danger of tying themselves in knots. When he was done, he ran across to his bed. 'It'll take a few minutes for every computer to respond,' he said, as the first wisp of smoke announced itself under the door. 'Then I'll unleash Spikey!'

'We must hurry!' said Gabriel. 'I never realised what a nuisance this *time* thing could be!'

'Wait 'til you see what flames can do!' said Norman, slipping on his protective footwear and rushing back to the console. 'Right...! We're almost there!'

As he raised his hand above the keyboard, a green, foul-smelling mist blasted into the room.

'You'd better get out of here!' bellowed the Devil, stepping from it. 'There's no advantage to be gained if you save the Universe but end up removing yourself from it in the process.'

'I don't do selfish anymore, remember?' said Norman. 'And now it's *you* who are too late!' He waved his raised hand defiantly. 'You're just a few seconds away from witnessing your own defeat! Enjoy!'

'But what about the spiritual paradox?' said the Devil.

'I don't have time for your games,' said Norman. 'It's pathetic. You're just trying to delay me. I can see right through your tactics.'

'But have you seen through Gabriel's...? Haven't you ever wondered how the spiritual paradox you created by demanding answers way above you soul's level was so easily resolved...? How a dilemma that you were told once threatened the entire fabric of the Universe simply *disappeared?*'

'I didn't need to know,' said Norman, looking at Gabriel.

'That doesn't sound like the old Norman Penkridge to me,' taunted the Devil. 'He would've *demanded* to know!'

'I don't want to be the old me,' said Norman.

'Well... how convenient for them,' sneered the Devil. 'Because, if you send that final command, you'll change in more

The tenant of 66a – the basement flat – had just finished a rather interesting period of internet surfing and had decided to round it off with a spot of devil worship. This usually involved him sitting in a pentagram in front of the gas fire and reciting some words from an Aleister Crowley novel. Nothing had ever happened... but it made him feel important... and he lived in hope.

He was in for a bit of a shock.

As he sat there cross-legged – his upturned hands resting on his knees – a strange odour began to invade the room. He stopped his incanting and opened his eyes.

A two-legged form – standing beside his pile of top-shelf magazines – greeted them.

'Beelzebub?' he croaked.

'Amongst other names,' said the Devil. 'But you can call me *Master*.'

66a's tenant panicked. He'd never got this far. For the life of him, he couldn't recall what it was he was supposed to do next. He'd been summoning the Devil for so long, he'd actually forgotten why.

'What is it you command of me, Oh Master?' he ventured... having heard it said once in a film.

'That's easy,' snarled the Devil. 'I want you to burn this building down.'

By the time Norman had completed his file upload, the smell of smoke was beginning to climb the stairs.

Oblivious to the danger, Oppenheimer had shut himself in his room and was pacing around it in ever decreasing circles, muttering to himself about family loyalty.

'Are we ready to go?' asked Gabriel anxiously.

'I just need to put my plimsolls on,' said Norman, looking around the room and sniffing the air. 'Can you smell that?'

'I don't do smell,' said Gabriel. 'But I assume you're referring to the fact the building's on fire.'

'What!'

14

from beyond Oppenheimer's open door, the landlord still trying to summon his mother.

'Mister Oppenheimer… are you alright?'

As the question was asked, a ball of orange light appeared behind Norman.

The sobbing ceased. 'Is that you, Penkridge?'

'Yes… and I was asking if everything was alright.'

'It is better than alright,' came a reply, bound with schizophrenic restraint. 'There is a man with a gun… and he is going to kill you with it… and that will remove all my problems… if you discount the bin men.'

'We must leave him,' said Gabriel softly. 'His vibrations feel extremely jumbled.'

'Mother?' sung out Oppenheimer. 'Is that you?'

'Oh no,' sighed Gabriel. 'Here we go again.'

Oppenheimer's tear-stained face appeared at the door, the years falling from it as he gazed upon Gabriel. 'Mutter!' he simpered. 'Ich bin dein Sohn, Joseph!'

Gabriel smiled back and edged up the stairs behind Norman.

'Mutter… why are you going with him? He is a very bad boy. He broke Uncle Helmut's hat stand!'

'I know, dear,' smiled Gabriel, sympathetically. 'I'll have words.'

'But, Mutter…! Lotty did the same and I never saw her again!'

'She wasn't right for you,' said Gabriel, feeling an urge to extend his role playing.

'Gabriel!' hissed Norman. 'Let's go!'

'Mutter!' screamed Oppenheimer, as the two disappeared up the stairs.

'Whatever you have to do, just do it quickly!' said Gabriel, as Norman closed the door to his bedsit. 'I fear I've been vibrating on the Earth plane far too long!'

'I just have to send the code for *Sex Wench* to a computer on the internet,' said Norman, sitting himself in front of the Ark's control panel. 'I've already converted the song. It'll only take a couple of minutes.'

As he spoke, their attention was drawn to a suited figure stumbling its way along the street.

'Hello, Norman!' Trevor greeted it. 'Looks like you're in something of a hurry!'

Norman would have returned the greeting had he not had more pressing things on his mind... or indeed, possessed the air in his lungs with which to do it.

'I'm just off to do battle,' said Trevor, in his customary, measured, back-of-the-throat voice.

'Anyone I know?' spluttered Norman, struggling for breath.

'The enemies of God,' answered Trevor chirpily.

Norman bent himself over and placed his hands on his knees. 'They may be closer than you think!' he wheezed.

'He's on to you,' mumbled Donald, through Chad's hand.

'Oh, good!' said Trevor, playfully unsheathing his sword. 'I've got eighty fellow knights waiting for me at Chipping Ongar. Perhaps I should give them a call and tell them to come over!'

'Eighty!' croaked Bob. 'They've got their own friggin' army! We're gonna need reinforcements!'

'I can't stop and chat,' gasped Norman. 'I've got something extremely important to do.'

'Got to save the Universe, have we?' joked Trevor, in his strangled lilt.

Norman inhaled deeply. 'Yes,' he said... and went inside.

Chad stifled a yelp as a set of teeth entered the palm of his hand.

'FOR MANY ARE CALLED, BUT FEW ARE CHOSEN!' shouted their owner, attempting to break free.

Trevor looked about himself uneasily... sheathed his sword... then hurried away, cursing the youth of today.

'I'm getting such powerful vibrations!' cried Donald. 'I've never known anything like it! I feel something's going to happen!'

'Spot on, Donald,' said Bob, knocking him out with a single punch to the jaw.

'Perhaps he's psychic after all,' observed Chad.

As Norman entered the hall, he could hear sobbing coming

The last time Norman had run for anything, it had been a baton in the school sports day four by four hundred meters relay. He'd only been included to make up the numbers and had looked in danger of being overtaken by his own shadow... though it was eventually the runners a lap ahead of him.

His side felt as if it was splitting in two, his lungs as if the air being dragged into them in huge gulps had been set on fire. Those he passed stopped and stared, though not in wonder at why he was running in the first place. They were more curious as to why he didn't just give up his tortured gait, and walk... given he would have gone much faster if he had.

The awkward slap of his feet reverberated from the buildings on either side as he stumbled his way into Armageddon Terrace.

Chad stared in bemusement as Bob came hurtling out of the front door.

'He's got armed friggin' guards in there!'

They both took cover behind the truck... Donald pulled unwillingly with them.

'You wanted proof this is the Templars' headquarters? Well... take a look at that!' Bob pointed at the figure surveying the street from the door he'd just flown out of. 'Is that a big enough *connection beyond friggin' coincidence* for you?'

Trevor Belchett – librarian, occupant of 66d and historical re-enactment enthusiast – stood on the step trying to remember which end of Armageddon Terrace he'd parked his car. After all, you didn't want to be wandering the streets dressed as a twelfth-century crusader knight any more than you actually had to. Teenagers could be cruel... even if you *were* in possession of a large sword. He adjusted his tunic and straightened the large, red *croix pattée* that had been faithfully reproduced on the front of it.

'I don't believe it!' whispered Chad. 'I thought the costumes over here were for the tourists!'

licence?'

'He doesn't have one!' shouted Xanthia, from her position wedged behind the helicopter's seats.

Norman felt his stomach freefall.

'Brace yourself, Babe!' yelled Stump. 'I'm going down!'

'Ooh... I think you'd better land this thing first!' she giggled.

Oppenheimer opened his door in response to the frantic banging on it.

'Give me the goddam key!' demanded Bob, his eyes ablaze with anger.

'You're not from the council, are you?' said Oppenheimer timidly.

'Very observant of you. Was it the accent or my total friggin' lack of manners?'

'It was more the street entertainment you appear to have involved yourself with,' answered Oppenheimer.

'You thought *that* was interesting!' said Bob, reaching inside his jacket and removing a gun. 'Now... GIVE ME THE FRIGGIN' KEY!'

'Oh Mutter... rette mich!' yelled Oppenheimer in terror.

'The key to Penkridge's flat,' said Bob coldly.

Oppenheimer staggered back into his room and inched his way towards a wooden bureau, his eyes transfixed on the gun being pointed at his head. 'I knew that boy was trouble!' he cried, scrabbling inside the writing desk for his pass key.

Bob snatched it from his hand as soon as it was offered and retreated backwards into the hall.

'I take it this means you haven't had a word with the bin men,' said Oppenheimer, in shock.

But Bob didn't hear him. He'd already started to climb the stairs, as Oppenheimer fell to his knees, weeping and calling for his mother.

Bob had only managed to get halfway up them when he froze. 'Shit!' he yelled, as he saw what was coming down the other way.

out into the road.

'THIS ABOVE ALL: TO THINE OWN SELF BE TRUE!' yelled the figure that flung itself at him and toppled him into the gutter.

'Talking of loonies,' sighed Chad.

'What are you playing at?' shouted Bob, as Donald grappled with his legs. 'We're supposed to be on the same side... remember?'

'GOD HATH GIVEN YOU ONE FACE AND YOU MAKE YOURSELVES ANOTHER!' shouted Donald.

'What the friggin' hell are you talking about?'

'SUIT THE ACTION TO THE WORD, THE WORD TO THE ACTION. I refuse to let you corrupt this gift of mine!'

'I'll corrupt your friggin' face if you don't get it away from my groin!'

'I won't let you do it! I won't let you take advantage of the spirit world!'

'I'll friggin' well send you there if you don't get off me...! Chad...! Give me a hand here!'

Chad grabbed hold of Donald's arms and pinned them behind his back.

'ET TU, BRUTE?' screamed Donald at the top of his voice.

Oppenheimer's curtain twitched again.

'This is ridiculous!' shouted Bob, brushing himself down. 'Right...! I'm getting inside that flat, if it's the last thing I do!'

With that... he crossed the road and disappeared inside number sixty-six.

'This Armageddon Terrace... It's just off the Bayswater Road?' yelled Stump, above the noise of the helicopter's rotor blades.

'That's right,' yelled back Norman. 'And I think we're almost there. That large area of green below must be Hyde Park. I can just make out the Serpentine.'

'In that case... I'll put this thing down there. It'll only be a few minutes from your door, if you run!'

'You know this means you'll probably lose your pilot's

Devil.

'I already have,' said Stump. 'You see... I cheated you. With my previous record, I was destined for Hell long before *you* intervened. I just figured what you had to offer might ease the pain before I got there! If you're ready, Norman... I'll get the keys!'

* * *

'You really need to use a non-abrasive metal cleaner on these,' said the ex-ironmonger, studying the handcuffs that had just been placed on his wrists. 'It'd bring them up a treat. In fact, you could say... the sparkle would be quite arresting!'

'Come along now, sir,' said the constable, leading him gently towards a waiting police car. 'You're gonna get yourself excited again.'

'Why? Are we off to the sales?'

'Sounds similar,' replied the constable, dryly.

'Ah... *cells!*' The ex-ironmonger applauded his attempt at humour. 'Very good, Officer. Very witty. Very...' His eyes widened. 'Tell me... have you ever considered a career in ironmongery? If so... I know of an extremely promising vacancy...'

As the last police car made its way out of Armageddon Terrace – its blue light flashing to warn other motorists that its occupants needed to get back to the station before the tea trolley finished its rounds – Bob stepped out from behind the truck and scratched the back of his head. 'What the friggin' hell was all *that* about?'

'You tell me,' replied Chad, joining him. 'It was your idea to come here.'

'D'ya think these Templars are out to destroy the hardware industry as well as the art market?'

'I think this country has more than its fair share of loonies... and it doesn't need *you* adding to its number!'

Bob surveyed the empty street. 'I'm not listening. We've wasted enough time. I'm gonna get this over with.' He stepped has heard me whisper. There are those who do my work for me, even in their ignorance. You are doomed to fail. You have found your voice too late! Even as we speak, my influence is at full strength outside the room which houses your precious Ark. It is about to be destroyed. You cannot stop them!'

Norman looked at Gabriel. 'Is this another of his tricks?'

Gabriel shook his head. 'I'm afraid those forces I warned you about are almost upon us.'

'But it would take me a couple of hours to get back there!' said Norman. 'I couldn't possibly do it in time!'

The Devil roared in triumph.

'Gabriel... I need your help!' implored Norman. 'I need to be transported home quickly. If I can just set the vibrations in motion before...'

'He cannot help you,' sneered the Devil. 'It's against the rules... Remember?'

'He might not be able to,' came a voice from the four-poster bed. 'But I can.' It was Stump's. 'All that *combination of the individual musical notes* stuff was beautiful, man... I can really identify with that. You've reminded me of why I formed a band in the first place. You're not so bad after all! I've got a helicopter out the back. I could get you to where you wanna go in no time.'

'I told you his soul could be touched,' said Gabriel, 'no matter how deeply it had been buried!'

The Devil span round to face his newest enemy. 'You talentless little runt. Who gave you permission to speak? Your soul belongs to me. You'll do as I command.'

'I think you'll find our agreement was for it to become *your* property on my expiring,' said Stump, standing up and adjusting his kimono. 'And seeing as how I haven't quite got there yet... despite some chemically induced close shaves... I figure I'm currently free to do with it what I want!'

'I'll take all this away from you!' howled the Devil, holding his hands outstretched.

'Fair enough,' shrugged Stump. 'But that would put you in breach of contract... and I'd get my soul back!'

'Do you think you can get the better of me?' shrieked the

'Then I'll appeal to his *mortal* side,' raged the Devil. 'If I win, Norman... you will too! I'll give you absolutely *everything* your heart desires. Success... fame... wealth... women... Yes... you can even have *Xanthia!*'

Xanthia looked coyly at the floor. Being the centre of attention again overruled the need for protest.

Norman met the Devil's gaze and held it. '*Everything?*'

'Simply name it,' the Devil tempted him.

'Alright, then...'

The Devil licked his lips.

'... I'd like to *belong*.' announced Norman loudly.

The Devil took a step back. 'What?'

'I said... I'd like to belong. For once in my life, I'd like to belong.'

'Is that it...? I don't understand!'

'Of course you don't,' said Norman. 'You're all about the individual... and I've seen the effect it has on people. You only succeed when you fool them into believing they are disconnected from everything else and that their actions need only benefit themselves. As you said... you're the other side of the lesson... and I've learnt what can be achieved when everything comes together.'

'*What* have you learnt?' scoffed the Devil.

'To appreciate that each individual brushstroke or musical note is essential to the masterpiece... but it's the combination of them all that gives it its beauty and purpose.' Norman turned to Gabriel. 'I used to think the answer lay in black and white... but now I know it's every colour imaginable... and some you even can't!'

The Devil wretched. 'I still won't let you succeed!'

'I don't see how you can stop me! If you're anything like Gabriel, physical restraint's going to be impossible! All you have is your poisoned logic... and we've just established that doesn't work!'

'You pathetic fool! You think my doctrine is nothing more than a way of thinking? Look around you, you insignificant imbecile. *Mine* is the word made flesh. Every soul on this planet form of the artworks they've inspired. And from where I've just been, they were all accessible at the same time! All I had to do was call back the memory of them and view them from the angle of their vibrations. As soon as I did that, I felt...' Norman paused and tried to remember what it was he *had* felt. His brow became corrugated. 'It's all very strange,' he mumbled. 'I can't quite remember what it was I...'

'Don't worry,' said Gabriel. 'The knowledge you acquired cannot be interpreted in this dimension. Your soul obtained it in its purest form. It's untranslatable. All that matters is that you're back here now!'

'But you still need the sphere of knowledge on this Earth plane,' said the Devil. 'And seeing as how I hold the rights to the master piece... I win!'

'Maybe not,' said Norman defiantly.

'What delusion is this? The master piece you seek is *mine!*'

'Fair enough,' said Norman, unperturbed. 'I'm more than happy to give you credit for its use.'

'*Credit?* What are you talking about? You obviously don't understand,' the Devil glowered. 'I *forbid* you to use it!'

'Of course you do,' said Norman. 'I wouldn't expect anything else. But all we need is its *vibration* to make the sphere of knowledge complete. That will happen when we place it into the program... with or without your permission.'

'You can't!' shouted the Devil. 'Tell him, Gabriel. You're forbidden from doing anything illegal! You're an Archangel!'

'He may well be,' said Norman. 'But *I'm* not!'

The Devil froze. 'That's...'

'Cheating?' suggested Norman. 'Well... how did the phrase go? "Cheating is nothing more than being smart and getting what you want on no one else's terms but your own". Isn't that what you said?'

'Tell him, Gabriel!' screamed the Devil. 'Tell him he's forbidden to go against the rules!'

'Well... I could,' said Gabriel. 'But I don't think it would do much good. He's the most stubborn mortal I've ever encountered!'

'WOE TO THE INHABITERS OF THE EARTH AND OF THE SEA! FOR THE DEVIL IS COME DOWN UNTO YOU, HAVING GREAT WRATH, BECAUSE HE KNOWETH THAT HE HATH BUT A SHORT TIME.'

'Not as short as yours, mate,' said the cab driver, demonstrating his own wrath. 'If you haven't got any money, you're not getting in!'

'But life is at stake!' protested Donald.

'Yes,' said the driver, impatiently. '*Yours!*'

As a four-poster bed and accompanying speaker stacks spun into focus, Norman's mind felt like it had been put into a liquidizer and puréed. The strange weight of his body caused him to collapse in a heap on the floor.

'Are you alright, Norman?' came a voice he recognised as Xanthia's. 'You haven't shit yourself again, have you?'

'Don't worry,' said Norman, gingerly picking himself up and trying to balance, 'I now believe it was only necessary for me to do that *once* in my life.'

Xanthia looked at him as if he had... all the same.

'Norman!' exclaimed Gabriel. 'How is this possible? I cannot believe you're standing here!'

'Neither can I!' snarled the Devil. 'What trickery is this? He must have received help!'

'I helped myself!' said Norman proudly.

'But you were supposed to acquire a knowledge of *everything!* You couldn't possibly have done that in so little a time!'

'My standing here having to suffer your disgusting halitosis suggests you're wrong,' countered Norman.

'How *did* you do it?' asked Gabriel.

Norman smiled. 'It occurred to me that you'd already collected all the answers I needed to know together in one place. They were contained in the sphere of knowledge.'

'But it doesn't exist!' hissed the Devil. 'That was the whole reason behind your task!'

'You're right,' said Norman. 'But its vibrations do... in the

24

you felt that existence to be. Scale was unimportant. It was an illusory trick of dimensions requiring measurement to experience them. The smallest individual particle mattered as much as the whole. For without it, the whole could not exist. Like a single, binary digit missing from the sphere of all knowledge... Like one lost soul preventing all others from becoming one again. *Everything* was important. *Everyone* was important.

And when you realised that... you'd found the reason for your three score years and ten.

What mattered then was what you did with them.

To be or not to be... that was the answer!

Now... could he have his feet back, please?

... Despite a warm glow flooding his thoughts, the coldness of eternity continued to dwarf them.

He wasn't even being allowed his *socks*.

Having understood *his* position in the scheme of things, surely he wasn't being expected to understand every individual connection?

... Apparently he was.

His non-existent heart sank.

Despite his new found enlightenment, he was back to square one. He was being asked to acquire a complete knowledge of *everything*.

And then a microscopically small brain cell joined hands with its neighbours, to confirm his theory and demonstrate that even the smallest particle of thought is essential to the greatest idea of all.

Norman's *being* grinned from non-existent ear to non-existent ear.

He'd had a flash of inspiration... and he was going home.

* * *

He was in the classroom again... an uncomfortable warm weight having stretched the crutch of his underpants. He felt his shame. He felt the derision of others. But he also felt their anxiety... as they realised that it could have been *them* standing in his position. And he noticed that those with the greatest anxiety were laughing the loudest. He could see the thoughts in their minds. It wasn't hate or cruelty... it was fear! And little Julie Swanson... holding her nose as she obeyed the teacher and dutifully opened the window. It wasn't teasing... she wasn't aiming an insult at Norman... she was just doing what she thought was expected of her by her peers. She was only trying to *belong*... like those who taunted him and made him a playground pariah. If they projected him as being on the outside, it affirmed that *they* were on the inside. It wasn't malice... it was weakness and ignorance.

And then Norman saw the chain of events the incident had prompted as if a flick book of pivotal moments. His ostracism... his becoming a loner... his discovery of computers... his obsession with learning their language... his acquiring the necessary skills... the appearance of the Archangel Gabriel in his bedsit... his being chosen to save the Universe.

They were all connected... each one a stepping stone to the next.

Gabriel was right. There was no such thing as random... especially when it came to people's thoughts and reactions. Everything was the result of something else... be it a preconditioned emotion or previous event. You could not separate *anything*. Everything was connected.

Hang on!

Was that it?

It didn't matter *where* you existed in the scheme of things... it just mattered that you *did*. Because, in doing so, you were a part of everything around you. And although that sounded glaringly obvious... it also meant that – in being connected – you were *responsible* for everything around you. There was no such thing as a solitary existence. Selfishness was denial. Your *being* affected everything else... no matter how small and insignificant organs... DNA... In fact... *all you need is love* was complete and utter bollocks. In terms of survival essentials, it probably ranked close to the bottom of the list.

He thought again.

Maybe he could steal an idea from one of the great philosophers... someone like Jean-Paul Sartre. Yes... that sounded good!

Okay...

... only one problem.

He didn't *know* any Jean-Paul Sartre.

A saying, then... The author was unimportant. Something monumentally deep... like...

I think, therefore I am.

... He waited for his feet to reappear, along with the rest of him happily balanced above them.

... The vastness continued to swirl all around him... although – to his astonishment – an image of the first time he'd encountered those words flashed in front of him as a reconstituted memory.

He was a student again, reading about Descartes in the university library. He'd picked up the book to impress a group of girls who were looking over in his direction and giggling. It was flirtatious giggling... the sort he'd never encountered before... or since.

He could see it all clearly. In fact... he could see it *so* clearly, he realised he could view the moment from every conceivable angle.

He observed it from the girls' vantage point and saw that they were looking over his shoulder at another male student. He was holding up an opened book on anatomy – displaying a diagram of a penis – whilst pointing at Norman and mouthing the words *"nob head"*.

This revelation caused other painful memories to flash in front of him... each one viewable from an infinite number of perspectives.

27

another outlet,' he suggested, with a shrug.

*   *   *

Norman's disembodied thoughts tried to calm themselves. How on earth was he going to get out of *this* one? The task ahead of him was all but impossible.

A logical thought tapped him on his non-existent shoulder.

Actually... it was *completely* impossible. If he weren't able to look into the black hole dimensions, how could he be expected to work out how everything fitted together?

Another logical thought tapped him on his other non-existent shoulder.

It was irrelevant. Even if he *could* finally make sense of what was before him, it would take so long to do so that what he was observing would have ceased to exist long before he had. The devil had truly won.

Another logical thought tapped him on his third non-existent shoulder.

Perhaps he could cheat. Perhaps he could come up with a single, all-encompassing thought that summed up how everything in the Universe worked. The sort of thing you saw on fridge magnets. Something like... *all you need is love.*

It was certainly worth a try. What was there to lose?

Alright...

All you need is love.

He waited for something to happen.

... Nothing did.

He tried again... but this time attempting to *believe* it.

... Nothing.

Perhaps that was too simplistic. After all... you also needed food... air to breathe... iron atoms in haemoglobin transporting oxygen in blood cells coursing through veins attached to vital

28

synaptic interrelations or my lack of stock. That would have created the ironic juxtaposition of states necessary for comedic misinterpretation!' He looked at the ground and tried to prevent a loud sob from racking his body. 'UNFORTUNATELY,' he screamed, 'I THOUGHT OF IT TOO BLOODY LATE!'

'PUT THE SCISSORS DOWN!'

The command had been issued from a loudhailer at the end of the street. Unseen by Chad and Bob... it had been quietly cordoned off, a phalanx of policemen looking on anxiously.

'I don't believe it,' moaned Bob, clutching his brow.

'PUT YOUR HANDS IN THE AIR AND WALK AWAY FROM THE VAN... I SAID, PUT YOUR HA_'

There was an excruciating squeal of feedback... followed by silence.

'I think it could be your batteries!' shouted the ex-ironmonger, shielding his eyes and trying to spot the loudhailer's operator. 'Have you had them in there long? You'd be amazed at the amount of people who come into the shop not realising drainage occurs... even if the appliance is switched off!'

There was further feedback.

'What have you got in there? Half a dozen size Ds... I should think. I'll see if I've got some in my van. If they're old ones, you can have them free of charge!'

The ex-ironmonger started walking towards the back doors of the van... then stopped.

He let out a slight guffaw.

'Did you hear that?' he chuckled. 'I said...if they're old ones, you can have them free of charge! Get it? Free of *charge*. If they were old... they wouldn't have any charge in them!'

The policemen behind the cordon gripped their truncheons tightly.

'He's going again, Sarge,' said a nervous constable. 'The doctors warned he might become unstable if he tried to make another sale.'

'Damn!' cursed the sergeant. 'What are we gonna do now?'

The constable gave their predicament some thought. 'I guess, in future... we'll just have to get the station's light bulbs from

29

being… You've ended its proud ancestral line of ironmongery and hardware supplies. Do you know how long it took my father to build up our extensive range of sticky-backed plastics? It was second to none in the Middlesex area! And where will people go now to get their keys cut? Had you thought of that? How will they get hold of life's essentials like adhesive towel hooks and grout cleaner? The repercussions don't bear thinking about! You have no idea what havoc you've wreaked!'

The ex-ironmonger reached into the van and produced a gleaming pair of scissors.

'Now it's payback time! I'm waiting here until you come down. You can't stay in there forever. You'll eventually need to come out to purchase ant repellent or bath sealant… and then I'll have you!'

Bob lent against the truck. 'This is the last thing we needed,' he groaned.

'You're probably wondering how I found you,' continued the ex-ironmonger. 'Well… I realised you'd have gone to the nearest outlet to purchase your precious computer memory… so visited it and asked if they remembered you… nerdish-looking kid… black glasses… carrying a brand-new crowbar and one hundred percent nylon toilet brush. When they heard about your behaviour, they were appalled and only too keen to provide your address. You see, Penkridge… we look after our own. Forget the Mafia… God help you if you ever cross the *Retailers' Association!*'

'What are we gonna do?' whispered Bob. 'He could be here for hours! If Penkridge returns, we'll have missed our window of opportunity to wrap this thing up without anyone getting hurt.'

'Look on the bright side,' said Chad. 'At least if our friend here kills him, it'll save you having to do it yourself!'

'You know the most annoying thing, Penkridge?' yelled the ex-ironmonger. 'As soon as you'd gone, I thought of a suitable rejoinder. All I had to say when you asked me if I sold computer memory was… "I'm not sure… my memory's not what it used to be!"… You see… I could either have been referring to my road in front of it. It had done so because its driver seemed intent on confronting the occupant of the room whose window he was now yelling up at.

'Are you in there, Penkridge?' he shrieked, having leapt from the driver's seat without acknowledging his close encounter. 'I know you can hear me!'

It was true Norman could hear him. Unfortunately – in his present predicament – Norman could also hear every other sound the Universe had ever produced.

'I bet you didn't think you'd be seeing me again!' the van driver bellowed up at the empty room.

Bob retreated back onto the pavement and edged behind the truck.

'You're a hard man to track down... but I found you in the end!'

Chad and Bob looked at each other... then at the writing on the side of the van. It read: *Fobbingtons' Ironmongers. Est. 1875. Quality Goods With A Smile.*

'I'm fucking well going to kill you!' yelled its driver.

The curtain below Norman's twitched.

'And I'm going to do it with a twelve inch pair of stainless steel, wallpaper scissors retailing at fourteen, ninety-nine!'

'Quality scissors,' observed Bob.

'But not for selfish reasons... I'm doing it for others.'

'That's refreshing,' whispered Chad. 'An altruistic psychopath!'

'My own humiliation, I can cope with... I may never work again... Paint brush display stands are anathema to me now... But I've had my reckless fun behind a hardware counter. What I can never forgive you for is destroying my *nephew's* career. He was only a lad. He'd hardly put a crease in his shop coat. Now your comments have finished him. He'll never feel the joy of completing his first window decoration... never experience the thrill of displaying a new range of airtight plastic containers... never savour the relief of an un-jammed till. And you've taken away my chance of ever seeing his picture in the trade gazette. But worse... you've shoplifted my family's very reason for

Only then will your soul be free to return.'

Norman peered into the vast billowing aggregation all about him. 'That's an awful lot of particles!' he gasped.

'As many as there could ever be,' said Gabriel.

'But what about saving the Universe...! I could be here forever!'

'That's what Lucifer was banking on. He tricked you. He used your own black and white logic to manipulate you. He knew you would languish here for eternity and that it would put an end to our plans.'

Had Norman possessed a face at that particular moment in time, it would not have been dissimilar to the one in Edvard Munch's painting, *The Scream*.

'*Eternity?*' he wailed. He got impatient waiting for a bus... let alone an existential answer as to why one might exist in the first place.

'Yes... which – coincidentally – is the circumference of what you're observing. That may give you some idea of the task that faces you. What you are seeing is everything that is... has ever been... or ever will be. All you have to do is work out how it all fits together. You'll excuse me if I don't hang around.'

'Wait!' yelled Norman. 'Aren't you going to stay and help me?'

'I wish I were allowed,' said Gabriel. 'But that would be against the rules. I'm afraid you're on your own now... with just the entire Universe to keep you company. Lucifer has won. I must go now and prepare for the consequences. Goodbye, Norman, and...... good luck.'

'GABRIEL!'

There was a cold, empty silence.

It was a silence that threatened to remain for eternity.

*   *   *

The van that skidded to a halt outside 66 Armageddon Terrace hadn't done so to in order to avoid Bob's new-found connection with the spirit world becoming permanent, as he crossed the particular answers you seek regarding your connection with Xanthia lie in the choreography of the dance between two of those dimensions... fate and chance.'

'Fate and chance are *dimensions?*'

'Extremely complicated ones. What you perceive as coincidence is nothing more than the pattern of their flirting folding back on itself and leaving a faint trace in your world. Most people are content to pass such occurrences off with a simple phrase such as *"it was obviously meant to be"*. But *you...*'

'It's just the way my mind works,' protested Norman. 'I like to know the rules.'

'Well... now they're all around you,' said Gabriel. 'You can understand them by observing the patterns they create.'

'But I can't *see* any patterns!'

'I told you... It's just a question of finding the right perspective.'

'But if fate and chance are dimensions with patterns... surely that makes me redundant? Every decision I *think* I make is a complete and utter waste of time! Everything's preordained.'

'The Universe dances to a strict choreography... that's true. But the greatest ballerinas are those who express themselves most within the confines of their steps. That is what free will allows your soul... *Expression.*'

'Then I'd like to express my desire to stop all this. I'd like to feel a pair of legs beneath me and a floor to stand them on. I'd like to go home now, please.'

Even though he couldn't see him, Norman felt the depth of Gabriel's pain.

'You really don't understand, Norman, do you? I warned you to be careful about what you wished for in your privileged situation. You have asked for something from the depths of your soul... and it must now be given to you. The problem is... it is beyond an explanation. What you have asked for is *understanding*... and that can only come from yourself. It is up to you to find the pattern in all this. You must discover how each individual particle relates to another... then put it all together. Only then will you be able to make sense of your place in it...

more that couldn't.

Norman no longer felt himself to be in the room. In fact… he no longer felt himself to *be*. It was as if he were a disembodied observer of a swirling chaos… so unimaginably vast he was no longer relevant. And yet… he *was* the chaos. He couldn't explain it. He was both the observer and the observed.

'It is not chaos,' came Gabriel's voice from all around him, as particles of dust and light billowed in the seething firmament. 'There is no such thing. It is merely a question of scale. Look from afar and it will appear as unpredictable as the patterns of the wind or the behaviour of water in an ocean. Look too closely and the rules that govern it will be outside your vision. But find the right balance and you will understand its workings and your place within it.'

'Its *workings?*' protested Norman, by way of a disembodied thought. 'But everything seems to be moving around at random!'

'A random event is just one the observer hasn't stuck around long enough to witness again,' said Gabriel. 'That, for you, is the curse of time. It's like a mayfly believing that *lunchtime* is a random event. God doesn't move in a mysterious way… God just moves in a very big one!'

As Gabriel spoke, another series of black flashes interrupted Norman's vision, causing an intense stabbing pain to invade his being.

'You must ignore them!' warned the Archangel. 'If your thoughts are drawn to them, they will be annihilated.'

'The black flashes?'

'Your thoughts.'

'But it seems that's all I am at the moment!'

'*Precisely…* Now is definitely not the time for obstinacy! They are the portals to dimensions you could not possibly understand… even in your current state. Think of them as mental black holes. You would not want to dip a toe in the real thing, so be careful where you place your curiosity.'

'My current *state…?* Now I'm *extremely* curious.'

'That is your problem, Norman… and, with it, mine. For the

34

'That's absurd!' exclaimed Norman. 'You're the cause of all the suffering in the world!'

'Am I?' said the Devil sharply. 'Have you ever stopped to think that one out?'

'Everybody knows it!' insisted Norman. 'It's what you're famous for!'

'I've just had bad press, that's all,' said the Devil, shrugging his shoulders. 'Look how much pain has been perpetrated throughout history in the name of *God!* Nobody carps on about *that*. Millions of souls maimed, butchered and caused immeasurable suffering in that name... but I'm the one with the image problem!'

'That's not our wish!' interjected Gabriel angrily.

'No,' said the Devil leeringly. 'But it's your *fault*.'

'The message has become corrupted,' said Gabriel. 'And you have helped fuel that corruption. And now that we are seeking to put it right, once and for all... it is you who are standing in our way.'

'I'm just playing the game,' pouted the Devil. 'Just like I was supposed to... Talking of which... I think it's time to play the next bit.' He looked directly at Gabriel. 'Your turn,' he smirked.

Gabriel tilted his head back and looked towards the ceiling in anguish.

'Oh... come on!' the Devil taunted. 'He demanded to know *everything!* Rules is rules!'

Gabriel turned slowly towards Norman, his face weighted with despair. 'I warned you about asking questions from the heart,' he said mournfully. He moved forward and placed a hand in front of Norman's forehead. 'I'm sorry... but this is going to hurt... and in more ways than you can imagine.'

Norman's brain was just about to object that hurt it could *imagine* was bad enough... when a searing pain shot through it, as if someone had dragged the blade of a rusted knife from its medulla oblongata right up into its occipital lobe. Flashes of black strobed across his vision... then were obliterated by a sudden, single burst of brilliant white light that sent his mind spinning in every direction that could be thought of... and a few and he's going in!'

* * *

'What does he mean *you're on the same side?*' demanded Norman angrily.

'It's not what it seems,' replied Gabriel.

'You can say that again! What the hell's going on?'

'His job was to tempt you... and he has succeeded.'

'But he said *you* sent him?'

'He means Heaven, Norman... He was once one of us... as in *Lucifer, the fallen Angel.*'

'Fallen doesn't come into it,' objected the Devil. 'I was pushed!'

'You lowered yourself to this level,' snapped Gabriel. 'You were only meant to test mankind... to make man stronger of spirit... not so weak he forgot he had one.'

'Can I help it if I'm good at my job?' the Devil sneered.

'There's that word again!' said Norman. 'What test?'

The Devil grinned. 'Ever wondered why God told Adam the one thing he couldn't touch in the Garden of Eden was a simple piece of *fruit?* Ever wondered why – if it was *so* forbidden – God put it there in the first place? The fruit itself was an irrelevance... It might just as well have been a *turnip.* It was simply a test of faith. You see... I'm the fruit made incarnate. I'm the negative side of faith's vibration. Without me, it can't exist... Without temptation, there's nothing for the soul to prove!' His eyes twinkled mischievously. 'I take it Gabriel's told you that the reason everyone's God doesn't appear in front of them and redeem their souls is because they need to learn how to do it for themselves?'

'Virtually word for word,' said Norman.

'Well... now you know why I've been sent down here. I'm the other side of that lesson!'

Norman flashed a questioning look at Gabriel.

'Oh... he knows I'm right,' said the Devil in response to it. 'He also knows that makes me an integral part of Heaven.'

his fingers as the idea gathered momentum. 'Look... it all makes perfect sense! Donald sent his letters to everyone immediately after the other side's suspicions were raised by your dumb phone call. They knew someone was onto them... but not *who*. So... what better way of flushing that organisation out than to write to every contender in a vague and rambling way, offering help? We fell hook, line and sinker! We didn't even question his being there at the exhibition that day we decided to visit. He fed us the line about the paintings disappearing... then was conveniently carried out!'

'But why would he do that if he were one of them? He led us to the fact there was a forgery on the wall!'

'No... he didn't! *We* discovered that for ourselves. He was trying to get us to accuse the organisers of meddling with the paintings that were all safely returned. How stupid would we have looked if we'd followed *that* one through? Psychic...? Try *sidekick*. He's working for the other side! I don't know why I didn't think of it before! Thanks to Donald, we've all but exhausted our credibility. Now... we go waltzing into that flat, remove this computer stuff and it turns out to be harmless and belonging to some poor innocent... we're *finished!*'

'Jesus!' groaned Bob. 'Talk about taking the anal in analytical too literally! You're so obsessed with logical thinking, you've stuck your head up your ass to see why there's a hole in it!'

'And you've gone soft on me! You're the *last* person I'd have expected to buy this mumbo-jumbo bullshit! You were the most obstinate, pig-headed, pessimistic cynic I ever knew!'

'Thanks!'

'And I'm missing that Bob! He wouldn't have been taken in for a second. Magic's only magic when you don't know how the trick's done. I'm sorry to shatter any childhood illusions you may have had, but rabbits don't materialise from hats... they get pulled from a hole in the table! Why bother complicating things when there's an easier explanation?'

'I don't need a hole in a table to produce *my* rabbits. They're carved in wood... behind that door. And I've got good news for you... That pig-headed, obstinate Bob is still alive and kicking...

But we're not talking *any* old hat stand.'

'Well... *that's* a relief,' sneered Chad.

'This one's special.'

'No shit...! Does it have supernatural powers?'

'Not quite.'

'What in hell, then?'

'Rabbits,' said Bob excitedly. 'It has rabbits!'

Had a clown in possession of a trumpet been nearby, he would have squeezed out five slowly deflating notes.

'Of course it has,' said Chad slowly.

'No... really! Carved around the base... At least... I *think* they're rabbits. Anyway... the point is... it's there in the hall *exactly* as Donald predicted. Given its uniqueness... it *has* to be proof he possesses psychic powers. And if he was right about the hat stand... he's got to be right about this address being the centre of Templar operations!'

Chad dragged a hand across his face.

'What's more... according to the landlord, this Penkridge guy's apartment is stuffed to the rafters with computer equipment! Now... we know they're not *stealing* the pictures, so they've got to be doing something *to* or *with* them. I'm prepared to bet my nuts those computers contain all the answers and evidence we need!'

Chad sunk his jowls into the palm of his hand. 'The trouble is... it's not just *your* nuts you're staking... and I still refuse to risk mine on this psychic crap. There's gotta be a rational explanation. Are you sure about these rabbits?'

'They're either cute little bunnies or badly carved turds. Either way... you do the math. The odds for them being there just as Donald predicted are too high to ignore.'

'There *is* another possibility,' suggested Chad.

'Shit... *Now* what?'

'Donald's in on all this. He's part of it. He's set us up and sent us here thinking we'd be gullible enough to swallow the bait.'

'For *what* possible reason?'

'To throw us off the *real* trail. We end up wasting our time, looking stupid and burying our careers for good!' Chad clicked

38

it?' he grinned.

*   *   *

'You took your time!' scowled Bob, as Chad alighted from the cab of the truck.

'*You* try getting hold of one of these things at short notice... Let alone driving it half way across London with the gear shift on the wrong side and having to avoid crowds of panicking protesters!' Chad dispassionately surveyed his surroundings. 'Is this *it?*'

'Sure is... and we need to get moving before our target returns!'

'Whoa...' said Chad, raising his hand. 'Before I risk making a complete and utter fool of myself... perhaps you'd like to explain *who* this target is and why the truck?'

'Okay... but we need to be quick... The address Donald gave me belongs to the building's landlord. The guy's as clean as a nun's wish list. But one of his tenants – a guy calling himself Norman Penkridge – has been receiving daily deliveries of large crates from that favourite courier company of ours...' he whistled a fanfare, '*Vault Vans!*'

'And what makes you think they're our paintings?' said Chad, unimpressed. 'That firm delivers to hundreds of addresses all over this city. That's been our problem!'

'Ah,' grinned Bob confidently. 'But not to one that contains what's at *this* address.' His grin widened. 'Our *connection beyond coincidence!*'

'And that is?'

Bob played the moment with a pause of self-congratulatory silence. 'A hat stand!' he announced proudly, after it had expired.

Chad stared at him in disbelief. 'Excuse me?'

'A hat stand.'

'No,' said Chad, shaking his head vigorously. 'A hat stand's what I *thought* you said.'

'No kiddin'... A hat stand as in *"a stand you put your hat on"*.

'Well... *I* am!' snorted the Devil. 'And *I'm* on his side!'

'Are you saying that me being here in this room right now with the object of my adult fantasies – who just *happens* to turn out to be the object of my childhood ones – is nothing more than a *coincidence?*'

'You've got him now!' spurred the Devil.

'And you can shut up!' shouted Norman.

'You must trust me,' answered Gabriel. 'There is so much you cannot understand.'

'Look out, Norman. He'll fob you off with another one of those pencils in a minute!'

'No, he won't,' said Norman resolutely. 'Because this time I demand to know *everything!*'

'Don't be ridiculous,' said Gabriel. 'It's not possible.'

'Then *make* it possible!' exploded Norman, his anger racing to the surface from every buried pore of his memory. 'Show me why it was necessary for a little boy to humiliate himself the way he did. Show me why he was forced to go through life the butt of everyone's jokes for nothing more than a moment's indiscretion. And tell me why he had to be reminded of it – just as he was starting to bury the past – in front of the very girl he'd always believed could've made it irrelevant. In fact... tell me why *anyone* has to suffer at all if God is a god of love! I WANT TO UNDERSTAND *EVERYTHING*... I DEMAND AN ANSWER!' He stopped... his eyes glistening... fists clenched... chest heaving spasmodically, as if the echo of a child's sob.

The Devil took a step back and smiled.

'Congratulations, Lucifer,' said Gabriel stoically. 'You've done your job well.'

'Of course,' said the Devil. 'That's why you chose me!'

Norman's chest stopped heaving.

'Oops!' said the Devil sarcastically. 'Have I let the cat out of the bag?'

Gabriel remained silent.

The Devil feigned a look of sympathy, as he observed Norman's expression of disbelief. 'Oh, dear! Didn't he mention we're on the same side...? It's not been your day, Norman, has made me sound kinda...' She fidgeted coyly. '*Sexy.*'

As far as Norman was concerned... he would've considered her sexy even if her name had been *The Right Honourable Sir Humpty Dumpty*.

'You see,' she pouted, 'my real name's... Julie.'

The space between Norman's head and everything else in the room suddenly lost its exactness. 'No!' He put his hands to it and gripped the sides of his hair as if to hold onto something solid. 'Not...'

Xanthia raised her eyes expectantly.

'Julie *Swanson*...? Saint Dymphna's Primary School...? First love of my life...? The object of all my unrequited passion...? The girl who held her nose to open the window and broke my heart?'

For Xanthia – née Julie Swanson – the penny finally dropped. 'Pooey Penkridge?' she enquired. 'The boy who shat himself?'

The Devil roared insanely.

'There was no need, Lucifer!' shouted Gabriel. 'No need!'

'No?' the Devil challenged.

'It's a wonder the poison in you does not corrode your very being.'

'You see, Norman,' said the Devil, waving the insult away with a contemptuous flick of his wrist. 'I rest my case. To him, the truth is poison. To me... it's a way for you to see how it really is and be free. Perhaps it's time you decided whose truth you'd rather follow?' He nonchalantly examined the fingernails of his other hand. 'Because, let's face it... if the whole Universe wasn't laughing at you before... it certainly is *now!*'

'Is it?' Norman quizzed Gabriel, his eyes dancing with anger.

'Norman!' exclaimed the Archangel. 'Can't you see what he's doing? He's playing a game. He's twisting everything!'

'What I see is that all my childhood I thought myself to be the butt of some grand, universal joke. And now – just as my adult years were beginning to suggest otherwise – it seems I've been told the punch line!'

'No one's laughing at you,' Gabriel assured him.

though I don't fink he did really. Everyone used to make fun of him. Mind you... he *was* pretty weird. Wouldn't talk to anyone.'

'Did you hear that, Norman? Everyone used to laugh at him. Poor child. Xanthia... What do you think became of him, I wonder?'

'Dunno,' shrugged Xanthia. 'Probably ended up a head case, what with all that rejection and stuff.'

'Do you ever think the whole *world* ended up laughing at him?' stirred the Devil.

'Guess so,' said Xanthia nonchalantly.

'And do you think the *Universe* was laughing at him?'

'Isn't that the same fing as the whole world?' said Xanthia, the strain of thought causing the makeup on her brow to crack.

'Oh, no,' the Devil replied. 'It's *much* more than that. I'm talking about everyone and everything. I'm talking about those who held his fate in their hands. I'm talking about those who made him... those who put him in that situation in the first place. I'm talking about a laughter that stretched as far as Heaven itself!'

'But I don't understand! I didn't know a Xanthia!' protested Norman.

'You what?' said Xanthia, nonplussed.

'And he never talked to anyone because no one ever talked to *him!*' insisted Norman, looking to Gabriel for an answer.

'I can't give you one you'd be able to understand,' Gabriel responded.

'But I didn't know her! I couldn't possibly have done! What's happening here? What's going on?'

'You're not the only one who resorted to a false name for the sake of their image,' grinned the Devil.

'Lucifer! Stop this!' cried Gabriel.

'Xanthia?'

'Go on... Ask her. Ask her what her real name is.'

Norman turned to her, his eyes pleading for him to be put out of his misery.

She lowered her head and started playing with her fingers. 'After leaving school, I decided to call myself Xanthia because it

'Of course you do,' grinned the Devil. 'And you shall!'

'NO!' shouted Gabriel.

'Remember the rules,' continued the Devil. 'First... we must be truthful. So let's start with your name!'

'What?'

'Your name. It can't get much easier than that!'

'Norman!' said Norman, perplexed.

'Your *full* name. After all... I believe sweet Xanthia here's under the impression you're Norman Templar.'

'My real name's Penkridge,' said Norman, his words directed at Xanthia as if an apology. 'Norman Penkridge.'

'There,' said the Devil. 'That wasn't so difficult, was it?'

'Penkridge?' said Xanthia, the cogs of her mind beginning to creak.

The Devil threw back his head and laughed loudly.

'I'm pretty sure I knew someone called Penkridge, once,' said Xanthia. 'And the person I'm thinking of *definitely* wasn't off the telly this time. Only... his name wasn't Norman.'

The Devil laughed even louder.

'Well... I can't actually remember what his *real* name was. You see, we used to call him...'

'O! WOE IS ME, TO HAVE SEEN WHAT I HAVE SEEN, SEE WHAT I SEE!' Donald had just managed to outrun the alcohol-sodden shell that once was Peter Snogden-Lambert.

The former gallery director might have stood a better chance of catching his intended target had he been able to run in anything remotely resembling a straight line. As it was, he had to make do with launching another empty vodka bottle towards Donald's fast-disappearing head, the sunlight glinting on a flapping veil of tin-foil as it slowly unravelled itself.

'Pooey.'

The Devil's laughter cracked the air like the tip of a whip.

'Yeah... that's right. I remember now,' said Xanthia, forgetting her predicament as she found herself the centre of attention. 'Pooey Penkridge. I suppose it was because he smelt...

43

by and watched!'... Who knows... she might even enjoy it!'

'Stop it!'

'And who cares if she doesn't... eh, Norman? You think she's with this idiot for his wit?'

'Stop it! Stop it!'

'What's the matter? Those shackles causing you pain again? You see, Norman... *that's* their game. *That's* what you're playing against. *They're* the opposition... not me! I'm on *your* side... I just want you to be free!'

'Enough!' shouted Gabriel, his aura flaring.

'Now who's interfering?' spat the Devil. 'Stick to your rules, Gabriel. The boy can make up his own mind. And if he's smart enough, he'll realise that it's *you* who have burdened him with his guilt. *You're* his enemy. *You're* the one he needs to fight against!'

'Remember, Norman,' pleaded Gabriel. 'Listen with your conscience!'

'Conscience?' sneered the Devil. 'That's the breeding ground for guilt! See how they're trying to trick you, Norman? Remember what I said about it being an uneven playing field? Well... there's even *more* to that unfairness than his loaded advice. Ever wondered why you find Xanthia *so* attractive... why she's haunted your fantasies for so long?'

'Lucifer! You have gone far enough!' shouted Gabriel.

'I have no limits,' bellowed the Devil. 'All I want is for him to know the truth!'

'It is not a truth he could understand,' said Gabriel.

'See how he patronises you, Norman! Apparently you're incapable of such a thing! I – on the other hand – encourage you to *discover* it. Whose side do you want to be on now?'

'What's he on about, Gabriel,' demanded Norman. 'What of Xanthia...? What truth?'

'There are things it would not help you to know,' replied Gabriel.

'Oh... you're not still peddling that *moving in mysterious ways* claptrap, are you?' the Devil sneered.

'I want to know about Xanthia!'

didn't need anyone's permission or approval? What if you understood that cheating is nothing more than being smart and getting what you want on no one else's terms but your own?'

'I don't need to cheat,' countered Norman. 'I'll achieve what I want in life by proper means.'

'Proper means?' sneered the Devil. 'And what might they be? Hard work?'

'If that's what it takes... yes!'

'You're pathetic, Norman. All those brain cells pulling together and you can't even work out that hard work means you've lost the game!' The Devil stabbed a finger at Stump. 'He's got a *fraction* of your brain power and he *won*! He beat you!'

'No!'

'YES! You admitted it. He's got everything you wanted.' The Devil turned towards Xanthia and licked his lips salaciously. 'And I mean... *everything!*'

'That's not fair!' protested Norman.

'I know,' cooed the Devil sympathetically. 'It isn't... is it? But here's another truth... *Life* isn't fair... Not the way you're expected to live it. Because – let's face it, Norman – you've hardly been given a level playing field to compete on, have you?'

'I don't know what you mean.'

'Think about it... They haven't exactly made it easy for you, have they? I mean... take all those hormones raging about inside your body. *You* didn't ask for them, did you? So they must be God-given. But you try using them. You're branded a sinner quicker than the time it takes your fingers to reach your trouser zip. Now... is that *fair*? What possible affront to God is it to experience that which God has given you? So... go on, Norman.' The Devil pointed at Xanthia. 'There's your dream... your nocturnal and diurnal fantasy... no longer teasing you from a poster, but in three-dimensional flesh and blood... just a quick unzip and liberating lunge away. No one's gonna stop you. He certainly isn't!' He nodded towards Stump. 'You have my supreme word on that! And who'll believe her if she complains? *"It was awful, your Honour!"* he parodied in a high voice. '*"I was violated whilst my boyfriend, Satan and the Archangel Gabriel stood*

'Now I'll tell you something that might shock you,' teased the Devil. 'Are you ready?'

Norman swallowed.

'I'll take that as a *yes*.' The Devil drew himself closer... the stench of his breath stinging Norman's eyes. 'Evil is simply telling the truth. The truth, the whole truth and nothing but the truth.' He pulled himself sharply away as if enacting the listener's horror. 'What can he mean?' he hammered. 'How could this be? You appreciate logic... so follow this.' He pulled himself so close that Norman could now feel the heat of his breath on his cheek. 'To be evil is simply to be true to yourself and act upon your feelings... Nothing more, nothing less. No lies... No deceit. How easy and pure of thought is that? Imagine the sense of liberation... of power... of *pleasure*... if you lived life exactly as *you* wanted, without those burdensome shackles of judgement... recrimination... and that heaviest one of all... *guilt!* Well... you can! For such restraints are not of the physical. They're in your head... nothing more than a way of thinking. So think them away! Go on, Norman... It's that easy! Liberate yourself! Do as was commanded. Refuse to bear false witness. It's time for the truth... for complete honesty. It's time to bare your soul!'

'I don't want to play this game!' said Norman, looking apprehensively towards Gabriel.

The Devil moved sideways to block his gaze. 'Norman! Do you seriously think you have a choice in the matter? From the minute they expelled you from the innocence of your mother's womb, and pulled you kicking and screaming from between her bloodied legs – dangling from the hand of a complete stranger, your vulnerability held up for all to gawp at – you became a player... whether you liked it or not. So what are you going to do? Sit on the sidelines and watch impotently from the substitutes' bench as the A team gets to play? Perhaps you're waiting in the hope you'll be asked to join in. Well... we can all do that! We can all sit and wait. The promise that something *might* happen is always a useful anaesthetic against the pain of knowing *nothing* ever will. But, Norman... what if you stood up and *insisted*... told them it was *your* team... *your* game... that you

'Don't listen to him, Norman… His words are poison.'

'So much for free will, eh?' the Devil scoffed.

Norman looked at Gabriel.

'I can't stop you from hearing him, Norman,' said the Archangel. 'All I ask is that you listen to what he has to say with your conscience. It's the one thing he cannot corrupt.'

'But what did he mean by *game?*'

'There are rules. His job is to make you think you can twist them to your own advantage… that there is an easier way than the way of God.'

'There is!' countered the Devil brightly. 'You are in the presence of living proof.' He thrust a talon-like finger at Stump. 'Think about it, Norman. He's everything you've ever secretly wanted to be… and everything you're not!'

Norman gave a half-hearted protest.

'No?' the Devil mocked. 'Well… Norman… you do surprise me! You haven't ever walked out onto the street and wished that people would actually *notice* you… think you interesting enough to want to talk to… tell you how wonderful you were, instead of passing by as if you didn't exist? Even excrement on the pavement gets noticed, Norman. But *you*…? And are you telling me that you've never played your favourite record at full volume and wished it were *you* standing on the stage performing it… its power in *your* hands… the gift of ecstasy to millions within *your* control… an adoring public gazing up at you as if you were… a *god?*'

'No!' objected Norman lamely.

'NO?' howled the Devil. 'Oh… come on! Thou shalt not bear false witness… It's one of the rules… remember?'

'Well… I might've… perhaps, once or twice…'

'Perhaps?' mocked the Devil. 'Once or twice?'

'Alright, then… Yes…! Yes, I have!'

'Ah…!' sighed the Devil, savouring his victory. 'Now we're *getting* somewhere! That wasn't so difficult… was it?'

Norman's face reddened. He was acutely aware of Xanthia staring at him – her mouth wide open – the expletive produced by the Devil's introduction still sitting gormlessly on her lips.

it! I kept my word... and now he keeps his.'

Xanthia looked enquiringly at Stump. He bowed his head without making eye contact.

'Now... seeing as we've established that the writer of the song belongs to me and, *ipso facto*, so does the song, I think we can agree that your attempt to obtain it is completely futile. Given your presence here is a complete waste of time, might I suggest "goodbye"?'

'But the song wasn't yours to trade!' exclaimed Norman. 'It didn't belong to you in the first place! It was just a vibration!'

'A vibration nobody wanted,' countered the Devil. 'A vibration so small and pathetic it was deemed unworthy of use by those who wished to praise their God. And what an irony there is in that! I simply saw an opportunity and acted upon it.'

'Opportunity?' cried Norman.

'Yes... to spoil their little plan!'

'You had no right!' said Gabriel forcefully. 'Your presence on Earth was to test man, not to interfere with the greater workings of Heaven!'

Norman's reeling senses were struggling to keep up. 'Test...? What do you mean... test?'

'You interfered by direct intervention, Lucifer! You know that is forbidden!'

The Devil looked his accuser square in the face. 'So, I cheated,' he shrugged coyly. 'I'm the Devil. What d'ya expect?'

'You had no right!'

'Test? What test?' Norman demanded loudly.

The Devil dropped his playful countenance and filled his eyes with an anger of such intensity they appeared to glow. The air in the room became charged... as if sharpened by a violent thunderstorm. 'I had *every* right!' he spat. 'You sent me here to provide an opposition. Well... congratulations... you've got it!'

'What's he on about?' asked Norman. 'What does he mean... *you* sent him? And what's this about *opposition?*'

'Think about it, Norman,' hissed the Devil. 'How can you have a game without one?'

'Game?'

already engulfing them.

'What's wrong?' asked Norman.

Gabriel seemed to be fighting the answer.

'Tell him!' jeered the Devil.

Gabriel remained silent.

'Not wishing it to be so will not alter what is,' the Devil smirked.

'What is what?' demanded Norman.

Gabriel's light flickered and dimmed slightly. 'He's sold his soul,' he replied mournfully. 'It's no longer his own.'

'I don't understand,' said Norman. 'How can he sell it? Sell it for what?'

'For all this,' gloated the Devil, stretching out his hands triumphantly. 'The fame, the fortune and the fans... Oh... especially the fans... the *female* fans!'

Xanthia swallowed her gum.

'You mean... he traded it for his *lifestyle?*'

'In a manner of speaking,' replied the Devil. 'You see... to be precise... he traded it for...'

Norman's mind threw up the answer a split second before it flew from the Devil's mouth... making it resound with even greater horror.

'A song!'

A wail – unheard by Norman – echoed through many dimensions.

'You mean...' Norman could hardly bring himself to utter the words.

The Devil gave a broad smile and raised his eyebrows in expectation and encouragement.

'*Sex Wench?*'

A gentle moan left Gabriel's lips.

'Well... what else?' scoffed the Devil. 'It was far too easy. There was this last piece of inspiration floating around unwanted, and I found the perfect vehicle for it. I promised him the chance to write something that would give his ego everything it ever craved. All he had to do in return was bequeath me his soul. He didn't even have to think twice about

49

both too traumatised to expel the expletives sitting on their lips. The Devil took a while to savour their terror, as if partaking of a particularly fine vintage wine. Stump, meanwhile, had sat himself on the bed and was observing the scene in front of him in silence and without emotion.

'You're forgetting one thing,' said the Devil. 'Your authority here is weaker than it might've once been. And for the record… it is *you* who have intruded upon *my* domain.'

Gabriel drew his head back, stung by such steely contempt. 'It seems you have become a victim of your own poison,' he responded. 'Vainglory has allowed your ego to fool itself. How can this be *your* domain when you are nothing but an unwelcome shadow upon it?'

'You misunderstand me,' said the Devil, completely unfazed. 'And though you underestimate my power and influence upon this world at your cost, I was referring to this room and its contents.'

Norman searched anxiously about himself. Surely the Devil wasn't referring to the *furniture?* Though the atrocious mix of antique fixtures and fittings alongside the battered paraphernalia of a rock and roll lifestyle might be regarded as offensive to an interior designer, bad taste was, at worst, a crime… hardly an evil.

'No… it's not the furniture, Norman,' said Gabriel testily, picking up the thought. 'You need to look deeper than that.'

'Not the…'

'Carpet? Have you taken leave of your senses?'

'Actually… I rather think they've taken leave of me!'

'He's referring to a soul. A soul that has had a shadow cast so heavily over it, I am unable to feel its vibration.'

Their eyes turned in perfect synchronisation towards Stump.

There came the sarcastic accompaniment of slow hand-clapping. 'Bravo,' crowed the Devil.

'So… *that's* why he can't see you!'

'It's much worse than that,' said Gabriel. 'There's not enough pity in the Universe to use upon this wretched being.' He looked at Stump with a sadness outweighing the heavy atmosphere reddish scales and thin, reptilian tail marked it out as anything but. Imperiously surveying its surroundings, it disdainfully sniffed the putrid air as if finding a part of the gagging aroma particular offensive. Its piercing, blood-red eyes settled on what it deemed to be that part.

'Gabriel,' it croaked, in a deep, guttural voice dripping with contempt and chafing the silence. 'It seems you're losing your touch.' It shifted its gaze towards Norman, giving him a cursory glance up and down.

As it reached the down part, Norman noticed two small horns protruding from the top of its skull and a thought – which he rather wished wasn't – shuddered through his mind.

'Is *this* the best you can do?' the creature sneered, its low voice burbling with the unpleasantness of gas escaping a feculent swamp. 'Have I made things so difficult for you that all you can find to put in my way is this pathetic runt? I gave you Caligula, Nero and Hitler... and you give me...' It looked the source of its repugnance up and down again. '*Norman Penkridge?* You disappoint me, Gabriel. But then... you always did.'

'What is your place here?' demanded Gabriel, attempting to establish his authority.

The creature looked at him mischievously. 'You mean... you haven't worked it out yet?'

'You have no business here!' Gabriel rebuked him.

'To the contrary!' countered the creature. 'I have business *everywhere!*'

And then Norman heard the name that confirmed his worst fear... shooting a sickening chill into the pit of his stomach and a hot flush across his goose-pimpled skin. As his legs began to wobble, his senses absconded, not wishing to associate themselves with someone resembling a hybrid of baked Alaska and a blancmange.

'This has nothing to do with you, Lucifer,' said Gabriel firmly. 'Remove yourself from here and leave us to get on with our work.'

Norman looked helplessly at Xanthia – who seemed to be looking helplessly at the visitor's rather impressive manhood –

temperature in the room plummeted.

Stump – who'd been attending to Xanthia – immediately looked up and switched his attention to a space to the right of Gabriel, from where a thick green mist was beginning to emanate. It brought with it a stench of such unimaginable foulness it caused Xanthia to cough and splutter, reviving her from her faint like a dose of smelling salts.

'Phoaah! Stump! Have you farted?' she moaned, indelicately wafting her hand in front of her face.

Stump was too preoccupied with what was occurring in front of him to answer. He was staring at the mist – which had grown denser – its stench so potent it made Norman's eyes water. It was as if someone had combined the aroma of a decomposed carcass... cat's urine... the earthy must of a dank cave... and thrown in some sulphur dioxide, in case nobody got the point.

'What is it?' spluttered Norman, the air in the room growing damp and heavy.

'You couldn't leave it alone, could you?' said Stump, without averting his gaze.

'Stump…! What's happening?' cried Xanthia, as she tried to make sense of the bizarre scene in front of her. 'There's an angel looking at me! Have we died or something?'

'You wouldn't take no for an answer,' continued Stump, emotionless. 'You just had to keep on pushing.'

'You can see the cloud?' asked Norman... for that is what the mist had become.

Stump didn't answer.

'What in Heaven's name is it?' implored Norman.

'It's not in Heaven's name,' answered Gabriel. 'At least... not anymore.'

*　　*　　*

The grotesque figure that emerged from the fetid cloud did so with a strutting arrogance born of its history. It moved on two legs and boasted predominantly human characteristics... yet its you… whatever he says to you will be in private.'

Norman looked at the Archangel uncomfortably.

'I'll save you the embarrassment,' said Gabriel. 'Don't even *think* it.'

'But…'

'Norman! You *know* I exist. Who do you think's been responsible for sending you all those works of art!'

'Templar Resources?'

'Norman… What's wrong with you?'

'You said Helmut and Gertrude were Mr Oppenheimer's parents.'

'They are!'

'Not according to him!'

'Don't do this, Norman! You're not thinking clearly. Something's happening here.'

'But that's precisely the point… *Nothing's* happening here. You said everybody saw something when you appeared… even atheists. So how come he's seeing and hearing nothing?'

Gabriel shook his head. 'I don't know. It's not a situation I've ever encountered before. But don't start losing your faith.'

'He has a soul… doesn't he? And you said that no matter how distant and buried it might be, there's always a part of it that will respond if you reach out and touch it. Well… go on, then… reach out and touch it!'

'That's the strangest part,' said Gabriel. 'I can't!'

'Why?'

'Because… I can't feel its vibration.'

'But you said *everything* vibrated.'

'It does… But it's as if something's interfering with this one.' A look of fear swept across Gabriel's face. 'Oh no…! Surely…' He looked at Stump and then back at Norman. 'Norman! Get out of the room as quickly as you can!'

'What?'

'NORMAN!' As Gabriel implored him to leave, the heavenly light flooding the room flickered and started to wane. Gabriel appeared to be fighting its diminution as if a struggle were taking place between him and an unseen force. The dangerous mate! You should be locked up!'

'There's something seriously amiss here,' said Gabriel.

'You can say that again!' agreed Norman.

'Alright... You should be locked up! Now... get outta here!'

Norman placed himself in front of Stump and raised his hands. 'Are you honestly telling me you can't see *any* of this?'

Stump's demeanour softened slightly. 'Look, Mr Templar... You've obviously got a problem. Maybe *you* can see what you say you can. Maybe the voices you hear seem real to *you*. But perhaps you should face up to the fact that it's all in your head... and go and get it fuckin' looked at!'

'I don't need to. Mr Oppenheimer saw it!'

'Your psychiatrist?'

'My landlord.'

'Your *landlord?* What the hell's he doing giving you psychiatric advice?'

'No... start again... Not my head... the *visitation!* I can't be mad... My landlord saw it too!'

'Your landlord saw the Archangel Gabriel?'

'Well... no... Not exactly.'

'*What* exactly, then?'

'He saw a girl.'

'A girl?'

'A woman... on my landing... I think he thought she was...' Norman's voice began to falter, '...a prostitute,' he said slowly, his thoughts examining the fragility of his own argument.

Stump looked at him compassionately. 'I rest my bleedin' case.'

'Don't listen to him,' said Gabriel firmly.

'Just like an angel,' said Stump.

Norman jerked his head. '*What?*'

'She looks just like an angel.' Stump's eyes gazed affectionately at Xanthia. 'She's strangely more attractive when her mouth's closed.'

'Would you excuse me a second?' said Norman. 'I need to talk to Gabriel.'

Stump waved his hand dismissively. 'Be my guest. I assure

broken glass is *everywhere!*'

Norman watched in astonishment as Stump proceeded to walk straight through Gabriel and towards the decimated television set at the other end of the room. 'Well… that's *that* well and truly fucked!' he said, staring at it and shaking his head.

'You're worried about the *television?*'

'Well… there's bugger all else to do around here! The nearest cinema's at least three quarters of an hour away… and as for a decent nightclub…' Stump cautiously investigated some of the debris with his big toe, then realised the room was missing the sound of gum being chewed. 'Xan?'

Norman looked searchingly at Gabriel as Stump proceeded to walk straight through him towards Xanthia's prostrate body. 'Why no reaction?' he asked the Archangel.

'I'd have thought that was bleedin' obvious!' Stump replied. 'She's fainted with the shock of the explosion! Perhaps I should call a doctor.'

'He can't see you,' said Norman.

'Why fuckin' not? I pay my taxes!'

'I was talking to Gabriel.'

'Who?'

'The Archangel Gabriel… The one standing in the middle of your bedroom!'

'Oh… don't start all that crap again! You can see I've got my hands full… Xanthia…? Babe…? Can you hear me?'

Norman's eyes begged Gabriel for an answer. 'I thought everyone could see *something.*'

'You're right,' replied the Archangel.

'Actually… that's where you're wrong,' said Stump, pushing Xanthia's cheeks together, as if making her lips bow inordinately might bring her round.

'You heard that?' asked Norman excitedly.

'Of course I did.'

'Then you believe me?'

Stump let Xanthia's head drop onto the bed. 'What is it with you?' he asked exasperatingly. 'You say something… I tell you you're wrong… and you interpret it as… *I believe you!* You're up to Norman's. 'Right, you little shit. You asked for it!' He took a step back and raised the guitar above his head again.

As he did so, a fountain of sparks shot out from the amplifiers powering the giant speakers on either side of his bed, a monstrous squeal of feedback providing accompaniment. The television set that had been on in the corner of the room – showing a local news item on Shakespeare-quoting vagrants – exploded, showering the room with fragments of broken glass.

A colossal orange ball of light appeared in the centre of the room and pulsated. The building's security alarm decided to try itself out... then promptly fell silent, following a large explosion somewhere in the basement.

Norman watched as the now familiar light expanded into a brilliance that caused him to become momentarily blinded, its power greater than anything he'd experienced before.

As he regained his sight, he found himself standing amongst a multitude of angels, cherubs and all the usual paraphernalia of Heaven that normally accompanied such visitations... except in far greater number. In the middle of it all stood Gabriel... with a presence of such magnificence that even Norman – who had grown used to seeing him – gawped in awe.

Xanthia let out a choked squeal... then passed out.

'What the fuck's going on?' said Stump, dropping his guitar and looking around himself. 'I don't believe it!'

'Neither did I, when it first happened,' said Norman.

'Look at it!' Stump had turned and aimed his line of sight directly at Gabriel's shimmering form. He started to move gingerly towards it. Cherub-laden chariots whizzed around him at giddying speed. 'There's stuff all over the place!'

'There sure is,' said Norman proudly.

'What am I gonna do?'

Norman was about to suggest that he ignore the protestations of his senses and surrender to the inevitable fact that he was witnessing a divine revelation, when the idea was derailed by the words... 'The cleaner only does Wednesdays.'

'*Pardon?*'

'Mrs Franklin... the cleaner. She only does Wednesdays. This more credibility in *Jack and the Beanstalk!*'

'I didn't expect you to believe me,' said Norman quietly.

'Well, that's a fuckin' relief!' sneered Stump. 'I might have a reputation for being wild... but I ain't fuckin' *stupid!* Now... seeing as you've had your fun... you've got to meet me and Xanthia... kindly take yourself and your designer suit to the front gates of my property and... fuck off!'

'I can't,' responded Norman resolutely.

'You fuckin' *can!* And if you don't... I'll get Sharky to come in here and give you a rather large and heavy hand!'

'He's not here,' said Norman calmly. 'You sent him to deal with the local inbreds... remember?'

Stump pulled back the pillow covering the panic button. 'I'm warning you. Get out now or I'll call the police!'

'How long was it?' enquired Norman. 'Within two hours, I think you said?'

Stump raised himself unsteadily on the bed and held his guitar as high above his head as the four-poster's canopy allowed.

'Careful, darlin',' cautioned Xanthia, as she disentangled herself from his trailing Kimono. 'You're not wearing any pants... remember?'

'Look,' said Norman, raising his hands. 'I've told you why I need the song. If you think I'm a nutter, then fine! Forget me buying the rights. All I'm asking now is for your permission to use it just once for the purpose I've explained. Then I'll leave you alone and never trouble you again. If I'm as mad as you think I am, it's not going to do any harm... is it?'

'He's right, Honey,' said Xanthia. 'Just tell him he can play it into his computer thingy and we'll be rid of him. We've got nothing to lose, have we?'

Stump lowered the guitar. 'No.'

'There you go, Mr Templar,' said Xanthia, as if addressing a child. 'Stump's said you can...'

'No!' yelled Stump over her. 'I meant... no... he can't use it!'

'But...'

'NO!' Stump jumped from the bed and pushed his face right

57

He momentarily froze.

'*Norman!*' a voice chastised him from the ether.

He hurriedly unlocked the door.

'You were in there so long, I thought you'd gassed yourself!' said Stump, as Norman joined him. 'Bit of a life altering experience was it?'

'I think you're about to find out,' muttered Norman under his breath.

*   *   *

'Chad... put your books down, tear up your friggin' library ticket and get your butt over here as fast as you can!' Bob pressed the phone tight to his ear so as to drown out the noise of a passing car. 'I've found the ultimate connection beyond coincidence! It proves beyond doubt that Donald was right all along...! ... No... I'll tell you when you get here... And we're gonna need a truck... a *large* truck. We've got some removals to do...... No... you'll have to sort it out yourself. I've gotta keep watch on this place.'

An old lady walking her poodle passed and exchanged a nodded pleasantry.

'Just friggin' do it!' yelled Bob into the phone. 'We've wasted enough time because of your scepticism! Now we've got a chance to shut down the Templars' base of operation and discover what this whole thing's been about! But we haven't got long... You betta hurry!'

*   *   *

'I told you he was a nutter, Babe! whooped Stump deliriously, once Norman had finished his explanation. 'William fuckin' Shakespeare... and the Archangel Gabriel! He's having a laugh!'

Norman was having anything but. His eyes were fixed on Xanthia, who was trying to disguise a smirk by chewing as rapidly as she could.

'A hundred percent solid gold loony!' crowed Stump. 'There's

58

washbasin and surrounding accoutrements visible through him.

Norman couldn't help feeling that a toilet seat was wholly inappropriate for having such an encounter... even if it had been previously anointed by the buttocks of his true love. But desperate times required desperate measures.

'I'm afraid it's not been going well...'

'I know,' interrupted Gabriel. 'We've been watching.'

'But I don't understand. I offered him *anything* he wanted!'

'It doesn't make sense to us either. All men have their price. It's one of the reasons their souls are still floundering here on Earth.'

'But you heard him! He's not interested!'

'He *was* interested in the truth,' said Gabriel. 'Maybe that is a price we should consider worth paying.'

'Surely you're not gonna tell him *everything*?'

'No... you're right,' said Gabriel. '*You* are. We *must* acquire the rights to his song or – at the very least – have his permission to use it. Even if he decides to tell the whole world, no one's going to believe him. They'll put it down to his excessive recreational habits.'

'But what if he still refuses?'

'He has a soul,' said Gabriel. 'Which means there is a part of him – no matter how distant and buried – that will respond. It is up to you to reach out and touch it.'

'And what if he doesn't believe me?'

Gabriel sighed. 'In that case... I'll appear in front of him with so many cherubs and rays of light he'll think he's died and gone to...'

'You all right in there?' came Stump's voice through the bathroom door.

'Yes, thanks!' responded Norman hastily.

'I'd better go,' said Gabriel. 'Good luck!'

The washbasin came into clear view again.

Norman stood up and flushed the toilet. The love of his life being only a mock-Georgian handle turn away, he quickly checked his appearance in the mirror. A laundry basket behind him caught his eye.

unconventional.'

'Well… you better start explaining! I'm beginning to lose my patience, and all I have to do is hit this button here,' he pulled back a pillow and pointed to a red, mushroom-shaped protuberance from the wall, 'and the Old Bill will be up here within…' He contemplated his position amongst the rural idylls of England. '…two hours.'

'I'm not sure I *can* explain everything,' said Norman. 'I'm going to need to speak to someone important first.'

Stump nodded. 'Very well. You can use the phone.'

'No. I need to use something else instead.'

'Not my fuckin' *car*?'

'I need to use your bathroom.'

Stump gave Xanthia another look of inquisition. She shrugged.

'Okay… But don't be long.'

'And be careful where you sprinkle,' called out Xanthia, as Norman took himself off into the *en suite*.

'I don't think he means to pee,' said Stump. 'He's gotta be using a mobile.'

'Perhaps he's gonna snort something for courage?'

'Or perhaps he's gonna rifle through your laundry basket!' teased Stump, rolling over and reducing Xanthia to a convulsing mass of flailing limbs.

'Gabriel… Are you there?' Norman sat on the toilet and waited for something to happen… metaphysically speaking, of course.

He wasn't sure if his progress was being observed from higher quarters or whether he should go home and wait for the Archangel to contact *him*.

Just as he was beginning to think the latter might apply, the small halogen spotlight above the vanity mirror flickered.

'Gabriel…? Is that you?'

The spotlight gave a *pop* and extinguished itself, just as an orange glow appeared below it. Gabriel's outline slowly materialised until he stood, fully formed… just the hint of a

'I told you,' said the other vagrant aggressively, his head nodding over the bottle he was clutching. 'You need to wrap your head in tinfoil.'

'An' how the hell would you know, Peter?'

The other vagrant stretched the lids of his closed eyes as if trying to access a distant memory. 'I knew someone once.'

'Oh... b'jesus... Don't be startin' all that again. If I hear another tall story about you and yer bloody art gallery, I'll swing for...'

'I had it *all* this time last week!' The other vagrant belched precariously and looked up. His eyes attempted to focus on Donald, but could only manage half the task. 'Don't I know you?'

Donald's recognition skills had been a little sharper. He was already backing away. Having hung around the galleries, he'd gotten to hear certain things.

'You look familiar,' slurred the vagrant. 'It'll come to me in a minute.'

Donald decided it would be better if he wasn't there when it did. He'd already been thrown off his bus, and the thought of another unpleasant confrontation delaying his urgent mission, didn't appeal.

He was halfway down the street when an empty bottle went whistling by his ear, followed by a scream of... 'Tucker-Jenkins... you utter *bastard!*'

* * *

'You're right to doubt me,' said Norman. 'I'm not a music publisher.'

Stump ran his hand through his hair and stared at Xanthia. 'I knew it! I bloody well knew it!' He turned back to Norman. 'So what are you? A fan? A nutter? I thought that chequebook gimmick was too good to be true!'

'Oh, no! That bit's genuine. I meant every word. You can ask any price for your song and it *will* be paid. It's the reason for me wanting to acquire it that's a little... shall we say...

Donald reversed his steps and peered into a narrow gap between the bins. Huddled together -underneath a temporary canopy of cardboard – were two vagrants sharing the contents of a bottle.

'What was that?' he enquired.

'Oh... b'jesus... don't make me say it again,' replied the larger of the two, in a broad Irish brogue. 'It's been poppin' into me head all day, so it has, and it's more than a poor man can take!'

'You too, then?' said Donald.

'Us two what?'

'No matter... It's Shakespeare, isn't it?'

'Hamlet,' replied the other vagrant, without bothering to look up.

'And if me good friend here says it's Hamlet... then Hamlet it is and definitely not Shakespeare!'

'And you've only been getting the one line?'

'Over and over again. I wouldn't mind... but I don't even understand what it means!'

Donald smiled sympathetically. 'Have you heard these voices before?'

'All the time, to be sure. But it's usually the banal kind of chit-chat that gives me something to keep me mind occupied. Now it's gone and occupied me mind!'

'You're psychic?'

'No... just mad. There's a lot of it around here. After all... sane people wouldn't be prepared to put up with the conditions *we* do. But the thing is... a lot of us *shouters* are all coming out with this same kinda rubbish. My best mate, Jimmy the Bins, has been *forsoothing* all over the bloody place... and there's a guy under the Westway flyover who's been coming out with whole...' he looked towards his companion for help.

'Soliloquies,' his inebriated friend obliged... with some difficulty.

'Yeah, to be sure. Those as well.'

'It's all coming to a head!' said Donald, his voice full of portent.

'It's bloody well all coming to mine... that's to be sure!'

'I think… it's about time Sharky got here with my sweets. I'm fuckin' starving!'

'Look!' said Norman, dropping any pretence of cool. 'What can I give you? Have the whole damn chequebook if you like! Do what you want with it! All I'm after is the one song!'

Stump stopped his playing and studied Norman. 'It's not just a song… it's my *life*.'

'Oh… I *see!*' A sense of relief slapped Norman around the face. 'You think you'd be selling your *identity*. Well… I assure you that all I'd own would be the *rights* to *Sex Wench*. It'd still be *your* song. No one could take that away from you. And you'd be rich beyond your wildest dreams!'

'I *am* rich beyond my wildest dreams… and so must you be if you're able to make such an offer. So how come I've never heard of your publishing company? Where have you suddenly come from… and what *exactly* are these plans you have for my song? How do I know you're not just some nutter desperate to meet me?'

'Or me,' chimed in Xanthia.

Norman blushed. This wasn't how things were meant to have gone. He'd offered Stump the Earth financially… but now he was asking for something that could prove far more costly… The truth.

He gave the matter some thought.

If money wasn't going to do the trick, he could hardly tempt Stump with a life of sex, drugs and rock 'n' roll. Maybe honesty was all he had left to offer.

*   *   *

'*There's a divinity that shapes our ends, rough-hew them how we will!*'

The voice that assailed Donald came from the direction of some rubbish bins he'd been hurrying past… which made a pleasant change from inside his head.

He stopped and tentatively called out. 'Excuse me?'

'There's a divinity that shapes our ends, rough-hew them how we will,' came the reply… a little firmer.

63

leaning towards Norman. The thought had suddenly struck her that his uneven teeth gave him character and a strangely rugged appearance.

'You can't be serious... I mean... theoretically I could cover the amount box with noughts.'

'You wanna put a one in first, though, darlin',' suggested Xanthia helpfully.

'Not just theoretically,' said Norman coolly. 'Do it for real.' He was surprising himself at how easy it was to give away someone else's money.

It was Stump's turn to look unsettled. His arrogant disinterest had faded. He wiped his mouth with the back of his hand and stared at the chequebook.

'Go on darlin'... write as small as you can!' Xanthia encouraged him.

There was a long silence.

'I told you, Mr Templar... *Sex Wench* is not for sale.'

The words came out of Stump's mouth in slow motion... went in one of Xanthia's ears and out the other, causing her to swallow her gum as they had a word with her brain... then enveloped Norman with a feeling of nausea and despair.

'No!' he protested. 'You don't understand... It has to be!'

Stump didn't respond. He was staring at his left hand, which he'd placed around the neck of his guitar.

'How can an unlimited amount not be enough?' exclaimed Norman. 'I'm offering you the chance to think of the most optimistic figure you could hope to earn from the song... then double it... *triple* it, even! All you have to do is reach out, pick up the pen and sign your name. I'll even fill the amount in for you, if you tell me how much you want.'

Stump started picking at a string on his guitar, keeping his gaze fixed trance-like on his chord hand. A two-note melody ground itself out of the speakers either side of him. It was *Sex Wench*... at half the tempo and with a fraction of its usual fire. But it still stirred the emotions... as if the melody of a powerful ballad, full of angst and suffering.

'What d'ya fink, Honey?' cooed Xanthia softly.

'I think he means pounds, Babe.'

'Two hundred and fifty thousand pounds for the rights to *Sex Wench* alone,' confirmed Norman.

'I don't think *that* would keep this one in clothes for six months!' laughed Stump.

Xanthia responded with a playful elbow in his ribs.

'Half a million... then.'

'Oh... So now we're up to *twelve* months!'

Norman waited a few seconds... then announced his next offer in a tone he hoped would suggest was his last. 'One... million... pounds.'

Xanthia stopped her chewing.

'Was that *two* million pounds?' asked Stump, tilting his head comically and waggling a finger in his ear.

'Yes,' said Norman. 'It was. Two million pounds... take it or leave it.'

Stump studied the knob of earwax perched on the end of his finger. 'Then... I'll have to leave it.'

Xanthia looked as startled as Norman.

'But you'd still receive a percentage of your royalties on top,' insisted Norman. 'And the song can't be earning you as much as it once did!'

'So why do *you* want it, then?' asked Stump sagaciously.

'Let's just say... I have plans.'

'So do I... and they don't include the sale of *Sex Wench*. I've told you... many have tried... all have failed. Whatever they offer is never enough... and I can't see how you could be any different.'

'You're wrong,' said Norman, fixing his eyes on Stump's. He walked slowly towards the foot of the bed and laid the chequebook out in front of him. Producing a fountain pen from his pocket, he uncapped it and ceremoniously placed it beside the chequebook. 'Name your price,' he said firmly.

Stump gave an embarrassed laugh. 'Yeah... right!'

Norman kept his gaze. 'I'm serious. Put in *any* figure you like and I'll honour it.'

Xanthia gently pulled herself away from Stump and started

Stump smiled knowingly and nodded his head. 'You mean…
Two Into One Will Go. An interesting slant on the theme of
eternal love triangles.'

'Is *that* what you're after, Mr Templar?' asked Xanthia, her
pouting lips teasing him as if she were in front of a camera.
'Two Into One?'

Norman tried to keep his voice… and his groin… steady.
'Actually… the song I'm really interested in is… *Sex Wench.*'

There was a moment of stunned silence… before Stump
burst into a fit of uncontrollable laughter. Xanthia squeezed his
arm affectionately and smiled.

'I bet you are!' he bellowed. 'You and every other fuckin'
music publisher under the sun!'

Norman stood his ground and soaked up the derision. But
they didn't have his trump card, he told himself confidently. He
reached into the inner breast pocket of his suit and pulled out
his chequebook.

'Don't tell me,' laughed Stump, 'you're gonna make me an
offer I can't refuse!'

'Well… yes… as it happens,' said Norman.

'Well… *no*… as it happens,' countered Stump phlegmatically.
'Listen mate… I don't wish to sound ungrateful … but have you
taken a serious look around you?' Stump raised his hands so as
to draw his guest's attention to his palatial surroundings. 'All of
this… everything you see… has been bought and paid for from
the proceeds of that one song. The best advice ever given to me
was to hold on to a hundred percent of the publishing rights.
You tell me why I should change the situation now.'

'The amount I could offer you?' suggested Norman.

'Been tried, mate. I've had 'em all down here at some point
trying to tempt me. And – with all respect – bigger publishers
than you.'

'Two hundred and fifty thousand,' announced Norman
assertively.

'Nah… I don't fink it was as many publishers as that, was it
Stump?' said Xanthia, her face straining to visualise a number
exceeding three digits.

she was meant to be draped.

'Are you Mr Templar, then?' chewed Xanthia with vigorous nonchalance.

Norman supposed he must be. It sounded better than Penkridge... and the last thing he wanted to do was disappoint her.

'I fink I knew a Simon Templar once,' she mused.

Stump looked at her with practised patience. 'No, you didn't, Babe. He was a fictional character on the telly.'

'Oh... right.' She looked at Norman. 'Is he a relation of yours?'

Norman was enraptured. He attempted a laugh and produced a strange squeak... on account of his top lip having become stuck to his teeth. *What a coquettish sense of wit she possessed*, he thought.

Stump was better informed. 'You just sit there and look good, Babe,' he ordered.

Xanthia – taking this as a compliment – found herself invited by Norman's quivering lip to inspect his teeth. *Why hadn't he been forced to wear a brace as a child*, she wondered? *If they were paving stones, there'd be a multitude of people on crutches suing the council.*

Norman – on the other hand – found himself invited by a stretched halter top... and fate... to inspect her breasts. They were magnificent, if a little... well... dare he think it... *smaller* than he'd expected. Sure, they stuck out like two Mount Everests holidaying in Belgium... but they still didn't quite live up to the hype.

Xanthia nestled her five-foot nothing frame against Stump and waited for someone to say something.

'Mr Templar wants to buy some of my songs. I was just trying to guess which ones.'

Xanthia sat up on her knees like an excited child at a slumber party. 'My favourite one's that song about the girl who can't decide which of two men she loves the most... and then they suggest she loves them both... at the same time... at *precisely* the same time!'

'He left earlier in a hurry. The news of your investigation seemed to cause him great concern.'

'Investigation?'

'Yah… about running an illegal business?'

'Yeah… of course.'

'He looked extremely worried.'

'I bet he did! D'ya know when he'll be back?'

'I do not read minds.'

Just as well, thought Bob. 'There's a lot of this equipment, you say?'

'You would need a truck.'

'And an extra pair of hands, by the sound of things. I'll have to call an associate. I take it you're not planning on going anywhere?'

'I wouldn't miss this day for the world!' gloated Oppenheimer.

'I'll be as quick as I can.'

'I wish our bin men were as efficient,' said Oppenheimer, as Bob shook his hand. 'Maybe you could have a word?'

Any remaining doubts that Donald's powers were bunkum were immediately quelled as Bob stepped out into the hall.

Staring him in the face was the ultimate *connection beyond coincidence*… and the absurdity of it made him laugh.

* * *

'Xanthia!' The name left Norman's mouth a nanosecond before the drool in which it was coated.

Babe froze mid-gum-chew and proffered her professional smile, unsure whether she'd been recognised as a celebrity or was meant to know the man now dribbling on her bedroom rug.

Norman tried to pull himself together. He'd always imagined that if he ever got to meet Xanthia he'd be extremely cool. He'd been wrong. He was, in fact, extremely hot.

'This is the guy from Templar Music Publishing,' said Stump, patting the bed next to him in case Xanthia had forgotten where

'We're talking big wooden ones.' Oppenheimer demonstrated with his hands.

'You mean *crates?*'

'Yah… that is the word.'

'D'ya have any idea what's inside them?'

Oppenheimer shook his head. 'Whatever it is… it must be of value. They are delivered by men with helmets and a van like a safe.'

'Security guards?'

'Yah… that is them.'

Bob tried to hide his rising excitement. 'And would this van happen to have a sign on it like this?' He used the first two fingers of each hand to make a *V*… then crossed them over each other.

Oppenheimer's eyes widened. 'Yah…! You know about this already?'

Had Bob not been impersonating someone from the council, he would've planted a kiss on Oppenheimer's head. 'Let's just say… we've had our suspicions!'

'Then, what are you going to do about it?'

Bob liked this man. He was so… *accommodating*. 'I'll need a little more information first… like… how many people are involved in his operation?'

Oppenheimer looked confused. '*Nobody* else… He has no friends. He runs it by himself. I think that is why he needs all those machines in his room.'

'*Machines?*'

'Electronic equipment… Computers… So many you would not believe. Every day they drain my electricity.'

'He's let you see his equipment?'

'Not exactly. But I have my pass key… I expect you'll be wanting to take this equipment away as evidence?'

Bob had never believed in Father Christmas, but he was beginning to suspect the rotund bearded-one might exist after all. 'I expect I will,' he grinned.

'I'll get the key.'

'He's not there now?'

'Are you from the council?'

Being American and unfamiliar with local government structuring, Bob kissed his luck. Was Oppenheimer expecting a member of some secret Templar council? Then again... it could be a trick. His answer required further caution.

'You mean... the council whose name should not be uttered so freely?' he said, with over-dramatic glances to either side of him.

'I mean... the council whose bin men drop more rubbish than they remove... and the one I called about my nuisance tenant upstairs... the one who's been running an illegal business from his room. Are you here to investigate him?'

Bob found the answer to *this* one far easier. 'You bet ya!' he beamed. 'Can I come in?'

'I wasn't expecting you until tomorrow morning,' said Oppenheimer, standing aside as Bob eagerly demonstrated that his last question had been a rhetorical one.

'No... I don't suppose you were. But we at the council take... "illegal business running" very seriously.' He glanced around an unexceptional room... devoid of Templars plotting at a table. Bob recollected Donald's earlier vision of a door *above* the one to the room he was now standing in. 'Your tenant *upstairs*... you say?'

'Yah... Norman Penkridge. He rents the flat on the first floor.'

Bob glanced at the ceiling... which appeared to be bowing slightly.

'For many years he was the model tenant,' continued Oppenheimer. 'A little odd, maybe... but kept himself to himself and was always polite.'

The classic description of a sleeper, thought Bob. *Remaining invisible until called upon to act.* 'And now?'

Oppenheimer's eyes shot heavenward in exasperation. 'Everything has changed! Hundreds of boxes... always the boxes... up and down my stairs every hour of the day. And we're not talking *little* boxes.'

'We're not?'

70

'Ah… right… let me guess… Would that be our next single…
I Stand Erected?'

The bush Norman was trying not to beat about had – like so
many in the vicinity of Soddem Hall – become predictably
phallic-shaped.

'No,' said Norman. 'It wouldn't.'

'Then you must be looking at *Turbo Tongue*. That's a blinder!
It's probably the fastest thing we've ever played.'

'Actually… it's…'

'*Hampton Caught*… It has to be! We don't normally play the
humour card… but with a line like… *I was so keen to flip her, I
caught it in my zipper*… how could we resist?'

Norman shook his head.

'*Vaseline Val?*'

'I don't believe I know that one.'

'*Vaseline Val… she's a slippery gal.*'

'No… Actually, it's…' Norman was about to utter the
hallowed words *Sex Wench* when his jaw hit his shoes.

Returning from her rebuild in the bathroom was *Babe*… now
more modestly attired in denim skirt, stiletto heels and an
overworked halter top. Except… it wasn't *Babe* at all… It was…

*   *   *

'Mr Oppenheimer?'

'Who wants to know?'

This – for Bob – was not as easy a question as the enquirer
might have supposed. For although the answer could be
supplied by anyone passing wind in the bath, he'd needed a
disguise… one that would enable him to explore the building
without creating suspicion.

It took the form of a clipboard… because that's what a
Governmental adviser on weevil infestation – needing to
thoroughly check every room of the building – would carry. He
knew it was weak… but it trumped a false beard and glasses.

An easier alternative was gifted him from the least-expected
quarter.

speakers, presumably so that he... and his neighbours half a mile down the road... could hear ineptitude at its loudest.

'Come on in mate and make yourself at home.'

Norman wondered how you did that in someone else's bedroom. Was he expected to clamber into bed with his host?

'The girlfriend's tarting herself up. When she's done... I'll get her to fix us a drink. What's yer poison?'

'A cup of tea... if it's not too much trouble,' replied Norman politely.

'*Tea?*' Stump gave the request some consideration. 'Radical... but what d'ya want *in* it?'

'A drop of semi-skimmed milk would be nice... if you've got it.'

'You don't want something... *stronger?*'

'Full cream?'

Stump let out a low whistle. 'Whoa... Down boy!'

Norman had just learnt that on the scale of rock and roll credibility, tea scored slightly less than zero. 'With a large splash of whisky,' he added... in an attempt to boost his rating.

Stump rubbed his hands together and grinned. 'Now you're talking! Babe...!' he yelled... his call eliciting no response. 'When you're done preening in the bathroom... go and fetch us a half pint of brandy and a tumbler of that special bourbon we brought back from the States. Oh... and stick a teabag in it!'

'Perhaps we could get down to business,' suggested Norman, thinking it wise to do so before he lost the power of speech.

'Whoa... You don't hang about, do you!' cooed Stump, impressed. 'They told me you were a whizz-kid. Obviously big on the whizz!'

'There's none bigger,' said Norman, warming to his role. 'I like to play hard and fast.'

Stump let out a whoop of appreciation and a poor attempt at a chord. 'I *like* it! That makes two of us! I can see we're gonna get on just fine! So... to business, then. I understand you're interested in some of my songs.'

'One in particular,' said Norman, deciding not to beat about the bush... or outstay his acting ability.

stale tobacco trailing behind him – the continuing silence broken only by the sound of his laboured breathing and the thump of Norman's heart.

Finally, Sharky and his stomach came to rest outside a door on which hung a sign warning... MAN AT WORK – DO NOT DISTURB beneath a picture of two stick-people copulating.

"ang on 'ere a second, mate... I'll see if 'e's decent.'

He knocked – entered – then reappeared a few seconds later... a loud, electronic hum accompanying him.

'Okay. You can go in.'

'And Sharky... be as quick as you can... I'm fuckin' starving!' shrieked a voice above it. 'And don't forget to tell those inbreds at the village shop to take the green ones out this time! You know my stomach's allergic to anything the colour of grass... It's fuckin' bad enough they're shaped like babies!'

'You've got it, boss,' shouted back Sharky from halfway down the corridor.

Norman pushed the door a little wider and followed the hum. *Think successful publishing mogul... Think successful publishing mogul*, he repeated mantra-like in his head.

An ear-piercing collision of bored hand on highly-strung guitar greeted his entrance.

'Er... Mister... Stump?' The words stumbled out of Norman's mouth much higher in pitch than he'd intended... and most *un-publishing-mogul-like*. But how *did* you address a man whose sobriquet conjured up thoughts of an unpleasant accident?

'The one and only,' acknowledged the occupant of a four poster bed situated at the far end of the room. This confirmation was followed by another high-decibel clash between musical intention and technical incompetence.

Norman gazed at its perpetrator. He was sat cross-legged on the bed... a shock of unkempt hair draped over an electric guitar, which was silhouetted against a pink kimono. This was Stump. The exemplification of rock and roll decadence... a modern icon of immoderation... a would-be confessor to profligacy, if only he knew what the word meant.

From the floor either side of his bed rose a stack of electronic

73

But such loyalty had been rewarded. As the touring schedule thinned in direct proportion to the band's hair, he'd been retained as a kind of rock and roll butler. His job description encompassed bodyguard, gofer, confidante, counsellor, court jester, chauffeur, cocktail waiter, snack chef, shoulder to lean on, shoulder to cry on, towel man, whipping boy, playmate, alibi and anything else that took Stump's fancy.

It was in his role as *keeper of the gate* – though not of the Queen's English – that he greeted the new arrival.

'You the publisher fella?'

Norman did his best to look important and nonchalantly unimpressed by his surroundings. The *Savile Row* suit helped... but the years preceding it didn't.

He nodded lamely.

'Follow me, then.' Sharky turned and disappeared into the building... leaving Norman to hasten up the steps after him in a manner *real* music publishing moguls would never have done.

His pursuit across the floor of the main entrance hall was witnessed by two suits of armour... their threatening pose softened somewhat by the large pair of Y-fronts each was wearing. They stood guard over a disparate collection of paintings exhibiting naked females, unrealistically proportioned racehorses, landscapes, more naked females, and an enormous, framed, blown-up photograph of Stump's posterior beaming at the camera from the stage of a packed, outdoor festival.

'He's in bed,' said Sharky, as Norman caught up with him, halfway up a magnificently cantilevered staircase.

'Is he ill?'

'Nope.'

Norman glanced at his wristwatch. It was three o'clock in the afternoon. 'A late night then, I suppose?'

'Nope.'

The rest of their ascent continued in silence... as did the journey along an eclectically furnished corridor. It wasn't often you found a piece of King Louis XIV furniture sitting alongside a 1950's jukebox... or a stuffed gorilla, come to that.

Sharky waddled briskly – as if trying to outpace the stench of

Though it was true he'd certainly had as much sex. He was mad, bad and... if you were a tortoise... extremely dangerous to know.

It was *this* man that Norman was about to come face to face with. Gabriel's *people* had arranged it. Stump – believing he was about to meet one of the hottest new music publishers in the business, intent on purchasing some of his back catalogue – had willingly agreed.

Norman pressed his nose against the smoked-glass window of the limousine.

The house itself looked like something out of a gothic horror story... its immense, jagged outline biting violently into the gently rolling English countryside surrounding it.

Norman had heard of Rolls Royces being driven into swimming pools. But the sight of a rusted, thirty-two seater tour coach sticking out of a huge, ornamental pond quite took his breath away. As did the interestingly shaped bushes that dotted the estate... demonstrating Stump's obvious fascination with topiary and a certain part of the male anatomy.

You wouldn't want to be the neighbours.

Norman's arrival brought out onto the steps leading up to the main entrance an imposing beer belly with man attached. This was Sharky... Stump's right-hand man.

Sharky had once been Stump's *left-hand* man. In less weighty days, he would crouch like an over-eager gun dog – stage left – in that no-man's-land frequented by roadies of neither onstage nor off... waiting for his master to think of something that wasn't as it should be. This could be anything from too much feedback to not enough... a dangerously low *Courvoisier* brandy bottle... or the need to detach a female member of the audience from his master's nether regions. He had perfected the art of doing whatever was required in one single movement, without stopping... always accompanied by a huge cheer from the audience.

Eagerness had eventually morphed into routine – the light-footed dash into a resigned waddle – as the additional weight of a couple of breweries around his midriff took its toll.

hold court in here.'

Norman was impressed. From the minute he'd passed through the imposing gates of *Soddem Hall*, he'd found himself immersed in the heady world of rock and roll excess.

This was Stump's home... he of *Sex Wench* fame... lead singer and main culprit for *Trouzerbulge*, the band who did for music what Genghis Khan did for world peace.

It was rumoured in diplomatic circles that their garishly coloured spandex trousers had once been the inspiration for a newly independent nation's flag. The truth was... despite the colossal popularity of their one major hit, the only thing their music was likely to inspire was a riot.

The drive leading up to the main house was like that of many stately homes... with one exception. Those that had managed to remain in the possession of the aristocracy tended not to have plastic blow-up dolls secreted amongst the branches of the overhanging laburnums greeting visitors. In fact... they tended not to have *many* things that could be found inside the grounds of *Soddem Hall*... Stump being one of them.

The man was living testament to the fact that you could come from the humblest of backgrounds, possess an amount of talent able to be demonstrated by a closely held thumb and index finger, and still mix it with the best. All that was needed was an unreasonable amount of belief in yourself... an aversion to shame... and, of course, the catchiest two-note melody that had ever been heard.

A gimmick also helped. His international notoriety had rocketed after an incident on stage when he'd been seen to bite the head off a tortoise. In truth... it had been a cleverly doctored Cornish pasty. But through a haze of dry-ice – and under the influence of anything that made their music more palatable – the effect was all too real. From that moment on, it became a regular part of the act and a highlight of the show... much to the disgust of parents, vegetarians and tortoises around the world.

He had become the Lord Byron of the twenty-first century... without the talent, good looks, decent rhymes... or the limp.

It bounced off the television screen, as the picture changed to similar scenes around the world showing other religious gatherings.

'Record congregations are being reported from around the globe... as people flock to their nearest church, synagogue, mosque or gurdwara in search of answers to the economic turmoil that looks set to blight everyone's lives,' announced a sombre voice-over.

Babe kept her eyes fixed firmly on her toenails... making short, quick flicks along them with a brush coated in baby pink nail varnish. 'I don't fink you should've done that. You should show a bit more reference.'

'What?'

'Reference... You know.' Her rate of gum-chewing increased as her companion fell back onto his pillows, laughing.

'I think you mean *reverence*, Babe.'

She tutted and waited for the bed to stop shaking before continuing her task. 'Whatever the fing is... you should show some. I fink it's quite nice those people have somefink to believe in.'

'They're only there because they're shit scared. They've spent their lives worshiping the great consumer God and – now he's let them down – they're looking for a psychological lifeboat.'

'I thought the Vatican was in Rome.'

'It is.'

'Well... that's nowhere near the sea.'

'What was that?'

'I said... it's nowhere near...'

'Not that... I thought I heard the gate alarm.'

'Probably... That'll be your appointment.'

'Appointment?'

'The publisher.'

'Shit! I forgot!'

'Shall I get the door?'

'Not dressed like that, you won't. Besides... what d'ya think I pay Sharky for?'

'Scoring yer drugs?'

'Besides that. Now go and put something decent on... I'll

that… it'd rubbish everything I've ever believed in!'

'Precisely what I told Donald. But maybe that's your problem. Maybe you're frightened to make a leap of faith.'

'*Faith?* That's just a more palatable word for *surrendering all logical reasoning*. You're only required to have faith in something if it can't be proved to exist. And, in my book… if something can't be proved to exist… it doesn't!'

'Well… maybe this 66b Armageddon just might! What have you got to lose by giving it a try?'

'My sanity… for one! Though – by the sound of things – you've waved *adios* to *yours* already! So, I'll tell you what… Why don't *you* check it out? At least when you discover it's complete bullshit, only one of us will look like an idiot!'

'We'll both look like idiots if we don't act quickly! You've always said we're a team. D'ya seriously think I should investigate this lead on my own? You've seen the news reports… It's getting pretty serious. This art thing has triggered an investment landslide. Those Templars are fuckin' with the system. We've gotta stop them before they screw it up all together! There isn't time to waste!'

'Yes there is,' said Chad coldly. 'There's my time. And you're doing it right now.' He picked up a book from the straightened pile. 'I'll tell you what… You find our Templars plotting around a table… or even the *remotest* connection beyond coincidence… you give me a call.'

*   *   *

The crowd were gazing eagerly up at the balcony and at its single occupant dressed in white, desperate for the words of comfort he seemed about to deliver. It was a scene that had been repeated many times throughout history… though this time, the numbers of those assembled in Vatican Square were larger than they'd ever been.

'Baah! Baah…! Look at 'em, Babe… Like bleedin' sheep, they are.' The owner of the voice lobbed the core of the apple he'd just been eating towards the outstretched hands of the Pontiff.

& Blount look and said nothing.

He didn't need to. Norman's mind had gone into freefall. 'Tomorrow morning… you say?'

'First thing.'

'If you'll excuse me… I have to go!'

*　　*　　*

'How many years have you and I been working together?'

It was a rhetorical question. Given those years, Bob knew to translate it as… *You might be gullible enough to be influenced by a man who has trouble influencing his own bladder… but don't insult me by believing that I might be too!*

'And tell me, oh learned one,' countered Bob sarcastically. 'What friggin' strategy have *you* come up with whilst I've been away doing something that might actually help?' He contemptuously kicked at a pile of books stacked close to Chad's chair. 'Because the last time I looked… your ideas file contained precisely jack shit!'

'Point one,' snapped Chad, brandishing the heavy tome he'd been digesting on ancient Masonic history. 'I'm currently working on solid, concrete, tangible clues… ones that don't require the intervention of a lunatic medium. Point two… Anything devised off the top of my head would be infinitely preferable to what's come out of that idiot's! And point three…' He bent down to tidy up the books Bob had just scattered. 'At this moment in time… *jack shit* is far healthier for what little career prospects we may have left than *deep shit*… because that's what we'll be in if we indulge any further in his madness!'

'Okay. So, on the subject of shit… what's this crap *you've* been working on?' demanded Bob.

'I'm trying to understand our opponents… get inside their minds,' answered Chad. 'Know your enemy well enough and you'll be able to predict their next move.'

'Never mind their next move… Donald's predicted their friggin' *address!*'

'How can he possibly have?' Chad scoffed. 'If I were to accept change.

'What's the matter?' gloated Oppenheimer. 'Not feeling so clever now?'

He wasn't. His offering had been designed to buy time... but the shape of his plan was beginning to look uncomfortably like that of a pear. 'You can't have me removed... I haven't broken our tenancy agreement!'

The confident widening of Oppenheimer's smile suggested that *Thackett, Hobson & Blount* had instructed him otherwise. 'Oh,' he sneered perniciously, 'but you *have*. You've been running a business!'

'That's not true!'

'Such a heavy schedule of deliveries suggests it is.'

'So take me to court,' said Norman, deciding attack might be the best form of defence. 'It'll cost you a fortune and take months, if not *years*, to resolve!'

'True,' said Oppenheimer with a shrug. 'That's exactly what my solicitor said.'

Norman found his landlord's calmness more unsettling than his anger.

'Which is why he suggested I contact the local council. I'm sure you researched the legalities of running a commercial enterprise from *residential* premises before you set it up?'

'I told you... there *is* no business!'

'The evidence would suggest otherwise,' said Oppenheimer, aiming an accusatory eyebrow in the direction of Norman's suit.

It suddenly felt very heavy.

'But the deliveries have stopped!'

Oppenheimer offered another shrug. 'Then the evidence would be that you *had* operated one. Either way... you're about to have some explaining to do. The council are sending someone round tomorrow morning to investigate. If they find your room equipped for anything else but that for which it has been rated, you will be prosecuted... and any equipment found, impounded.'

'Impounded? They can't!'

Oppenheimer gave another *not according to Thackett, Hobson* encased inside a suit and tie was at his Aunty Flo's funeral. He'd been a week short of his fourteenth birthday and the suit, a week short of its third… its trousers and sleeves about six inches short of everything else. All the other mourners had dressed in black. Unfortunately for Norman, safari suits tended to come in tones of beige… and junior ones with a compulsory, large, gold-coloured belt buckle prominently displayed at the front. Even the vicar had winced. As he'd stood watching his Aunty Flo disappear into a hole in the ground, Norman had wished a large one would open up and swallow *him*.

But now it was different. The suit fitted… and how.

He'd just been *made-over* by the trendiest outfitters in London and was looking and feeling a million dollars… and hopefully every bit the image of the successful, music-publishing whiz-kid Gabriel had instructed him to become. He'd even ended a lifetime's slavery to glasses… having embraced the world of the contact lens.

This was a new him. He not only *looked* different… he *felt* different.

'I can't stop, Mr Oppenheimer. I've got an extremely important meeting to attend. I just thought I'd make a peace offering.' He confidently proffered the bottle.

His benevolence wasn't returned.

'Peace…? You think a bottle can bring me *peace?* For so many months I have had to suffer the noise of your business… the constant intrusions into my home… your rudeness… the erosion of my authority… not to mention a top-quality stair carpet… and you have the cheek to suggest it might all be forgotten with a *drink?'*

'It *is* a bottle of *Bollinger,'* said Norman positively.

'I don't care if it's a bottle of *Champagne!* You're finished here!' Oppenheimer drew a wounded smile. 'You're also too late. This morning I instruct my solicitors to get you removed. They tell me that this should not be a problem, given your *activities.'*

Norman lowered the bottle. Before its offering, he'd felt like a million dollars. It was now something approaching loose

81

It took a few seconds for Oppenheimer's brain to register what was in front of it... his body instinctively recoiling from the object thrust outwards. 'W... what's the meaning of this?' he stuttered, his widened eyes playing for thinking time.

The figure impassively removed his sunglasses and indicated with his eyes towards the object in his outstretched hand. 'Surprise!' he sang in a looping pitch. 'This is for you!'

Oppenheimer's face collapsed. He stared at his visitor, unable to believe what he was seeing.

The figure stepped forward.

'Oh my God!' yelled Oppenheimer, clutching at his chest.

The three shepherds sat impassively, staring out at the barren terrain.

'Do you know something,' said Shepherd One, breaking an excruciatingly long silence. 'I've got this awful feeling in the pit of my stomach.'

Shepherd Two glowered at him. *Typical*, he thought. *He's at it again... The other month it was trimmed wicks. Now it's stomach pains. Always showing off!*

'You should've gone before we came up here,' said Shepherd Three.

Half an hour passed.

'No... I don't mean like that,' said Shepherd One. 'I mean... like an ominous feeling of impending disaster... like something's going to happen... and it's not pleasant.'

Shepherd Three turned apprehensively... just in time to see Shepherd Two lunge at Shepherd One yelling, 'You're not wrong there... you egotistical bastard!'

'Norman!' cried Oppenheimer, dropping his arms. 'You nearly gave me a heart attack! I was not recognising you in your fancy clothes! What is the meaning of this?' He shot his rapidly darting eyes from Norman's businesslike attire towards the bottle of champagne being thrust towards him.

The corners of Norman's mouth quivered with suppressed pride. He hardly recognised *himself*. The last time he'd been wide open.

The figure entered the building and hesitated.

There was a door to his right, on which cracked plastic numbers and a solitary letter informed whoever cared to know that this was 66b.

The figure put on a pair of sunglasses – inappropriate for such gloomy conditions – then turned to face it… carefully positioning himself so as to be ready when the door opened.

The fingers of his right hand gripping tightly around the object he'd been carrying, he raised his arm so as to bring it to head height.

Arm outstretched… he used his other hand to knock sharply three times.

A muffled voice preluded the sliding of a security chain.

The figure drew a deep breath.

The door opened.

'CRY "HAVOC!" AND LET SLIP THE DOGS OF WAR!' Donald winced and slapped his own face. 'Shut up you fool! You've only got yourself to blame for this mess!' His trembling hands flitted across the over-burdened bookcase. 'I WAS TALKING TO MYSELF!' he shouted. 'BUT WHILST WE'RE ON THE SUBJECT… YOU CAN SHUT UP TOO! IT'S BAD ENOUGH WITH THE SHAKESPEARE!' He momentarily paused his search of the battered spines to adjust a huge turban of tin foil, which had been hastily wrapped around his head. 'I need to think!' he groaned. 'I must have silence!' Resuming his search, another outburst sent a cluster of cats scampering. 'LO! NOW MY GLORY SMEARED IN DUST AND BLOOD!' He clamped a hand to his mouth… but the words insisted on coming. 'Mmm Mmmm Mm Mmmm Mmm Mmmmmm Mmmm Mm!' Finding what he was looking for, he removed a tattered A to Z from the shelf and hastily flicked his way to the back pages. 'Armageddon… … A… Arm… Armada Court… Armadale Close…… I have to put a stop to this!'

savings into something tangible – have decided that hard currency is preferable to... hard times.'

'I understand that this panic amongst the public has led to some pretty ugly scenes,' commented a voice from the studio.

'That's right,' nodded the reporter. *'As banks instructed their high street branches to close early this morning to avoid a worsening situation, reports increased of skirmishes up and down the country. It appears it's just got harder than ever to contact your bank manager!'*

'But just how serious is the situation?' quizzed the studio voice. *'Are we looking at a financial Armageddon?'*

'I put that very question to this company's CEO half an hour ago, when I interviewed him in his office a few floors above where I'm standing now. He intimated that the next hour would be critical for the survival of his company. Like everyone else... he's praying that this freefall ends and things start to go up.'

'Something just went down!' shrieked the studio voice, with alarm.

'Pardon?' The reporter's hand shot up to his earpiece.

'Behind you! Something just went down behind you!'

The reporter turned to observe a large window boasting a panoramic view of the city. *'What was it?'*

'I can't be sure,' quaked the studio voice. *'But I believe it was wearing an Armani suit.'*

*　　*　　*

Unusually dark skies and the threat of what they might bring had ensured Armageddon Terrace was deserted, as a black limousine with darkened windows rolled to a halt outside number sixty-six.

Within seconds, a suited figure – holding something that glistened in what little light there was – emerged from the back and, without bothering to survey his surroundings, strode purposefully towards the building's front door. It was never kept locked, providing the tenants with easy access to the inner hall but precious little in the way of security.

The car's engine remained running... the door at the back,

politely to stop?'

'I… I don't know… I mean… I never thought…'

'Thanks for your help, Donald. I dunno how you do it… but you're one hell of an original guy! If this thing works out, it'll be mainly thanks to you!'

'No…! You can't!' shouted Donald, placing himself in front of Bob to block his exit. 'This information was given to me in good faith. My gift is meant for the *benefit* of mankind… not a weapon to be used *against* parts of it!'

Bob stabbed a finger at the television still showing pictures of turmoil from the world's stock markets. 'And you think what's happening out there at the moment is benefiting anyone?' As he spoke, the image of a panicked queue outside a bank appeared as a newsflash on the screen.

'*That…?* That's only about money. You're talking about human *life!*'

'I'm talking about orders, Donald. I'm talking about the way the world *really* works… about security… about not allowing people to step out of line. Somebody has to keep it all together.'

Donald's head shot to the left. 'I *KNOW* YOU SAID HE WAS A COMPLETE SHIT…! I JUST THOUGHT YOU WERE BEING BELLIGERENT!'

'Jesus! It's bad enough being insulted by the living!' said Bob, circumnavigating his deprecator's conduit.

'You can't do this!' shouted Donald, as Bob made his way towards the front door. 'I trusted you…! I even lent you daddy's trousers!'

*　　*　　*

I'm standing here on the twelfth floor of one of the world's largest investment houses,' announced a television reporter, with professionally-managed concern. *'Shockwaves – from what looks like being the biggest market crash in history – are set to undermine the very foundations on which it stands. It seems that every economist's worse nightmare – a worldwide run on the banks – has finally become a reality. Smaller investors – opting to convert their*

'What's happening?' asked Bob anxiously.

'Whitebait thinks the third digit's not a digit at all. He says it looks more like the letter *b*. And – having given it another look – I'm inclined to agree with him.'

'Sixty-six b...? What's that... the Beast's brassiere size, for Christ's sake?'

'I think it means we're not going to die,' replied Donald calmly. 'It might also be the address you're after... 66b Armageddon.'

'*Armageddon*...? Is that a street... a road... a district?'

'Oh, I'm sure you can find that bit out for yourself. I shouldn't think there are too many options in the London A to Z.' Donald slowly rotated his neck. 'I've done my part. Now, if you'll excuse me... I'm feeling rather tired. It's enough to send you to an early grave, all this conversing with the dead.'

'No problem!' said Bob, jumping up enthusiastically. 'I've got what I came for. All I gotta do now is convince my partner this information is worth acting upon... which could be the hardest bit!'

'And what might that entail?'

'Persuading him to drop every bit of logical reasoning he's ever had... I should think.'

'I meant... what *action* will you be taking?'

'Well... if you *have* given us the address where this scam's being masterminded from, all we gotta do is get over there and eliminate the problem.'

Donald scratched his head. '*Eliminate?*'

'Best you don't dwell on that bit. But, you needn't worry... We'll be discreet.'

'What do you mean *discreet?*' asked Donald, concerned. 'What's there to be discreet about?'

'Can't have people tinkering about with the fragile balance of the world's investment systems, can we?' Bob made a move towards the door. 'They need to be stopped at all costs.'

'At all costs...? You mean... you're going to eliminate *people?*' gasped Donald, horrified.

'Well... what did ya think we were gonna do? Ask them

Bob stopped his shaking. 'Does one *figure* at any point in the Book of Revelations?'

'Not to my knowledge. And if it did... I'm sure it would have something more apocalyptic than *rabbits* around its base.'

'*Rabbits?*'

'Well... I *think* they're rabbits.' Donald's hands gripped the edge of the chair, his body jolting backwards. 'Oh no... Please... no!'

'Another hat stand?'

'The Beast!'

'Chasing the rabbits?'

'HERE IS WISDOM. LET HIM THAT HATH UNDERSTANDING COUNT THE NUMBER OF THE BEAST; FOR IT IS THE NUMBER OF A MAN; AND HIS NUMBER IS SIX HUNDRED THREESCORE AND SIX!'

'You can *see* him?'

'Numbers... Numbers on a door!'

'Six, six, six?'

Donald's face was pale and etched with fear. 'Yes,' he gasped, his lips barely moving.

'Well... I'll be fucked!'

'You may well be,' said Donald, his eyes dropping from the top of his head. 'You were right the first time,' he trembled, his gaze cutting straight through Bob's. 'They're showing me... the end of the world!'

Bob stared at him in disbelief.

Donald looked shattered. 'I knew it was something big. I had no idea it was *that* big!'

Bob sank back into his chair, his mouth agape. It started moving in pronounced slow-motion, his front upper teeth making their way onto his bottom lip as the top one drew back. 'F...u_'

'WAIT!' yelled Donald, grabbing Bob's arm. 'WHAT'S THAT?' His eyes darted to and fro, focusing on a spot only visible to him. 'WHAT D'YOU MEAN... "IT'S A B"?' Donald tilted his head. 'HMMM... DO YOU KNOW...' The terror drained from his face. '... I THINK YOU MIGHT BE RIGHT.'

'What've *they* got to do with it?'

'AND HE GATHERED THEM TOGETHER INTO A PLACE CALLED IN THE HEBREW TONGUE ARMAGEDDON!'

'Armageddon?' exclaimed Bob. 'You're seeing the end of the world?'

'Actually… I think it's the end of a road… There's a building… and a room with a number on it. I can't quite make it out.'

Bob grabbed him by the shoulders. 'You must, Donald! Try harder! This is extremely important!'

Donald's face contorted with the extra effort. 'Nope… it's no good. They're just not able to give it to me. Something's stopping them.'

'Try taking your hat off!'

Donald exposed his head… then shook it slowly. 'It's no good… It's just not coming.'

'Is there anything else you can see?'

Donald groaned. 'Stairs… There are stairs leading downwards.'

'Can you go down them for me?'

'I'll try.' He groaned again, but much louder this time. 'There's something at the bottom.'

'What?'

'I don't know.' Donald's eyes flickered beneath their lids. 'Oh my God…! It's *hideous!*'

'What is it?' said Bob, shaking him backwards and forwards. 'What are you seeing?'

'It's *awful.*'

'Describe it to me!'

'It looks like…'

'Yeah?'

'It looks like…'

'What?'

'… a hat stand!'

'But what *exactly* is it?'

Donald took a closer psychic look. 'A hat stand.'

'Well?'

'He says he doesn't know. None of them do. They're only getting the odd snippet of information. Apparently, there's so much excitement and activity taking place on the higher planes, it's causing certain vibrations to leak out onto their level. They're just grasping at them and channelling them through me. The trouble is... it's all disjointed and without any form. And when they *do* get something more coherent, they all start shouting at once... and then nothing makes any sense. It's hell... what with that and the Shakespeare.'

'*Shakespeare?*'

'I can't help it. His words keep popping into my head.'

'Perhaps you should be using the other side of the tinfoil?'

'All I can tell you is that these happenings involve the illicit procurement of artworks from around the world... and that they're being sent to a single location somewhere in the centre of London. There's been an unprecedented surge of spiritual activity occurring there over the last few months... Quite remarkable!'

Bob leant forward. 'Now we're getting somewhere! Can you be more specific about this London location?'

Donald looked at him apologetically. 'I'm not sure I can.'

'Could you try?'

Donald's eyes fluttered up into their lids. He gripped the bridge of his nose between his thumb and forefinger. 'Horses!' he said... after a moment's contemplation. 'I'm getting horses!'

'A stable perhaps?'

'There are four of them.'

'Four stables?'

'Horses.'

'Hyde Park? I've seen some being ridden around there.'

'Not by *these* riders, I hope!'

'Why...? D'ya know 'em?'

'Not personally. They're called Death, Pestilence, Famine and War.'

'I take it we're not talking surnames.'

'We're talking about the Four Horsemen of the Apocalypse.'

'Well… it hasn't fallen off yet.'

'I meant the tinfoil.'

'I'm not sure. I can never figure out if it's the shiny or dull side you're supposed to use on the outside.'

'These voices… You actually hear them like I'm hearing you?'

Donald considered the question as if never having given it any thought before. 'Not exactly… They're more a suggestion of a voice that has a will of its own.' He jerked his head to the left. 'THANK YOU…! THERE'S NO NEED TO DEMONSTRATE… HE CAN'T HEAR YOU!'

'Was that one?'

'Whitebait. He thinks he's being helpful. I KNOW IT'S HARD TO HEAR YOU WITH THE TELEVISION SWITCHED ON… THAT'S THE POINT…! Do excuse me… NO… I WON'T SWITCH IT OVER… I DON'T CARE IF THERE *IS* A COOKERY PROGRAM ON THE OTHER SIDE…! I'VE GOT A GUEST!'

Bob waited his turn.

'YES…I KNOW HE'S THE ONE I COULDN'T STAND…! BUT HE'S ASKING FOR OUR HELP NOW.' There was a pause. 'YES… THANK YOU… HE HAD THEM CLEANED!'

'If it's inconvenient, I could always come back.'

'You stay where you are!' commanded Donald. 'If you give in to them, they'll *never* leave you alone! IF YOU DON'T STOP BOTHERING ME, I'LL STICK MY HEAD IN THE TUMBLE DRYER AGAIN!'

'I'll cut to the chase… seeing as you've got your hands full.'

'Head,' Donald corrected him.

'Quite… Look… I dunno how this spiritual thing works… but I'm prepared to accept that it does.'

'That's very gracious of you.'

'I'm also prepared to accept that you got hold of information outside our usual sphere of understanding. If it's Whitebait who's responsible for that, perhaps he could tell me why all this friggin' shit's been going down.'

Donald's eyes flickered impatiently. 'HE'S AMERICAN… CONSIDER IT A COLLOQUIALISM!'

'I didn't say I've changed it.'

'But you're having doubts.'

'Look… I've got a helluva lotta questions that need answers. I thought if I came to see you, I might be able to find some… one way or another.'

'We're all looking for those,' said Donald, his attention momentarily distracted by the flight of a wood pigeon from a nearby tree. 'There's much strangeness afoot in both worlds at this particular moment in time. I'm getting more psychic information than I can cope with!'

'That's what I wanted to talk to you about,' said Bob.

Donald glanced furtively about the drive. 'In that case… you'd better come in.'

An old black and white television had been left blasting away in a corner of the study, its speaker struggling to cope with the demands being made of it.

'*It looks like being a day of chaos on the world's stock markets,*' announced the suited presenter, an electronic tickertape of negative figures scrolling in front of him. '*It began as markets opened a few hours ago to rumours of an unprecedented number of aggressive take-over bids between some of the world's leading multinational corporations. Those affected initially saw their stock values soar. But as hunted turned hunter, counter bids have sent the markets crashing with the uncertainty. Analysts say they have never seen anything like it. It follows already weakened confidence caused by the recent collapse of the art market, which many believe to be a catalyst for the current situation. Predictions are for a turbulent day ahead.*'

'I only keep it on to block out the voices coming at me from the other side,' said Donald, acknowledging the television.

'Is that why you're wearing the metal hat?' braved Bob, risking mention of Donald's unorthodox headwear.

'Got absolutely nothing to do with it,' said Donald. 'It protects me from falling masonry. Mind you… it does help keep the tinfoil in place.' He lifted the helmet to reveal a crumpled, improvised skullcap beneath. 'See?'

'Does it work?'

and write a cheque. If it's greed that persuades him – rather than altruism – then so be it. He'll end up paying back far more than he receives in the long run... believe me.'

'But... a*ny* amount?'

'The price is irrelevant. You can draw as many noughts on a piece of paper as you wish. In the eyes of the greater Universe, that's all they are.'

'And how will I find him?'

'Our people will arrange that. The rest will be up to you.'

*   *   *

'Ah...! I was wondering when I'd see you again!' Donald opened the door wider, allowing a number of cats to escape into the drive. 'I take it you've come to give me a progress report.'

'Not exactly,' said Bob, trying hard not to stare at the Second World War helmet perched on Donald's head.

'My trousers, then?'

'I've had them cleaned,' Bob handed him a carrier bag.

'You shouldn't have gone to the trouble.'

'They were doing a *two-for-the-price-of-one*.'

'... Ah' said Donald slowly, recalling the reason behind their loan.

'Actually... I was also wondering if I could have a word with you.'

Donald peered over his visitor's shoulder... and at the empty car parked on the drive. 'Alone?'

'Let's just say... my partner's a little more sceptical of your special abilities than I am.'

'Oh... I *see. That* kind of talk... I'm surprised. I'd have put you two the other way around in the *Doubting Thomas* stakes.'

'That's because he's politer than I am.'

Donald looked to his left and nodded. 'Whitebait says it's the first time he's agreed with you.'

'What's more,' said Bob, 'I've surprised *myself*.'

Donald's eyes twinkled. 'So what happened to change your mind?'

thought it?'

'I guess all that remains now is for me to digitise the track and add it to the others,' Norman beamed up at him.

'Before you do... I need to know who created this song.'

Norman picked up the discarded CD case and examined its inner sleeve. 'According to this... it was Stump.'

'What?'

'You mean... *who*. He's the singer of the band.'

'Is he dead?'

'No... he always sounds that way.'

'Then before we proceed any further, we must get his permission.'

'You're kiddin' me!'

'I told you, Norman... we're not allowed to break any laws. It makes no difference whether they're the fundamental laws of the Universe or those pertaining to copyright.'

'*Copyright?*'

'Yes... If he wrote the song, we must have his permission to use it. We've had to do the same thing for every other work of art you've encoded. Only – in those cases – as their creators were in spirit form, they were hardly in a position to refuse!'

'So... what are you going to do? Appear in front of him like you did me? I can't wait to hear the band's next album, if you do!'

'That won't be necessary. It's *you* who'll be doing the asking.'

'*Me?*' Norman looked horrified. 'But how am I gonna get to meet someone like Stump? And what am I gonna tell him if I do?'

'You could tell him the truth.'

'But he'll think I'm mad!'

'More than likely... and all the better from our point of view if he does. Just so long as you get permission to use the song.'

'I don't think it'll work.'

'Then offer to *buy* the song. Or at least the copyright. Once we have that, we can do whatever we like with his work.'

'But what if he refuses?'

'Everyone has their price. All you have to do is ask him *his*

'Wait 'til we get to the chorus! That's the bit that *really* gets you!'

Had the first-time listener been under the impression that a band couldn't play any faster or louder, *Trouzerbulge* proved them wrong. With a technique owing more to amphetamines than any musical training, the band launched into hyperdrive.

Norman – overtaken by the excitement – threw his fist into the air and began singing at the top of his voice. '*Sex Wench...! Sex Wench...! Gonna strap yer to my workbench!*'

Gabriel bowed his head.

The words were carried on a two note melody which had all the finesse of a police siren.

But it worked.

Gloriously so.

The pounding rhythm beneath and uninhibited exuberance of the performance produced an effect to match anything Wagner or Tchaikovsky could put against it.

'Have you heard enough?' yelled Norman above the caterwauling.

'More than enough,' said Gabriel, raising his head.

'Shall I turn it off?'

'Please!'

Norman obliged and waited expectantly as Gabriel breathed in the silence.

'Well?'

'Yes... Very well, thank you. I'm glad it's over.'

'Sorry if it was a bit loud. Only... you really need to feel the full effect.'

'I certainly did that. And when I said it's over, I wasn't referring to the song. I was referring to our quest. You've done it, Norman! I don't know how... but you've found the missing piece!'

'Yo!' Raising his hand in the air, Norman launched himself towards the Archangel in an attempt to give him a high-five. Gabriel – sensing what was intended – raised his in response and watched as Norman fell through it and onto the floor.

'*Sex Wench*,' groaned Gabriel, shaking his head. 'Who'd have album somewhere. Do you wanna hear it?'

'I suppose it's worth a try,' sighed Gabriel resignedly. 'If it *were* to be the master piece, I'd feel the vibrations immediately.'

'You'll feel the vibrations even if it's not!' laughed Norman. He hurried over to an untidy pile of compact discs on the floor and began sorting through the cases like an over-oiled threshing machine. 'Here it is!' he exclaimed... finally holding one aloft. '*Songs to Shag By, Volume One.*'

The concept behind the album was totally wasted on Norman. But its price had been reduced in a sale... and he could always dream.

He loaded the disc into his music system... selected the relevant track and hit play. The stillness of the room was violently defiled by a noise comparable to that of a machine gun being let off in a giant biscuit tin. After a few bars, it came to an abrupt halt... the relief on the listener's ears mugged by a drum break suggesting its instigator had fatally caught a ricocheting bullet and fallen over his kit.

Then it started up again... the throbbing bass line so banal it sounded like the CD had become stuck. It was only when the vocals – or more accurately, air-being-forced-through-a-tortured-larynx – were introduced into the proceedings that the listener realised this was not the case... and probably wished it were.

The singer appeared to be in pain... a condition he seemed determined to inflict upon others.

For the band's part... they sounded like they were trying to get to the end of the song as quickly as possible... which was hardly surprising, given the vocals.

It was audible adrenalin... the angst of youth played out by men who had long since left it behind and should've known better. Their one-finger salute to Father Time was to continue squeezing into unfeasibly tight trousers and wearing badly applied mascara.

'Are you feeling anything?' shouted Norman above the cacophony.

'*Despair*... might be a good place to start,' answered Gabriel.

Norman's face became contorted with the strain of thinking. Gabriel was about to suggest he stop before he did himself an injury when it erupted in an expression of revelation.

'I've got it!' he cried. 'Not the lyrics... the *song*! Not a couple of *letters*... but a couple of *notes*! That's what we're looking for! A melody consisting of just two notes!'

'It's possible,' said Gabriel. 'But how many inspiring melodies do you know that fit that criterion?'

'That were written about twenty years ago?'

Gabriel nodded.

'And were powerful enough to inspire others?'

'*Many* others. Its appeal would have to have been universal. Small wonder the piece hung around unclaimed for so long. It would seem an almost impossible task to achieve.'

'Depends on who your audience were!' grinned Norman. 'Surely not!' he mumbled to himself.

'Surely not *what*?'

'No more than two notes... and a pretty big hit?'

'Enormous.'

'Then I may have the answer!'

Gabriel looked unconvinced.

'*Sex Wench!*'

'I beg your pardon?'

'*Sex Wench...* a phenomenal track by the heavy metal band *Trouzerbulge*. It contains the most repetitive melody you've ever heard.'

'I can't imagine the lyrics are much better.'

'Who knows? You can't hear those anyway... But it's an absolute classic! There's something about the track that just makes you feel... well... kinda... *good*.'

'I suppose that's a start,' said Gabriel.

'The song was a massive hit around the world. The band's only one, in fact. It became a universal anthem... used in films and adverts... It's even sung at football matches... though the lyrics are less polite.'

'I shudder to think.'

'Quite... I've got a copy of the original on a compilation

it became are just as small as the piece itself?'

'I suppose so.'

'And that means we should be able to locate it just by thinking logically!'

'Ah... logic!' smiled Gabriel. 'That quaint method of perception available to those who only have a few dimensions to do their thinking in. I wish the Universe were that simple, Norman!'

'But we're not looking for this master piece in the whole of the Universe. We're looking for it in this "quaint" backwater of a dimension.'

'There you go... a textbook example of its application. You even managed to slip in its twisted derivative... sarcasm.'

'But I'm right, aren't I? Even though this master piece was so small... it must've been used to produce something that inspired the whole world. If it wasn't big enough for a painting or a book, perhaps it ended up as a poem?'

'Still too big. You'd probably be talking no more than a couple of letters.'

'There you go!' said Norman brightly. 'That narrows our options even more!'

'It's impossible that two letters could have such a profound effect upon the listener,' said Gabriel. 'Or *any* effect... come to that.'

'What about Old MacDonald?' asked Norman.

'Who's he?'

'He had a farm.'

'Where?'

'In a song. I'm talking about the lyrics. They go... *Old MacDonald had a farm.*'

'Apparently.'

'And then they go... *e... i... e... i...*'

The Archangel raised his eyebrows sympathetically.

'*O... Shit...* One too many,' said Norman.

'Quite... which means we'd be looking for something universally awe-inspiring which has two-thirds the lyrical depth of *e... i... e... i...o...* Any other bright ideas?'

omnipresent?'

'It's such a bad term, that,' mused Gabriel. 'It gives the impression God's everywhere at the same time. Whereas, technically... God's *everything* at the same time,'

'Then... how come God can't tell you what's happened to this little bit of everything?'

'That's the complete and utter mystery. We should be able to feel it resonating somewhere. The problem is... we can't!'

'What... not even the slightest rumble?'

Gabriel shook his head.

'Okay... So, what do we do now?'

'I don't think we can do anything,' said Gabriel softly. His wings folded in on him and his head dropped.

This wasn't the response Norman had expected. 'Just a second...! Are you suggesting we give up?'

'It's not a case of giving up, Norman. If there's no way of knowing what and where this *master piece* is... then nothing more can be done.'

'You might think that!' retorted Norman. 'But I haven't come this far to throw in the towel! There *has* to be a way to locate this last piece!'

'If the whole of Heaven is unable to find it, I think you'll have to accept that there isn't,' said Gabriel. 'Ironic, isn't it... that the smallest piece should turn out to be the most important? I think there's a lesson in there somewhere.'

'I'm not interested in lessons,' snapped Norman. 'I'm interested in seeing this thing through to the end. If you can't tell me what the piece was used for, I'll just have to scan every notable work of art there is until I find the right one!'

Gabriel looked at him affectionately. 'Even if it were physically possible... I think your tenancy agreement would have expired long before you'd completed your task. Besides... this *master piece* is so small, it would have been impossible to have produced anything as grand as a painting from it.'

'A miniature... perhaps?'

'Still way too big.'

'If that's the case,' said Norman, 'surely the options for what

'You were going to your big meeting,' Norman reminded him.

'That was ages ago,' said the Archangel. 'Much has happened since then.'

'No it hasn't.'

'Not in your dimension, perhaps.'

'Oh... I see.'

'We have a problem, Norman.'

'You mean... *another* one.'

'It eclipses all the others.'

'I was rather fearing it might,' sighed Norman.

'To put it at its simplest... there's a piece missing.'

'Of what?'

'Vibration. It seems it was so infinitesimally small that nobody knew of its existence. Furthermore, it wasn't accounted for because it was a remnant of a greater piece.'

'I'm not quite with you.'

'It was the bit Schubert never got to use when composing his *unfinished* symphony. He'd unwittingly transcribed the bulk of a huge vibration to produce the first two movements... then found himself with such an infinitesimally small amount of inspiration left, he failed to get any further. He assumed he'd hit a writer's block. It was while he was prevaricating about what to do next that he was called home.'

'To Austria?'

'Heaven.'

'... Ah.'

'The bit that was unused remained in the ether. But being so small – and of little inspirational value to anyone – it floated around ignored.'

'You said "floated"... Past tense.'

'That's because it was finally used for something about twenty of your years ago.'

'*What* something?'

'That's the problem... We don't know!'

'You don't know?' exclaimed Norman. 'But I thought you guys knew everything! I thought God was supposed to be

99

get interesting!'

Norman heeded the warning... rooting his plimsolls firmly to the floor.

'Any minute now!' said Gabriel expectantly.

'I'm ready!'

A car alarm sounded in the distance.

Norman scrunched his eyes shut and waited.

There followed a long period of.......... absolutely nothing.

'Shouldn't my socks be smoking by now?' he asked, after the absolutely nothing seemed to be taking longer than it should.

'I don't understand,' said Gabriel anxiously. 'Are you sure everything's working properly?'

Norman cautiously opened one eye. 'Yep,' he said, taking a tentative peek at the screen. 'I'd be getting an error message if just *one* of the computers had failed to respond.'

'But the sphere of knowledge isn't materialising! There has to be a mistake!'

'Not from this end,' said Norman confidently. 'I've checked and rechecked my program a hundred times. It's as much a masterpiece as any of the works of art I've encoded.'

'Well... s*omething's* wrong,' insisted Gabriel, circling the room in a state of agitation. 'I suggest you shut everything down whilst I endeavour to find out *what*.' He halted by the door. 'I shall have to convene a Grand Council of Heaven. There are those who will have had a better viewpoint of what just occurred. They may be able to shed some light on the matter.'

Norman opened the door. 'Good luck!'

'Luck is Heaven wishing you well,' said Gabriel, exiting towards the stairs. 'You can rest assured we have plenty of that.'

Norman brought the door to a close with the full weight of his disappointment. 'Another cup of tea, then,' he muttered to himself.

He was just about to move when he heard a voice.

'Norman... It's Gabriel... open the door!'

He quickly did as he was told. 'Have you forgotten something?'

'No... why?' asked Gabriel, floating past.

100

few minutes for the other computers to respond.'

'There's no hurry. We have waited through many of your centuries for this moment. Minutes are of no significance. It's all the same where we come from.'

'It must make boiling an egg extremely difficult,' observed Norman. He finished typing. 'Okay... plimsolls!' Gabriel watched in bemused silence as he made a dash for his bed... dived headlong underneath... and began throwing out a multitude of objects... finally emerging with a beam on his face and some battered footwear held triumphantly aloft.

'I knew they'd come in useful if I kept them!'

'Put them on quickly and brace yourself!'

Norman fumbled with the laces. 'It's okay. I've one final command to give before the process can complete.' He stood up. 'So... who's gonna get it this time?'

'Get *what?*'

'The sphere of knowledge. Who's gonna find themselves the most popular bloke at their pub come quiz night?'

'That's not for you to worry about,' said Gabriel. 'And you're making two assumptions. One... that it will be a man... and two... that it will occur in your lifetime.'

'Might it not?'

'That depends on whether you survive this,' said Gabriel matter-of-factly.

Norman felt his stomach somersault.

'Don't worry. That was a joke... Never let it be said that Heaven doesn't have a sense of humour.'

'I know from personal experience that it does,' sighed Norman. He inputted one last command into the console and held his finger above the *enter* key. 'Now for the final vibration!' He brought his finger down with theatrical majesty.

A large image of Spikey burst onto the screen... bouncing up and down to the sound of synchronised *boings*. 'I thought it'd be quite amusing to have him be the one who ultimately saves the Universe... so he's programmed to represent the final vibration! What d'ya think?'

'I think you should hold onto that table. Things are about to you... it is.'

Norman seated himself at the Ark's console. 'I feel there ought to be some form of ceremony before we start... You know... a speech or something to mark the occasion.'

'I think enough words have been spoken already,' said Gabriel. 'I suggest a prayer might be more appropriate. You've got an awful lot of Heavenly attention focused on you at this particular moment. There'll never be a better time for one!'

'But given the momentous nature of this event for mankind... shouldn't you utter some profound words of wisdom?'

'You mean, like advice?'

'If you like.'

Gabriel gave the matter some thought. 'Alright,' he said, looking down at Norman's bare feet. 'I suggest you go and put your plimsolls on.'

'I can hear pretty well without them, thanks,' said Norman, somewhat perplexed.

'No... you don't understand,' said Gabriel. 'That *was* the advice.'

'Plimsolls...? If we're talking dress code... don't you think a suit and tie might be more appropriate?'

'Only if they're made of rubber.'

'*What?*'

'An elastic, polymeric substance made from the latex of one of your planet's tropical plants.'

'Sorry. Grammatical error... *Why?*'

'Because the sphere of knowledge will start to form in the fifth dimension of this very room. When it does... there will be an enormous discharge of a force best compared to the one you know as *static*... only... *considerably* stronger. It'll be breathtaking to behold, but it can also be extremely...' Gabriel considered his next word carefully.

'Hair-raising?' prompted Norman.

'Amongst other things. So keep your feet firmly on the floor.'

'Understood!' Norman composed himself. 'Right... Here we go!' He began inputting instructions into the console. 'It'll take a condone the breaking of a law, no matter how trivial the transgression! Our plan could not continue under such circumstances. It would break a far greater law... one that says free will is sacrosanct and that nothing should be done against another's wishes.'

'I'm not doing it against their wishes,' protested Norman. 'I just haven't told them! I'm simply *borrowing* unused computer space for a while.'

'But without people's permission,' countered Gabriel.

'If they don't know about it, they can't object! Things get imbedded in computers all the time when connected to the internet. Permission isn't asked... it's simply taken for granted. That's the thing about cyberspace... there *are* no laws. What I've done is no different to what happens to millions of computers every second of every day. Nobody will suffer and we'll get the chance to produce our simultaneous vibrations!'

Gabriel considered the argument carefully. 'I'm not happy about this. Are you sure there's no other way?'

'Not unless *you* can come up with one. Besides... don't you think it's appropriate that the whole planet will be involved in saving itself... even if unknowingly?'

'I suppose I might be persuaded to see it that way,' said Gabriel grudgingly. 'Just so long as this outside assistance doesn't increase the risk of failure.'

'We'll know the answer to that soon enough. I've only used computers I've identified as being kept permanently online. But you never can tell.'

'It's imperative we keep the vibrations going for as long as necessary,' warned Gabriel. 'There will come a point where they begin resonating with one another... rebuilding the original sphere of knowledge. It's crucial that nothing happens to interrupt this process. Were such a thing to occur, the assembling vibrations might become unstable and shatter into pieces again. I cannot stress how dire the consequences would be if this happened. Do you understand?'

'Absolutely. So... is this it?'

Gabriel drew a deep breath. 'Failing another scare from

'We don't have to. It already exists.'

'It does?'

'Yes... It's called the internet.'

Gabriel bowed his head. 'Norman... this conversation is playing havoc with my vibrations. Perhaps you'd be kind enough to explain.'

'Distributive computing,' obliged Norman.

'That's a *term*, Norman... not an explanation.'

'Okay... it's like this... Every second of every day, millions of computers around the world are switched on but not being used. Apart from the minuscule amount employed to keep them ticking over, their processing power goes to waste. That's an awful lot of power! Imagine the potential if it were harnessed. Well... that's just what SETI did. They...'

Gabriel raised a hand.

'The Search for Extra Terrestrial Life,' elaborated Norman. 'They need to process vast amounts of incoming data from their monitoring devices in order to discover if intelligent life exists elsewhere.'

'Couldn't they just acknowledge the billions of stars in the Universe and use common sense?' asked Gabriel, nonplussed.

'That's not the point. The point is... they devised a screensaver for volunteers that analyses sections of this data when their computers are idle and returns the results via the internet. It effectively produced the world's first global super-computer. Other projects have since followed... allowing calculations that would take a single computer thousands of years to complete, to be done in a matter of days. That's distributive computing.'

'And this is the method you intend employing?'

'I've already employed it! Only... I couldn't get people to install a screensaver without them knowing what it was being used for. So I cheated a little and installed it without their knowledge.'

'You mean you *hacked?*'

Norman twitched. 'Not quite the way I'd put it.'

Gabriel looked mortified. 'Norman! You know I cannot

Mister Prometheus made for the door.

'He's biting my ear!' shrieked Mister Atlas, from beneath the table.

* * *

'The greatest moment of consequence in the history of all that has been and ever will be is finally upon us,' announced Gabriel grandly.

Norman slurped his tea.

'The wisdom of the Universe has been captured and our faith in you justified.'

Never had a cup of tea tasted so good. Norman took another mouthful to hide his look of smugness. 'That's very kind of you to say so... but we haven't done the tricky bit yet.'

'*Tricky* bit?' Gabriel's confidence wobbled.

'Yep... the bit where all those separate strings of noughts and ones get to be played back at *exactly* the same time.'

'I take it this isn't a problem?' said Gabriel anxiously.

'It was always a problem,' replied Norman. 'The amount of computing power required to achieve it is mind-numbingly phenomenal! The sheer size of the...'

'The complexity of the task we set you is well-recognised!' interrupted Gabriel. 'You're not going to tell me that you don't have enough of this *computer memory,* are you?'

'No... I'm not.'

'Thank goodness for that!'

'I don't have enough processing power.'

'WHAT!'

'It'd be impossible! I'd need an aircraft hangar full of equipment to achieve the result!'

'But why didn't you say so from the beginning!' exclaimed Gabriel. 'If it was beyond your ability to do such a thing, you should've warned us!'

'Relax,' replied Norman coolly. 'I didn't say it was beyond my *ability.* I simply said... I don't have enough processing power.'

'Then we must construct a system that does!'

audience's look of bemusement for one of captivation. 'This…
er… two-faced siren,' he continued, encouraged, 'who lures the
ship of capitalism with the beauty of her song… then unleashes
a destructive force that… erm… smashes every timber of it into
driftwood.'

'What on earth's he on about?' cried a voice.

'That temptress,' answered Mister Atlas, 'who becomes an
adulteress and makes a cuckold out of capitalism… *Competition!*'

There was an *almost* collective gasp of horror.

'And you know what that means.'

A chord of dramatic silence sounded.

'Winter sales?' suggested Mister Epimetheus.

'Worse… Permanently lower prices!'

There was an assortment of cries and whimpers as the
horror of such a concept sunk in. When it had, pandemonium
erupted… as those around the table turned on one another,
seeking to find out who the guilty parties were. Long
simmering business grudges surfaced as fingers were pointed,
and soon the air was thick with insults and threats of hostile
takeovers.

Mister Dionysus – seizing the moment – threw his robe over
his shoulder to reveal an objectionably insufficient thong… then
dived headlong at the unsuspecting Mister Atlas shouting,
'Come on, poetry boy… let's see what you're *really* made of!'

'You're all crazy!' yelled Mister Prometheus above the
uproar. He rose and turned to leave.

'Not so fast, Prometheus!' cried Mister Zeus, grabbing him
by the shoulder and spinning him violently around. 'This is all
your fault!'

'Mine?' exclaimed Mister Prometheus, knocking his accuser's
hand away. 'It's greed that's brought you all to this. Except now
it's working against you instead of for you. You've only got
yourselves to blame. And this contrived, Olympian-like world
of yours… If it crumbles, it'll be for the very same reason the
original Olympus lost its power… People stopped believing in
it!'

'If we fall, you'll fall with us!' screamed Mister Zeus, as

seem to be having trouble with that sentiment. Perhaps you'd care to enlighten us?'

A disparate collection of eyes attached themselves to the hapless Mister Pan. 'I... I thought it might be judicious to... unload a little of my art stock,' he stammered. 'My actions – on their own – should not have had any effect on the market.'

Mister Zeus sharpened his gaze as if pulling a whetstone over a blade before an impending castration. 'But they weren't on their own... were they, Mister Pan?'

'It would appear not,' conceded Mister Pan uncomfortably.

'Indeed... For it seems that others assembled around this table also thought it prudent to do likewise... acting on privileged information for their own, personal gain.'

A number of heads bowed.

'I shouldn't need to remind you of the consequences. The art market is in freefall and – as a result – other areas of investment are beginning to lose their footing. The very pulse of capitalism has been weakened... that pulse which ensures the triumph of optimism over pessimism... the supremacy of confidence over fear... the beat of positive against negative... the rhythm of *to win or not to win*... TO BE OR NOT TO BE!' Mister Zeus stopped at the zenith of his rant and exhaled painfully. 'The nightmare scenario we dreaded is knocking on our door... and it is *we* who invited it here!'

There were individual murmurs of dissatisfaction from around the table.

'Were we simply to stand by and do nothing?' asked Mister Poseidon boldly, refusing to be cowed. 'What is the point of acquiring information if it's not then acted upon? Some of us had more to lose than others.'

'Our power is in our unity!' snapped Mister Apollo angrily. 'It is not that you acted... but that you acted *selfishly*. As one, we are infallible. Divided, we will pull ourselves apart!'

'And by acting selfishly,' contributed Mister Atlas, 'you have brought a spectre into our midst that will eat at our bones until there is nothing left to devour.' Mister Atlas – possessing a tendency to indulge in a bit of poetic hyperbole – mistook his

107

'I think you ought to put the knife down before I answer that.'

Snogden-Lambert lowered his arm.

'I think there's been a rather unfortunate misunderstanding,' said the Monsignor as delicately as he could. 'I think you might want to take a look in that envelope over there.' He pointed to the one he'd been forced to drop.

Snogden-Lambert narrowed his eyes and backed over to the door. He picked up the envelope and slit it open with the letter opener. 'It's a certificate of authentication.'

The Monsignor nodded.

'For the Turner.'

The Monsignor nodded again.

'But I don't understand. Does this mean you've found it?'

The Monsignor grinned inanely.

'Then... where is it?'

Monsignor Hoff's eyes slowly went towards the remains of the painting.

Snogden-Lambert twitched.

If embarrassment had a sound, it would have deafened them both.

'Oh... fuck,' said Snogden-Lambert quietly.

'Yes... I think that about sums it up,' said the Monsignor.

*　　*　　*

Mister Zeus raised his considerable frame and cast an ominous shadow over the boardroom table. 'We have styled ourselves on the Greek gods,' he boomed, 'because the destiny of this planet is in our hands... When we act, the world *reacts*. Such a power must be considered both a blessing and a curse, for it is not one to be used unwisely.'

There was a collective nod of consensus.

'And when we act... we must act *together*.'

Most continued nodding their heads in agreement... but a few abstained and looked at one another sheepishly.

'Mister Pan...? You, and one or two others in our midst,

got their head stuck through a painting and about to get their arse kicked!'

The Monsignor rapidly extricated himself from the Turner and stared at the gaping hole through which he had just pulled his head. 'We must surely be able to repair this,' was all he could think to say.

'You reckon?' said Snogden-Lambert, picking up a letter opener from his desk and approaching the easel again. 'In that case…!'

The Monsignor, fearing further assault, scampered out of the way.

The gallery director launched himself at the painting, attacking it with a succession of downward lunges, ripping at the canvas until it resembled a plate of tagliatelle.

'This isn't happening!' exclaimed the Monsignor, grasping at his head in horror.

'Well… according to Miss Gusset… I'M AFRAID IT IS!'

'But why?' begged the Monsignor, tears welling in his eyes. 'It's a masterpiece!'

'Oh, yes,' agreed Snogden-Lambert. 'Whoever painted this was extremely talented, I'll give you that!'

'What do you mean, *whoever painted it…?* You *know* who painted it!'

Snogden-Lambert stopped what he was doing and turned to face the sprawled Monsignor with a look that would haunt the clergyman's sleep for many a year to come.

'Are you insinuating I was in on this?' he snarled, waving the letter opener threateningly.

'Turner! I meant the artist Turner!'

'I know who painted the original, you idiot … I was referring to this forgery.'

'Pardon?'

'This cruel attempt to discredit me! This sick reminder of my torment!'

The Monsignor placed his head in his hands. 'You haven't been told, have you?' he said slowly.

'Told? Told… what?'

standing at the door, clasping a large envelope. 'Oh, good... I see you got my note!'

'You sick bastard!' shrieked Snogden-Lambert, throwing it to the ground and charging at him like an enraged bull.

It was not a situation the Monsignor found himself in every day. In fact... it was not a situation the Monsignor found himself in *any* day. It was why he couldn't think of anything else to do but stand there and wait for the inevitable impact. In his experience, directors of national art galleries usually greeted him with a handshake.

This one lunged at his neck, sending the two of them tumbling backwards into the reception area.

'Shall I call security, sir?' shouted Miss Gusset.

'No thank you, Miss Gusset. I'll kill him on my own!'

'Have you gone mad?' choked the Monsignor.

'According to your note... yes!' cried Snogden-Lambert, initiating a headlock.

'I thought you'd be happy to see the painting,' gasped the Monsignor as he was yanked to his feet.

'I've seen enough of it already. But maybe you'd like to take a closer look.'

The next thing the Monsignor knew, he was being hurled across the office, the painting and easel filling his vision at a worrying rate of knots. 'I'm a man of the cloth!' he yelled.

'Then you'll feel at home with your head wrapped in canvas!' roared Snogden-Lambert, letting go.

The Monsignor shut his eyes as his destination became inevitable. He felt a brief pressure on his head... then everything was still.

He gingerly opened them to find the painting had gone.

It took a few seconds for him to realise that it was, in fact, exactly where it had been. It was just that he was now wearing it around his neck. 'You're mad!' he screamed.

'Oh... worse than that!' said Snogden-Lambert, panting heavily. 'I'm bloody furious!'

'No, you don't understand... you need help!'

'I don't think so,' sung Snogden-Lambert. 'It's not *me* who's

When he realised it wasn't, he stopped.

When he realised who it *was*, he froze.

'Miss Gusset! Tell me this is a dream!'

'It's a dream,' said Miss Gusset obligingly.

'Oh... thank God! For one awful minute I thought this was all real!' He contemplated his predicament... before his stooped frame stooped even more. 'Oh... God... It *is* real, isn't it?'

'It is as far as I'm concerned, sir. Would you like a cup of tea?'

Snogden-Lambert fumbled in his pocket and pulled out a plastic container full of pills. He flipped off its lid and – without bothering to count them – deposited a number in his mouth.

'Are you alright, sir?' asked Miss Gusset anxiously. 'Only... you seem a little...'

'I'm fine thank you,' mumbled Snogden-Lambert through his mouthful. 'Or at least I will be when these things kick in. Everything's under control. I feel incredibly relaxed.' He spoke the last two sentences as if reciting a mantra and shuffled into his office. 'What the hell's that wretched thing still doing in here?' he exclaimed, catching sight of the painting on the easel.

Miss Gusset shrugged. 'Dunno, sir. It was here when I got in. But there's a note to go with it.'

'As if I need reminding! Someone's sick idea of a joke, no doubt!' He walked over to the easel and picked up the Monsignor's message. '*My apologies you'll be viewing this alonee.* Alonee? What the hell's *alonee*?'

Miss Gusset tutted. 'I knew it wasn't spelt like that.'

Snogden-Lambert thought awhile. 'Oh, right... I see! A *loony! My apologies you'll be viewing this a loony. Your mind, it's been certified!*' His voice quivered with rage. 'Who wrote this offensive garbage, Miss Gusset?'

'I did,' came the timid reply.

'*You?*' he bellowed. 'In that case... you're sacked...! Get out!'

'No... what I mean is... it was Monsignor Hoff. He told me to do it!'

Snogden-Lambert's face exploded. 'Monsignor Hoff?' he yelled.

'Did I hear my name?' The Monsignor, perfectly on cue, was

Authenticated, it had been placed back on the easel in his office as a surprise.

No one was to say a word. Mrs Fanshawe-Whittingham had insisted on being the first to break the good news as he entered the office. But, unfortunately, the excitement had triggered one of her migraines and she was currently laid up in bed.

A temporary replacement had been requested, the agency sending out their most experienced secretary in that line of work... Miss Gusset.

She was sitting nervously at her desk when the phone rang. 'Hello?'

'Hello... This is Monsignor Hoff. I'm supposed to be meeting Mr Snogden-Lambert in his office shortly to present him with a certificate of authentication for the Turner. However... I'm running late. So could you leave a message for him next to the painting, just in case I don't make it in time?'

Miss Gusset rested the phone on her shoulder and reached for a pen. 'Certainly, sir. What would you like me to write?'

The Monsignor – mindful of previous events – took care to speak as clearly as he could. 'My... apologies... you'll... be ... viewing... this... alone... ... To... ease... your... mind... it's... been... certified.'

Miss Gusset was sure *alone* was spelt with one *e*. But if Monsignor Hoff stressed it was two, then two it was... and he could take the blame.

She wrote out neatly in her best handwriting... *My apologies you'll be viewing this alonee. Your mind, it's been certified.*

Miss Gusset had just completed painting the nails of her left hand when Peter Snogden-Lambert made a cautious entrance into reception.

He was almost unrecognisable, the parts of his face that weren't hidden by an outsized pair of sunglasses looking drawn and haggard... his gait, that of a man well beyond his years.

He attempted to manufacture a smile, assuming the figure sitting at the desk to be the stalwart Mrs Fanshawe-Whittingham.

112

'I'm simply saying... there's stuff out there we don't know about.'

'We don't know about it because there's nothing *to* know!'

'In that case... why have our own boys been running a remote viewing project for decades? We've got guys on the payroll who claim to see things happening half way around the world... just by closing their eyes and concentrating.'

'Yeah, right... but not into the future! And certainly not communicating with the dead! I dunno how that remote shit works. Perhaps they're picking up on other people's brainwaves, or something. Who knows? What I do know is that it's fallible... otherwise you and I would be out of a job, replaced by rooms full of weirdos taking naps!'

'We very nearly *are* out of a job! And all I'm saying is... maybe Donald's picking up on other people's brainwaves too. He's just interpreting it the only way he knows how.'

Chad shook his head derisively. 'You've changed your tune, haven't you? One minute the guy's a complete and utter loony... and now you think he's the answer to all our prayers. You'll be believing in angels sent from Heaven next!'

Bob rose from his chair and drained the last of his coffee. 'Okay... then I'll ask the question again.' He banged the cup down on the table. 'Where the *hell* do we go from here?'

* * *

There was quite a buzz about the gallery.

Word had circulated that Snogden-Lambert was expected to be making a return to work that day after his "holiday". Word had also circulated that it was provisional... the proviso being that if he showed the slightest signs of strain, he would be asked to leave. Furthermore, permission had only been granted after Monsignor Hoff had magnanimously agreed to drop his complaint against him.

Some questioned the wisdom of such an early return... though all agreed the discovery of the genuine Turner would be a great tonic for his rehabilitation.

have. We need a result fast.'

'It's not the speed of the result that bothers me,' said Chad, looking up. 'It's the *nature* of it. This termination angle doesn't sit easy with me.'

'It happens all the time,' said Bob. 'It's how the real world operates. Just think of it as self-preservation.'

'Don't you mean *desperation*? And what exactly are we preserving?' Chad placed his head in his hands again.

'Dunno 'bout you... but I'll be preserving my future.' Bob took another mouthful of coffee. 'You know what really puzzles me about all this? How did our friend Donald know what was going on in the first place? I mean... he sent his letter to us warning of a plot *before* the paintings were removed. There's no way he could've foreseen what would happen to them. According to Snogden-Lambert... he warned *him* before the paintings were even *loaned!*'

'Well... according to Donald,' mumbled Chad sarcastically through his hands, 'he heard voices!'

Bob toyed sheepishly with the handle of his cup. 'I know you'll think I'm crazy... but do you think he might just have?'

Chad pulled his hands away from his face and stared at his partner in disbelief. 'Are you losing it? The guy's a whacko. You're very own words!'

'Yeah... and *you* said he may just be right.'

'About the missing paintings, Bob! And only because he saw them go! It was nothing more than coincidence he had what he thought was a premonition and then happened to be in the right place at the right time! There are crackpots all over the world making bizarre claims. This one just got lucky!'

Bob stared hard into his cup. 'You don't think there's a possibility he might *really* have some kinda psychic ability?'

Chad lurched back on his chair. 'I don't believe it! You're not telling me you believe in all that crap!'

Bob kept staring at his cup.

'You do... don't you...! Look, Bob... there's a logical explanation for everything. The minute you start looking beyond that, you've lost it.'

'Best not.'

Flowers smiled.

'It's nothing illegal!' added Norman hastily.

Flowers gave a comforting wink.

'You won't say anything to anyone... will you?'

'My lips are sealed,' promised Flowers. 'Which is just as well, given what I'm about to tell you. We 'ad a couple o' Yanks sniffing around the pub opposite our depot yesterday. The chaps go in there for a swift 'alf at lunchtimes. These guys were asking questions about certain deliveries... deliveries that sounded like the kind you've been receiving. We're often offered *incentives* to divulge information that could be valuable to the criminal fraternity... but – for obvious reasons – the approach is always made extremely discreetly. These guys were anything *but*.'

'Do you think anyone said anything?' asked Norman anxiously.

'I made sure they didn't,' replied Flowers, giving another comforting wink. 'They're a pretty loyal bunch of lads... but I can't guarantee their silence on this one forever. It may be something or nothing. But I thought you ought to know.'

'Thanks, Flowers. You've been a good friend. I'll make sure I have this last one ready for you to pick up tomorrow, if that's okay.'

'It'll be a pleasure. And Norman... mind 'ow you go. Whatever it is you're involved in... these guys seemed pretty determined to find you!'

* * *

'So... where do we go from here?' Bob took a large gulp of coffee and wiped his mouth with the back of his hand. 'We've drawn a big fat zero from *Vault Vans*... and the exhibition ends tomorrow.'

'I'll think of something,' said Chad, burying his face in his hands. 'I just need time.'

'Only one problem,' said Bob. 'That's precisely what we don't

It'll be returned tomorrow and you can put it back up on your wall.'

'Just in time for Mr Snogden-Lambert's homecoming,' said Mrs Fanshawe-Whittingham. 'It'll be just the tonic he needs. It's been a difficult two weeks for him by all accounts. The doctors said it was touch and go whether he'd ever pull through enough to return to work. But he's a fighter.' Her breasts swelled a little. 'When it's been authenticated, I'm going to have the painting placed here in his office and break the good news to him myself. It'll be a wonderful surprise. I can't wait to see his face!'

'He's a lucky man to have you, Joan' said Hedonist, turning to leave.

Mrs Fanshawe-Whittingham stared coyly at the ground. 'Mind how you go, Chief Inspector.'

'*Ex* Chief Inspector,' he corrected her.

'You'll have to leave by the back entrance, I'm afraid. Our night watchman unexpectedly handed in his notice this morning and we haven't had a chance to replace him yet.'

Hedonist smiled. His slippers awaited.

*　　*　　*

Norman opened his door to find Flowers standing beside a solitary crate.

'I thought I was through 'aving to lug these things up yer stairs,' the security guard wheezed. 'I was under the impression deliveries to this address 'ad come to an end.'

'They have now!' beamed Norman. 'And I can't tell you how glad I am to receive *this* particular one!'

'It's a painting, ain't it?' said Flowers nonchalantly. 'Like all the other crates.'

Norman tried to mask his shock. 'What makes you say that?'

'Well... yer wallpaper was a bit of a giveaway,' said Flowers, acknowledging the artistic adornments covering Norman's bedsit. 'Not to mention their shape. Quite valuable ones, I should think, given we've been involved. Though what you've been doin' wiv 'em, I can't imagine!'

to commit themselves anymore to what is now viewed as a volatile market. It appears that the days when such paintings could be considered a safe bet are finally over. It's not yet certain how this will affect the rest of the markets, but it seems that Van Gogh's Sunflowers have finally begun to wilt. This is Tammy Gruenbaker for Channel Seven's business report... Steve.'

Steve's equally well-manicured face turned into a blank screen as the remote control fell from AKA Mister Prometheus's hand.

He reached for his phone and stabbed frantically at the dial pad. 'Cheadle... is that you? Listen... I'm giving you and that idiot partner of yours one last chance to rescue your careers... Get your sorry butts back over to England and sort this thing out once and for all. Only, this time, you're not answering to the department...you're answering directly to *me*. This is now a black project that's been graded *invisible*. The rules have changed. Use whatever force you think necessary to put a stop to this mess. Get as dirty as you like... It's not answers I want anymore... it's *termination*. Death or glory... Do you understand?'

*　　*　　*

Chief Inspector Hedonist (retired) stared at the painting on the easel, a satisfied grin on his face.

'I expect you're feeling pretty chuffed with yourself,' said Mrs Fanshawe-Whittingham, handing him a cup of tea.

'As a matter of fact, Joan, I am! The gallery's got its painting back and I've maintained my one hundred percent clear-up record. It turned out to be a pretty easy one to crack in the end. Bit of a shame really. I rather fancied getting my teeth into something again.'

'Biscuit?'

'No, I meant... oh, I see!' he took a Bourbon Cream from the plate thrust under his nose. 'Someone will be picking this up shortly. My *employers* have insisted on having it independently authenticated to prevent any further accusations of impropriety.

117

had the bedsit to himself. Without the crates he'd come to regard as passing friends, he'd have to make do with the hundreds of pictures of paintings now obliterating every surface.

As it dawned on him that his task was near its end, the full force of his labours hit him and he collapsed, exhausted, onto the sofa to contemplate his fate.

What if the missing painting was never found?

His brain refused to answer, preferring to contemplate the soft cushions beneath him and the fact there was now time to appreciate them.

As he did so, his thoughts detached themselves from reality.

He was floating through a cotton-wool world where everything had the texture of a warm, cosy duvet.

'Hello,' said the Sandman.

'Hiya,' mumbled Norman.

'I haven't seen you for a while. I've been by a number of times but you weren't at the stop.'

'Sorry... I've been busy.'

'Never mind,' said the Sandman. 'Hop on board.'

*   *   *

'It's for you.' Mrs AKA Mister Prometheus handed her husband the phone and made herself scarce.

'Mister Zeus...! ... Yes... I've got it on now... ... No... I'm watching the Yankees versus the... ... Oh, I see... Channel Seven... I'll take a look...... Yes... of course... I understand.' He quickly disengaged the call and fumbled with the television's remote control.

Channel Seven had a tan-from-the-bottle presenter sitting at a desk, behind whose head flashed a large graphic reading: ART PRICES PLUMMET.

A spokesperson for one of the world's leading auction houses claimed today that the sudden release of hundreds of old masters onto the market had caused a glut and resulted in a downward spiral in prices. Investors in Japan and the Middle East say they are unwilling drummed his fingers on the desk. 'I'm sticking an *investigation closed* notice on this one. I shall inform those who seek my advice that we have absolutely nothing to worry about.'

Chad looked at his superior in disbelief. 'Nothing to worry about? You think this is the end? You think they went to all that trouble for no reason whatsoever? They've set something up here! And if we fail to understand *what*, God knows where we might end up!'

'I *know* where you're ending up,' said AKA Mister Prometheus dispassionately. 'It's over, gentlemen... and I'm not just talking about the case.'

* * *

'Is that it?' asked Norman, examining the three small packages he'd just been handed.

'That's all there was at the depot,' said Flowers, handing over his clipboard for signing.

'I think your days of lugging heavy crates up my stairs might finally be coming to an end,' said Norman. 'I guess we won't be seeing much of each other again.'

'The crates, I'm extremely 'appy about,' said Flowers. 'The other will be a shame.' He paused awkwardly... debating as to whether to initiate a parting handshake.

'Will I see you tomorrow?' asked Norman, handing back the clipboard.

Flowers shrugged. 'There's nothing marked on the roster.'

'Right.'

Flowers turned to leave.

'By the way,' said Norman. 'There's one thing I've been dying to ask you.'

Flowers seemed pleased at having an excuse to loiter. 'Fire away!'

'Why do they call you Flowers?'

The delivery guard looked at him blankly. 'It's my surname.'

'Right... Well... goodbye, then.' Norman closed the door.

For the first time since the chequebook incident, Norman

pattern we can read anything into to me.'

'Depends where they were being sent.'

AKA Mister Prometheus looked at his men with weary resignation. 'Tenacity in the face of overwhelming odds can be a virtue, gentlemen. But it can also be a pain in the ass. What makes you think they were being sent *anywhere*? All you've done is followed an unmarked van. You could've been chasing laundry! You have precisely one minute to persuade me why I shouldn't have you discharged from this organisation for professional incompetence... and it better be good!'

'Okay,' said Chad, throwing a file he'd been clutching onto the desk. He thumbed his way quickly to a paper displaying columns of figures. 'Take these time discrepancies for the absent paintings. They *prove* these works of art were moved to a single location before being returned. They even enable us to pinpoint *where!* If you assume my central location theory to be correct... it would have to be closest to the area where the exhibits were missing for the shortest period of time and furthest from those reporting the *longest* absence. All the other times should correlate proportionally, providing us with a mathematical connection beyond coincidence... And they do! The figures work out perfectly. And that central location looks like being somewhere in the country you've just pulled us from. Now... I admit we still don't know *why*... but given our curator friend is denying that exhibits are even leaving the *building*, there's gotta be something occurring that they don't want us to know about. That's why they've gotten their influential big guns to break cover and attempt to disrupt our actions. If we could just find the *exact* coordinates of this central location, we'd be able to...'

'Time's up, gentlemen,' said AKA Mister Prometheus, leaning back in his chair and placing his hands squarely on his desk. 'You're too late. Most of these exhibitions are coming to an end and we've had no more reports of any further activity in that area. Apart from one single forgery – which appears to be an isolated and unconnected incident – this whole affair looks like being able to be filed away as *benign*. The irony being... the only damage done has been that caused by you two!' He hadn't! You'd already managed to accuse one of the Vatican's top representatives of being responsible for an art forgery... along with the man he entrusted to run his exhibition... a man who seems to have friends in *very* high places. Once again... you've ingloriously forgotten the meaning of the word *covert!*'

'We needed a break. We thought if we stirred these Templars up, they might do something in haste and drop their guard.'

'Oh... you've certainly stirred them up! Unfortunately for you, some of their friends in high places saw fit to complain to some of *our* friends in high places... and now they're not being so friendly. On top of which... I've got the British protesting about our abuse of their sovereignty and a furious Catholic lobby stalking congress, baying for my blood! How much more did you want the thing *stirred,* gentlemen?'

'They're riled because we're on to them,' asserted Chad.

'Them?' scoffed AKA Mister Prometheus. 'Do you know who *them* are?'

'They're a secret sect.'

'Try *society*, Cheadle. One which – when confronted with the appearance of a forgery in their keep – doesn't turn tail and run... but insists on calling out of retirement one of England's finest and most respected detectives to investigate the matter. Hardly seems like they're trying to keep anything secret to me!'

'But you can't deny the presence of the forgery!'

'*One*... Cheadle! Just *one* forged painting... despite sending our inventor friend and his goddam gadget – at your insistence – to numerous exhibitions around the globe. What a holiday *that* man's had! The cheeky bastard's even sent us a postcard... with a *rabbit* on it!'

'But we're not the only ones who've witnessed the removal and replacement of exhibits. This agency has now received consistent reports of similar activity around the world. It's gotta mean something!'

'Similar, but not the same. Your paintings were only absent for a day or two. In some of the cases you're referring to, the exhibits went AWOL for over a week. That doesn't suggest a

'Perhaps you were just speaking faster,' suggested Norman, trying not to smile.

'Ah! That's where I've got you!' sneered Oppenheimer triumphantly. 'It doesn't work. Listen…! Hippopotamus, hippopotamus, hippopotamus, hippopotamus, hippopotamus, hippopotamus, hippopopamus, hoppopopamus… See…! It can't be done!'

'Fascinating,' said Norman. 'But perhaps you'd manage it if you didn't have your face wedged in my door.'

'Bah!' said Oppenheimer, pulling away. 'Try for yourself if you don't believe me!'

'I think I'll give that a miss, thank you.'

'You think you're a smart boy, don't you? But I have news for you. You won't make a fool of me much longer!'

'Look, Mr Oppenheimer,' said Norman, deciding a conciliatory tone might remove the landlord from his door a little faster. 'The delivery of crates is coming to an end. I've nearly finished what I'm doing. Soon, things will return to normal and you won't have to worry about African wildlife in your electricity cupboard.'

'That is where you are wrong,' countered Oppenheimer menacingly. 'You have thought it amusing to challenge my authority. Things can *never* return to normal. If I can't remove you from my premises, I'll find another way to make you pay!'

With that, he left… leaving Norman to ponder what the name for a baby hippopotamus was.

* * *

'I can't believe we're going through this again!' bellowed AKA Mister Prometheus at the two men staring at the carpet. 'You went to interview a man on a bridge and ended up insulting the entire Catholic Church! I sent you to England to redeem your reputations… not *bury* them!'

'But why call us back? We weren't finished!' protested Bob.

'That's what *worried* me!' exclaimed AKA Mister Prometheus. 'God knows what you would've ended up doing if I

122

66c Armageddon Terrace now resembled a miniature art gallery. Norman – having become quite the art connoisseur – had taken to printing off scaled-down copies of the paintings and sticking them to his walls.

At first, he'd arranged them in chronological and geographical order, the front of the bedsit given over to European classics. Anything from the impressionists and beyond followed a route to the bathroom... whilst art suggesting an *ethnic* tag, brightened up the kitchenette.

Then he'd decided it didn't matter. After all... such classifications were just a convenience for the art historian. They either moved you or they didn't.

It had been a week since the problem of the forgery had surfaced. He'd heard nothing from Gabriel since. But the deliveries had continued... though the amount of visual samples was dwindling as their audio counterparts increased.

The reduction of heavy traffic on the stairs should have come as a relief to Oppenheimer, and might have done had it not been for one thing... Hippopotami.

'Fourteen!' he yelled, trying to force his face into the narrow gap in the door. 'In fact... thirteen and a half to be precise!'

'You can't get half a hippopotamus,' retorted Norman, trying to drag an already absurd conversation into even more ludicrous territory.

'Of course you can!'

'Alright, then... what's it called?'

'It's not called anything. It just *is!*'

'Doesn't sound convincing to me,' taunted Norman.

'It's not the animal... it's the word! And today I've counted thirteen and a half of them!'

'I still don't see how a hippopotamus can be divided into two. There are five syllables to start with.'

'I ended up with an extra *hippopo*,' insisted the landlord. 'That's between a *hippo* and a *hippopot*. Thirteen hippopotami and a hippopo!'

'Crystal, Mr 'edonist. But I'm afraid it ain't that easy.'

'You'll find a way,' insisted Hedonist, 'believe me.'

'No… you don't understand… it's *who* it was stolen for that's the problem. I'm not gonna name names – no matter what you threaten me with – but it's a pretty big one as names go. I don't think he'll wanna part wiv 'is pride and joy so easily. Not when it's cost him so much to have it 'anging on 'is wall in the first place.'

'Then you'll have to make sure he doesn't know it's been returned, won't you?'

'I beg yer pardon?'

'I've got a perfect copy upstairs, Klepto. You can have that one… *gratis.* I believe it belongs to your friends anyway. All you've got to do is swap it back for the original. Given the gallery never noticed the difference, I doubt he will either!'

'And how the 'ell do we pull that off, Mr 'edonist?'

'I'm used to answering that sort of question *after* it's been done. You've already had one go. Just think of that as a dry run.'

'But this would be against a major villain. Those sort are far more careful about their property. They're only too aware how many unscrupulous types there are knocking around!'

'I don't want excuses. I want the painting. Just make sure my one-hundred-percent record stays that way… or it won't be only your job you'll find yourself losing!'

'Alright, alright!' said the night watchman, holding up his hands. 'You know I'll do my best for you, Mr 'edonist, or my name ain't Charles Carter-Smith.'

'It isn't!'

'Yeah… well… you know what I mean.'

'There's *one* thing, Klepto. At least you won't have to worry about him reporting the matter to the police if he *does* get to find out what you've done.'

'It wasn't the police I was worried about!' came the sullen reply.

*　　*　　*

124

placed his hand inside his tunic and started fiddling nervously with his Saint Dismas medallion. 'You've got it all wrong, Mr 'edonist. I'm an innocent in all this!'

Even the portraits on the walls winced.

Hedonist straightened up and drew a smile the way one might draw a sword. 'All *what*, Klepto?' he said slowly.

There was an excruciating silence whilst the night watchman's brain tried to work out which way to run.

'I'll help you, shall I?' said Hedonist calmly. 'You were *persuaded* against your better judgement to participate in a little, harmless picture swap. You didn't think it would hurt anyone, otherwise you would never have agreed... so help you God. Only... now the deed's been discovered, you're in a rather awkward situation. Do you tell the nice, ex-policeman all you know and, therefore, help ensure its safe return... but incriminate yourself in so doing and risk the danger of being labelled *a grass*... or do you lie through your slimy teeth – as is your habit – and face the wrath of a man whose reputation means more to him than anything your crooked little mind could imagine? Do you know what I'd do if I were in your shoes...? I'd ask myself why a retired Chief Inspector has been drafted out of retirement to work on this particular case. I'd probably come up with the answer that this must be *extremely* important to some people, and that the consequences of it not being solved don't bear thinking about for anyone standing in the way. Now... how did I do?'

'Uncanny, Mr 'edonist. It must be a gift.'

'No... This is a gift, Klepto. Strange as it may seem – and against my own inclination – my people aren't interested in punishing those who've perpetrated this particular crime. They simply want the painting back. That gets you nicely off the hook. Now... given you undoubtedly know who those perpetrators are, I suggest you get in touch with them as soon as you can and let them know that I'll be turning the whole soddin' underworld upside down if I have to, to get to the bottom of this one... and it'll be them who'll incur the wrath of every villain who gets inconvenienced if I do. Is that clear?'

'I told you… once a thief, always a thief. And if we're looking at being *honest*… that occupation's genetically bred into your family. What did we call your little firm back at the yard? Ah, yes… I remember… Klepto and Son. By the way… how *is* that boy of yours?'

'Temporarily detained.'

'At Her Majesty's pleasure, no doubt?'

'Well… certainly not 'is mum's!'

'No, I'm sure not… And dear old Brenda… how's she?'

'Temporarily detained.'

Hedonist allowed himself another smile. 'See… nothing really changes, does it? But hang on a second… how come I didn't get to see your dishonest mug this afternoon?'

'I'm a night watchman, Mr 'edonist. I don't do days.'

'But you do have a personnel file… or a least, you should have.'

The night watchman tried to engage his eyes elsewhere.

'I take it the fact it was missing from my pile had nothing to do with you?'

'I don't know what you're talkin' about, Mr 'edonist… truly I don't.'

Hedonist drew himself closer to his prey. The years appeared to fall from his face as he transmogrified into Hedonist of the Yard. 'I'll tell you what I'm talking about, shall I? I'm talking about the one thing that made my years of dealing with nasty slime like you worth all the effort. I'm talking about my hard-earned, highly cherished one hundred percent clear-up record. I'm talking about my *reputation*.' He placed his face as close to the night watchman's as he could without making inappropriate male-to-male contact. 'I've put men behind bars who'd eat you for breakfast. I've had some of the hardest villains known to man in my custody, begging me to charge them and put them out of their misery. I've solved cases your devious brain couldn't even comprehend. If you think I'm going to lose it to a two-bit criminal like you, you're more stupid than you look.'

Charles Carter-Smith neé '*Klepto*' Carter felt his legs buckle. His face had just been touched by the breath of a legend. He

126

Chief Inspector 'edonist! With all respect, sir... ain't you supposed to be dead?'

'Retired,' Hedonist corrected him. 'It's the same thing... only you're forced to wake up every morning.'

'So that means you're no longer a copper, then,' said the night watchman, with sudden enthusiasm.

'Once a copper, always a copper,' replied Hedonist. 'And once a thief, always a thief... eh, Charlie?'

The night watchman said nothing.

'Perhaps you'd like to take a guess at why I'm here?' suggested Hedonist.

'You're taking advantage of our pensioner's discount?' tried the night watchman.

'Very funny... Charlie *Klepto* Carter, as I live and breathe. I knew there had to be a rat in the building, somewhere!'

The night watchman looked about nervously. 'Shhhh! Not so loud! I'm Charles Carter-Smith 'ere, if you don't mind Mr 'edonist.'

Hedonist recoiled his neck. '*Carter-Smith*...? What's all that about, then?'

The night watchman gave a sheepish look. 'Smith was me wife's maiden name... see? So I thought I'd add it to mine for a touch o' class. It 'elps me fit in wiv the nobs 'round 'ere.'

'You don't think elocution lessons might've been a better bet?' said Hedonist dryly.

'I might if I knew what they were. Is it anything to do wiv electrical wiring?'

'You haven't changed a bit, have you?' said Hedonist, shaking his head. 'Apart from your identity. Now... I wonder why you should've gone to the trouble of doing that?'

'Like I told you, Mr 'edonist... It 'elps me fit in 'round 'ere.'

'Helps you avoid your employers finding out you have form, more like.'

The night watchman tried his best to look hurt. 'Please, Mr 'edonist. That's all in the past, that is. I'm going straight now... honest!'

'You don't know the meaning of the word,' scoffed Hedonist.

files. 'He's a great man. It's just that he's been under a lot of pressure recently. I should never have gone to the Isle of Wight.'

Hedonist sniffed the air. 'Would you care to elaborate on *what* pressures he might've been under, Joan?'

Mrs Fanshawe-Whittingham stopped what she was doing. 'I'm sure it's no secret they're of a financial kind.'

'Do you mean *personal* financial problems, Joan?'

Mrs Fanshawe-Whittingham looked horrified. 'I was referring to *professional* cutbacks, Mr Hedonist! And I hope you're not insinuating that Mr Snogden-Lambert had anything to do with this sordid matter.'

'I'm not in the business of insinuation, Joan... I'm in the business of finding evidence. And in my book – until I do – *nobody* is above suspicion.'

'Then you'll have to count me among your suspects, Mr Hedonist,' said Mrs Fanshawe-Whittingham prickly.

'Oh, don't worry, Joan,' said Hedonist, putting on his coat. 'You're way up there with the rest of 'em!'

Hedonist's footsteps echoed in isolated grandeur as he made his way through the now emptied halls towards the exit.

A cubbyhole – discretely positioned away to the right of the main doors – housed the night watchman.

'Just a second, sir... I'll get the key,' came a voice from inside.

'Thank you. If you would.' Hedonist exercised his toes inside his shoes and lazily glanced around the foyer.

'You're obviously new 'ere, sir,' said the night watchman, shuffling out. 'It's easier at this time of night if you use the rear ent_' He froze mid-sentence, as the two men's eyes connected.

'Well, well, well,' said Hedonist, in a well-practised delivery.

The night watchman dropped his head quickly and fumbled with a large bunch of keys. 'I'll just get the door unlocked, sir, and you can be on your way.'

Hedonist gave a wry smile. 'Do you know something? Suddenly I think I'd rather stay awhile.'

The night watchman screwed up his eyes. 'Bloody 'ell...!

hippopotami for the dial to revolve once... and God help his tenant above if that number decreased!

* * *

Hedonist wearily dragged his cupped hands down over his face and tilted his head back.

He had just finished interviewing the last of the gallery's staff... but not one of them had aroused an iota of suspicion in him.

Yet he knew it *had* to be an inside job. Such was the security surrounding the paintings, it would have been impossible for any to have been switched without someone's knowledge within the building.

In his experience, it was extremely rare for crimes of this magnitude to involve people who had never previously been tempted from the straight and narrow. The employee who turned a blind eye or provided sensitive information, had probably done so before and usually exhibited signs of wealth beyond their wage packet. But most importantly of all... they could not help giving away, when interviewed, those tell-tale signs that behavioural scientists and good coppers interpret as *person under pressure*.

The trouble was... Hedonist hadn't seen any.

None of the staff had previous form... all were long-serving and trusted employees of a closely knit working environment... and all seemed genuinely shocked that such a thing could have happened right under their noses.

This was not going to be easy.

'So that's the last of 'em, is it, Joan?'

Mrs Fanshawe-Whittingham nodded that it was.

He glanced at his wristwatch. 'In that case... I'm off home to get some tea. Of course... I haven't had the chance to speak to Mr Snogden-Lambert yet, but by all accounts, I'd get precious little sense from him right now if I did.'

'He'll bounce back,' said Mrs Fanshawe-Whittingham loyally, leaning over the desk and scooping up the scattered personnel

He knew the crime had been perpetrated here and not at the exhibition as soon as he'd shaken Mr Le Blanc's hand.

As he examined the rows of paintings stretching through into numerous rooms, he quickly realised that access to these valuable items was all too easy. It was the getting-them-off-the-wall-and-out-the-front-door bit that was the trickiest. Harder still, was doing it without anyone noticing. And as hard as it would have been to smuggle a painting *out*, that problem was doubled by the fact its replacement had to be smuggled *in*. There were surveillance cameras in every corner of every room, and the entire gallery was wired to the most sophisticated of alarm systems.

And that's when he realised how it had been done.

*　　*　　*

Joseph Oppenheimer stared intently at the dial on his electricity meter and tried to ascertain if it was travelling faster than it had the day before.

Along with the mystery crates that had been yo-yoing up and down his stairs over the weeks, there had been yet more boxes of electronic equipment. The difference was... they had been going up without coming back down, and – unless his troublesome tenant was eating the stuff – it was surely being used at *his* expense.

He couldn't remember the word he was supposed to utter to mark the passing of a second. He tried counting *one thousand... two thousand... three thousand...* until realising that this unit of measurement depended on how fast he spoke.

So he substituted it for the word *hippopotamus...* counting as fast as he could without taking a breath in-between. He figured there was a maximum speed at which it could be spoken with clarity... even after hours of practise.

It proved successful until he became dizzy and the word *hippopotamus* turned into *hopapopamus...* whereupon he lost count.

After much trying, he finally deduced that it took seventeen being a victim of zero tolerance could be.

But it was not just his unflinching dedication to duty that facilitated a meteoric rise through the ranks. Whispers in the canteen suggested it was also due to a readiness to roll up a trouser leg in private and adopt a funny handshake in public. This was a side he kept to himself. He took oaths of allegiance very seriously... especially those that involved unmentionable things happening to his body should he spill the beans.

He might have risen to greater heights still, had he not refused further promotion on the grounds it would take him away from the action. This only brought further admiration from his colleagues... as well as a flood of *wish-you'd-change-your-mind* cards from most of London's villains.

He was the copper's copper. A fair cop, if ever there was one.

But all that was history. His mantelpiece was now home to a set of golden handcuffs tackily mounted on a mahogany base, a plaque on the front wishing him *all the best from the lads at the station.*

He'd come away from the force with this keepsake, a pension, a lifetime of memories and, most treasured of all... his one hundred percent clear-up record.

But the latter was now under threat.

For he'd been persuaded by powers beyond the powers that be to put his slippers to one side, dust off his pocket-book and investigate the surfacing of a forgery. Furthermore... not only was he to find the original, he was to present it to those powers beyond the powers that be before its return to its rightful owners.

He couldn't go back on his word. It had been given with a very special handshake.

Hedonist stood in the main hall of the gallery and breathed in his surroundings. He liked to imagine himself inside the skin of his criminal. It gave him a more accurate perspective. He was renowned for spending hours at a time just standing quietly at crime scenes, not so much trying to understand how the perpetrator had done it... but how the perpetrator had done it so as not to get caught. That gave him the edge.

the ear from his dad and a certificate of commendation from the local constabulary.

School gave him the perfect opportunity to hone his law-enforcement skills. From the more serious misdemeanours like smoking and extortion of first-years' pocket money to lesser ones like cheating at marbles and violation of the school dress code... he reported them all. By the time he'd left, he'd reduced such incidents to zero... along with his circle of friends.

He sailed through police training school... counting as the proudest day of his life, the moment he first stepped out on the beat with a truncheon that could finally do *real* damage.

But that truncheon was quickly swapped for plain clothes, as he set about solving some of the nation's most notorious crimes.

It was Hedonist who was responsible for putting behind bars such infamous men as Glasgow's Jack *'The Utter Bastard'* McRatchet... Liverpool's Frank *'The Murdering Psycho'* Cleaver... and the Home Counties' Crispin *'The Frightful Rotter'* Heatherington-Ashe.

Regarded as something of an honour in the underworld for villains to have their collar felt by the great man, some even grassed *themselves* up to obtain credibility.

He was the first to advocate a policy of zero tolerance, long before it was fashionable with politicians or referred to by that name. In his day, the obsessive and wholesale pursuit of those developing dyslexia when it came to the letter of the law became known as *Hedonism*.

Awards and commendations punctuated a spectacular career, it being widely held in police circles that he would've been knighted for services to law enforcement, were it not for fears that – during the ceremony – he might attempt to arrest the Monarch for possession of an offensive weapon.

His obsession with work eventually led to the break-up of his marriage. Not because of the endless hours spent alone in the office when all others had gone home... but due to an incident one Christmas Day, when he arrested his wife for being drunk and disorderly, having helped herself to an extra portion of sherry trifle. He found out the hard way how painful

'We must be positive,' said Gabriel. 'Don't forget the power of thought.'

'Then... maybe encoding something so close to the original will still work?' Norman suggested.

'Absolutely not! Should the end vibration be just one cycle out, the sphere of knowledge will fail to materialise... as will our chance of saving the Universe.'

'I'm glad you don't do negative,' groaned Norman despondently. 'So... I guess we're sunk.'

'Not if we can locate the original.'

'And how are we gonna do that?'

'Not *us*... but friends of ours.'

'You mean Templar Resources?'

'I mean... friends in possession of knowledge that enables them to communicate with us from time to time. Whilst they attempt to recover the painting, you must carry on with your work in the hope they succeed.'

'And if they don't?'

'Then we *are* sunk,' said Gabriel. 'Ark and all.'

* * *

Though now retired, former Chief Inspector Hedonist still smelt like a policeman. It was a curious mixture of serge and disinfectant, instantly recognised by tracker dogs and those leaving premises with things that didn't belong to them.

He'd been *on duty* for as long as he could remember, donning his first outfit at the age of eight. It had plastic handcuffs and a hollow truncheon that bent in two when used on Grandpa Hedonist for failure to signal whilst manoeuvring a walking frame.

His first citizen's arrest was performed two weeks later on Mr Pugh – his next door neighbour – who he caught watering his dahlias during a hosepipe ban. Mr Pugh was fined fifteen shillings and sixpence by the magistrate, shamed on page four of the local newspaper and died of a heart attack... brought on by stress, the doctors said. Hedonist junior received a clip around

133

call in the British police!'

'We'd rather you didn't,' said Chad, moving towards him.

'I fail to recognise your jurisdiction over this matter,' said the Monsignor, placing his finger on the intercom's button and leaning forward to give instructions to Mrs Fanshawe-Whittingham.

'Perhaps I could be of help here,' said the curator, swiftly placing his hand on top of the Monsignor's. 'We should not act in haste.'

The Monsignor looked at him with surprise.

'There are many reputations at stake,' the curator continued, acknowledging Chad and Bob. 'We must proceed with a certain amount of... *caution*.'

'So what do you suggest?'

'That an investigation is undertaken... by the right people... people who would be sympathetic to the delicacies of the situation.'

'And they are?'

'The police, of course... But I have contacts within their most senior ranks who will assist in whatever way they can... and discreetly so.'

'Then I suggest you call them right away,' said the Monsignor. 'We need this matter resolved as quickly as possible!'

'We do indeed,' said the curator solemnly.

'I've heard the Algarve is very nice this time of year,' said Mrs Fanshawe-Whittingham, placing a comforting hand on the stretcher. 'I'll get some brochures and send them to your wife.'

Peter Snogden-Lambert said nothing... his glazed eyes following the contours of the ceiling as he was carried away, the sound of Mendelssohn's Funeral March playing in his head.

* * *

'A *forgery?*' gasped Norman. 'It seems no sooner do we fix one problem, than another raises its head!'

switched whilst it was in your charge?'

'Absolutely not!' said the curator firmly. 'We've adopted the highest security precautions. Such a thing would've been impossible.'

'I think not,' contested Chad. 'What about when they were sent off to be cleaned?'

The curator stiffened. 'Sent off? What makes you think they were *sent off*?'

'We saw a van leave your premises,' said Bob.

'Vans come and go from our building all the time. But what has that to do with the paintings? They're cleaned in-house.'

'And was this particular painting *cleaned*?' asked Chad, pointing at the forgery.

'I'm not sure,' answered the curator sharply. 'Why don't you ask Mister Tucker-Jenkins?'

Snogden-Lambert clutched his hands to his head. 'That man again...! Why do I keep hearing his name?'

'He's not important,' said Chad.

'But he was right!' cried Snogden-Lambert, wide-eyed. 'He tried to warn me...! He said they would try to steal my paintings...! I should've listened to him...! I should've listened!'

The director no longer appeared to be addressing those in the room. He was engaging his own personal demons.

'I can assure you,' said the curator confidently, 'that the paintings that were temporarily removed from their positions were the exact same ones that were replaced. I would be happy to swear this on oath or under any test of honesty you might devise.'

'That won't be necessary,' said the Monsignor. 'It is obvious the forgery was given to us by this gallery.'

Under normal circumstances, Snogden-Lambert would have had much to say in response. Under *whimpering-whilst-body-is-being-painfully-contorted* conditions, he was oblivious to the accusation.

'Furthermore,' the Monsignor added, 'I find myself asking why it is I'm standing here with representatives of an *American* agency, whilst no one has yet suggested the obvious... that we we meet again… I take it you're not here in your capacity as art journalists this time?'

'CIA' said Chad.

'Yes… I thought your interest in the same painting as our protestor was too much of a coincidence.'

'Protestor?' enquired the Monsignor.

'A gentleman by the name of Donald Tucker-Jenkins,' explained Chad.

'God preserve us!' cried a voice from a crouched position behind the desk. 'Not that lunatic! What's *he* got to do with anything?'

'It's he who alerted us to this matter in the first place,' said Chad. 'Without him, we wouldn't have discovered the forgery.'

'But he hears voices!' exclaimed Snogden-Lambert.

'We know,' said Chad.

'He wraps his head in tin foil to keep the noise down!'

'*That,* we didn't know,' said Bob.

'He's responsible for ruining my intercom!'

'That's nothing,' said Bob. 'He's responsible for ruining my *trousers!*'

Snogden-Lambert peered from behind the desk. 'How did he do that?'

'I got shat on,' said Bob.

The curator gave a questioning look towards the Monsignor.

'The filthy bugger!' gasped Snogden-Lambert.

'Gentlemen!' shouted the Monsignor. 'It doesn't matter how the forgery was discovered… What matters is how we resolve this mess.'

'I want my painting back!' snapped Snogden-Lambert childishly.

'You may well already have it back,' countered the Monsignor. 'Who's to say that the picture on the easel is not the exact one we were given?'

'We don't make a habit of hanging forgeries on our walls,' snarled Snogden-Lambert.

'Neither do we!' The Monsignor turned to the curator. 'Mr Le Blanc… is it at all possible this painting could have been panicked look towards the two agents.

Bob shrugged.

'That's preposterous!' he bellowed. 'Why... I've never heard anything so ridiculous in my life!'

The Monsignor had... and most of it in that very room. He watched as the gallery director floundered like a fish pulled from the water.

'Are you seriously suggesting...? Why... I mean... who would...?'

'Perhaps you gentlemen have something to say on the matter,' said the Monsignor, turning and addressing the two agents.

Chad stepped forward. 'There is a third scenario,' he ventured.

Snogden-Lambert was thankful for an excuse to stop puffing out his cheeks.

'It could be that those in charge of running the exhibition are behind this... that you are *both* unwitting victims.'

'Yes!' said Snogden-Lambert, clasping his hands together with relief. 'Yes...! That's probably it!'

The Monsignor seemed less impressed. 'In that case... we should ask them.' He made his way towards the door. 'Given the seriousness of this matter, I requested that the exhibition's curator accompany me here. He's waiting outside.' He placed a hand on the doorknob.

'No!' shrieked Snogden-Lambert, sticking out *his* in terror. 'What if he's armed!'

The three men stared in disbelief as the gallery director dived behind his desk.

'Pull yourself together!' barked the Monsignor. 'These are serious accusations being made.' He jerked the door open. 'Mr Le Blanc... would you mind joining us, please?'

The curator made an entrance more befitting of an elder statesman... his white suit and beard complemented by a white cape, its magnificent silver clasp hanging around his neck like a badge of office.

He paused on seeing the two agents. 'Ah... gentlemen... so

situation,' he said, as calmly as his simmering emotions enabled. 'And seeing as how – since our last meeting – you've made representations to the authorities to have me removed from my position here...' He paused and tried not to think about the small bottle of pills that had started cooing his name from the drawer of his desk, '...you'll excuse me if I don't have an awful lot of sympathy for you.'

The Monsignor stretched his neck, but remained silent.

'It seems the boot is on the other foot now,' continued Snogden-Lambert, emboldened. 'You might've once regarded me as a fool... but it is not I who find myself in this embarrassing situation.' His look of measured calm had been replaced by a vindictive sneer. 'Not looking so high and mighty now... are we?' He rose to his feet, his voice getting louder and more aggressive. 'It seems my doubts about you have been vindicated... my initial scepticism well-founded... You have chosen a dangerous adversary, Monsignor Hoff... It's a foolish man indeed who crosses swords with a Snogden-Lambert!' He tilted his head back with a look of triumphant contempt.

In his mind, his words were being magnificently weighted by an orchestra powering its way through Wagner's *Ride of the Valkyries*. In the minds of everyone else in the room, they sounded better suited to the accompaniment of a psychotic xylophone player's unaccomplished attempt at a child's nursery rhyme.

The Monsignor calmly rose to his feet. 'And it is a foolish man who thinks himself above suspicion,' he replied firmly.

'What's that supposed to mean?' retorted Snogden-Lambert.

'Well...' said the Monsignor, examining his fingernails. 'It strikes me as curious that you are so eager to have the Church implicated in a case of deception before you have considered the alternative scenario.'

Snogden-Lambert looked at him askance. 'Alternative scenario...? What on earth are you on about, man?'

The Monsignor looked straight into his accuser's eyes. 'That the painting was a forgery *before* you gave it to us.'

Snogden-Lambert's air of superiority crumbled. He shot a

previously been forced to the ground and given an unusual perspective of firearms.

He too now suffered nightmares.

'I'll hold your calls and be at my desk if you need me,' said Mrs Fanshawe-Whittingham, with matronly efficiency.

Snogden-Lambert nodded his appreciation, and waited until she had left the room before speaking again. 'I don't believe you know these two gentlemen,' he said, casting his line of sight over the Monsignor's left shoulder. 'They are the CIA operatives of whom I spoke on the phone.'

The Monsignor turned with surprise to find Chad and Bob standing quietly at the far end of the room.

'I've taken the precaution of checking their identities, of course,' continued Snogden-Lambert. 'It can save an awful lot of embarrassment later... as I'm sure you are only too aware.'

Monsignor Hoff glanced unhappily at the carpet again... then found his gaze drawn towards an easel, on which had been placed a large painting.

'It's a Turner,' said Snogden-Lambert in response. 'But then you must know that, given it was painting number one hundred and seven in your exhibition.'

'Ah... the painting in question,' said Monsignor Hoff, stony-faced.

'Indeed... And when I said it's a Turner, what I should've said is that it *was* a Turner... at least, it was when it last left this gallery.'

The Monsignor wrung his hands. 'I take it you've sought independent verification of these gentlemen's claims?'

'Of course,' said Snogden-Lambert aloofly. 'It's been examined by a panel of experts who have unanimously concluded that the painting is indeed... a forgery.' His eyes caught the Monsignor's and challenged them for a reaction.

The Monsignor responded with extreme gravitas. 'If that is the case... this puts us in a very awkward situation.'

Snogden-Lambert re-squared his already squared pencils, his hands showing signs of a slight tremor.

'I think, by that, you mean it puts *you* in a very awkward

whispered in his ear.

The boy's eyes widened in horror.

'Guess you'll be running along, then,' prompted Bob.

The boy nodded up and down with a silence rarely witnessed in children of his age... then turned and ran.

'Alfie?' yelled the child's mother, chasing after him.

'I have a way with kids,' said Bob, getting to his feet. 'Now... how are we doin'?'

'It's genuine,' said the gadget's owner. 'Just like all the others.'

Chad stared at the floor in a stupor.

'He's not used to being wrong,' whispered Bob.

The gadget's inventor looked away with embarrassment... then aimed his machine at the next picture in line as an excuse for something to do.

Click.

Beep.

'Well... I'll be fu_'

*   *   *

'*Monsignor Hoff is here to see you, sir,*' came a crystal-clear voice from the brand-new intercom.

Peter Snogden-Lambert squared up his pencils and stared ahead. 'Send him in please, Joan,' he said crisply.

The door of the office opened to reveal Mrs Fanshawe-Whittingham alongside the man who'd been featuring heavily and unpleasantly in his dreams over the past few weeks. It had taken an awful lot of counselling – and the return of the trusty Mrs Fanshawe-Whittingham – for him to even contemplate entering his office again.

It had also taken a lot of medication.

'Monsignor Hoff... I'm relieved you could make it at such short notice... Come in.' Snogden-Lambert signalled towards the chair in front of him, but did not rise to greet his visitor.

'I could hardly ignore your request, given the circumstances,' said the Monsignor grimly.

As he entered, his eyes alighted upon the spot where he'd

'This is a particular favourite of mine,' said the machine's inventor as he recalibrated its parameters. 'It beautifully demonstrates the opposing forces of man's psyche... the battle between good and evil... the juxtaposition of nobility and savagery within the human soul, the...'

'Is it real or not?' interrupted Chad tersely.

'Stand back.'

Click.

Beep.

'Thank you.'

'...Well?'

'It's another rabbit!'

Chad walked himself around in a tight circle. 'I don't understand,' he mumbled, sweeping his hand over his hair.

'Surely that's good news?' said the gadget's owner, perplexed. 'It's exactly what it's meant to be!'

'Let's try painting one hundred and six,' said Chad, ignoring him. 'Maybe Donald got himself confused about the numbers. At least we definitely know *that* one was removed... And can we drop the goddam rabbit metaphors!'

The Hay Wain was hanging precisely where it should... a crowd of admiring onlookers having gathered in front of it, nodding appreciatively and touching their chins.

The gadget's owner raised himself on tiptoes to get a clear view.

Click.

Beep.

'You're not supposed to take photographs,' said a small boy standing behind them.

'Run along, sonny,' smiled Bob artificially. 'It's alright.'

'No, it's not,' insisted the boy. 'There's a sign over there that says so.'

'We're Americans,' said Bob. 'We can't help it. It's in our blood.'

'You're still not supposed to take photographs.'

Bob softened his smile and bent down to the boy's level. 'Talking of blood...' He yanked the boy's head forward and

141

accompanied by the muffled sound of uncontrollable sobbing.

* * *

'OK,' whispered Chad. 'Start with painting seventy-four and work your way up through the sequence.'

The man next to him held a camera-like gadget up to his eye and focused on the painting in front of them.

Click.

Beep.

'Is *that* it?'

'Sure is,' drawled the man laconically. 'The dog only needs one sniff of the rabbit.'

'And how long before we know if the rabbit's in disguise?' enquired Bob.

The man examined a small readout on the back of the machine. 'You wanna know now?'

'Sure.'

'It's a rabbit.'

'Are you saying this painting's *not* a fake?' asked Chad incredulously.

'One hundred percent the genuine article.'

Chad looked at his partner. 'Perhaps it's not set up right.'

The machine's inventor gave him a disdainful look. 'I'll do it again if it'll make you any happier.' He lifted the gadget to his eye for a second time.

Click.

Beep.

There was a pause.

'Still a rabbit... and I can stand here clicking away 'til kingdom come and it ain't gonna turn into a gopher!'

Chad grasped at the nearest of his scattering thoughts. 'Maybe our source was wrong about this painting... Let's check out the next one on the list.' He moved off hurriedly, leaving the others to catch him up.

They did so in front of painting number ninety-eight... a magnificent white horse being savaged by a lion.

his head and waved it wildly at Norman. 'It was you, wasn't it?' he shouted, tears welling in his eyes. 'You're the one!'

'Listen,' said Norman, slowly retracing his steps past creosote and wood stains. 'I'm not quite sure what's going on anymore.'

'Neither is Uncle Raymond,' spat the assistant. 'You saw to that! He's had to retire on medical grounds... and he was only forty-five. If I can't make a go of it, it'll end six generations of ironmongery in our family. He's now a shell of a man. The doctors say he'll never be able to fire a pricing gun again. All because you asked if he sold computer memory!'

'It was a joke!' said Norman.

'Precisely,' said the assistant, advancing towards him. 'You broke the unwritten rule of ironmongery. *We're* the ones who make the quips!'

Norman thought he might have slipped into one of those other dimensions Gabriel had told him about. 'I'm sorry,' he said, raising both his hands in what he hoped was a dimensionally universal gesture of surrender. 'Unwritten rules are very hard to read!'

'Very funny,' said the assistant, taking an angry swipe at a display of multi-purpose lubricant. '*So* funny, you should be a... wait a minute!' His look of anger turned to one of horror. 'Oh... now I get it!' His stared widened. 'You're one of us, aren't you! Sent by a rival outlet to sabotage our business!'

Norman shook his head... more in disbelief than denial.

The assistant ignored him. 'So... whose shop coat do you wear...? One of those large nationwide chains', no doubt!'

Having reached non-stick pans – as well as the end of his tether – Norman made a dash for the door. Stumbling out into the street he turned and shouted through the window. 'Call yourself an ironmonger...? Your Uncle Raymond would be ashamed of you...! At least he would've asked me if I wanted a left or a right-handed one!'

'Damn!' mouthed the assistant through the glass, slapping a hand to his forehead.

'You're a disgrace to the profession!' yelled Norman.

A box of assorted galvanised hinges crashed against the pane,

'Why... have you lost it?' said the assistant.

Norman looked at him blankly. 'Lost what?'

'Your soldering iron.'

'I never had one in the first place. That's why I've come in here!'

'No... it was a joke,' explained the assistant hastily. 'You said... I'm looking for a soldering iron, and I said... why... have you lost it?'

Norman caught himself standing with his mouth open. 'Right... Well... have you got one I can buy?'

The assistant lost himself in thought again.

'*Hello?*' said Norman, trying to get a response.

'Buy, sir?' said the assistant stiffly. 'You'll have everyone thinking this is an ironmonger's.'

Norman looked around himself in disbelief. 'It is...! Look... do you want my business or not?'

The assistant folded with a look of embarrassment. 'It's no good,' he whimpered. 'I'm just not cut out for this job. Uncle Raymond made it look so easy. He always claimed to have at least three quips for every item on sale.'

'I know,' said Norman. 'I heard some of them.'

'He was brilliant,' said the assistant admiringly.

'He wasn't *that* good.'

'He put *me* to shame,' said the assistant.

'That's true,' agreed Norman. 'But even he was fallible. His weakness was failing to have a riposte for something he *didn't* sell.'

The assistant's expression froze. Norman – thinking he was about to be entertained with another side-splitting display of teenage repartee – waited for the response.

'How did you know that?' the assistant asked coldly, his eyes suggesting all was not well.

'Erm...' Norman thought he'd withhold his reply... as the boy had leapt the counter and was angrily storming towards a display of brooms.

Selecting a large yard brush with synthetic yellow bristles and plastic end attachment for wall hanging, he raised it above going.'

'We've already checked that possibility,' replied Mister Prometheus. 'Unfortunately, they're independently owned.'

There was a collective shudder of disgust.

'Do you still think this is an art scam?' enquired Mister Pan painfully.

'I should have an answer to that tomorrow,' answered Mister Prometheus, 'after my agents have checked the authenticity of some paintings we've been alerted to.'

Mister Pan wiped his brow.

'We must keep our nerve,' advised Mister Zeus. 'As a collective, we are infallible. When we discover where our enemy hide, they'll feel the full anger of the gods! There's only one group of people allowed to mess around with this world on such a global scale... and that's us!'

There was a collective gnashing of teeth.

* * *

Much to his frustration, Norman's trusty hand-held scanner had finally succumbed to its colossal workload. A cursory inspection revealed a cracked circuit board. It was a simple enough problem to repair... if you possessed a soldering iron.

As Norman did not, he found himself revisiting his local hardware store.

There was a different assistant behind the counter... a young lad barely out of acne. He'd been whistling cheerfully to himself as he filled a compartmentalised tray with various types of washer.

'Morning, sir... Can I help you?'

'I hope so,' said Norman. 'I'm looking for a soldering iron.'

The assistant stopped what he was doing and appeared to be giving the matter far more thought than was necessary.

Norman waited for a response, until the lack of one prompted his own. 'I guess you've such a wide range of items, it must get rather confusing!' he said, hoping conversation might bring the lad back into the land of the living.

the brains of the scanner and was busy downloading its data.

'He's an odd one,' whispered Mickey. 'I don't think he's all there. Boy of his age... you'd think he'd get a *proper* girlfriend.'

'Don't knock it,' said Flowers. 'There's nothing wrong wiv 'is cash. Besides... I've grown quite fond of 'im.'

Mickey examined the bundle of notes in his hand. 'Will you be needing the services of our other cousin?' he asked. 'The one who specialises in marketing gimmicks?'

'No, thanks,' said Norman. 'I've got what I needed.'

'It doesn't have to be a Christmas card,' suggested Mickey, turning his attention to the statue's breasts again. 'He does a nice line in table mats.'

* * *

'Were it not so serious, this would be a farce!' shouted Mister Zeus, above a collective babble of agitated voices. 'Now you're asking us to believe that our enemies are descended from a bunch of twelfth century knights!'

'I'm not asking you to believe anything,' said Mister Prometheus, determined to stand his ground. 'As our information changes, so do the facts. I am merely passing them on. I make no assumptions as to the motives. It is *you* who have seen fit to do that. I can only report what I'm getting back from my operatives in the field.'

'And where might that be?' asked Mister Poseidon facetiously. '*Camelot?*'

There was a collective snort of derision.

'You must excuse our scepticism,' said Mister Atlas. 'But the mass hypnotising of the world's religious leaders? I ask you... is it likely?'

'I don't see why not,' replied Mister Prometheus, unfazed. 'My organisation's been looking at the possibilities of doing something similar for years!'

'These *Vault Vans*...' joined in Mister Zeus. 'Are they a company that one of us ultimately owns? If so... we'll have their paperwork examined to ascertain where these deliveries are what it was she was up to.'

'Was she alright?'

'She was once they'd dosed her up with medication.'

'Did that improve her memory?'

'No... but it did wonders for the frostbite.'

As a set of swing doors approached, their distance equated against Mickey's speed suggested the trolley was about to be used as a battering ram.

Norman dashed ahead and just managed to hold them open in time. 'She's rather delicate,' he explained, as Mickey passed him with a disdainful look.

The maze of corridors was traversed at breakneck speed to the accompaniment of sharp intakes of breath every time a corner was negotiated.

Much to Norman's relief, Mickey finally swung the trolley into an open lift and hit the button for the sixth floor.

They'd only gone as far as two when it stopped.

The three men exchanged nervous glances as the doors opened and a doctor joined them.

'Oh dear,' he said, staring at the trolley. 'Lost one, have we?'

'Yes,' said Mickey quickly. 'As stiff as a statue.'

The doctor looked at him aghast. 'Have some feelings, man. That's somebody's loved one under there!'

Mickey caught the doctor's eyes wandering towards the plinth. 'Her suitcase,' he explained. 'She thought she was going home today, poor thing... She'd packed it, ready to leave.'

'Tragic,' said the doctor, as the doors opened onto the third floor and he got out.

'That was close,' gasped Flowers.

'Can you imagine if he'd lifted the sheet!' said Norman, trying not to.

Flowers and Mickey looked at each other, paused... then took a synchronised sharp intake of breath.

'Nice set of jugs,' said Mickey, as he and Flowers watched a rotating image of the statue on a screen.

Norman wasn't listening. He'd wired a laptop computer into

147

paused at the top of the stairs.

'A word of advice,' whispered Flowers, before their descent. 'If we get into difficulties... try and avoid the repaired 'at stand!'

'Quick... put these on!'

Flower's cousin, Mickey, threw a porter's coat at each of them... then swung his trolley around to the back of the van.

'Archaeologist are we?' he said, as the doors opened to reveal its cargo.

'I told you not to ask,' said Flowers sharply.

'Only... we get a number of 'em up here with objects that require investigating. Though never at midnight... curiously enough.'

'And never with cash, I should think,' countered Norman.

Flowers smiled. 'Two hours you say?'

Mickey nodded. 'Absolute maximum! If anyone disturbs us, we're doing tests... okay?'

The three men lifted the statue onto the trolley and draped it with a large, white sheet.

Mickey stood back to admire their handiwork. 'Shame about the plinth.'

'I take it that'll fit in your machine,' said Norman.

Mickey tilted his head and drew a sharp intake of breath. Norman assumed this to be another genetic hand-me-down. 'There's only one way to find out,' he said, pushing the trolley towards the building.

'How's Aunty Ada?' enquired Flowers, as they headed for a service entrance.

Mickey took another sharp intake of breath. 'Not too good... Her memory's getting worse. We got a call last Christmas saying she'd tried to escape from the home again. Apparently, she smuggled herself out in Santa's sack... then legged it across the courtyard to the front gate. Being Christmas, it was unmanned. Nobody noticed she'd gone until they discovered her cracker un-pulled the following morning.'

'So where did they finally catch 'er?'

'The front gate. Seems as soon as she reached it, she forgot was a tactic he employed when faced with situations in which he was clearly out of his depth, but didn't wish to appear so. It was meant as a surrogate wince, with a sagacious hint of foreboding attached. He'd last used it as the crate had been lifted from Nobby's mangled body and one of the paramedics had caught his eye. 'This changes things a bit,' he said, shaking his head. 'I'll 'ave to call me cousin again.'

'But it shouldn't be any different to having a *real* body scanned,' insisted Norman.

'Maybe so... But I don't think yer lady friend 'ere can walk as fast. We're gonna need an 'ospital trolley at the other end... not to mention an extremely large blanket!'

'There's something that intrigues me,' said Norman, as he tilted the statue's head towards himself and prepared to take the weight. 'You've never asked me what's in the crates you've been delivering.'

'Not allowed,' said Flowers laconically, grabbing hold of the base of the figure.

'But aren't you curious?'

'It's against company policy to be curious,' replied Flowers. 'The rules state we don't ask and we don't wonder. It's better for security that way. I'm not even supposed to be calling you by yer first name.'

'If it were me, I'd be dying to know.'

'Alright then... What's in the crates, Mister Penkridge?'

'None of your business.'

They shuffled towards the door.

'And what do the rules say about helping customers transport semi-naked women in the middle of the night?'

'I don't believe that's included,' said Flowers. 'So I guess it must be alright!'

'And your cousin... will he be equally as unconcerned?'

'On the contrary,' answered Flowers. 'He's *extremely* concerned. But it's amazing how cash can soothe the nerves. Must be a genetic trait, that.'

Having manoeuvred themselves out onto the landing, they

did it take?' he asked pensively.

'They asked for ten... but we 'ad 'undreds to choose from. Those scanners 'ave to photograph you from every conceivable angle in order to build up a three-dimensional image.'

'They do... don't they,' grinned Norman. 'And this cousin of yours... the one who's friends with the scanner technician... can he arrange private commissions?'

Flowers looked at him curiously. 'Why... you thinking of 'aving your own card done?'

'Let's just say... I've got a young lady who might be interested in having her measurements immortalised!'

'In that case... I'll ask 'im. But if the 'ospital found out, he'd lose his job.'

'I'd make it worth his while.'

'That'd be... *both* our whiles, would it?' asked Flowers delicately.

'In more ways than you could ever imagine!' said Norman, with a huge smile.

It was approaching midnight when Flowers next knocked on the door.

He was alone.

'I've got a hire van outside... just like you asked,' he whispered furtively. 'Though I don't know why we couldn't 'ave taken your lady friend in me car.'

'There's something I haven't told you,' said Norman, ushering him in. 'She's a little on the heavy side.' He grabbed hold of a duvet covering the statue and yanked it clear.

'Blimey!' exclaimed Flowers, eyeing the figure up and down. 'Ain't it amazing what you get at garden centres these days!'

'It's the patient,' said Norman.

'The what?'

'The one who needs to be scanned.'

'You're kiddin' me...! But I thought...'

'It shouldn't make any difference,' said Norman quickly. 'And at least we know she'll lie perfectly still!'

Flowers tilted his head and took a sharp intake of breath. It

150

connection beyond coincidence! And now we have it, we know where to apply pressure without fear of making another mistake! Once we've confirmed those replaced paintings are forgeries, we'll work on the curator and see which way he jumps. With luck... it'll be in the direction of whoever's at the head of this thing.'

'Who needs luck when you're a genius like me!' Bob grinned smugly. 'I think it's time I took a bow.'

'I think it's time you sat down,' said Chad. 'I'm starting to feel ill.'

* * *

'Here's something for you,' said Flowers, handing Norman an envelope.

Intrigued... Norman opened it and removed a Christmas card. 'I believe in being ahead of the game... but this is ridiculous!' he said, puzzled.

'Look at the front!' insisted Flowers, unable to contain his excitement.

Norman found himself staring at the X-ray image of a human body. Judging by the huge amount of non-translucent scaffolding holding it together, it had obviously suffered appalling injuries.

'Nobby?' winced Norman.

Flowers nodded enthusiastically. 'You 'aven't seen the best bit yet! Go on... give it a tilt!'

The reason for Flower's childlike exuberance became apparent as soon as Norman did as instructed. Nobby and his injuries rotated against the angle of the card.

'That's brilliant!' said Norman, rolling the image backwards and forwards. 'How did you manage this?'

'Another of my cousins,' said Flowers proudly. 'He works for a company specialising in marketing gimmicks. All we 'ad to do was supply 'im with a couple of frames from Nobby's scan and 'e did the rest. Good... ain't it?'

Norman continued playing with the card. 'How many frames

leisure… even down the phone!'

'It all sounds pretty wacky to me,' strained Bob, above the sound of bubbles forcing themselves out of the water.

'Those lights were wacky, Bob. And there's nothing wacky about hypnosis. It's been around as long as history itself.'

More bubbles ensued.

'Maybe Professor Hummingbone was right,' continued Chad. 'Maybe those Templar knights picked up more than ancient secrets of geometry on their crusades. Perhaps those "deeper and darker truths" he talked about included knowledge of mind control. We know flashing lights can affect the brain. Maybe that's why they went to such great lengths to create the effect they did using crystals. Having the necessary geometric skills, they simply combined the two disciplines. There's no doubting our Templars were resourceful!'

After a brief silence, a loud splash from the bathroom was followed by an ecstatic cry of 'EUREKA!'

Chad pushed the door open to find Bob standing upright in the bath… the broadest grin on his soap-covered face.

'I've got it!' he beamed. 'I've got our ticket back in from the cold! I was right! Curved balls do work now and then!'

Chad's bemused gaze dropped to his partner's nether regions. 'I think you're being unfair on yourself, Bob. They're not *that* deformed.'

'I'm talking about my call to the Mennonites. Resourceful Templars… *Templar Resources!* That's the name of one of the companies on their call log! I *knew* I'd heard the name Templar before when the professor mentioned it! Someone put a call through to them shortly after they received mine. We ran a check on them, but the name drew a negative. With nothing untoward on our files, we assumed they were a religious supply company. You know… bibles, prayer cushions… that kinda thing.'

Chad took a moment to digest the information… then clenched his fist in celebration. 'You've done it, Bob… You've finally justified my faith in you all these years! You've found what we've been looking for. That perfect, indisputable used to detect anything that might be counterfeit. It works on the same principle as iris recognition... measuring and logging millions of points on a picture, then comparing them at a later date to ensure it's the same one. He claims its measurements are so accurate, it'd be impossible for an expert faker to get even a couple of points to match. What's more... the original scan can be made from a photograph or auction house brochure. The scale doesn't matter, as it's the ratios between the points that count.'

'I take it this gizmo's portable?'

'Portable and compact... so it can be used without anyone knowing. He's gonna preprogram it with images of the originals we're investigating... so we'll know which paintings are forgeries as soon as he points and clicks.'

'And *then?*'

'We tread *extremely* carefully. We're way beyond our jurisdiction here. But the last thing we wanna do is hand this over to the Brits. This is our chance to come in from the cold, Bob. We're not gonna mess up this time. It's possible the Churches are innocents in all this. If so... the political ramifications of us steaming in with accusations don't bear thinking about!'

'*Innocent?* If the paintings are being stolen, surely they're the ones doing it!'

'Not necessarily. They may be the ones holding the exhibitions... but could've been duped into doing so by others.'

'So... why the secrecy if they've nothing to hide?'

'That's for us to find out. Look... we know those lights affected everyone who saw them. What if that fifteen minutes of silence was the result of a mass hypnotic trance? Think about it! You'd have control of some of the most influential men on Earth!'

'But how could you control people if nothing was said?'

'Maybe they were being set up to receive a hypnotic trigger... one that could induce an identical state later on. Remember that electronic interference we got? Maybe that was it! You'd only have to repeat it and you could indoctrinate your subject at

153

had increased, he'd resorted to hurling abuse from the hall at Flowers and his associates, and threatening to call the police. But having failed to stop them, he'd turned his vitriol towards the source of his problem... Norman.

His castigation was unequivocal.

Norman simply retaliated by insisting that he was not breaking any of the conditions in his tenancy agreement.

Oppenheimer disagreed... warning he'd consult a lawyer and see about getting his troublesome tenant evicted... as well as the cost of a replacement stair carpet. In his opinion, there was nothing more odious than a tenant who thought he knew his rights. If he'd known Norman would end up developing a sense of worth, he'd never have allowed him into the building in the first place!

His tirades rapidly descended into screaming fits, as his words fell on deaf ears. Norman absorbed the insults with a skill honed to perfection during his formative years... his insouciance made that much easier by the fact most of them were now being delivered in a foreign language.

But it was a distraction Norman could do without. His work schedule was punishing... the gruelling lack of sleep starting to have an adverse effect on his ability to think clearly and rationally. He was convinced this was the reason he hadn't been able to resolve the problem of the statue.

His three-dimensional quandary remained. He couldn't see a way around it. And – if he couldn't do that – all his efforts and sleepless nights would be in vain.

* * *

'So, when are they flying this inventor guy over?' shouted Bob, fishing between his legs for a bar of soap.

'The day after tomorrow,' replied Chad, through the half-open bathroom door.

'And this machine of his... it really works?'

'Apparently so. He originally designed it for the insurance market, to confirm the authenticity of paintings. But it can be

Thanks to cockney rhyming slang... this point regarding exclusive association of a surname fails miserably if the examples of Brahms and Liszt are used in conjunction with each other.

Such recognition is fame indeed. You can strut around the afterlife knowing that – in terms of achievement – you couldn't have done much better.

And then it is put to you that you really ought to go back down and have another go. You might have done well in the household-name stakes... but what about the drinking, gambling and womanising that went with it? Wouldn't it have been better – the karmic argument goes – if that success had been established living on top of a bleak mountain, using a pseudonym, and without encouraging the ego?

Oh – and by the way – when you do return... you'll have to start again as a complete nobody, with zero recollection of your previous achievements. You might get lucky and inadvertently stumble upon your old self whilst visiting a hypnotherapist... but a spell of hospital incarceration would undoubtedly ensue when you tried to claim your royalties.

With a current planetary population of over seven billion souls, the chances of you doing better in the *look-mum-I'm-famous* stakes are extremely thin.

So... should you stay or should you go?

Curiously... it's also a dilemma that must face every ordinary ex-mortal who – whilst not having achieved anything more than a well-tended allotment or sadly impressive collection of beer mats – quite liked themselves as they were, thank you.

Norman wondered who *he* had been in a previous life. He wondered what heinous crimes he'd perpetrated to be given the life he was currently having to endure. And had he been connected with Xanthia somewhere along the existential line? Was that why he felt such a strong pull towards her? Perhaps her magnificent breasts were merely icing on the karmic cake.

And then there was Oppenheimer... Where did *he* figure in the eternal cycle of souls? What previous misdemeanours was *his* karma trying to work out?

The man had become unbearable. As the traffic on his stairs

This exposure to so many masterpieces was beginning to have an effect on him, the luxury of examining them in such detail providing a fascinating insight into the world of the creative mind.

When Norman first observed the paintings, he'd seen nothing more than the images they conveyed. But now – having run his fingers over the contours of the paint, exploring the movement of the brushstrokes – he realised they revealed the direction of an idea and the moment in which thought was given form. It was as if he'd broken through the two-dimensional constraints of the canvas and connected with the artist's mind.

He'd entered the fifth dimension.

The more he looked, the more he understood. And as he understood, he realised he was being spoken to… and what was being said was exquisite.

He also felt he was being watched. Not just by those Heavenly entities who had a vested interest in his success… but by those whose work he had been entrusted with. He surmised that – given he was handling the actual source of their immortality – they were probably floating around him in spirit form, nervously keeping an eye on their intellectual property. At least… those who had not yet signed up for a spell of reincarnation.

It was this last point that gave root to an intriguing dilemma. What did the extremely famous dead person think about reincarnation?

After all… there you are, having managed to spend your Earthbound existence making such a name for yourself, it eclipses all others using the same one. For example… hear the name Mozart and you immediately think of Wolfgang Amadeus, the child genius… whose musical compositions will still be performed right up to the moment the sun is finally switched off. You are hardly likely to question *which* Mozart… or call to mind by mistake, Adolf Mozart – a Leipzig chimney sweep – whose life of flues and brushes was never chronicled, as nobody gave a toss.

'And where can we find these people?'

The professor looked nonplussed. 'The one thing about being a secret society, dear boy, is that no one's supposed to know who you are! You could always join the Freemasons and work your way up!' The professor smiled to himself. 'It's rather an irony that one of their symbols is a mason's trowel... given you seem to have come up against a brick wall!'

Chad was less sure he had. He'd now linked a modern-day secret society with the builders of the temple, who – if in possession of advanced skills of geometry and mathematics, as the professor had suggested – would've been able to fashion crystals that could split light as required. Furthermore... their signature was identical to the one on the curator's signet ring. Everything was falling into place. It wasn't a wall the trowel had built... it was the foundations.

'You've been more helpful than you can know,' said Chad, warmly shaking the professor by the hand.

'I have?'

'Perhaps that boyhood fantasy of yours was not so far-fetched after all.'

The two men left Professor Hummingbone to work out where he had gone right... the age-lines on his face suddenly a little less obvious... the turn-ups on his trousers, a little less needed.

*   *   *

The stairs at 66 Armageddon Terrace had taken on the characteristics of a conveyor-belt, supplying a relentless stream of artworks to encode. But Norman's task, though repetitive, had become anything but boring. In the last few days, he'd been up close and personal with works by Degas, Vermeer, Renoir, and Canaletto, as well as a couple of Modiglianis. He'd also encoded numerous stunning works of ethnically diverse origin whose creators were totally unfamiliar to him... all whilst accompanied by a cornucopia of music, created by some of the greatest composers ever to inspire the soul.

157

mathematics... as well as deeper and darker truths that they kept to themselves. This may not be as far-fetched as it sounds. For the Templars suddenly became great builders... constructing some of the greatest fortresses and churches of their time. It is also an interesting fact that – just a few years after their return from the Holy Lands – an inexplicable explosion of Gothic architecture enveloped France and led to the building of some of the greatest cathedrals ever seen on a scale previously unimaginable. From what you have shown me, it is more than probable they had a hand in the construction of *your* temple. The inscription would have been their way of signing their work, much the same way a painter does... Did it appear to be placed at a significant point?'

'You could say that,' replied Chad.

'There you go!' said the professor. 'Being an extremely secretive order, it's small wonder the archives contain no mention of this particular work of theirs.'

'And these Templars...' said Chad, 'what became of them? I mean... are they still around now in some guise or another?'

'Ah... that's where it gets even *more* interesting! By the end of the thirteenth century, they had become so phenomenally rich and powerful that they were regarded by many as a threat. So much so, in fact, that King Philip IV of France – on the pretence of them being involved in sacrilegious and blasphemous initiation rites – had fifteen thousand of them arrested in a single day... many being tortured and killed. That day was Friday the thirteenth of October 1307... and so great was the shockwave it sent throughout Europe, it's why Friday the thirteenth has been regarded as portentous ever since...! As to them being around now... it's said that Freemasonry has its origins in Templar society, and that many of its secret rituals and purposes have roots that go back to that time. Its name derives from the guilds of stonemasons and cathedral builders of the Middle Ages... so the link appears less than tenuous. Given that the Freemasons are very active today... it's possible that the highest and most secretive of their order may still have knowledge of your temple.'

'Of course.'

'In that case...' The professor produced a pen and some paper, '...as precisely as you can.'

Chad carefully drew the symbol he had seen and handed it to the professor.

The professor knew immediately what it was he was looking at... his head nodding up and down so vigorously he was in danger of unwinding his hair.

'That explains it! The *croix pattée*.'

'The what?'

'The emblem of the Templar Knights. They adopted it after the Synod of Troyes gave them official recognition in 1128.'

'Rewind that a second for me, professor. The emblem of *who*?'

'The Templar Knights. Nine French noblemen who took it upon themselves to go to the Holy Lands as part of the Crusades. They eventually grew in number to around twenty thousand, establishing a secret order that would become one of the most powerful and richest in Europe.'

'*Templar*,' said Bob, chewing the word in his mind. 'It's got a familiar ring to it.'

'Their influence is everywhere,' said the professor. 'Our own Temple buildings in Fleet Street were once owned by them and now carry their name.'

'But what were a bunch of French knights doing carving their emblem into the temple at Arwan El Kahab?'

'Well... that's where it gets interesting! Many believe the original Templar Knights travelled to the Holy Lands in search of the lost secrets of the ancients. The crusading part was arguably just a front, as they appear to have done very little of it. It was widely believed that earlier civilisations – such as the Egyptians – possessed a secret knowledge enabling them to build the monumental structures that are found around the world. With the decline of these societies, it became lost. It's possible the Templars set about trying to find it by searching for various relics and manuscripts. Many believe they succeeded, acquiring ancient secrets pertaining to geometry and countrymen that "an expert is one who knows more and more about less and less". You've definitely come to the right person given the narrowness of your enquiry. I'm afraid you'll just have to take my word for it, gentlemen… There are no records for Arwan El Kahab.'

'But what if I was to tell you that certain people alive today have a knowledge of this place?' said Chad, undaunted.

'Then I would say it's been empirically gained and that you ought to talk to *them*! I'm sorry I can't be of any more help to you than that. It's so nice to get a chance to put what's been stored up here over a lifetime of study…' he rapped his head with his knuckles, '…to a more practical use. I've always dreamed of it being like it is in the movies… where an academic is visited and provides information to help solve a great mystery…' He paused awhile… looking wistfully over his half-moon glasses at a point either somewhere in his youth or somewhere on the edges of senility. A glazed smile etched itself on his face.

Bob coughed.

'Yes… well…' the professor blurted. 'When I heard you were from such an *august* body as the Central Intelligence Agency, I rather hoped my boyhood fantasy had finally come true! Alas… it seems that is not to be. Never mind… there's always tomorrow!'

Bob couldn't help feeling that was an extremely optimistic viewpoint given the limited amount of tomorrows the professor appeared to have in him.

'I take it there's nothing else I can help you gentlemen with?' he asked wishfully.

'Actually… there might just be,' said Chad.

Professor Hummingbone's body lifted itself up inside his suit. 'Oh… really?'

'There was an inscription at the temple… the only one we came across… a cross carved into one of the stones… though not the usual Christian style.'

'Would you be able to draw it for me?' asked the professor, hurriedly opening his briefcase and rummaging inside.

wrapped around a liver-spotted pate... badly.

'Professor Hummingbone?' enquired Chad.

'I was the last time I looked in a mirror,' he replied.

Given the state of him, Bob wondered when that might have been.

'So you gentlemen are from America?' said the professor cordially. 'Some very good friends of mine, the Finchamptons, live in Seattle on the East coast.'

'Can't say I know them,' said Bob. 'But if it wasn't for the two and a half thousand miles in-between, they'd be practically neighbours.'

The professor smiled. 'Yes... it's a big country, isn't it? Don't think I could live there myself, though. I'd miss the sense of history.'

'Yeah... but the shopping malls are great,' returned Bob.

The bemused look on the professor's face suggested the agent's sarcasm had gone right over his head... which is more than could be said for his hair. 'Well... you gentlemen certainly aroused my curiosity with your telephone call. I've been trawling through a number of manuscripts trying to discover a reference to this temple you enquired about. The problem is... I've been unable to find a single one! I've spoken to a number of my learned colleagues, but they also confess to having no knowledge of it. That's not to say it doesn't exist, mind.'

'We know it exists,' said Chad. 'We've been there.'

'Oh!' said the professor, somewhat taken aback. 'I see... Then, you'll know that the area in which you say it's located is a vast and desolate one, ideally suited for escaping the attention of the outside world... including scholars! Many sects chose such places to establish themselves in order to be free from persecution and unwanted interference. Unfortunately... it also made them inaccessible to the archivists of the time, not to mention those who've followed since. In the case of your temple at Arwan El Kahab, it seems to have eluded them completely!'

'But I assume there must be records *somewhere*,' said Chad.

'If there were, I'd certainly know about them,' replied the professor. 'I've always enjoyed the quote by one of your fellow here, we're keeping ourselves on the case. And, as long as we're doing that, we still have a chance to redeem ourselves!'

Bob gazed out of the window. 'I spy with my little eye, something beginning with... *A*.'

'Answers?'

'Nope... Another traffic warden... Let's go!'

*   *   *

The offices of the antiquities department looked more ancient than some of the exhibits in its charge, a fact also true of many of those working there. But it was a petite, bespectacled girl in her late twenties who approached the two men as they stood waiting.

'Professor Hummingbone will see you now,' she said, smiling politely.

The smile Bob returned had less to do with courtesy and more to do with a pick-up in a nightclub. 'Shame about the glasses,' he whispered, as they followed her.

'Your concern's understandable,' commented Chad. 'She can see how ugly you are.'

Much like his partner's pursuit of the truck the previous day, Bob kept his attention fixed firmly on the girl's tail end as she led them through a series of interconnecting rooms stuffed with the trappings of academia. Plain, labelled, vanilla boxes seemed to have cloned themselves and taken over every conceivable space.

Reaching a door marked *meeting room*, she pushed it open, gave another of her smiles and headed off back from where she had come.

'Do enter, gentlemen,' came a voice from inside.

It belonged to a man stubbornly refusing to recognise the concept of retirement, his suit doing the same. A crumpled, bottle-green bow tie sat above a bulging waistcoat, the turn-ups on his trousers suggesting a considerable loss of height since first acquiring them. Those remnants of wispy, silver hair that had decided *not* to jump an obviously sinking ship, had been mental decline.

'There's been something bugging me ever since we left that temple! The trouble is… I've been unable to put my finger on exactly what it was. But you did… literally… the night we stayed at the *Hotel Bedouin*… Remember? You ran it along the frame of that picture and complained. Think, Bob! What did you complain about?'

Bob cast his mind back. '*Everything*… knowing me.'

'In particular.'

'I think I preferred the previous game. It was easier… and you were less frightening.'

'Okay, then… something beginning with… *P*.'

'Prices?'

'No.'

'Plumbing?'

'No… Dirt!'

'That's a *D*.'

'*P* for Pollution, Bob. Dirt… dust… grime or bird shit! It's all the same thing!'

Bob lifted the lapel of his shirt and spoke into it. '*Earth to Chad… Earth to Chad*.'

'Look… Those crystals we discovered… perfectly aligned to create that fantastic display. Doesn't it strike you as odd, that in a temple known to have been abandoned for centuries, they sparkled into action without a hint of anything dulling them?'

'The *whole* thing's odd… if you ask me.'

'It was no freak occurrence, Bob. Someone *ensured* they were in that condition… Someone *had* to have cleaned them! And that makes the light show relevant… and with it the temple… and April, twenty-third! We have it, Bob… our connection beyond coincidence!'

'Then… what's next?'

'We do our research… confident we're heading in the right direction. We find out who built that temple and what they were about. And what better city to do it in than this one! It's packed with archaeological repositories and experts. And there's an added bonus… As long as we're able to justify our staying

'Vault Vans?' exclaimed Bob. 'They've gotta be kiddin'. Your wallet's more secure than that truck!'

'I think you'll find they're referring to the one coming *out*,' said Chad, as a seriously riveted security van swung into the road and made off in the opposite direction, the emblem of two overlapping *Vs* indelicately saluting them from the rear doors.

'At least we can be certain our man's dropped off something valuable,' said Bob.

'The trouble is... unless we develop X-ray vision, we've no way of knowing which truck to follow next.' As Chad spoke, a van identical to the last exited from the yard and made its way past them. 'I'll tell you what... they've either got a severe lack of brains or a helluva lotta balls using a *kosher* delivery firm to transport their spoils!'

'Precisely... It don't make sense. They're leaving a trail of paperwork that could be traced and used as evidence. You know what I think it proves?'

Chad took a long look at his partner. 'That they're even dumber than you?'

'That all this is legit. Perhaps they really *are* getting the paintings cleaned.'

'Oh... come on! Even if they needed to, don't you think they'd do it in-house?'

'We're talking priceless works of art,' said Bob. 'You don't just give them a quick squirt of polish and a wipe with a duster! Perhaps we're chasing our tails here. Perhaps the only dirty work that's occurring involves the use of a restorer's rag. Maybe we should accept that dust is a fact of life, churches don't cheat, Tucker-Jenkins is fully-baked as opposed to half... and that all of this is a complete and utter waste of time.'

'Dust!' shouted Chad, banging the steering wheel exuberantly. 'You're right! Dust *is* a fact of life!'

Bob looked at his partner, as if witnessing the first signs of mental decline.

'Dust is our connection beyond coincidence! Or, at least... the *lack* of it is!'

Bob looked at his partner as if witnessing the *second* signs of the large metal shutter on the side of the building they'd been observing. 'Anyway… what was it?'

'Parking warden.'

'They're not called parking wardens over here… they're traffic wardens.'

'Whatever… P or a T, she's showing an unhealthy interest in our car.'

Chad jerked his body upright. 'I spy with my little eye, something beginning with M.'

'Monetary penalty?'

'Movement!' Chad reached for the key in the ignition and started the engine.

'Relax. If she gives us a ticket, we'll deposit it in the bin at the airport.'

'Not from her, stupid… from the entrance opposite!'

The large metal shutter was slowly rising, exposing the bowels of a delivery bay. As soon as the shutter reached maximum height, a small, unmarked truck emerged and nosed its way out into the one-way street.

'Don't lose it!' said Bob, scooping up the empty polystyrene cups from the dashboard.

'As if!' said Chad, pulling out smartly behind. 'I've got a feeling our careers are riding on that truck!'

The pursuit commenced at a reasonable pace, the driver of the truck weaving his vehicle in and out of lanes with the confidence of a man familiar with the route he was taking.

Chad kept tight to its tail end, determined not to be caught out by an inconsiderate motorist or traffic light coming between them. It did little for Bob's nerves, his faith in ever seeing home again resting solely on his partner's ability to react to the truck's brake lights before they became imbedded in his forehead.

Finally – and much to his relief – the truck slowed and turned into a large, gated compound.

Chad pulled over and watched as the van disappeared. '*Vault Vans*,' he read, from a sign above the compound's entrance. '*We take the fright out of freight.*'

Chad dropped his head back onto the headrest of the driver's seat and gave the matter some thought. 'Porch,' he said lazily.

'It hasn't got a porch,' said Bob, taking another look at the building they had been taking a look at for the last four hours.

'What's that above the entrance, then?'

Bob squinted. 'An overhang.'

'That's a kinda porch.'

'Something beginning with *P* doesn't mean *something kinda like something beginning with P but actually beginning with O*, does it?'

'Alright... Poster. There's one advertising the exhibition on the front of its doors.'

'Nope... not poster.'

Chad chewed his lip. 'People.'

'Nope.'

'Pollution.'

'*Pollution...?* How the hell can you *see* pollution?'

'What d'ya think all that grime on the stonework is?'

'Dirt.'

'Yeah... from pollution!'

'Not necessarily... The pigeons have had a fair say in the matter.'

'I'm talking about the black bits... not the white!'

'Whatever... The answer ain't pollution.'

'Pigeon, then.'

'Nope.'

'Pigeon *shit?*'

'Nope!'

Chad let out a sigh and drummed his fingers on the steering wheel. 'Pedestrian,' he said wearily.

'Close.'

'Pavement.'

'Nope.'

'Okay... I give up.'

'You can't give up!' said Bob indignantly. 'I've just spent the last thirty minutes working out that *T* stood for tourist!'

'That's because you're more stupid than I am.' Chad gazed at paintings are at risk and will get these to you as a priority. We must process them all before this interference is successful. I'm afraid you'll find precious little time for sleep over the coming days.'

'No change there,' sighed Norman.

Gabriel's attention switched to the statue in the centre of the room. 'Ahh… Canova's *Venus Italica*. Is she coming or going?'

'That's where *my* bad news comes in,' Norman grimaced. 'I need to hang on to her for a while. I've got to find a way to convert a three-dimensional form into binary.'

'*Five*-dimensional,' Gabriel reminded him.

'I don't suppose you have any suggestions?'

'Actually… I do. It's this… You'd better find your solution quickly.'

Norman allowed an impure thought to parry the remark.

Gabriel flinched.

'You're not back to your mind reading tricks again, are you?' asked Norman suspiciously.

'No need. I felt *that* one's vibration! It's obvious you've got a problem on your hands. You must inform those who are awaiting the statue's return that it will be delayed.'

'And how do I do that?'

'Send a note back with the other crates. Explain you need to hang onto it… but say nothing more. Address your message to *Templar Resources*. That will take care of it.'

'The same organisation whose name is on all the delivery documents,' commented Norman.

'The very same.'

'And who are also the account holders for the chequebook you gave me,' he fished.

Gabriel said nothing.

Norman prepared his next question.

'The good guys,' said Gabriel. 'And let's leave it at that.'

*   *   *

'I spy with my little eye, something beginning with… *P*.'

minutes to pick up the crates from the previous day's delivery. But there was a problem.

The statue was standing in exactly the same state of undress as she had been when Norman first set eyes upon her. Whilst the contents of the other crates had been processed and repackaged, his three-dimensional dilemma stood silently in the middle of the room, calmly looking the other way.

He'd spent the last twenty-four hours racking his brains as to how he could reduce her curvaceous beauty to a code of noughts and ones, but had been unable to come up with the answer. He knew failure wasn't an option. If she'd been created from a segment of vibration, she *had* to be returned to that form for his task to succeed.

He let out a groan.

'Are you alright?' came a voice from the other side of the door.

He glanced at his watch. 'Flowers? Is that you? You're early!'

'It's Gabriel. I need to speak to you!'

The briskness with which the Archangel entered the room indicated further problems. 'I have bad news,' he said, confirming it.

'Funny you should say that,' muttered Norman.

'Remember I warned you there were dangerous forces afoot who might seek to impede our mission?'

'I'm hardly likely to forget.'

'There's no *might* about it anymore. Suspicion has fallen on our scheme for obtaining the paintings… which could result in some of them no longer being made available to us.'

'*Suspicion?*'

'Certain individuals have picked up the wrong end of the stick… but the stick, nonetheless. If they succeed in denying us just *one* of the paintings we require, we'll be unable to complete our task. Just one work of art that can't be encoded, Norman… that's all it will take for us to fail!'

'Strangely enough… I was thinking that *very* thing before you arrived.'

'You must redouble your efforts. We have identified which

168

concerned with such matters. I have people to do that sort of thing for me.'

'Then I suggest you get on the phone and call them,' advised Mister Prometheus. 'If paintings have been loaned to these exhibitions, they must be retrieved immediately.'

'It's not that easy,' said Mister Pan. 'I'll first need to get my personal assistant to call my financial management team... who'll need to call their creative investment subsidiary in order to find out which accountants were authorised to employ an investment broker on behalf of my art holdings. The investment broker should then be able to inform me which company they hired to instruct an agency to employ an art management expert to decide on which institutions should be allowed to exhibit my investments. These institutions may well have subcontracted their exhibitions... meaning it may take some time before I can do anything.'

'And this is the same for all of you?' enquired Mister Prometheus in amazement.

There was a collective nod.

'Then I suggest you start immediately,' he advised.

'But before we do,' interjected Mister Zeus firmly, 'I wish to say one final thing. It is not Christianity or Hinduism, Islamism or Judaism that is the biggest religion on Earth... It is materialism. It will take a while before its foundations feel the force of any attack against it. Remember that when you go about your business. We must act with decisiveness. But above all... we must not panic.' He sat back, impressed with the sound of his own voice. 'I propose this meeting be adjourned,' he announced.

'Seconded!' said Mister Pan hastily.

'Carried!'

There was a collective scramble for the door.

*   *   *

Norman sat slouched on the sofa – face in hands – his body language screaming despondency. Flowers was due in fifteen

'We face our toughest challenge,' announced Mister Zeus sombrely. 'We must act decisively to prevent this Armageddon.'

'So... Mister Prometheus,' said Mister Hercules. 'What does your Government intend doing about it?'

'My Government doesn't know about this situation yet,' came the answer. 'I assumed you'd want to be the first to know.'

'Quite right,' said Mister Zeus, stroking where a beard might be if he'd had one. 'We don't want to cause a panic outside of these walls. The first thing we must do is ensure our own interests are made safe. Mister Pan... I believe this might be of greater concern to you than it is for some of us.'

Mister Pan – who had been growing steadily ashen-faced throughout the whole proceedings – rose to speak. 'It is no secret that I have favoured art as one my main investments... yes.'

'Then I must ask the question,' said Mister Zeus, 'could you, or any other members of this council, have unwittingly contributed paintings to these exhibitions?'

'This is the worrying thing,' replied Mister Pan. 'I am unable to answer that right now.'

'But surely you must know what you own?' said an astonished Mister Prometheus. 'We're talking about world masterpieces here!'

'Do you mean what *I* own... or what *companies* that I own, own? Or perhaps you're talking about what companies that are owned by companies that I own, own? Or perhaps you're talking about...'

'He gets the picture,' said Mister Zeus, waving his hand dismissively.

Mister Pan sat down. 'You see, Mister Prometheus... even the works of art that we choose to display for our own gratification are copies. The originals are securely locked away in protective vaults, being far too valuable a commodity to hang on walls. But we usually concede to requests by major galleries and museums for their loan... such exposure maintaining an interest in those particular works and thereby increasing their value. It is not I who decides, being far too busy a man to be

The effect such a scenario would have on some of the wealthiest individuals on the planet began to dawn on those sitting around the table... who happened to be some of the wealthiest individuals on the planet.

'Art portfolios would be decimated over night!' exclaimed Mister Helios in horror. 'Paintings would be worth nothing more than the canvas on which they were painted!'

'Entire corporations with investments in the market could go the wall!' added Mister Hercules.

'People might even start to question the value of other investments!' suggested Mister Cronus.

There was a collective whimper.

'The whole of Capitalism could be at stake!' cried Mister Epimetheus.

There was a collective panic.

'Ladies and gentlemen!' shouted Mister Zeus above the ensuing pandemonium. 'Our namesakes would not have recognised such a mortal emotion as fear! *We* are the ones in control. Our power is supreme. It is up to *us* to put a stop to this outrage!'

His outburst brought a frangible calm to the room.

'Maybe, at least now,' he continued, 'we have the answer as to *why*. If Capitalism were to collapse, who would people turn to for answers in the ensuing turmoil? Their gods, of course! In one fell swoop, the religions of the world would have brought about the death of materialism and a monumental increase in their congregations!'

There was a collective drop of the penny.

'They must be stopped at all costs!' yelled Miss Aphrodite, getting up onto the table and brandishing her handbag.

Mister Prometheus felt he should remind them that their *Death of Capitalism* scenario was just a theory. But the sight of Miss Aphrodite breathing heavily and licking her lips caused him to reflect on the wisdom of such a move. Besides... the thought had occurred to him that they might just be right. After all... it was not only the *first* theory he'd heard that made any sense... it was the *only* one.

'I told you it was a bad idea,' glared Bob, as they exited the rusty gates at speed and turned onto the narrow lane that had brought them there. 'We're gonna be a complete laughing stock back at Langley when word gets out we gave him a second chance. What were we thinking of?'

Chad kept his steely gaze fixed on the road ahead. 'Maybe it won't.' He pushed his foot hard on the accelerator as the lane widened.

'And how do you work that one out, Wonder Boy? It's only going to take another of his letters to headquarters... once he starts complaining we didn't take him seriously.'

'Then maybe it's time we did!'

Bob stuck a finger in his ear and waggled it. 'Am I hearing you correct? Have you finally taken leave of your senses?'

'Listen,' said Chad, turning and transferring his gaze to his partner. 'What if he's right? What if they've been removing the paintings and replacing them with fakes. That would give them even more time to cover their tracks. No one's gonna check a painting for its authenticity whilst it's hanging up in an exhibition... especially one organised by a church. And what if this is going on in every religious exhibition around the world?'

'Would you mind keeping your eyes on the road,' said Bob stiffly. 'I've already ruined one pair of trousers today.'

*　　*　　*

'So it *is* an art scam?' Mister Zeus rose to his feet and clenched his fists.

'We can't be one hundred percent certain at this point in time,' replied Mister Prometheus, 'but it's certainly beginning to look that way.'

There was a collective feeling of alarm.

'Do you realise what this means?' said Mister Poseidon, nervously. 'If confidence in the authenticity of paintings by the great masters were shattered, it would lead to a complete collapse of the world's art market!'

The collective wobbled.

'Just out of interest,' said Chad, as they stepped outside into the relief of fresh air. 'What do *you* think has happened to the paintings?'

Donald stared at him awkwardly. 'How do you mean?'

'I mean... where do you think they are right now?'

'I *know* where they are,' said Donald, surprised.

His reaction was as nothing compared to Chad's. 'You *know*?'

'Yes... of course I do! They're hanging on the walls of the exhibition.'

'The exhibition...? But you told us they were *missing!*'

'I told you they'd been removed,' said Donald. 'I never said anything about them not having been put back again!'

Chad looked at him in astonishment. 'But what about Constable's *Hay Wain*? We saw that was missing with our own eyes!'

'You may well have done. But I expect it'll have been put back by now,' said Donald matter-of-factly. 'Just like all the others.'

Chad struggled to find his next words. 'So what's all this been about?' he exclaimed, throwing his hands up in despair.

Bob put his in the ample pockets of his plus fours and stared at the ground.

'I thought *that's* what you were going to find out!' replied Donald. 'Just because the paintings have been put back doesn't mean they haven't been tampered with. For instance... how can we be sure they're the originals? Haven't you thought of that?'

Chad grappled for an answer.

'Are you *sure* you don't want me to help you?' asked Donald, peering at him suspiciously.

'Quite sure, thank you,' murmured Chad. He beckoned Bob with a cursory nod and headed for the car.

'You can hang on to the trousers until we meet again,' cried Donald cheerily after them. 'They really do suit you!'

His comment went unacknowledged.

'I KNOW HE LOOKS BLOODY RIDICULOUS,' shouted Donald to his left. 'I WAS JUST BEING POLITE!'

want to put them on the defensive... do we?'

Both agents relaxed.

'I KNOW IT WAS OUR DISCOVERY... BUT THESE GENTLEMEN ARE HERE TO HELP US!' Donald shouted at the top of his voice.

His outburst caused Bob to spill his coffee and the drenched cat on his lap to launch itself to the floor. But not before it had dug its claws deep into his leg.

'Shit!' he yelped.

'It happens sometimes,' said Donald.

Chad sniffed the air. 'And what's *that* smell?'

Donald pointed to a little brown message the cat had left on Bob's lap before vacating it.

'Oh, shit!' groaned Bob.

'As I said,' shrugged Donald. 'It happens sometimes.'

The chequered plus fours Donald fetched from upstairs had belonged to his father. Bob – refusing to wear anything that had seen service anywhere remotely near Donald's own loins – had been forced to settle for a compromise. It was either them or a choice of heavily embroidered evening gowns once belonging to Donald's mother.

'They're a bit baggy about the crutch, but the colours are really you,' said Donald, tilting his head. 'Shame about the shoes and socks, though.'

'No sweat,' glared Bob. 'You won't catch me doing anything more than looking outta the car window in these.'

'You will take care of them, won't you?' pleaded Donald. 'Only... they were the ones father was wearing when he passed over.'

'You mean... to the other side?' choked Bob.

'Well... yes... That and the sign saying *Danger, No Vehicles Beyond This Point.*'

'Now, remember,' advised Chad. 'Leave this matter to us. No more chaining yourself to radiators.'

Donald nodded his compliance and showed the two men to the door.

'Neither,' said Donald. 'I was referring to Lancelot the poltergeist. He's very good at it... creating an atmosphere of confusion. It's probably a throwback to his earthly life.'

'Was he once a knight?' enquired Chad.

'Twice a bloody day, if you'd let him! Now... about the paintings.' Donald rummaged about inside the pocket of his trousers and produced a crumpled piece of paper which he carefully unfolded and smoothed across his knee. 'I've observed three other exhibits removed from the exhibition. One hundred and seven... ninety-eight... and seventy-four.'

Donald found himself being stared at blankly.

'That's *Lion Attacking a Horse* by George Stubbs... William Blake's *The Ancient of Days*... and a painting by Turner which I didn't catch the name of,' he elaborated.

Chad took a sip of his coffee and a moment to reflect. 'I'm no art connoisseur... but even *I* recognise those artists. We must be talking *extremely* valuable masterpieces here.'

'The best!' said Donald, his eyes brimming with enthusiasm. 'Now you can see why I've adopted such drastic measures to get my voice heard.'

'Well... you've finally got yourself an audience,' Chad assured him. 'And you can rest in the knowledge your efforts have been worthwhile.'

'Rest?' exclaimed Donald. 'There's precious little time for that! We must discover what's occurring to these great works before it's too late!'

Donald's use of the pronoun "we" didn't sit easily with the two men opposite him.

'You're gonna have to leave this to *us* now,' said Chad. 'We don't wanna alert those involved that we're onto them.'

'But they know I am!' insisted Donald. 'I've got the bruises to prove it!' He lifted a trouser leg to demonstrate.

Chad chose his next words carefully before unleashing them on Donald's feelings. 'Let's just say... they don't know of *our* involvement. And in order not to lose the advantage of surprise, it would help us if you stayed away.'

Donald mulled the idea over. 'Good point,' he said. 'We don't

'The thing that interests us is your claim that *other* paintings have been removed from the exhibition's walls.'

'One second!' said Donald, raising his hand. 'I'm extremely uncomfortable about your use of the word "claim". It suggests an unsubstantiated argument.'

'Then you *can* substantiate it?' said Chad eagerly.

Donald considered the question. 'Not really. But I don't think you gentlemen would have bothered to come all the way here to my home if you weren't prepared to at least accept my word.'

Chad nodded.

'In which case,' continued Donald, 'I shall tell you what I know.' He cleared some papers from an armchair hiding beneath them and beckoned for his guests to be seated on the *chaise longue*.

As the two men gingerly complied, a number of cats took it as their cue to jump up and search out a comfortable lap.

'AT LEAST THEY'RE BEING FRIENDLY!' said Donald loudly. He looked quickly at his guests. 'By the way... I was talking to Whitebait this time... and not about the cats.'

A mangy looking tabby – having chosen Bob as a resting place – was having second thoughts. He lifted his paws awkwardly as he debated whether to settle.

'I don't think he likes me,' said Bob.

'No, he doesn't,' said Donald bluntly. 'He thinks you're arrogant, self-opinionated and a tiresome cynic.'

'You communicate with cats as *well* as the dead?' remarked Chad.

'Oh, sorry,' said Donald, looking at the one auditioning Bob's lap. 'I thought you meant Whitebait... There you go... He's up to his old tricks again.'

'I take it you mean Whitebait and not the cat?'

'What?'

'Up to his old tricks?'

'Is he?' said Donald, with a look of astonishment. 'I didn't know he did tricks.'

Bob stared at the floor and drew a deep breath. 'Are we talking about Whitebait or the cat?'

176

'So would they,' said Donald. 'Lancelot's a poltergeist.' He placed the tray on a small table and handed out the drinks. 'Now... what can I do for you gentlemen? I assume you've had a change of heart since we last met.'

'That was an unfortunate misunderstanding,' said Chad awkwardly. 'We now believe you really *do* have information that could be of use to us.'

Donald bent down and allowed a couple of the cats circling his feet to scent his hand. He gave one a friendly pat on the bottom. Bob thought he'd give the biscuits a miss.

'You see how they've got their tails between their legs?' said Donald.

'Really? They look like they're all in the air, to me,' observed Bob.

'I was talking to the cats,' said Donald, eyeing him superciliously.

Bob lodged his tongue in the side of his cheek and deferred to Chad.

'We'd assumed from your letter that you were willing to help,' Chad obliged.

'Was... and am. I'm glad to see you've finally seen sense. I know some might say I'm a little odd...' He paused for a reaction indicating the contrary, leaving Chad and Bob to wonder why he'd stopped talking. 'But even madness does not imply idiocy. When you look at a madman, you are not necessarily looking at a stupid man. It is a wise man who knows the difference!'

'That's why we're here.'

'Fair enough. So... what exactly is it you wish to know?'

'We witnessed your demonstration the other day,' said Chad.

'Which one? There have been many.'

'*Manacled Man and Radiator*,' prompted Bob.

'Ah!' A smile swept briefly across Donald's face. 'Just a minute!' He bent over so as to view the two men upside down. 'So it was *you!*'

'Correct... And you were absolutely right about painting one hundred and six.'

'Well, of course I was!'

mixed with an assortment of other eye-watering aromas they thought it best not to try and identify.

'It's the damp,' explained Donald, seeing them suffering. 'The house never gets aired… what with me being away so much on my mission. I'll leave the door open a few minutes.'

'I don't think we'll be keeping you that long,' said Chad, placing a finger to his nose in the vain hope the smell of skin might counteract the malodour.

'Nonsense,' said Donald dismissively. 'You'll at least have a cup of tea. I'll put the kettle on.'

'Make that a coffee,' said Bob. 'And how about we drink it outside?'

'I'll bring it to the drawing room,' said Donald, ignoring the comment and opening a door that led off from the hallway. 'Make yourselves at home, gentlemen.' He energetically ushered them through. 'I shan't be long.'

A number of cats – who'd been using the drawing room as a resting place – sprang from their positions and followed him as he disappeared.

'Jesus!' said Bob. 'What a friggin' stench! Have you ever smelt anything like it? When he said he talked to the dead, I didn't think he kept their corpses in the house!' He walked to the far end of the room and fumbled behind a large set of dusty, green velvet curtains for a window to open.

The drawing room was littered with newspapers and magazines – many bundled and tied up with string – alongside numerous boxes of books. To the right of a covered piano was a dilapidated, purple *chaise longue*, covered in cats' hairs and definitely not looking to be sat upon. The walls were lined with dozens of old photographs… many showing Donald as a surprisingly dapper young man, involved in various activities with his parents. The rest comprised framed pictures of ironing boards, a fact which totally perplexed the two observers.

'I hope you take your coffee black,' said Donald, returning with a tray. 'I'm afraid Lancelot drank the last of the milk.'

'No problem,' said Chad. 'Can't stand the stuff. I'd much rather the cats had it.'

The only reason there wasn't a hint of flaking paint on the wooden beams that interlaced the decorative brickwork was because there wasn't a hint of paint to flake. It had gone the same way as the gravel. And many of the small, diamond shaped panes making up the leadlight windows had at some point been broken and replaced with cardboard wrapped in polythene bags. What at first glance appeared to be a long, thin window box below the roof of the house – in which were being cultivated various tall grasses – turned out, on a second, to be the guttering. Had the building been a hospital patient, it would instantly have been admitted to intensive care.

It would also have probably died.

'Do you think this is meant to happen?' asked Bob, waving a detached doorbell under Chad's nose.

Chad shrugged and rat-a-tat-tatted their arrival on a large, brass door-knocker cast in the shape of an ironing board.

There came a brief spell of shouting from inside the house, followed by the sound of sliding bolts.

The large, dark-oak door creaked painfully on its hinges, opening cautiously to reveal Donald surrounded by a retinue of cats and attired in clothes for which the word *casual* would have been not only wholly inappropriate, but also an honour. There were so many holes in his cardigan that there was less of it than there was more, and he was shoeless... ten grubby, un-manicured toes greeting their visitors through an exhausted pair of socks.

Despite his appearance, Donald had been expecting them. 'Gentlemen... So, we meet again!' He pushed the cats out of the way with his foot. 'You'd better step inside.'

The thing that struck Chad and Bob – as they accepted his offer and entered a gloomy interior – was the smell. This was not struck as in a sudden or unexpected impression entering one's consciousness. This was struck as in a large freight train hitting you full on as you ran as fast as you could towards it. It was hard for them to place its bouquet on account of the fact they were desperately trying not to breathe in. When they did... they were assaulted by the stinging redolence of cats' urine

How could he possibly encode what was in front of him? When Gabriel had asked him to devise a way of capturing images in a binary format, he'd naively assumed they would all be two-dimensional. As he stood captivated by the statue in front of him, he realised what a massive mistake that had been.

*   *   *

The first thing that impressed visitors to Donald Tucker-Jenkins' residence was the length of the drive, meandering its way from the quiet country lane through a canopy of sycamore and ash. The second, was the size of the house to which it led.

Bostock Tucker-Jenkins – Donald's father – had been big in ironing boards. So much so, that a shudder had coursed through the entire industry on the announcement of his untimely and tragic death. Questions had been asked in parliament... or to be more precise, *one* had. It was this:

'Does this house agree that the death of Bostock Tucker-Jenkins is a huge loss to the ironing board industry?'

It did... but it needn't have worried. The ironing board industry continued to go from strength to strength, despite the introduction of cheaper models, whose ratcheting systems and methods of cover attachment left a lot to be desired.

The first thing that *least* impressed visitors about Donald Tucker-Jenkins' residence was its condition... which, coincidentally, was the first thing that least impressed visitors about Donald himself.

The drive – which had once known gravel – opened out into a wide circle in front of the house, an ornamental fountain standing apologetically in the centre. Its water had long since ceased to flow... weeds the only thing now sprouting from its pipes.

Had the two gentlemen getting out of the car not been visitors from abroad, they might've recognised the house's exterior as mock-Elizabethan. It didn't take a knowledge of English architecture, however, to recognise it as being in dire need of repair.

Trusty crowbar in hand, he set about unlocking the crate's secret... methodically working his way around its outer edges until he'd loosened the front panel. Prising it far enough open to slip his fingers inside and grab hold, he gave a sharp tug.

It was more than was needed.

The panel detached itself with surprising ease, sending him sprawling backwards, a shower of polystyrene balls bursting out and covering the best part of the carpet.

Still embracing the panel, he peered over its top.

Standing gracefully within the wooden confines of the crate was a semi-naked woman – perfectly formed – her hands clutching a simple dress against her body, her bare breasts just visible above it. She had spared Norman's embarrassment... or perhaps it was her own... by having turned her head to one side as if something of more importance had caught her eye. She exuded a classical beauty... her ringletted hair tied back in the tradition of ancient Rome, her perfect skin the colour and texture of marble.

'And who might *you* be?' he muttered quietly.

She didn't reply.

She didn't move either... though Norman deduced that this was due to her feet being firmly attached to a small marble plinth.

For the first time, Xanthia's stare from her poster made him feel uncomfortable. Up to that point, hers had been the only breasts to grace his bedsit. But they weren't three-dimensional. The statue's *were*. They also seemed far more ... *civilised*. They just happened to be part of her... as opposed to her just happening to be part of them.

Norman rested the lid of the crate against Xanthia's face and stepped forward to study his visitor.

Reaching out, he ran his fingers along her exquisitely smooth shoulders... following the contours of her neck until they came to rest beneath her delicate jaw. Had her skin been warm and soft, she would not have been any more beautiful.

He wondered what the binary equivalent of 36-24-36 was... and then the hammer fell.

and let his mind swim in its current.

Now, he'd been given that chance... landlord permitting.

The incident with Lotty had troubled Oppenheimer greatly. Whilst finally managing to convince himself it had been a sleep-induced hallucination, the fact he'd envisaged her going into Norman's room only increased his animosity towards his newly troublesome tenant. That and the constant, heavy, ten o'clock traffic up and down the stairs eventually brought him out of his room, manically waving Norman's tenancy agreement in the air. But – as Norman politely pointed out – there was nothing in its copious reams of small print that covered the subject of personal deliveries. Oppenheimer had stabbed his finger at a clause forbidding use of the premises for commercial purposes and another relating to *nuisance activities*. But seeing as Norman categorically denied the first and claimed that any attempt to restrict him receiving *essential items* would be seen by a court as *infringing his human rights*, the landlord was forced to retire and lick his wounds... wounds which festered as the days passed and the deliveries continued unabated.

Free from further interruption, Norman made excellent progress. As his encoding technique improved, so did the number of works he was able to process each day.

But it was the arrival of an unusually proportioned crate that finally threw a spanner in the works. Even Flowers – blissfully unaware of what it was he was delivering – commented on it being different to the others. As wide as it was deep, its major dimension lay in its height. It was also extremely heavy.

'Bloody 'ell!' he said, wiping the beads of perspiration from a ruddied brow and arching his back in discomfort. 'What on earth 'ave you got in this one, Norman? Feels like a set of paving stones!'

The truth was, Norman didn't know. *Perhaps it was a collection of bricks,* he mused... *a piece of modern art, maybe?*

Closing the door more hastily than usual, the "ten" of Flower's cheery "see you tomorrow at" was absorbed by its other side.

'Elementary, my dear Papadopoulos,' Chad smiled. 'Remember that letter he wrote? Well... I don't know about you, but I reckon his home address might be a good place to start.'

* * *

Art had never been a passion in Norman's life. Its subjectiveness placed it outside his interest zone, preferring, as he did, things that were black and white, ordered and defined.

Numbers were good. They could be added or subtracted, divided or multiplied with an absolute certainty. Take one plus one, for instance. It always equalled two. No matter whether you did the maths standing on your head, under water or floating in a vacuum. It was an immutable law... comforting and dependable. There really *was* safety in numbers.

The same applied to computer code. It either worked for you or it didn't. If A meant B should do C, C would *always* be the result of A on B. There were no margins of doubt around the foundations of logic. You knew where you stood, and where you stood was solid.

But colour? Who could say if yellow was bolder than red, green weaker than blue? And what made a painter determine which way their brush should go in order to capture a feeling? How did a composer know which note followed next? What was right and what was wrong? What made them decide?

As the days passed – and Norman found himself privileged to be alone with some of the greatest works of art in history – he began to realise that such decisions, when artists got them right, could obliterate all traces of technique and thoughts of construction. They took on a power beyond analysis.

There was a magnificence in that which scared him. It scared him because he didn't understand it. But at least he'd come to know the reason.

He'd never understood art because he'd never bothered to *think* about it. He'd never taken the time to stand in front of a painting and drink in its impact... or listen to a piece of music

'Our curator friend has exactly the same thing on his signet ring!'

'Coincidence?'

'You know I'm always wary of that. But it's gotta be worth a closer investigation... see if we can prove a connection *beyond* coincidence.'

'So how do you suggest we go about it?'

Chad prepared himself for a reaction. 'You're not gonna like this... but first we have to find Donald.'

Bob stopped abruptly and stared at his partner in amazement. 'Tucker-Jenkins? You can't be serious! What the hell do we need *him* for?'

'Information,' Chad replied calmly.

'*Information?* The guy's a complete wacko! He's not playing with a full deck. His elevator don't quite reach the top floor! Need I spell it out any more? He claims to talk to the friggin' dead!'

'Yep... mad as a box of frogs, I agree. But even madmen have eyes, and are just as qualified to be in the right place at the right time as the sanest of observers. Now... given he was correct about painting one hundred and six, it's fair to assume he's right about there being others that have gone missing from the walls. I also happen to share his view that it's odd paintings are being removed for cleaning from a temporary exhibition. What better way to buy time whilst they're smuggled out of the country? At the point where people realise what's going on, it'll be too late to do anything about it.'

'I'm not happy,' said Bob.

'Neither would I be with that face of yours. But listen... All we need to know from him is exactly how many paintings have disappeared and which ones. Then we're done.'

Bob winced at the thought of further contact. 'If we *must*. But we can hardly go back there and ask to see him without alerting the other side to who we are. That's if they haven't thrown him out already!'

'We don't need to.'

'Really? So how d'ya reckon we're gonna find him?'

that needed dealing with.'

'Yes... we saw him,' smiled Chad sympathetically. 'Quite a character, by the look of things!'

'I have another name for it,' said the curator coldly. 'He's been plaguing us since our exhibition opened. But it's the first time he's seen fit to *attach* himself to any of it. Now... what can I do for you?'

Bob clasped his hands together. 'I was rather hoping to do an article on Constable's *The Hay Wain* before returning to the States, but am distraught to discover it's been removed for cleaning. I was wondering if I might be able to see it before we fly back?'

'That particular picture seems to be causing quite a bit of interest today,' remarked the curator. 'As you rightly point out... it's in the process of being cleaned and should be returned shortly. I'm unable to give you a definite time, but trust it shouldn't be absent for more than a few days... I hope that answers your question.'

'It does in deed,' said Bob, offering out his left hand. 'Thank you... you've been most helpful.'

The curator responded, but realising a discrepancy, awkwardly swapped his right hand for his left. 'What magazine did you say you were from?'

'I didn't,' said Bob, shaking it firmly.

'Okay... so what about the curator's ring?' asked Bob, as they exited the building. 'I take it you got a good enough look this time?'

'I did... and I reckon it might provide us with our first major lead. Remember that stone abutment I climbed up to when we were at the temple? The one with the crystal attached to its end?'

Bob nodded.

'It had a cross carved into it. Nothing unusual there, given it was attached to the wall of a temple. But this wasn't any ordinary cross. Its ends were splayed outward.'

'What of it?'

'Unfortunately for myself and my boyfriend Danny, it seems your only exhibit by this renowned artist is absent from the wall. We were wondering why this was, whether it's a temporary situation and if so, exactly when we would be able to see it? I was hoping to include reflections on the painting in a piece I'm currently writing.'

'I see, sir,' said the attendant, not seeing at all. 'I'll have to get someone who can help you.' He reached for his radio and fiddled with it as if its buttons possessed the power to electrocute him. 'Hello... control...? This is... erm... attendant... er... five. I've got a gentlemen and his... *friend* with me who has a query regarding one of the paintings. He's from an important magazine... so could you get me...'

'The curator,' instructed Bob, looking nonchalantly away to his left.

'Yes... the curator... that's right... over.'

'*Do you want him out there?*' crackled the radio.

Bob looked back and nodded heavily.

'Yes... yes we do... over,' confirmed the attendant, nodding in sync.

There was a pause.

'*He says he's busy... You'll have to make do with his assistant.*'

Bob shook his head and thrust out an insulted palm. 'It has to be the curator. We've travelled all the way from America for this!'

'No... he says it has to be the curator,' repeated the attendant, shaking his head whilst maintaining eye contact with Bob. 'He's travelled all the way from America.'

'*Hang on a second.*'

The attendant smiled inanely to fill in time.

'*Okay. He'll be with you in a minute... over and out.*'

'He'll be with you in a minute, sir... over and out,' relayed the attendant.

'That's very kind.'

It was nearer five before the white-suited curator finally emerged from the door marked "private" and approached them.

'I'm sorry to keep you gentlemen waiting. I've had a problem

'You haven't heard the last of me!' he threatened horizontally.

It was as he was being removed to a door marked *private* that he caught sight of the two men who'd been standing at the front of the crowd. 'I know you, don't I?' he enquired of their upside down faces.

The two men said nothing.

'It'll come to me in a minute!' shouted Donald, as he was bundled through the door.

'I thought we'd seen the last of him,' said one of them, looking around the room.

'When you suggested we stay another day and check out the exhibition, I never thought I'd find it so entertaining!' said the other. 'Our idiot friend's obviously very persistent.'

'And maybe not such an idiot, despite what happened on Waterloo Bridge. Did you see what was on the curator's finger?'

Bob turned to where the curator had been standing, but the man had disappeared. 'What?'

'I need to get a closer look before I can be sure.'

'Leave it to me,' said Bob, scanning the hall for an attendant who looked least qualified to answer his next question. Having espied one of senior years, struggling to stay awake on his chair, he made a beeline for him.

'Sir... Excuse me.'

The attendant sat upright with a jolt. 'Halt... Who goes there?' he shouted... then looked rather sheepish.

'My name is Crispin Van der Beer,' said Bob, pretending he hadn't noticed. 'I'm from the extremely important and influential American art magazine *Yankee Doodles* and was rather hoping to see a Constable.'

The attendant tried to appear focused, but was having difficulty working out where he was. Moments earlier, he'd been cowering behind his old school desk, having turned up for a double period of maths naked. 'Have you tried the police station, sir?'

'He's a painter.'

'Oh... sorry, sir. Yes, of course.'

187

proceedings.

'Your knowledge of the saints is of no concern to me,' responded the assistant curtly. 'The fact you have chosen to interrupt the public's enjoyment of these fine paintings... *is.*'

'I'm telling you,' yelled Donald, 'the reason for this exhibition had been built on pretence!'

'Would you kindly keep your voice down, sir.'

'Conspirator!' shouted Donald, stabbing an accusing finger at him.

'You're being ridiculous,' retorted the assistant.

The two men at the head of the crowd looked at each other and smiled.

'Oh, I am... am I?' said Donald, his widening eyes suggesting he was about to unleash uncomfortable information. 'Then... perhaps you'd like to tell me – and all these good people standing here gawping – why it is that paintings have been going missing from your walls ever since this exhibition opened?'

'That's absurd!' smiled the assistant weakly, his comment addressed more towards the crowd than his accuser.

'Is it?' Donald challenged him. 'Then I suppose I'm imagining the fact that painting one hundred and six – which yesterday was John Constable's *The Hay Wain* – is now a rather grubby patch of magnolia wall paint with a light fitting above it!'

'Get that bloody chain off him,' demanded the assistant under his breath as Donald beamed a smile of triumphalism at the crowd. 'The painting you refer to, sir, is being cleaned,' the assistant announced loudly.

'But they're not yours to clean,' insisted Donald.

The assistant turned towards the crowd as a large pair of bolt cutters appeared. 'That's it, ladies and gentlemen. Our impromptu floor show is over. I'm sure you'd now prefer to study what's on our *walls* rather than our floor!'

There was a polite splattering of applause from a group of Japanese tourists as the crowd dispersed.

Donald was disconnected from the heating system and grabbed by his hands and ankles.

that of *over-manning*. For he shares his horticultural chores with ten others, one of whom is... wait for it... our old friend, Saint Fiacre.

It would seem that if you're a syphilitic taxi driver who takes your mind off your piles by doing a spot of gardening, Saint Fiacre is the man for you.

Finally... there are the positions that leave you wondering if there is also a patron saint of scraped barrels. These include the patron saints of fainting... recently dead people... fear of the lord... hopeless cases... disappointing children... unattractive people... the patron saints against hesitation... twitching... oversleeping... nettle rash and – even more obscurely – the patron saint of leaping.

But surely the award for the most absurd and menial patronage of all must go to Saint Benedict, who – alongside his overseeing of cave scientists – also has the glorious distinction of being the patron saint of servants who broke their master's property.

Saint Christopher never had it so good.

Unsurprisingly... or maybe, *surprisingly*... nowhere in the above appears the name of Saint Pedalo, alleged patron saint of beach entertainment... a point not lost on Donald Tucker-Jenkins.

'Never heard of him!' he shouted, as a huddle of security staff fussed around his prostrate body, trying to ascertain the thickness of chain he'd used to attach himself to the radiator.

The exhibition's curator looked on impassively, content to let his assistant deal with the matter. Not for him the prospect of raising a crease in his immaculate white suit or ruffling a hair of his immaculate white beard. His hawk-like gaze distanced him from the shallower smirks of other onlookers.

Donald had chosen to stage his protest in the exhibition's main hall. A considerable crowd had gathered... some in the belief they were witnessing an unusual piece of performance art. Two men in particular were showing a keen interest in the

Welcome to the world of patron saint multi-tasking.

Whilst the majority only have to concern themselves with a single cause, there are multi-tasking superstars like Saint Michael the Archangel, whose remit encompasses no less than forty separate ones.

It's worth bearing in mind that none of these saints had any say in the causes that were allocated to them. One can assume that for those representing peace or wisdom, it was a very proud and empowering moment. But spare a thought for poor Saint Guy of Anderlecht and take a brief moment to imagine the expression on his face when discovering he'd been made the patron saint of outbuildings.

But even *he* might have considered himself lucky when compared to those associated with certain occupations. For whilst saints representing doctors, lawyers, sailors, and even beggars have been kept busy throughout the centuries, one could hardly say the same thing of Saint Benedict, patron saint of cave scientists. Then again, there *is* a danger in that type of work that suggests a possible need for saintly intervention... unlike those in Saint Raymond of Penyafort's charge... medical record librarians.

For some – like Saint Christopher – the merchandising possibilities are immense. For others – like Saint Margaret of Cortona, patron saint of reformed prostitutes – they are not.

A thought should also be spared for Saint Adrian of Nicomedia, whose conscience must be something of a battle ground... holding, as he does, the title "patron saint of arms dealers".

Saintly minds must also be tested when assigned a cause *against* a particular species of God's creatures. Whilst one might justify being the patron saint against rats or snakes, could Saint Ulric *really* hold his head up high at afterlife gatherings when introduced as patron saint against moles? Perhaps – seeking safety in numbers – he seeks out Saint Magnus of Füssen, patron saint against caterpillars... and Saint Sebastian, patron saint of gardeners.

The latter illustrates another issue concerning patronage...

life.

The drawback, of course, is that you have to be dead to qualify. But given that your life will have been spent promoting that which follows after it, this shouldn't present too much of a problem.

Being a patron saint is like being an ordinary saint... only, more glamorous.

Mention the name Saint Dismas, and it probably conjures up the image of an extremely devout man from so far way-back-when that the last *S* in his name could equally well be exchanged for an *L*. However... mention he's the patron saint of thieves and suddenly the guy starts to look a lot more interesting.

He also starts to look a lot less dead.

For if you're one of those unfortunate enough to require his services, you would pray to him in the fervent belief that he was listening and might act on your behalf. To what level Saint Dismas is supposed to assist those he represents, one can only wonder.

Such patronage provides the otherwise faceless saint with a ready-made, off-the-shelf identity.

Think of Saint Christopher – the patron saint of travellers – and you instantly get the image of a man of the people... someone you wouldn't mind sharing a car journey with. Visualise Saint Jeremy – patron saint of people called Jeremy – and you immediately think of... well... probably somebody called Jeremy.

The three examples so far encountered not only suggest contrasting levels of work, but also the possibility of a hierarchy... a league table of patronage, if you will. For whilst Saint Christopher has his image plastered on everything from key fobs to car fresheners, motoring gloves to medallions, when was the last time *you* saw a dashboard figurine of Saint Fiacre, patron saint of haemorrhoids?

Then again, you just might... for Saint Fiacre also happens to be the patron saint of taxi drivers, a link which bears reflecting upon. Curiously, he is also the patron saint of syphilis... one which doesn't.

'This was due to Nobby 'aving prevented it from 'itting the floor.'

'But that's also good news... isn't it?'

'Not for the parts of Nobby's body that did the preventing, it ain't. We're talking both his tibia and fibula, pelvis in the singular and ribs in their multitude... not forgetting his inappropriately named *right humerus*. The man's got more metal screws in 'im than a flat-pack chest of drawers. I've never seen anything like it. His X-rays make him look like a badly made model glider!'

'You've seen them?'

'Better than that. My cousin's a security guard at a private 'ospital. He's mates with the technician that operates one of those fancy three-dimensional scanners. We sneaked Nobby in the other night and 'ad 'im done. We're gonna feature 'im on the front of this year's works' Christmas card.'

'It'll make a change from reindeer, I suppose,' said Norman. 'Still... at least *you* seem to have escaped relatively unscathed.' This was something of an educated guess on Norman's part, given he could only see Flower's head above the crate he was standing behind.

'Mustn't grumble... mustn't grumble. I'm just sorry we trashed the 'at stand. Rather unfortunate place for it to be. Not least because I swear I've seen a part of it on Nobby's X-ray. I shudder to think where the entry point was! Still... he's currently in bed on sick leave and I'm 'ere having worked up a mighty sweat... so maybe he wasn't the unlucky one after all!' Flowers nodded at the crate in front of him.

'Surely you haven't dragged that thing up here on your own?'

'As if!' laughed Flowers. 'I've sent Nobby's replacement down to keep an eye on the fourteen others we've got for you. Talking of which... if you'll excuse me, we'd better start fetching 'em up.'

*　　*　　*

On first consideration, being appointed a patron saint of anything might be deemed the ultimate achievement of a pious

'I just want to clarify one point,' said Chad calmly. 'Are we correct in believing that the information you were about to impart has been delivered to you from the spirit world?'

'Absolutely,' beamed Donald, rearranging his clothing.

'In that case, Mister Tucker-Jenkins... thank you for your time... and rest assured, we'll be making a full report of this meeting to our superiors.' Chad signalled to Bob that they should leave.

'But I haven't told you anything yet!' exclaimed Donald, as the two men began to walk away.

'It's OK,' shouted out Bob. 'If we need to know anything, we'll get in touch with Whitebait via an Ouija board!'

Donald was left standing on the pavement, more than a little confused. 'I don't think that's a good idea,' he shouted out after them. 'He's just told me he's not very good at spelling!'

* * *

'Morning, Mister Penkridge!'

'Flowers! I didn't think I'd be seeing *you* for a while!'

'You can't keep a good man down,' said Flowers cheerily, removing a pen from behind a bandaged ear.

'Glad to hear it...and I'd rather you called me Norman, seeing as how we'll probably be seeing a lot of each other over the coming months.'

'Well, Norman... do you want the good news or the bad news?'

This was a choice Norman always hated making. If he went with the good first, the impending bad would invariably cast a shadow over it. But if he opted for the bad – in order to end on a positive – the positive might not be as positive as the negative required it to be.

'It makes no difference,' he said resignedly.

'Alright... The good news is that the crate we removed from yer premises... admittedly a little quicker than anticipated... was undamaged by the incident.'

'And the bad?'

'I beg your pardon?'

'The transmitter! You were talking to someone!'

'Ah... that.'

'Yeah... *that!* Who were you talking to?'

Donald didn't particularly want to say. It always seemed to lead him into trouble. Then again... things couldn't get much worse.

'Whitebait,' he said, noticing his vest was on back to front.

'Is that his codename?' yelled Chad, standing over him as Bob searched behind his back for wires.

'I don't think so,' replied Donald. 'I shouldn't think he needs one in the spirit world.'

Chad and Bob stopped what they were doing and looked at one another.

'I can ask him if you like?' offered Donald over their silence.

'*What* spirit world?' said Chad cautiously.

'Well, I think there's only the one, dear boy,' Donald replied.

'You were talking to... a *dead* person?'

'Well... he'd hardly be there if he were alive, would he?' said Donald.

The driver of a passing taxi – which had slowed down on the far side of the bridge – wound down his window and called out. 'Oi... are you alright mate? Do you want me to call the police?'

'It's OK!' shouted back Bob. 'We've got everything under control!'

'I wasn't talking to you,' said the cabby. 'I was asking the fella you're kneeling on!'

'I'm alright, thank you,' said Donald politely. 'I know these people.'

'Perverts!' shouted the taxi driver, speeding off.

Bob looked up at his partner. 'Raving fruitcake,' he mouthed, removing his knees from Donald's shoulders.

Chad stuck out a hand for Donald to grab hold of. 'I think there's been a slight misunderstanding,' he said, pulling him onto his feet.

'That's a relief,' sighed Donald, brushing himself down. 'I thought for a minute you boys didn't believe me!'

with… the verbal, I don't have to!' He gave Bob an icy stare.

'It's alright, Donald… we're on the same side,' said Chad. 'If someone's after you, we can arrange for your protection. But we need to know what it is you're mixed up in. So… if you wanna go somewhere else to talk we…' He stopped mid-sentence, realising Donald was no longer listening to him. 'Are you okay?'

'If you gentlemen will excuse me a moment,' said Donald. 'I shan't be long.' He turned and checked the traffic in both directions, then hobbled across the road to the other side of the bridge.

'What's he up to?' asked Bob.

'I dunno. But look… go easy on him. From the state of his appearance, I'd say he's obviously involved in something heavy. Looks like he's been on the run for quite some time. Don't scare him. We need to hear what he has to say.'

They watched as Donald began pacing backwards and forwards in a state of extreme agitation.

'*Now* what's he doing?' groaned Bob.

'There's something odd going on here,' said Chad uneasily.

'Too friggin' right!'

'No… Look… he's talking to someone. I think he's been wired!'

'Shit!' Bob glanced nervously at both ends of the bridge. 'It's a trap! We've been set up!'

'They couldn't have lured us into a worse place!' exclaimed Chad, looking at the only alternative route of escape. 'How good a swimmer are you?'

'If I'm jumping off this thing, he's coming with me!' yelled Bob, taking off across the road.

Chad was surprised by the balletic grace with which Donald hit the pavement as Bob lunged at him.

Donald was surprised he'd lunged at all. 'I thought you said we were on the same side!' he bellowed, as a pair of hands reached inside his coat.

'Where is it?' shouted Bob angrily, frisking him.

'Where's what?'

'The transmitter!'

195

'I've got a bad feeling about this, Bob.'

As the man got within a few metres of them, he slowed his approach and bowed his head.

'What's he up to?' asked Bob bemused.

'It's *his* idea,' grimaced Chad.

As the figure drew level, he stopped. 'The... moon... is... bright... tonight,' he said, with heavy deliberation.

Bob shot a pained glance into the cloud-filled sky.

'Just go with it,' whispered Chad. He cleared his throat. 'Yes... One can see its light reflected in the water.'

The man looked at him hesitantly, but said nothing.

'Yes... One can see its light reflected in the water,' repeated Chad, only this time louder.

'On!' said the man, with annoyance. 'You're supposed to say... One can see its light reflected *on* the water!'

'Sorry,' said Chad. He cleared his throat again. 'Yes... One can see its light reflected *on* the water.'

'I mean... surely it's obvious to anyone that moonlight would be reflected *from* the surface as opposed to below it.'

'It's a little hard to tell,' chipped in Bob, 'on account of the fact your British weather's obscuring the friggin' moon!'

'That's not the point.'

'Look... are you Donald Tucker-Jenkins or not?' enquired Bob brusquely.

'I am he.'

'Good... then cut the crap and tell us what this is about so that we can get to our beds.'

'There's no need to take that attitude with me, young man!' said Donald indignantly. 'I'd rather be in bed myself. I'll have you know my body's a mass of bruises thanks to the information I'm privy to.'

'Are you telling us you've been got at?' asked Chad, placing a restraining hand on Bob's shoulder.

'Got at...? In what way?'

'Attacked... Have you been attacked because of what you know?'

'Frequently,' replied Donald. 'But the physical I can cope

196

morning, transatlantic flight had lowered their enthusiasm for the perfect picture-postcard view that stretched out in front of them. To the west, Big Ben stood guard over the ancient Houses of Parliament... whilst to the East, the illuminated dome of Saint Paul's punctured the night sky, a watery ribbon of coloured lights shimmering between the two. But this was of little consequence to men who'd rather have had a view of their feet tucked under the blanket of a warm, hotel bed.

'I'll give him this,' said Bob, stamping his against the pavement to keep their circulation flowing, 'our friend Ronald's certainly got a sense of drama.'

'It's *Donald,* apparently... and his surname's *Tucker-Jenkins.*'

'Whatever... I reckon the guy's been watching too many black and white spy movies. All we need now is a thick fog to descend and Orson Wells to friggin' swagger out of it!'

Chad surveyed both ends of the bridge. The traffic was still quite busy, but the passers-by had trailed off to the occasional one or two making their way home after a night of revelry.

'Are you sure we've got the right place?' asked Bob, placing his hands in his pockets and hunching his shoulders against the cold.

'The middle of Waterloo Bridge... East side... midnight,' recited Chad verbatim.

'And how are we supposed to recognise him? Will he be wearing a white carnation and carrying a copy of *The Times?*'

'He insisted on *The Guardian,*' said Chad impassively.

'Shit,' groaned Bob, shaking his head.

As they waited, a number of false alarms appeared and disappeared.

Finally – as they were beginning to give up hope – a lone figure approached briskly from the south bank.

'Not this one either,' remarked Chad, discounting it without fuss. 'Looks like a vagrant.'

'How many vagrants do you know with flowers in their buttonhole?' said Bob, peering through the gloom.

'You're not gonna tell me he's got a paper?'

'Under his arm.'

painting. As a point of interest... that's what triggered an upsurge in experimental art towards the end of your nineteenth century. All the good bits of inspiration had been used by then. The only pieces left were small, incomplete fragments. The Impressionists started making use of them first – moved to create *something* – but lacking sufficient vibrations to provide anything of great detail. But such was the power behind even those smaller strands, the images still caught the imagination of the world. After that, it was down to the Cubists to try and make something coherent out of the dregs. One has to admire their ingenuity. The same situation occurred in music. It's small wonder Schoenberg raised eyebrows. There weren't any decent bits left!'

'I always wondered why the public were taken in by conceptual art,' said Norman. 'I guess it was produced from the tiniest fragments of all.'

'To be honest... we don't know *what* all that was about,' admitted Gabriel, shaking his head. 'It's a complete and utter mystery to us, that one.'

Norman looked at him awkwardly. 'I don't wish to be rude... but I'm going to have to kick you out. It looks like I've got an early start tomorrow and I need to get to bed.'

Gabriel remained static, his thoughts transported elsewhere at the prospect.

'Did you hear what I said?' prompted Norman. 'I'm going to have to kick you out.'

Gabriel sighed wearily as he broke from reflecting on his earlier encounter with Oppenheimer. 'Couldn't I stay a little longer and watch you sleep?' he asked apprehensively.

*　　*　　*

Waterloo Bridge at midnight was not the warmest place to be standing. Despite it being summer, the wind was blowing a chill across the Thames, and the two men leaning against the low wall that stopped foot passengers from falling in were suffering more than they usually might. A ridiculously early

'Oh...' said Gabriel uneasily.

'Don't worry. Nothing heavy. I was just wondering... Assuming I'm going to have to encode some of Shakespeare's work, given it figures so prominently in the scheme of things... what am I to encode?'

'The words, of course,' said Gabriel nonplussed.

'Yes... I know *that*. But how? Do I do it from a recording of them or an actual written document? Because if it's the latter, aren't we going to need the original manuscripts? You're surely not going to tell me you've located those!'

'It makes no difference what you use,' said Gabriel. 'The result will be the same.'

'But that's impossible!' frowned Norman. 'The codes couldn't *possibly* be identical.'

'I know this is a little difficult to grasp,' said Gabriel, 'but they don't *have* to be... as long as the vibration produced creates the same effect. Think of it like attempting to determine the nature of water from a vast ocean. You could use a thimbleful from the shore or a tankful from its deepest depths. Either way, the result would be the same. Only, here, we're talking about inspiration. Words – unlike art and music – are less subjective. Their meaning is less prone to interpretation, so the vibration can be less specific. You can be just as moved reading the words of Shakespeare from a book as you can watching them performed on a stage. I appreciate the actual workings behind these vibrations are difficult for you to comprehend... but to quote from one of those vibrations in question, "there are more things in Heaven and Earth, Horatio, than are dreamt of in your philosophy"!'

'But the Mondrian and Schoenberg test pieces *were* identical,' said Norman. 'How could *that* have happened?'

'Simple... and rather fortuitous, given what we were able to use them for,' Gabriel replied. 'It just so happened they were inspired by the same piece at *exactly* the same time. It's the only case we know of. The chances of such a thing occurring were obviously helped by the fact it was a very short strand. It's also the reason for the atonality of the music and simplicity of the mistaken me for someone else,' he said politely, trying to alter his vibrations a little.

The radio in Oppenheimer's room changed stations.

'I don't think so,' insisted Oppenheimer. 'I bought you that dress... But that was... so long ago!'

'Must dash,' said Gabriel, taking advantage of Oppenheimer's stupefaction and legging it up the stairs. 'It's me! Open the door!' he sung out nervously, as he reached the landing.

Obliging, Norman heard the sound of a body collapsing to the ground in the hall below as the Archangel quickly sought refuge.

'That was close!' said Gabriel, glancing around the room. Its appearance had changed dramatically since his last visit. It now resembled mission control. Banks of hard drives stacked one upon another were vying for space alongside a host of computer screens lined up in rows along the floor. 'You've been busy,' he observed.

'I'm afraid I've given the chequebook a bit of a bashing,' admitted Norman, kicking a pile of empty boxes away with his feet so as to clear a space for Gabriel to stand. 'Welcome to The Ark!'

'I beg your pardon?'

'The Ark. That's what I've called my new computer system. I thought it was appropriate, given I'm gathering up binary digits of inspiration, two by two, and storing them in order to save the world!'

'Very clever,' said Gabriel. 'Is it ready to sail?'

'Aye aye!' asserted Norman.

'Good... In that case, we'll start you on fifteen paintings a day and see how you cope.'

'Don't worry about me,' said Norman. 'It's Mister Oppenheimer who's in for a bit of a shock.'

'I think you'll find he's already had it,' said Gabriel. 'I wouldn't concern yourself with him. He'll have more important things on his mind for a while.'

'I've got a couple of questions,' said Norman, deciding to let the cryptic comment pass.

variety, Oppenheimer had grown increasingly concerned about their use, given his tenants enjoyed unfettered access to the electricity supply.

He'd taken to observing the wheel of his electricity meter, in an attempt to ascertain if it was going around faster than normal. But such was the strain it put on his eyes, he decided to take a nap... though not before thumbing through an old scrapbook he'd found stored in the cupboard in which the meter was housed. It contained time-stained pictures of himself and Lotty... her soon-to-be-lost innocence a perfect match for his own.

As he started to fall asleep in his armchair, she drifted into his melting thoughts and took him by the hand.

No sooner had he touched it... he was rudely brought back to reality by the crackling of static from a radio that had been quietly playing a Viennese waltz.

A movement in the hall caught his eye. He'd left the door ajar to keep track of Norman's movements.

'Who's there?' he croaked, rubbing his face.

'It's alright... it's only me,' came a soft reply.

Oppenheimer lifted himself from his chair and staggered towards the hall. As he pulled back the door, his disorientated mind reeled in shock as the figure of a young woman turned to face him.

'I'm visiting Mister Penkridge,' said Gabriel uncomfortably. 'He's expecting me.'

Oppenheimer's face froze in disbelief.

'The door was on the latch,' pretended Gabriel. 'I let myself in. I hope you don't mind.'

A tear appeared in the landlord's eye and threatened to fall.

'I'll go straight up, shall I?' said Gabriel.

Oppenheimer stretched out a hand as if to greet a ghost. 'Lotty,' he murmured breathlessly. 'Is it really you?'

Gabriel felt powerless. It wasn't up to him how people chose to interpret their angels.

'But it can't be... you look... so young!'

Gabriel backed himself slowly up the stairs. 'I think you've

This wasn't difficult. The vetting procedure he applied was so rigorous and restrictive, his tenants comprised life's losers and loners... traits he was determined to preserve.

For starters, there was Melvin Thedbury, who'd rented 66e – the eaved attic room – for the last twenty-three years. At six foot five, Melvin now walked with a permanent stoop.

66d was sanctuary for Trevor Belchett, a librarian whose hobbies included taking part in historical re-enactments and dreaming about planning a model railway. To Oppenheimer's horror, Trevor had briefly entered into a relationship with a fellow librarian. But this ended acrimoniously when she was persuaded to defect by a French bowman at the battle of Agincourt.

Little was known about the unemployed occupant of the basement flat... which was probably just as well for him. *His* hobbies included Satanic worship and downloading pornography from the internet. He hardly ever went out... and, when he did, always looked extremely pale and drawn.

Then there was Norman.

If ever Oppenheimer could be accused of having a favourite, it would be him. He reminded the unpopular landlord of himself when he was a younger man... lonely, unattractive and full of dreams... until Lotty and her "liberation" by the American army had shattered them.

But he'd seen an unwelcome change in his favoured tenant over the last few weeks. He'd become secretive and, even more alarmingly... confident.

As for Norman's mystery female guest... From her manner of dress, it was obvious money was exchanging hands somewhere during the evening. The strangest thing was, he was unable to picture her face. He vowed to take a closer interest should she decide to show it again.

He didn't have to wait long.

The stairs had seen their busiest day, Norman having traversed them for the greater part of it with a range of recently purchased goods. Noting they were mainly of the electrical else's… where logic was pessimistically warped and success only measured against the failure of others. It was a world where minimum social interaction was preferable, especially when it came to those renting his rooms.

His dislike of people wasn't only reserved for non-paying guests. It happily encompassed the whole of mankind… especially the half of it that was female. Not that he didn't appreciate a shapely pair of legs – as Gabriel could testify – or a species that could weaken his own by simply fluttering their eyelids.

Appreciate them… yes. *Trust* them… no.

He'd done so twice before and both had let him down.

The first had been his mother… an angel incarnate and hard act to follow. Unfortunately, she was no longer incarnate… her comforting bosom having stopped heaving when Oppenheimer was barely into his teens. Her sudden demise had left him devastated and confused… partly as to why she'd left him so prematurely and partly as to why his Uncle Helmut no longer felt the need to visit.

But that bosom had been replaced – in a far less maternal manner – by the bagel-haired Lotty. Lotty had graced his childhood years with her innocence… until she'd lost it with anything *but* grace when a group of American servicemen became stationed nearby.

Traumatised by the discovery that not all stories have a happy ending, he'd left his country for pastures new, which eventually turned out to have the address *66 Armageddon Terrace.*

The trouble with pastures new is that they eventually turn out to be nothing more than pastures old visited for the first time.

In post-war England, his accent had singled him out… the thin, pale epidermis that stretched itself frugally over his wiry frame barely able to deflect the ridicule and prejudice it inspired. So he'd retreated behind the four walls of his own empire, determined that those who paid on a monthly basis to be his subjects would never end up having a better time than him.

part, I want you to keep quiet about it. I don't want my judgement being called into question... do you understand?'

'But it smacks of desperation to me,' said Bob, shaking his head.

'That's because I *am* desperate!' shouted AKA Mister Prometheus. 'And so should you be. We all need results here! Let's not forget the reason you're standing in my office and not blazing a trail out there somewhere in the field. So now I'm giving you a chance to put that right. You're being assigned to this case because it's all I'm prepared to trust you with at the moment. This guy might turn out to be the biggest idiot in the world... but at least *you* two won't have trouble recognising that particular characteristic!'

'I take it this part up here is his address,' said Chad, still trying to decipher the letter.

AKA Mister Prometheus calmed himself. 'Apparently so. The only drawback is... it's an *English* one. So you'd better take your raincoats.'

'But it's summer over there, too, sir!'

'Precisely. We'll contact him and arrange a neutral rendezvous. You'll be given the details as soon as you land. Any other questions?'

'Just the one,' said Chad. 'What's his name?'

'It's a little hard to tell,' said AKA Mister Prometheus, acknowledging the letter. 'His signature's worse than his handwriting. But we think it's Ronald Tucker-Jerking.'

'Doesn't look like a *T* to me,' said Bob, scrutinising it closely. 'Looks more like an... *F*.'

'In which case,' said Chad, 'he's *definitely* a lunatic!'

'I've booked you on the earliest flight tomorrow,' announced AKA Mister Prometheus, finally lighting his cigar. 'Give my regards to the Queen.'

*   *   *

For a simple man, Joseph Oppenheimer could be extremely complex. He inhabited a world slightly parallel to everyone the shore! Now... what *else* can you give me?'

There was an awkward silence.

'That's what I thought!' AKA Mister Prometheus pulled a sheet of paper from his filing tray and thrust it across the desk. 'Feast your eyes on this, boys, and tell me what you make of it.'

The two men examined what was a hand-written letter.

'Looks like a spider's crawled through your inkwell and gone for a jog,' offered Bob, in reference to its writer's abysmal handwriting.

'I don't have an inkwell... take a closer look.'

They peered intently at the document, struggling to decipher it.

'I'll save you the effort... We received it a couple of days ago. At first glance, I assumed it to be the ramblings of a lunatic... only a very persistent one. It seems the President, Vice-President and half of Congress have received similar communications, along with our colleagues at the FBI. The writer claims to have knowledge of a plot to steal works of art from galleries around the world. He admits he doesn't know when or how this will happen... and the rest of his letter seems rambling and vague. But this is the thing... He's convinced the Vatican are involved in the conspiracy.' AKA Mister Prometheus paused and looked at the two men eagerly. 'Well, boys... what d'ya think?'

'I think your first assumption was correct,' said Bob. 'It's the ramblings of a lunatic.'

AKA Mister Prometheus shifted restlessly in his chair. 'I know, I know... That's what everyone else believes. The trouble is... I *need* to make progress on this case. Now... whilst this guy might not be the neatest writer in class, he's certainly sailing close to where we are at the moment. In the clear absence of anything else to go on, I think you guys should check him out.'

'What... you want us to talk to him?' exclaimed Chad.

'Precisely. But here's the important bit.' AKA Mister Prometheus gave a cursory glance towards the door and lowered his voice. 'Seeing as how this might be considered by some in the department as a rather *questionable* move on my

Chad checked his partner again. 'It's a little more than a theory, sir. It's an inescapable *fact*. Every bit of information we've received confirms the same thing. From Rio to Rome, Delhi to Detroit... the whole of the religious world's at it... persuading anyone who is anyone to loan them valuable works of art. These are then being displayed at hundreds of exhibitions taking place simultaneously around the globe. It's all they seem to be bothered about at the moment. There's absolutely nothing else on their agendas.'

'Yeah... yeah, I know all that,' said AKA Mister Prometheus irritably. 'The answer that no one seems to be able to furnish me with right now is... *why*.'

'But does it matter, sir?' interjected Bob. 'I mean... it hardly seems to be threatening national security.'

AKA Mister Prometheus chose his next words carefully. 'I've got associates who think that it might.'

'*Associates?*' queried Chad.

'Government type people,' coughed AKA Mister Prometheus into the back of his hand. 'They seem to think this whole thing might have something to do with manipulating the price of art.'

'We're ahead of you there, sir,' said Chad. 'The possibility of it affecting the markets has already been explored. Whilst the experts acknowledge prices could go up as a result of demand caused by increased global interest, they also suggest they might fall through overexposure and consumer fatigue. The consensus of opinion is that the two will balance each other out in the long run.'

'So where does that leave us?' asked AKA Mister Prometheus, chewing the end of his cigar 'I mean... what the hell are these guys up to? Is this some kinda religious internecine art-exhibition-of-the-year conflict?'

'I'm still convinced our answer lies in the Mennonite file,' said Bob, taking advantage of the moment and stepping forward.

AKA Mister Prometheus's eyes flashed a warning. 'If you knew how thin the ice was you've just skated onto, Papadopoulos, you'd be wanting to tiptoe your sorry ass back to 'why am I converting what's already been converted?'

'Because therein lies our salvation,' answered Gabriel. 'We are going to encode every creative work that was produced from the original sphere of knowledge and store the information in your computer. When that is done, we will use those binary codes to regenerate the sphere's original vibrations as a single event, thereby recreating it. Reconstituted, we'll be able to use it on another candidate... and this time we'll make sure we check the calendar!'

'*Brilliant*,' drawled Norman, his jaw hung in admiration.

'We thought so too,' Gabriel beamed.

Norman felt a rush of vigour such as he'd never experienced before. 'Then what are we waiting for? Let's not waste any more time. Let's get on with it!'

Gabriel glanced at the shredded chequebook by Norman's feet. 'In that case... I'd better have another word with our financial backers.'

* * *

'You're probably wondering why I've called you boys in.'

'If it's about the time I've been spending on the Mennonite file, I can explain,' said Bob uneasily.

'Relax.' AKA Mister Prometheus fumbled with an unlit cigar. 'I'm after your advice, this time... not your balls.'

Chad and Bob glanced at each other cautiously.

'Yeah, I know,' scoffed AKA Mister Prometheus, waving down their surprise. 'I've got a whole goddam department out there telling me what's what and I'm asking *you* two!'

'Does that mean we're valued again?' ventured Bob, testing the waters with a cheeky grin.

'No, Papadopoulos ... it does not! It means Cheadle here is. You're just the baggage I have to accept comes with him!'

'And how can I help, sir?' asked Chad, a little too eagerly for Bob's liking.

AKA Mister Prometheus leant forward. 'For starters... I wanna know your take on this art exhibition theory.'

vibrations in the dimension of mind? Well... given that vibrations are the result of energy passing backwards and forwards between two points... if those points are digitally expressed, thoughts can be represented as a binary code... complex though that code might be.'

'Yes... I suppose they could,' said Norman, reflecting on the idea.

'As can a painting or piece of music... as demonstrated by your program. The bit you're going to have to trust me on is that the binary codes for both the thoughts and the work inspired by them are identical. This shouldn't come as such a surprise, given the mathematics of the Universe are all around us and even art cannot escape its rules. It is no accident that a note one octave below another is the frequency of the higher note halved. Change the wavelength of light and you change its colour. It's all inexorably linked. The works of art you have been receiving are mathematically precise encodings of the Universal truth. The observer experiences this truth as the mind subconsciously does its sums. The human brain works more like a computer than you may think. Artificial intelligence is nothing new. Man created it eons ago. Intelligence is nothing more than a code generated by his soul to create the illusion of self. Reality is to the soul what a computer-generated virtual world is to reality... a series of cells switching themselves on or off to create a believable illusion. Brain cell or electrical cell... it's all the same. Your life is simply a complicated string of ons or offs! To be or not to be... As far as the brain cell is concerned... that is the answer!'

Norman felt a menthol-flavoured rush of thought sear through his mind. It was crisp and clear and had the same effect on his thinking as a blast of ice-cold air might on his body. He felt he'd just been told the secret of life... which was hardly surprising, given that, in a roundabout way... he had.

'Of course, there's a lot more in the detail,' said Gabriel. 'But given as how you could never comprehend it, there's little point in trying to explain.'

'But as far as the works of art are concerned,' asked Norman, millions of souls have been drawn to his works and feel a deep-seated connection with them. They're not just good stories... they're a subconscious reminder of Universal truths... which is exactly what we'd intended in the first place.'

'But what happened to all these other bits of the sphere? Are they still out there floating in the ether somewhere?'

'The answer to that provides the final part of my explanation. For, you see... these fragments were dispersed around the globe – hovering on the edges of that dimension I refer to as mind – awaiting the thoughts of men to pick up on their vibrations and recognise them as divine inspiration. Those who did, and who possessed creative talents, encoded what they experienced in a way that could inspire others. From Rembrandt to Renoir, Mozart to Mahler... these *sensitives* captured in their creations echoes of a much-forgotten past, expressing them to those who experienced their work. Slowly, through the centuries, the meaning of life was plucked from the ether and given form. It was no accident that there was an explosion of creativity at the end of the sixteenth century which led to a blossoming of the arts... other than our own mishap, that is! This process continued until the last fragment was caught and encoded... the sphere of knowledge having been finally transferred to the material plane in a way we had never intended.'

'And these artists and composers... were they aware of what they were involved in?'

'Not a clue. How could they have known? Those with faith recognised their inspiration as divine simply because their souls saw the hallmark of a higher being stamped on what they had discovered. But others seemed happy to bask in the glory it brought them, convinced of their own genius. Either way, it didn't matter. What is important is that the sphere of knowledge now exists in material form.'

'You're not going to tell me that all the paintings put together form some kind of educational fresco, are you... with a musical accompaniment to go with it?'

'Not quite. Remember I told you that thoughts produced

unfortunately ten days too early. There is no allowance for imprecision when it comes to the workings of the Universe. Quantum physics regards nanoseconds as cumbersome units. A week and a half was totally out of the question. His spiritual clock hadn't quite ticked enough to prepare his mind to accept the vibrations in their entirety. That's why the sphere of knowledge fragmented. He just didn't possess the ability to receive it all.'

'But if he didn't receive it all, he must've got some of it... surely?'

'Oh, yes... bits and pieces... Quite a lot of them, in fact. How else do you think a man of such humble beginnings and rudimentary education could write so fluently and masterfully about everything from the affairs of court and the minds of the aristocracy to the constitutional intricacies and ways of the law. It's long been a sense of wonderment to us that no one seriously questioned how he was able to do this! Admittedly, a few have raised their voices in the past... but they have been conveniently ignored. One wonders where the rest of humanity actually thought he *did* acquire such vast knowledge from. Not surprisingly, he often wondered himself... especially when he found himself inexplicably an expert on military life, seamanship, mythology and even falconry!'

'So... what happened next?'

There was a pause whilst Gabriel stared past Norman's ear again. 'Henry VI... parts I, II and III,' he replied dispiritedly. 'For – having failed to receive that part of the sphere of knowledge that would have had him act upon his thoughts and become a leader of men – he turned his attention to the pen, unwittingly using the fundamental truths behind the workings of the Universe to fill the mouths of actors with words that have reverberated through time in another way.'

'So let me get this straight... You're saying that the works of William Shakespeare are based on the bit of the sphere of knowledge that didn't fragment?'

'Certain parts of them, yes... even individual lines in some cases. The rest he filled in as any writer might do. That is why idea had our blessing... even though it caused uproar amongst many who believed the Church had stolen ten days from their lives! We even managed to spot – in advance of our delivery deadline – that Gregory had only removed ten days from the calendar instead of the fourteen needed to put things right... Don't ask!' he added quickly, raising his hand. 'Something to do with the Council of Nicaea in the year two hundred and thirty-five.'

Norman gave another dishonestly intelligent nod.

'Finally the day arrived... the marking of twenty-one years of existence for the entity known as William Shakespeare, and the moment when the sphere of knowledge we had so painstakingly created could be transferred into his being. As the exact point in space-time occurred, the process was set in motion... the sphere of knowledge transferred to the correct location... and then it happened.' Gabriel froze, his forlorn expression reminding Norman of one of the onlookers in Rembrandt's *tea tray*. He was reliving the moment... and it obviously wasn't a happy one.

'*What?*' asked Norman gently.

'It shattered,' replied Gabriel, looking straight ahead. 'The sphere of knowledge... with the answers to everything as well as our prayers... was dispersed into the ether in thousands and thousands of fragments. We had failed... and do you know why?'

'The English calendrical system?' postulated Norman.

'Precisely,' said Gabriel. 'Or should I say... *imprecisely*. For England didn't decide to adopt the Gregorian calendar for another one hundred and seventy years. How were we to know? We understood Shakespeare's birthday to be April the twenty-third and calculated our timing accordingly. But we were working on Vatican time... Unfortunately for the wider world, William and the rest of England were batting for the other side. This discrepancy in calendar dates was our undoing. The concept of time has always been a distant stranger to us, Norman. Perhaps we should have got to know it a little better.'

'But did you manage to hit him with this thing?'

'With pinpoint accuracy! We scored a direct hit... but

211

he probed.

'The English calendrical system,' repeated Gabriel. 'It proved to be our downfall... and the biggest irony of all was that the problems we encountered were initiated by one of our own representatives here on Earth.'

'You're going to have to explain this one a little more clearly,' suggested Norman. 'Shall I get my pencil?'

'Not necessary,' replied Gabriel. 'It's painfully easy to understand... which makes it all the harder to bear. Up until October the fourth, in the year fifteen hundred and eighty-two, the Western world relied on the Julian calendar to mark its dates. This assumed there were three hundred and sixty-five and one quarter days in every year. The quarter was important because, with the inclusion of a leap year every four years, it squared the solar circle, as it were. But the quarter was also *wrong*. For as we know, a solar year lasts precisely three hundred and sixty-five days, five hours, forty-eight minutes and forty-six seconds.'

Norman demonstrated that it was possible to nod intelligently and dishonestly at the same time.

'This meant that the seasons slowly regressed against the days on the calendar... though not so slowly it wasn't noticed. For although eleven minutes and fourteen seconds might not be missed in any one year by an illiterate blacksmith, it worked out at almost one day per century... and the diarists were beginning to have their suspicions, the astronomers were becoming embarrassed and the astrologists were hiding their heads in the shifting sand. In an attempt to rectify the situation, Pope Gregory XIII took it upon himself to lose ten days and balance the books by omitting the leap year at the turn of every century... unless that year was divisible by four hundred... excepting ones divisible by four *thousand*... Are you still with me?'

'I'm running as fast as I can,' said Norman. 'So... are you saying you didn't know about this calendar change?'

'Oh, we knew about it,' answered Gabriel. 'Given the old system was playing havoc with the timing of holy festivals, the

212

'Precisely... So, in order to achieve this, we created a huge sphere of vibrations from the dimension of mind, containing all the wisdom of the Universe. Transferred to the material plane, it would be dropped onto the chosen one at the precise moment his soul completed twenty-one years of incarnation. It was a colossal undertaking. One that – due to the laws that govern such things – could never be repeated.'

'You had someone waiting?'

'Of course. Not that he knew anything about it.'

'He must've been someone pretty special!'

'No... That's the point. He was extraordinary in his ordinariness. His parents were neither rich nor poor... powerful nor without influence. They were called John and Mary, names not a million miles removed from those of other parents I once had dealings with. His own was William, a common name for where he was born. In fact, the only thing that stood out about him was his surname. It had quite a memorable ring to it... which we thought might come in useful.'

'And what was that?'

'Shakespeare,' said Gabriel wistfully.

Norman couldn't have looked more dumfounded had he taken lessons. 'What...! Not *the* William Shakespeare?'

'If you mean *the* one from Stratford-upon-Avon... yes,' replied Gabriel.

'*The* William Shakespeare... as in... "*to be or not to be*"?'

'An ironic way of putting it, but yes... the very same.'

Norman stared at the Archangel, open mouthed.

'It was all a question of coordinates, you see,' said Gabriel plaintively. 'The soul had to be precisely located in space and time for it to work. We knew William's birth date... and Stratford-upon-Avon hadn't appeared to have moved.'

'So what went wrong?'

Gabriel looked away. 'The English calendrical system,' he answered, with something approaching a wince.

Norman felt himself caught in the "*pigeon*" syndrome again. Only this time, matching a phrase that sounded anything like the one he'd just heard had to be impossible. 'I beg your pardon?'

driven barriers between them. Mankind externalised faith the same way it externalised its mind and soul. So we decided it was time for a new beginning… time for a new *Saviour.*'

'But hang on a second!' interrupted Norman. 'Wouldn't that just add to the problem? I mean… wouldn't a new Saviour be yet another prophet ploughing another path?'

'This would be someone different, Norman. A Saviour like no other. Such would be his presence amongst men that his authority would be unchallenged, touching every mortal soul with the power of his message. The beauty of his words would cause detractors to be struck dumb and his wisdom would make him the consort of kings. His light would shine so bright as to eclipse all those that had gone before him and unite the world's religions. It was the perfect plan.'

Norman gingerly stuck a finger in the air. '*Was?*' he observed delicately.

Gabriel stared wistfully past Norman at a thought hanging somewhere in the air. 'Yes,' he said softly. 'We encountered a slight mishap.'

'You mean… it went *wrong?*'

'It went *very* wrong,' said Gabriel, snapping himself back to attention. 'The idea was to create this new Saviour from the soul of an ordinary mortal. You see… in the past, we'd sent advanced souls to the Earth to teach you to advance your own. But their purity of thought meant they were unable to foresee how those teachings might become corrupted. A mortal would not have this problem. He would be able to think like those he taught, being wise to the scheming of those who equated attaining knowledge with attaining power. He would be able to fight fire with fire. In the words of your own century, Norman… he would *kick arse!*'

'He wouldn't be wearing sandals, then?'

'Not unless they were metal ones with an optional attachment for a large set of spurs. But he *would* come vested with an incredible ability. For this was our strategy… We would imbue this mortal with the knowledge of *everything.*'

Norman whistled his respect.

shouted Donald at the top of his voice.

This was followed by a whelp of pain as a size eleven boot – wrapped around a size ten foot – landed on his behind.

'You will recall me previously telling you how the souls of men lost their way,' said Gabriel, 'and that more-advanced ones were sent to walk amongst them, in order to help them rediscover it.'

Norman nodded.

'They were the prophets... those in the history of your planet who shone a light for others to follow. Some have become known for all time... though there were many others who failed to leave their mark.'

'I suppose those would be the *losses*,' quipped Norman irreverently.

'They are losses indeed,' said Gabriel sternly. 'But those that succeeded in their mission brought upon the world a problem we did not foresee... *Religion!*'

Norman pulled his head back as if reacting to a punch. He placed a finger in his ear and shook it vigorously. Surely he'd misheard the word. It must've been another that sounded similar. The trouble was... he couldn't think of one. The nearest he could get was *pigeon*... and this hardly solved the problem. 'Excuse me,' he said tentatively. 'But I thought you said...'

'I did,' confirmed Gabriel.

'But isn't religion a *good* thing?'

Gabriel looked horrified. 'Are you *serious*? Whilst it's true there are many paths to enlightenment, we never meant for Man to erect fences between them all! And some of those paths have been claimed as one might claim a piece of real estate. It was when we saw the fences becoming fortressed walls that we decided something needed to be done about it. We have watched in disbelief as religions have fought one another... not for what they believed in... for that was ultimately the same... but simply for *how* they believed. The message has become twisted. Where harmony and understanding should have flourished and brought souls together, dogma and doctrine have consciousness, they have allowed their ego to convince them that mind is a *part* of them, not they a part of *it*. Your subconscious knows the truth and has maintained the link. But ignored, your dreams have become nothing more than the entertainment of sleep. You have forgotten how to listen to your deepest thoughts and no longer recognise the dimension in which they exist.' Gabriel paused awhile to let Norman catch up. 'I suppose you're wondering what all this has to do with the paintings?'

'I didn't like to say,' admitted Norman.

'Well... you see... they are the thoughts of one dimension captured forever in another. The artist – be they painter, musician or other – delves deep into the dimension of mind and encodes what they discover so that others can experience it too. That is what inspiration is. Good artists capture the questions these insights provoke. But *great* artists capture the *answers*.'

'Are you saying that the Rembrandt I had in my room was one of those answers?'

'It was an answer encoded by an inspired genius the only way he knew how... to represent it in two-dimensional form. And what irony in that! Perhaps Norman Junior shouldn't feel so limited after all! That answer has since resonated in the psyche of millions who have gazed upon his work. And this is true of all the works of art you will have to encode over the coming months. They are all interpretations of answers... all encoded snippets of the mysteries of Heaven.'

Norman tried hard to digest what he had just been told. Inspiration had always been as hard for him to understand as logic was easy.

'Now we get to the most important part,' said Gabriel, drawing closer. 'No other mortal has ever been so privileged as to understand the inner workings of Heaven as you are about to.'

Gabriel paused.

'I'm ready,' said Norman excitedly.

'HARK! HARK! THE LARK AT HEAVEN'S GATE SINGS!'

this room was first created in the dimension of mind, starting life as a thought. Your bed... the chair... the table on which your computer stands... all first existed as an idea. They could not have come into being any other way. And it is no different for everything else you perceive in the Universe... those things that you consider *natural* being fashioned from the thoughts of what you know as *God*. That is why *mind* is the most powerful and most important dimension of them all. It has no boundaries. Even Norman Junior has access to it.'

'But surely not everything I think can materialise?' contested Norman.

'Actually, it can,' replied Gabriel. 'Though not necessarily in the dimension you wished for it in.'

Norman looked at him bemused.

'I'm afraid that's another pencil moment, Norman. Just accept there is magic in your mind. Which is why you must be careful with your thoughts. As you have already found... they are extremely powerful things. And there are rules attached to them as universally absolute as those on which your science is built. Take *gravity*, for instance. As particles of matter are attracted to one another in the physical Universe, so particles of thought – and the vibrations they produce – have a similar attraction in the mental one. Thoughts of love will attract the same and – just as a mighty planet is formed from the gravitational swirl of dust – utopian environments could be created on Earth if such positive thoughts were allowed to work unhindered. But – by the very same rules – thoughts of evil beget evil... and from them, darkness grows. Although this process cannot be viewed in the dimensions of space and time, its effects are felt there. Thus is the nature of creation.'

'I have that power in *my* mind?' exclaimed Norman.

'Of course. But you must lose the idea of self when considering the fifth dimension. Great minds think alike because they *are* alike. There is only one mind... the universal consciousness. But as you know, the souls of mortals have immersed themselves so deeply in the physical plane they have forgotten they are connected. Distracted by the vanity of self-

'Just one thing,' said Norman, waggling it pensively in the air. 'You said I was a *couple* of dimensions up on Norman Junior. Surely you meant *one?*'

'Your question conveniently leads me to the second part of my explanation,' said Gabriel, looking around the room. 'Take that book over there.' He pointed towards a well-thumbed paperback lying on Norman's bedside cabinet. 'How many dimensions do you think it has?'

'Well... that depends on which dimension I'm in when I do the counting,' said Norman smugly. 'But a few minutes ago I would have bet on three.'

Gabriel shook his head.

'No... wait a minute! Four...! There's *time!* It's as measurable a dimension as the other three, only rendered invisible by the fact we move along with it in perfect synchronicity!'

'Very good,' Gabriel acknowledged. 'But it has another dimension that's within your grasp to comprehend. A *fifth...* and, without doubt, the most important of all. For it's the closest I can get to explaining Heaven to you. It's something you ignore on Earth as a dimension in its own right... which is highly ironic, given it was this very dimension in which your Earth plane was created.'

Norman stared hard at the paperback.

'It's the dimension of *mind*, Norman, or if you prefer... the dimension of *thought*... the dimension you inhabit when reading the words inside. It's the dimension to which you are taken and from where the writer has come... a dimension of ideas... of expression. It's free from the constraints of time and space and, therefore, a dimension of infinite possibilities.'

'That's an awful lot of possibilities!' opined Norman.

'Infinitely. For it is the dimension in which everything that exists was first created from the power of the spirit.'

Norman's face indicated signs of a cerebral struggle.

'It's simple,' affirmed Gabriel. 'Spirit is the energy of what you call God and the life force from which everything is made. Mind is the dimension in which that energy is fashioned and brought into existence. Look around you. Everything you see in can jump up and down inside the box as well as move left and right. But that is all he can do. That is all he understands. But it is not a problem for him because that is all he *needs* to understand. However... now go ahead and stick your pencil through the paper so that it penetrates his world.'

Norman inserted the pencil, as instructed, just to the right of Norman Junior's body.

'Now,' said Gabriel. 'What happens if Norman Junior attempts to move in that direction?'

Norman stared at the paper. 'I guess he's stopped from moving by the pencil.'

'Correct. But given he only has an understanding of two dimensions, how does he reconcile this fact? He cannot see the pencil, as it is a product of a third dimension... a dimension he cannot possibly understand... there being no way of demonstrating it to him in his two-dimensional world. To us, the explanation is perfectly clear. But Norman Junior – no matter how intelligent – will never be able to comprehend the reason for the invisible blockage.'

Norman considered his namesake's predicament.

'From where I stand, Norman, you are but a couple of dimensions up on your two-dimensional counterpart. When it comes to the multi-dimensional Universe, you have no more way of understanding those other dimensions than Norman Junior does the pencil. They are beyond the language of your thoughts.'

Norman remained silent.

'You will come to expect answers that I could not possibly translate. These will be the pencils that pass through your world. You will just have to accept that they are there.'

'Am I allowed to know *how* many extra dimensions there are?' asked Norman cautiously.

'The answer to that depends on which dimension you happen to be in when you do the counting,' replied Gabriel.

'That'll be the first of those pencils, I suppose,' said Norman, removing his from Norman Junior's world.

Gabriel nodded.

ceiling closed in on itself, strangling the shafts of light and returning the room to its original ordinariness.

Norman rose to his feet and examined the plaster where the hole had been. It was exactly as it should be... Solid.

'How did you do that?'

'It's a question of dimensions,' explained Gabriel. 'Something I'm going to have to explain in detail if you're to fully understand the purpose of our mission.'

'But what about the paradox?'

'We've found the perfect solution to that.'

'You have? What is it?'

'All in good time, Norman.'

'But you said...'

'Ah, ah!' Gabriel quickly raised his hand so as to silence him. 'Let's not create another one!'

The thought of his underwear taking to the skies again was enough to quell Norman's intrigue.

'Firstly... you will have to accept that there are some things that will forever be beyond your comprehension,' said Gabriel. 'This is not an attack on your intelligence, but a simple truth. The brain through which you are viewing your current existence is incapable of comprehending the majority of dimensions that exist within the Universe. That is a fact.'

Norman's brow registered a protest.

Gabriel's overruled it. 'If you have trouble understanding *that*, you will never understand what is to follow. But I shall try and explain as simply as I can. Have you a pencil and paper?'

Norman nodded and hurriedly fetched both from a drawer beneath his desk.

'Draw yourself a square,' Gabriel commanded.

Norman did as he was told.

'Now draw a simple stick figure inside it. For the purposes of this demonstration, we will call this fellow Norman Junior.'

Norman looked at the Archangel warily, then constructed Norman Junior using four straight lines and a circle.

'As you can see,' said Gabriel, 'existing on a piece of paper, Norman Junior inhabits a world of only two dimensions. He

avoiding antagonising a potentially dangerous loony in public...
which is next to another one in the brain called *preserving your
personal anonymity despite wearing a silly uniform and knowing it.*
It was this last area that Donald unwittingly trampled upon in
his next exchange.

'Don't you look at me as if I'm mad, young man! It's alright
for people to whistle along to that nauseating pan-pipe crap
your employers force into our ears. But the minute I do the
equivalent to what's occurring in my head, you flex your
muscles...! HOW THE HELL DO I KNOW...? And I'll tell you
another thing whilst we're obviously *not* having a
conversation... WHAT...? NO, I WON'T ASK HIM...! GO
AWAY...! LOOK, I WON'T TELL YOU AG_ ... OH,
ALRIGHT... AS LONG AS YOU GIVE ME SOME PEACE IF I
DO!' Donald drew himself closer to the bemused guard and
cleared his throat. 'Whitebait wants to know why they've given
you a hat that's too small for your head when the rest of your
uniform is clearly too big.'

As he found himself lying prone amongst a pile of scattered
trolleys, Donald was saved from a follow-up kicking by the
timely passing of two pensioners... *geographically* speaking, that
is.

'Ooh... look at that, Doris... They must be filming for the
telly!'

'So they must, Edith. If I live to be a hundred, I'll never
understand the thought process behind these modern adverts.'

'I know exactly what you mean, dear... And you'd think
they'd have given the Nazi a better fitting costume.'

'Even Heaven is allowed to celebrate now and then,' said
Gabriel in response to Norman's wide-eyed wonderment.

'Does that mean I'm back on the case, then?' A shooting star
came close to singeing Norman's seven-day-old beard.

Gabriel raised his hands and directed his celestial entourage
towards the hole in the ceiling. 'You could say that.'

As the last chariot disappeared into the mist beyond, the

peeled back as if clouds parting, shafts of blazing sunlight streaming down upon his tortured face. The most sublime music he'd ever heard swam into his ears, a couple of glorious *hallelujahs* breaststroking in for good measure. Miniature winged horses leapt through the gap in the plaster pulling golden chariots, on which rode naked cherubs... or were they seraphs...? reins in hands. Others floated serenely about the room strumming on golden lyres, blowing into long horns and some just pointing wistfully at nothing in particular. A dazzling display of shooting stars whizzed about between them whilst a number of smiling angels looked on from the heavenly portal. And in the midst of it all – with wings magnificently outstretched in a silent display of celestial authority – stood Gabriel.

'You've chosen well, Norman,' he announced, above the music. 'And in so doing, you have proven yourself worthy of our solution to the spiritual paradox.'

'How the hell am I gonna explain all this to Mister Oppenheimer!' shouted Norman, ducking as the wheels of a chariot threatened an impromptu haircut.

'It's familiar, but I can't quite place it!' insisted Donald.

The supermarket's security guard stood in front of him, hands on hips, blocking his re-entry.

'The music I'm getting!' Donald looked to his left and shook his head. 'I KNOW THE IDIOT CAN'T HEAR IT...! THAT'S WHY I'M TELLING HIM!' He addressed the guard again. 'It's a little bit like Vivaldi's *Gloria*.... only... even *more* uplifting!'

The security guard said nothing. He didn't do speaking. He was only good for following suspicious looking individuals around the aisles... or keeping up the morale of the checkout girls by giving them the odd wink and occasionally – if crime incidents around *tinned fish* and *cooking sauces* were low – handing out the wire baskets to save people bending down. He would love to have uttered the words "move on please, sir" to the ranting stranger in front of him... but somehow the words stuck between the thought and the action in an area called times, he was now unconvinced he was convinced.

If he wasn't circling the table, he'd be sat in front of it, sweating and shaking as he rocked himself backwards and forwards pleading for the decision to be taken out of his hands.

But his prayers remained unanswered.

It was now day seven and Norman's tortuous vacillating over what could be considered rightfully his now encompassed the subject of his own mind. He no longer felt in control. A schism had developed in his thinking process. On the one hand, there was his moral conscience – the more familiar Norman – telling him that he was being watched and judged and that his soul was in danger of selling itself for a few pieces of silver. But on the other, was the promise of a new, more *exciting* Norman... and, more importantly... Xanthia!

She stared from the poster, awaiting his decision.

The time had come.

It was now or never.

He knelt in front of the chequebook and closed his eyes.

'Forgive me!' he murmured, reaching out and grabbing hold of it.

Somewhere in a supermarket checkout queue, Donald Tucker-Jenkins bellowed out at the top of his voice. 'BLESSED IS THE MAN WHO ENDURETH TEMPTATION, FOR WHEN HE IS TRIED, HE SHALL RECEIVE THE CROWN OF LIFE!'

He was confused as to why he'd just done so... though not half as much as those standing next to him. The words had just popped into his head and out through his mouth, without bothering to hang about and discuss the matter with his brain.

There wasn't much discussion from the security guard, either, as he briskly marched Donald to the entrance.

Norman stood up with the chequebook in both hands and kissed it. Then, turning his head away, he ripped it into pieces and sank back on to his knees, sobbing.

As his first tear christened the carpet, the bedsit ceiling

223

the terrain more rugged and menacing. He could no longer hear the children giggling. As panic began to grip him, the path ahead dropped sharply into a deep chasm, from which tongues of flame and swirling sulphurous smoke billowed up towards him. He'd turned to escape, but the stones of the path crumbled beneath him. His limbs reluctant to cooperate, he'd found himself trapped in a futile, slow-motion scramble to escape. Glancing down at his new trainers failing to keep pace with the disappearing ground, a crowbar had whizzed by the side of his head, crashing into the searing heat below and sending a shower of sparks into the air.

He knew he was next.

Someone shouted at him. They'd been standing on a ridge above, waving and calling his name.

It was Oppenheimer.

'Norman!'

He'd awoken in a pool of sweat to the sound of his landlord banging on the door, his feet tangled up in the bed sheets.

Rent days were always a difficult time, usually filled with excuses designed to elicit a few days' grace. Oppenheimer had looked startled as his bleary-eyed tenant had thrust a fistful of notes at him without the usual tales of impecuniosity. He'd also looked suspicious.

The remaining five days turned out to be more of a nightmare than the crumbling path, as Norman became embroiled in a torturous battle with his conscience. He'd eaten little, slept even less and had remained inside the four walls of his bedsit, uninterested in anything else that might be going on outside. In other words... his usual routine.

Temptation and the chequebook – placed on an occasional table, ceremoniously positioned in the centre of the room – had been his only companions.

Having spent hours circling it – first one way, then the other – he'd managed to convince himself that he was now the chequebook's rightful owner and that it wouldn't make a scrap of difference to those in the spiritual realm if he used it. The problem was... he'd had to convince himself of this fact so many him an intelligent, sensitive man... who just happened to be driving a top-of-the-range Ferrari. Not that there was anything wrong about eyeing her body. He gave that last thought even more thought. He would get himself some contact lenses. Then he could wear the sort of sunglasses that wrapped themselves around your head and made you look interesting. Clip-on shades were so passé. He'd get his teeth fixed. He was sure he had more than was actually necessary. Someone had once likened his orthodontic profile to Highgate cemetery. He would undergo plastic surgery... get his ears pinned back... nose remodelled. There was even an operation that gave you pectoral implants.

She wouldn't recognise him... if, in fact, she'd known what he looked like in the first place.

Come to think of it... he probably wouldn't recognise *himself*.

Fired by such an encouraging thought, a surge of adrenalin coursed through his body as temptation whispered that it could all be for real.

If only...

As the real world began to slip away, he'd found himself standing in the grounds of a Mediterranean villa... Xanthia playfully chasing their five children around the garden in slow motion, their white taffeta clothes billowing gracefully as they giggled as only excited children can... Xanthia's perfectly formed teeth exquisitely framed by her smile of utter contentment... her divine breasts bouncing... bouncing... bouncing... whilst a group of envious businessmen stood behind a hedge, desperate to get a look.

It was perfect. For the first time in his life he was happy.

Then a shadow had crossed his face as a cloud rudely intruded, blotting out the sun and the colours around him. Someone had taken hold of him by the arm and told him it was time to go. He was to leave his family there and follow the faceless stranger.

At first he'd done as he was told, turning and following the figure along a narrowing path which wound its way down a small mountain. As he walked, the path had grown steeper and until the flesh of detail had been pared to the bone.

It was on the second day that something had entered into the bedsit, giving them something else to focus on.

It materialised slowly, though he could not see it... grabbed hold of him with a vice-like grip, though he could not feel it... and whispered sweetly to him, though he could not hear it.

Temptation.

Exciting and vibrant, its siren song promised to put the colour that had briefly spattered his monochrome existence, back again. It promised him happiness... it promised him status and – above all – it promised him... Xanthia!

She had looked out from her poster, her pouting lips and *hold-me-Norman* eyes begging him to come and whisk her away from the drudgery of endless photo shoots and cheap daytime celebrity quiz shows. She was his for the taking... if only he succumbed.

It couldn't be easier.

The chance of a lifetime sat on his desk... all twenty-something pages and a couple of stubs, conveniently signed and simply waiting for him to fill in the blanks.

For a nanosecond, his conscience raised a polite finger and offered an objection. But the babble of excited voices in his head drowned it out. Think what he could do with the money! Think of all the fun he'd have! If he couldn't earn respect, he'd buy it. He'd be interesting... fêted... admired. He'd even be... *popular!*

Hadn't Gabriel told him he could do what he liked with the cheques?

Yes... that was the very phrase he'd used. All that had been requested was he did what was asked of him. Well... he'd certainly done that. It wasn't his fault his help was no longer required.

Suddenly, spiritual paradoxes didn't seem so bad.

He'd gone to bed that night fantasising about how he could use his new-found wealth to catch Xanthia's eye... along with the rest of her. She was probably used to being wooed by rich businessmen. But they only had eyes for her body. He would be different... and she would recognise and respect that, seeing in

There was a collective look of discomfort.

'I've seen and heard enough!' shouted Mister Zeus, demonstrating so with a thump of the table. 'Mister Dionysus... kindly sit down and – for decency's sake – avail yourself of an undergarment in future... As for you, Mister Prometheus... you will go immediately from this meeting and discover the true purpose behind these exhibitions. We need to act decisively. We cannot allow our thinking to become clouded by theories and supposition. Mister Cronus is right. Whatever is afoot, we need to be ahead of those...' He hesitated awkwardly.

'Feet?' suggested Miss Themis helpfully.

'Exactly... So you will not disappoint us in your search for an answer. Their God help you if you do... for we certainly won't! We expect you to report back to this meeting as soon as you have it. Leave no stone unturned, Mister Prometheus... or you may end up under one yourself! Is that understood?'

There was a collective stare of menace.

'Perfectly,' came the answer.

*   *   *

It had been a difficult seven days for Norman.

The morning after Gabriel's abrupt departure, two couriers had arrived precisely on the stroke of ten to pick up the re-crated Rembrandt. He'd half expected... or was that hoped... that he would open the door to find yet another crate standing there awaiting his signature, and that Gabriel would materialise shortly afterwards as if nothing had happened, hurrying him to get the picture encoded as more were on their way.

But it wasn't to be.

As he'd watched the two men struggling down the stairs, an enormous weight of sadness had descended upon him.

The following days had dragged by with unbearable heaviness, the first twenty-four hours caught in a numbing void of self-criticism. His mind had been unable to settle on anything, his thoughts racing backwards and forwards over the events of the past few days, examining and re-examining them not only are we doing everything we possibly can to find an answer to that question, but will actively investigate all other links presented to us. Meanwhile, I can only report that, to date, we've found no evidence of wrong-doing. Their intentions seem refreshingly altruistic. As far as we can ascertain, these exhibitions are without profit and purely for the enjoyment of the general public.'

There was a collective gasp of disgust.

'Without profit?' exclaimed a horrified Mister Hephaestus. 'Isn't it bad enough these people thrust the concept of God upon our planet without following it with yet another monstrous idea?'

The collective shuddered.

'Perhaps they're looking to artificially stimulate the world's interest in art,' suggested Mister Apollo, through narrowing eyes. 'That would produce an increase in demand, thereby raising its investment value. And who'd be the major beneficiaries? Given how much of it they own... *themselves!*'

There was a collective moment of breath-holding as the thought was digested.

'You know... I think Mister Apollo is right,' finally exhaled Mister Pan. 'They're attempting to drive the market!'

There was a collective sudden desire to increase art portfolios.

'Just a second, just a second!' exclaimed Mister Prometheus, waving his hands so as to flag down the idea. 'Now who's making assumptions? We *must* stick to the facts, ladies and gentlemen!'

'Facts of *what is* are of no use to us!' interjected Mister Cronus testily. 'We need facts of *what will be*. If the market moves, we need to be ahead of it!'

There was a collective murmur of agreement.

'I think Mister Prometheus is holding out on us!' proclaimed Mister Dionysus, rising to his sandalled feet and throwing his robe across one shoulder. 'There's obviously more to this than he's letting on! I think I should wrestle him to the ground and force him to come clean!'

patiently, 'but the link is real enough. Every scrap of intelligence we've gathered points to the same thing. Individuals and organisations around the world in possession of valuable works of art are being persuaded by various religious communities to loan them out. It's happening everywhere we've investigated… without exception. So… in the absence of any other link to connect them, we *must* assume that this is what they met at Arwan El Kahab to discuss.'

There was a collective stunned silence.

'Never assume anything,' said Mister Helios, with measured delivery. 'As my grandmother used to say, *"it makes an ass out of you and me"!*' He scoured the room for collective appreciation of this sage piece of octogenarian wit.

There was collective contemplation.

'Excuse me,' interrupted Miss Themis politely. 'Shouldn't that be *"it's* made out of ass, u and me"?'

There was a collective cough of embarrassment.

Not according to Mister Helios's grandmother, it shouldn't. 'It seems to me, Mister Prometheus,' he continued, undaunted, 'that you have simply looked out of your window, observed birds flying in the sun and come to the conclusion that it is the sunlight keeping them in the air!'

There was a collective careful scrutiny of the analogy this time, followed by a collective gentle nod of consensus.

'Even if we are to believe your summation is correct,' added Miss Aphrodite, an imposing woman whose hawk-like features were sharp enough to rip an opponent's confidence to shreds, 'you have yet to explain *why* these art exhibitions are being held.'

There was an even bigger collective nod of consensus… due, in part, to the fact it mostly comprised men who'd rather voluntarily remove their own manhood than disagree with Miss Aphrodite and suffer her doing it for them.

Mister Prometheus shifted uncomfortably and turned to face her *careful-what-you-say-next-as-I've-had-to-battle-twice-as-hard-to-get-where-I-am-today-than-anyone-sitting-around-this-table-with-a-penis* stare. 'I can assure you ma'am,' he verbally tiptoed, 'that

229

far?'

Chad looked away sheepishly.

'Would I be right in thinking... *Hello* and *goodbye?*' Bob scoffed.

'It's obviously a statistical anomaly,' muttered Chad. 'I need to analyse a bigger sample.' He quickly turned his attention back to his own screen, pretending not to notice Bob's interrogating stare.

'*What* is?' said Bob, rising from his desk. 'What have you got there?'

Chad drew himself nearer his screen so as to obscure what it was displaying. 'I told you... we need to analyse a higher proportion of data before we can trust any results.'

'Bullshit!' said Bob, pulling him back by the shoulders. 'You've been working on that thing with an entire team of analysts for days. So... what are we looking at here?' As he read the screen, Chad's shoulders dropped resignedly. 'You cannot be serious!' Bob drawled. 'Does that top result say what I think it says?'

Chad nodded slowly.

*   *   *

'Art Exhibitions?' The vein on Mister Zeus's forehead bulged to the point of eruption. 'Do you take us for complete idiots, Mister Prometheus?'

He didn't... not complete ones, anyway... and hadn't expected the news of his findings to meet with anything but the reaction it just had. Once more, he felt the collective stare burrowing beneath his epidermis.

'Perhaps you'd like to run by this meeting *exactly* how you arrived at the conclusion that the only link between those who attended the gathering at Arwan El Kahab... other than their misguided belief in an afterlife... is a sudden philanthropic interest in displaying works of art to the public!' demanded Mister Poseidon, his face stretched with disdain.

'I know it's difficult to accept,' answered Mister Prometheus message across to those in power would be to write and tell them exactly what was going on... or, more accurately... disjointed fragments of what *might* be going on.

* * *

'So... are you any the wiser?'

Bob grudgingly turned from the computer screen he'd been studying and faced his inquisitor.

'I mean... we're in this mess because you believed that telephone stunt of yours would produce results. I was just wondering when they were gonna materialise.'

'I'm working on it,' said Bob defiantly. 'Granted... whoever I spoke to at the end of that line was smarter than I gave 'em credit for and switched-on enough to use a different line to contact the brains behind this whole thing. But they would've wanted to do so as quickly as possible. That's why I'm cross-referencing every single call made from each individual line belonging to their *entire* organisation. It might be a mammoth task, but it's only a matter of time before I have what I'm looking for.' He tapped the screen confidently. 'The answer we're looking for is in there somewhere.'

'Well... take much *more* time doing it and we'll probably find ourselves facing further demotion,' Chad warned him.

'Further demotion?' Bob looked at his partner incredulously. 'What're they gonna do? Give us a mop and bucket?'

'Don't joke about it. We need to come up with the result of our careers if we're to justify me protecting your "reckless" arse!'

'Well... I haven't exactly heard *you* shouting *eureka* since we've both been searching for it!' Bob exclaimed.

'At least I'm following procedure,' countered Chad.

'Oh yeah... I was forgetting... trying to find your precious connection beyond coincidence!'

'Don't knock it, Bob. It's built on a sound, logical principle... locating keywords that appear in disproportionate quantity in their communications so as to indicate what they're up to.'

'And what has that sound, logical principle come up with so

231

people couldn't see him anyway. For Donald, it usually meant more tumbling onto pavements.

The problem was that the messages being received, whilst audibly loud and clear – to Donald at least – were fragmented and without sense.

Take, for instance, the copious amounts of Shakespeare he suddenly found himself reciting. Although Whitebait was unable to see where the words were coming from, it didn't stop them coming. Worse still were the strange snippets of conversation alluding to the removal of great works of art from their rightful places and a vast conspiracy by the religions of the world.

None of it made any sense. But given he believed them to be warnings of some sort, Donald felt compelled to do what he could to put a stop to it. Maybe... finally... this would be his atonement for failure to save his parents from their automotive fate.

Unfortunately, no one appeared to be taking him seriously. Perhaps – he surmised – he was approaching the wrong kind of people. He needed to get his message across to those who would have the ability to see the bigger picture... those who'd finally be able to do something about it.

The policeman at the large security gates that blocked off Downing Street and kept it safe from media-dangerous, trouser-stained vagrants was extremely polite. He informed Donald that the Prime Minister would be unable to see him without an appointment. However... this could be gotten by writing to his office and requesting one... though he could by no means guarantee that one would be granted.

Donald – finding it exceedingly refreshing to encounter such a non-judgemental attitude towards his unorthodox appearance and even more unorthodox message – thanked the officer for his civility... then barged past him in an attempt to rush the gates.

It was as he was being thrown into the back of the police van that he came to the conclusion that the only way to get his vent their spleen… had they still possessed one… mischievously encouraged to do so by Whitebait.

As a younger man, Donald had briefly flirted with show business, pursuing a career as a stage spiritualist. Not that he needed the money. He'd inherited his parents' vast estate after they were killed in a tragic accident. Donald, having been *forewarned,* had tried to convince them that picnicking at Beachy Head – before his father had fixed the handbrake on the Austin Healey – was a big mistake.

His mother had subsequently appeared to him from the other side, apologising for not taking him seriously and asking him to cancel the milk and papers.

His stage career was short-lived, due to the nature of information Whitebait saw fit to provide Donald's eager, yet vulnerable, audiences. On many occasions, deceased husbands were encouraged forward by the guide to tell their grieving widows not to worry as they were far happier dead than they'd ever been when alive… and there was the time when an inconsolable and recently bereaved young man was told by the deceased father he'd idolised to forget the tears as he wasn't really his.

Things finally reached a head when Whitebait summoned forth a spirit calling herself Great Aunt Felicia, who – in front of a packed village hall – urged a senior member of the audience and Chairperson of the Women's Guild to end her assignations with a Mr Herbert Bucket… as Mrs Bucket was starting to get suspicious.

Donald never trod the boards again.

There followed many years of mutual tolerance between medium and guide, a steady flow of other-worldly traffic ensuring the relationship continued, if no longer for public consumption… unless you happened to be standing in the middle of a crowded shopping precinct, that is. For the spiritual traffic had finally gotten out of hand. The steady flow had become a torrent and the strain was beginning to show. Donald and Whitebait frequently found themselves airing their differences in public which, for Whitebait, meant little… as *guesting* at the kind of hospital that felt it necessary to fit locks on the *outside* of their doors.

He'd inform the doctors he could hear voices in his head. Then – just because *they* couldn't – the assumption would be made that he was mad. But as he more than vociferously pointed out... if *they* were able to hear them, the voices wouldn't be in his head... they'd be in the *room*.

He'd always heard them. As a child, his parents had tolerated his "imaginary friends", putting them down to an overactive imagination or some genetic hand-me-down from great-grandpa Birtwistle. Barmy – as he was known to family and friends – had taken, in his latter years, to believing he was a chicken. They would have had him treated. But according to Barmy's sister, Lillian, the eggs came in useful.

As Donald grew, his "friends" remained... not that they had anywhere else to go. For they were of the spirit world... souls departed, yet still craving earthly contact. In their reluctance to let go, they'd grabbed hold of the nearest mortal attuned to their frequencies and were now using him as a kind of spiritual telephone.

One in particular had formed a close bond and volunteered himself as Donald's spirit guide. Such guides are common amongst those claiming to contact the dead... most with a sense of romance and mystery surrounding their previous lives. From Native Americans... with names poetically derived from nature... to Egyptians from the time of the Pharaohs... whose names feature poetically placed vowels. You even find the odd individual purporting to come from Atlantis, whose name contains no vowels whatsoever. In Donald's case, however, it was an ex-trawlerman from Grimsby who now went by the name of Whitebait.

Unfortunately – for one from the spirit world – Whitebait was exceptionally unspiritual... which was also unfortunate for Donald. For rather than receiving the wisdom of those who'd passed over and were able to espouse the meaning of life – having discovered the meaning of death – he was forced to endure the rantings of every unsettled spirit who wanted to haven't decided what to do with the two of you yet. But whilst I do, I'm suspending you both from field operations and confining you to desks. You can help collate the mountain of information that's coming in from our eavesdropping program. See if we can make sense of all this rubbish. Perhaps it'll be a salutary reminder of how much information can be gathered when it's done so *professionally*.'

Chad flinched from the sting of the last remark and bowed his head.

'That will be all, gentlemen.' AKA Mister Prometheus blew a long trail of cigar smoke into the air and nodded towards the door.

'Thanks for sticking up for me in there,' said Bob, as the two men embraced the calmer atmosphere of the corridor.

'You heard him,' said Chad, without looking at his partner. 'We're a team. I'm simply following the rules. But from now on, if you want us to continue working that way… fifty-fifty… equal partners… straight down the middle…… you do *exactly* as I say… *Understood?*'

*　　*　　*

As days went in the life of Donald Tucker-Jenkins, this wasn't one of his best. He'd just received his fifth manhandling of the afternoon – bringing his tally for the day to nine – and was beginning to wonder why no one was prepared to listen to what he had to say.

This wasn't, however, strictly true.

They *listened*… the majority, politely at first. But even the most courteous smile eventually became strained at the edges, a few turning to outright snarls as he found himself roughly ejected from a range of cultural establishments.

It was occurring with such regularity, he'd developed a method of tumbling onto pavements with as much dignity as possible.

It had been the same on occasions when he'd found himself

demanding to know what this united God squad are up to... and you go and pull a stunt like that! Covert means covert, gentlemen. It doesn't mean taking chances and thinking you can influence how the opposition will react. Our Anabaptist friends can't be certain it was us who called them, but I guarantee you they'll be certain they're extra vigilant from now on... and that's only gonna make our job harder.' He leant forward. 'You listen to me... My balls are firmly on the line with this one.' He squeezed the device and sliced the tip off the end of his cigar.

Bob winced.

'And I don't mind telling you that I've grown extremely attached to them... as has my wife.'

The truth was Mrs AKA Mister Prometheus couldn't have cared less if Mister AKA Mister Prometheus's dangly bits suffered the same fate as the end of his cigar. But as a senior member of the CIA's directorate of operations, spreading misinformation was a habit.

'Now – thanks to you – my ownership of them is starting to look a little tenuous!' AKA Mister Prometheus applied a flame from an imitation firearm to the end of the cigar and took a series of stuttered drags. 'What I can't understand is this... We all know Papadopoulos here is an idiot. But *you*, Cheadle. I had great things planned for you. You were one of my best!'

'It's not Chad's fault,' said Bob, stepping forward. 'I take the blame entirely. I did what I did without consulting him.'

'Not good enough!' barked AKA Mister Prometheus. 'You're a team. You're supposed to work as a team. *We're* supposed to work as a team. The minute anyone starts thinking they can go it on their own, that's when the whole thing collapses. I've spent my life trying to keep the forces of anarchy at bay. Now it seems they're happily at work in my own department!'

Chad chanced a sideways glance at his partner. 'Perhaps we should investigate Bob's idea, sir. After all, I believe there could be method in his madness.'

'No you don't, Cheadle. You're just trying to cover his reckless ass and, with it, your own. Well, let me tell you... that ass has now got my foot wedged firmly between its buttocks. I

Gabriel's image began to melt, as if mist warmed by an emerging sun.

'Nice shoes, by the way,' came his fading voice.

'They were on special offer!' called out Norman. But his words felt foolish as they tumbled out of his mouth and into an empty room.

*   *   *

The corridors of power are very straight and very long. They are illuminated by strip lighting and lined by doors distinguished only by meaningless combinations of letters and numbers. You have to know where you're going. If you don't... it probably means you're a spy. But at least – in this particular building – you wouldn't be out of place.

Those corridors had seemed a little longer than usual as Chad and Bob made their way to the room in which they were now standing. It was considerably better furnished than most of the others, the thick, beige carpet and deep-buttoned plush upholstery giving the room an elegance that was better suited to a late nineteenth-century drawing room.

'I can't believe I'm having this conversation with *you* two. What the hell did you think you were playing at?'

The question came from the figure sat behind a highly-polished walnut desk. In another room... and another life... that figure would have been recognised as Mister Prometheus. In this one, such recognition would instantly have resulted in his arrest.

'You were given the temple surveillance job because you were the best guys for it. Now you've gone from elite to laughing stock in the time it took for the sun to fry your brains. The problem is... *I'm* not laughing.'

Neither were Chad and Bob.

'You have no idea how much personal pressure I'm under on this one,' said AKA Mister Prometheus, producing a small metal object from the drawer of his desk and placing it around the end of an unlit cigar. 'I've got the whole world on my back

237

the Spirit to be one again. If we were to give you an unfair advantage, your soul will have been cheated of its chance to grow and return with all the others. It will have disqualified itself and be lost. Such a thing is unthinkable to Heaven, as all souls could never be unified again. By so forcefully demanding an answer, you have created a problem that is as great as the one we set out to solve!'

'Would saying sorry help?' asked Norman contritely.

'Desires are powerful things, Norman. You cannot see it in your world, but they are like waves that ripple out through the ether, carrying their own form of energy. They cannot be stopped. Nor can the consequences of their motion. That is why you should be careful what you wish for.'

'Then I'll wish for things to be as they were a few minutes ago! That way, the paradox can be ignored!'

Gabriel remained sombre. 'I wish it were that simple. A prayer from the deepest reaches of the heart cannot be overturned by a contrived one, no matter how good its intention. If you could but see them, the difference in the size of ripples is breathtaking!'

'But I'm serious! I'm truly sorry now I know what a mess I've made of things!'

'Precisely. You're sorry because of what I've told you. Already your soul is being unfairly influenced. I must leave before I do further damage.'

Norman detected an extra translucence to the Archangel's appearance. 'You're not fading on me, are you?' he asked anxiously.

'I'd like to think we'll meet again,' said Gabriel. 'Your irreverence seems to give me a curious warmth.'

'But what about the stairs... You're supposed to be a woman.'

'See what I mean?'

'Is that it? What about the fate of the Universe?'

'We may have to look elsewhere for a solution.'

'Then, what should I do about the cash I've withdrawn?'

'Your conscience will give you the answer to that. And just in case you were wondering... you can keep the ironmongery.'

'I must leave you now,' said Gabriel. 'We may not see each other again. If that is the case, I'd like to say that it's been... interesting.'

'Hang on a second!' said Norman, the anger in his voice turning to panic. 'Are you telling me, that's it?'

'I'm afraid the final answer to that must come from a higher power than me,' said Gabriel solemnly. 'If the answer is yes, the painting will be collected from you in the morning and you can return to your material pursuits, forgetting that any of this ever occurred.'

'I think that might be a little difficult!' declared Norman. 'Besides... all I wanted was an explanation!'

'And – as you so vociferously pointed out – you have every right to demand one. There is a Universal truth in the tenet "*ask and ye shall receive*". It is one of the immutable laws... one of the *rules*, you might say. I am therefore bound by those rules to oblige you. And therein lies my problem. You have created a spiritual paradox.'

'I have?'

'You've asked for something that cannot be delivered.'

'But surely that's not unusual? Millions of people must make unrealistic demands every day when they pray. I bet they don't all find their underwear imbued with the power of flight!'

'All prayers are answered, Norman. It's just that sometimes that answer is *no*. What you have done is *challenge* the answer. Now we have a problem. It is one of the reasons direct contact with your dimension is so rare. It is fraught with the danger of such paradoxes.'

'Now I'm even more confused,' Norman groaned. 'What's the paradox I've created?'

'Your soul is in its present incarnation to learn. The true value of that lesson is in its struggle to do so. To simply *give* you knowledge beyond your soul's rank would interfere with the universal scheme of things. After all... if it were that easy, the God people have envisaged to represent the Truth as, could simply appear in all Their glory and tell them how it is. Self-learning is the very essence of existence and the only way for

'But what harm could it…'

'Faith, Norman!' interrupted Gabriel loudly.

Norman was buffeted by a gust of wind.

'And if that is not enough for you, you will have to accept my words as a divine command!'

The atmospheric conditions inside the room had become decidedly unpleasant. They were the sort that had wind farm owners hoping they'd not skimped on lubrication. A full blown gale was now raging inside the bedsit. Discarded magazines and some items of clothing were being circled around the two antagonists as the vortex engulfed them. Even Gabriel seemed to be feeling the effects, steadying himself as his wings battled the force of the wind.

Norman's eyes bulged with exasperation. He'd had enough of being told what to do. 'Then what about *free will?*' he shouted above the commotion.

A flash of lightning seared through the room.

'Norman! Be warned! You must not go any further!'

It was too late. Norman had become caught up in the excitement of his own anger. For the first time, he sensed he had Gabriel against the ropes. 'You said we were given free will in order for us to express ourselves. Well… that's what I'm doing… I'm expressing myself. I'm *demanding* an answer!'

An even greater flash of lightning illuminated the room… then everything fell still. A pair of Y-fronts that had been circling energetically above them plummeted to the ground.

'Oh dear,' said Gabriel, with overpowering solemnity. 'I wish you hadn't just said that.' The light about him waned and his wings folded as if conscious of their own weight.

Norman examined the crashed underwear. 'Does this mean I've won or lost?'

Gabriel looked at him mournfully. 'Under any other circumstances, I would remind you that things are never so black and white. But under *these* circumstances, I fear they are very black indeed.'

Norman hadn't been aware of a mark… but something about Gabriel's countenance suggested he'd just overstepped one.

They are currently arranging to have sent to this address some of the finest works of art ever created. Which is why you must accept things as they are and get on with your work before negative forces disrupt them.'

'There you go again!' said Norman angrily. 'What forces? Who are they and what can any of this possibly have to do with saving the Universe!'

'That's a very big question,' said Gabriel. 'The problem is... it requires an even bigger answer.'

'Then perhaps the quicker you start explaining, the quicker I'll be able to get on with my task and finish whatever it is you're up to!'

The atmosphere in the room changed. Norman felt a cold gust of wind attack his legs.

'You must stop this now,' said Gabriel sternly.

Norman had only just started. He was tired of the Archangel's condescension. After all... wasn't it himself who'd been doing most of the hard work? Divine beings probably didn't need sleep. He, however, had made great bodily sacrifices to deliver the program on time exactly as specified. The least the Archangel could do was explain the purpose behind that sacrifice. 'I'd still like an explanation!' he asserted.

The wind about his legs began to swirl.

Gabriel stood his ground. 'I'm afraid, it's not that simple. It would require more than mere earthly knowledge for you to fully comprehend... and that cannot be.'

It made no sense to Norman. 'Why? Why can't it be?' A stiff breeze began circling the room. 'You're here in front of me, aren't you? You could explain in words I'd understand.'

The air in the room was now becoming turbulent. The papers on his desk began to rustle.

'Knowledge of certain things could be dangerous, Norman.'

'I'll take that chance.'

The papers lifted and scattered.

'The chance is not yours to take,' said Gabriel firmly. 'And the danger of which I speak lies beyond your comprehension. You must trust me and leave it at that.'

didn't mean anything by it. Perhaps if you'd given me a better copy, I'd have recognised the religious theme and been more respectful.'

'Copy…? What on earth are you on about?' Gabriel twitched uncomfortably. 'This is the *original!*'

Norman was growing used to surprises. But Gabriel's disclosure was something else. 'You can't be serious?' he gasped, fumbling for the edge of the bed and attempting to sit without sending the mug of tea flying.

'I have never been more so,' replied Gabriel. 'Especially given the amount of preparation it's taken to get it to you.'

'But…' Norman gingerly removed the offending crockery, 'a genuine *Rembrandt!*'

'Precisely.'

'And the Mondrian?' enquired Norman weakly. 'Was that also…'

'An original,' confirmed Gabriel. 'As will be all the visual works of art you will receive over the coming months. Surely you didn't think we'd bother to go to all this trouble just to encode *copies?*'

'That's just the problem,' said Norman. 'I don't know *what* to think anymore… And I certainly don't *understand!*'

'You don't need to,' said Gabriel. 'All that's important is that you do as instructed.'

'But I *want* to understand, don't you see?' protested Norman, getting to his feet. 'I need to know why there's a genuine old master on my bed impersonating a tea tray. I mean… how on earth did it end up getting here… and isn't someone going to miss it?'

'Not if our plan runs smoothly,' answered Gabriel.

'But what's next? Van Gogh's Sunflowers?'

Gabriel considered the question. 'I believe they're due around about week three.'

'What…! This is ridiculous!' Norman threw his hands up in the air. 'How can this be possible?'

'I've already explained,' said Gabriel patiently. 'There are others here on Earth who have been instructed to assist you.

faces of those in the crowd. It was as far removed from Mondrian's coloured squares as you could get.

It wasn't the sort of thing Norman would've hung on his wall... but the skill with which the artist had created the light impressed him. It showed a mind that had taken the problem of how to achieve such an effect... solved it... applied it... and won.

He could relate to that.

The remainder of that afternoon was spent carefully scanning and stitching sections of the canvas together until the scene – in all its glory – sat recreated on his computer screen.

Just as he finished, Gabriel announced himself on the landing. Oppenheimer was nowhere to be seen.

'I was wondering,' said Norman, on opening the door, 'how you might cope with a beaded curtain. I mean... if you think about its molecular structure, one could...'

'I see you've made a start on the first of the paintings,' said Gabriel, floating by and purposefully ignoring him.

'The robber and the gallows...? Bit of a morbid subject, isn't it?'

'Robber and the gallows?' exclaimed Gabriel, shocked.

'Well... I assumed he was a robber. They've obviously hung him for some reason or other.'

Gabriel looked at him indignantly. 'It's Jesus being removed from the cross!'

'*Cross?*' Norman peered closely at the canvas lying face up on his bed. 'So it is,' he said, adjusting his squint.

'And what in Heaven's name is that on top of it?'

'Exactly! The picture's so dark in that area, you can't make out what it's supposed to be.'

'Not on top of the cross, Norman... on top of the *painting!*' Gabriel was referring to a half-finished mug of tea precariously perched on the canvas.

'Don't worry. If it leaves a ring, I'll wipe it off.'

'Wipe it off! Have you any idea what you have here in your room?' The feathers of Gabriel's wings rustled as if caught by a stiff breeze. 'It's Rembrandt's *Descent from the Cross!*'

Norman studied the image with indifference. 'I'm sorry. I

pounds, please.'

Norman had ordered a lot of them.

'Will you take a cheque?'

The assistant's facial expression – which had hitherto suggested he might be better suited to work in a funeral parlour – began to crack. Norman thought the man was about to sneeze, but caught the full blast of a roar of laughter... so loud, the rest of the shop turned to see what was occurring. Laughter in a computer store is far rarer than laughter in a hardware store. It probably has something to do with the prices that are charged.

'That's very good, sir,' wept the assistant deliriously.

In an embarrassingly long display of hysterics, he removed from his system years of frustration at having to wear a shirt and tie, and thus missing out on the glamour and authority of a shop coat.

His composure eventually regained, he informed Norman that he would have to wait for delivery until after the cheque had cleared, and that this could take a number of days.

The choice for Norman was simple... He didn't have one.

Norman's last port of call was to replace the battered plimsolls that were failing to prevent the pavement from coming into contact with his socks. Strangely enough, their replacements looked remarkably like expensive, top-of-the-range trainers... a difference he hoped might get overlooked come judgement day.

It was late afternoon before Norman was finally able to tackle the second crate that had been delivered... his reward, the discovery of yet another artist's canvas carefully packaged inside.

Considerably larger than the first – measuring approximately four feet by five – it depicted a macabre scene... a naked man being removed from what looked like a pair of gallows, whilst a group of onlookers swooned nearby. A cloth – laid on the ground to receive the body – was being illuminated by a golden light, which also bathed the victim, his helper and some of the

The assistant looked vacant. Try as he might, his brain seemed unable to come up with a suitable riposte... *Computer memory*... There had to be some form of badinage he could indulge in with this one, surely... *Computers...? Memory...?* No... it just wasn't there... He looked mortified. He'd always prided himself that there wasn't a single item in his shop he couldn't attach at least three gags to. The trouble was... he didn't get much practice when it came to items that *weren't* stocked. His eyes began to water. 'Seventeen pounds fifty, please,' he croaked.

Norman left him contemplating his future in the industry... as well as a long lie down.

The assistant at the computer store didn't do jokes... though it might have been better if he had. Norman thought it possible he'd been the recipient of a humour-bypass operation at some point in his life, but wasn't going to ask in case he couldn't see the funny side.

'Internal ones or external ones?' asked the assistant sullenly, in response to Norman's request for hard drives.

For those who do not understand anything about computers... this remark in no way displays a clever or inventive exploitation of the comic potential of language via an absurd subversion of the logical state... whatsoever.

'I'm not sure,' chanced Norman. 'My memory's not as good as it should be!'

For those who do not understand anything about computers... this *does*.

The assistant looked at him blankly.

'External,' said Norman soberly.

'Fast seek time?'

'The fastest.'

'Maximum storage capacity?'

'Absolutely.'

'Anything else?'

'No, thank you.'

'That'll be fourteen thousand, six hundred and eighty

the long weight.

Norman smiled sympathetically. 'Just the best one you've got, please.'

'Ah… In that case… you'll be wanting the deluxe model, sir.'

'*Is* there such a thing?' asked Norman.

'Caters for the discerning criminal, upwardly mobile thug and fashion conscious vandal.'

'And what makes it deluxe?'

'Its price,' quipped the assistant.

'I'm also going to need a hammer.'

'Would that be a left-handed or right-handed one?' The assistant suddenly stopped himself and squeezed the bridge of his nose. The strain of selling chain by the metre was finally beginning to show. It wasn't easy being an ironmonger. Sure… everybody *thought* it was… especially when they were served by your pre-pubescent son on a Saturday afternoon. But didn't they realise he was being *trained*? For you had to be an expert on everything from quick dry glues, masonry paint, weed killers and the adhesive potential of sticky-backed plastic to the use of bio-friendly slug repellent and cold water dyes. He'd never quite recovered from having to go metric. 'I'm sorry, sir… where was I?' he mumbled.

'A hammer?' prompted Norman.

'Ah, yes… That's hit the nail on the head,' said the assistant, back to his old self. 'Bet you'll have a smashing time with this!' He reached to his side and lifted one off a hammer-shaped display stand. 'Will that be all, sir? Only… I've got a great deal going on washers at the moment… You get a free hole inside every one!'

'I need a new toilet brush,' said Norman warily. 'The old one's taken a bit of a battering.'

'Shit happens,' joked the assistant, producing one from beneath the counter. 'Drives you round the bend, doesn't it? But I'm sure you'll be well-flushed with your new one…! Anything else?'

'Not unless you sell computer memory,' replied Norman.

There was an awkward silence.

up. He managed to get as far as the first four hundred, then left it to blind faith and the cashier's integrity... though he pretended to be keeping pace with her blurred index finger just in case she was thinking of taking early retirement at his expense.

The pavements were annoyingly full of pedestrians. Norman hated having to second-guess their intentions, usually ending up in a pathetic dance with a complete stranger or careering into the heels of someone who didn't understand the concept of linear motion.

He finally took sanctuary in a hardware store, the assistant behind the counter expertly demonstrating a brand of humour that has become as much a tradition of selling ironmongery as needlessly-worn shop coats sporting assorted pens in outer breast pockets.

'Left-handed or right-handed one, sir?'

Norman stared at him, perplexed.

'The crowbar... Do you want a left-handed or right-handed one?' This was one of the more easily applied quips in the ironmongers' repertoire... able to be used in the sale of anything from watering cans to coffee cups. He'd even once applied it to a transaction involving a twenty-four foot, extendable, aluminium ladder with patented safety lock. In fact... he was now unable to sell *any* item without resorting to a level of wit that would have Oscar Wilde turning in his grave. Though as Oscar might have said... had he thought of it... There is one thing worse than turning in your grave... and that is turning in your grave and discovering that you're not actually *dead*.

It might be possible that this affliction – known in the trade and amongst long-suffering Do-It-Yourselfers as *Ironmongers' Syndrome* – is hereditary and perpetuated by family-run businesses. Alternatively, the cause could be viral... transmitted via the handling of pricing guns and out-of-date seed catalogues. But it is far more likely to have developed over a period of time in response to first-day apprentices requesting sky hooks, cans of tartan paint and that rib-splitting perennial...

Only, this time... you won't be in a position to argue back.'

Bob exercised his jaw and stared at the ceiling fan. 'I take it you didn't ask if my call had produced any results?'

'Oh... it's produced results alright,' said Chad brusquely. 'We're going home... and I don't think it'll be to a warm reception.'

* * *

To look or not to look?

Norman felt the bank's security cameras scrutinising his behaviour as he waited at the counter.

He'd just presented the cashier with a cheque to cash... and presumably because of the amount involved – he'd decided to add an extra nought at the very last moment – she'd scuttled away to make the necessary enquiries.

The cameras were staring directly at him, daring him to stare back.

What to do? If he pretended he hadn't noticed, might it raise suspicion as to why he was trying to avoid their gaze? But if he looked directly into them – so as to prove he had nothing to hide – might the unseen eye behind wonder why he was so concerned about their presence in the first place?

He waited in a kind of boss-eyed limbo, speculating as to whether the entire bank's staff was crowded behind a monitor, analysing his every move.

Someone managerial-looking briefly popped their head around a screen... gave him the once over... then disappeared.

Finally... the cashier returned, her expression noncommittal. 'How would you like the money, sir?' she asked.

'Very much... thank you,' The etiquette of banking was something of a stranger to Norman.

She raised an eyebrow. 'Which *denominations?*'

'Oh... I see... Er... whatever you've got.'

The cashier's eyebrow remained raised, as she pulled a number of bundled notes from a drawer and proceeded to count through them with a speed that left Norman struggling to keep *start.* 'I'll go and check the post,' he said excitedly.

'PUT MONEY IN THY PURSE!'

Donald finished shouting and looked up. To his astonishment, the bus had completely emptied.

*　　*　　*

'Congratulations,' said Chad, addressing the slumbering bundle beneath the blanket. 'The shit's well and truly hit the fan.'

Bob's face reluctantly emerged and grimaced at the light streaming through the window to the unwelcome accompaniment of a nearby souk. He glanced at the ceiling fan revolving above Chad's head, giving the appearance of a halo. 'The plumbing in this shit-hole *that* bad?' he mumbled, closing his eyes and preparing to sink beneath the blanket again.

A towel hit him in the face.

'Better get yourself washed and dressed. We've got problems.' Chad positioned himself in front of the washbasin and wedged his shaving equipment between the taps.

'You're not wrong there,' yawned Bob, raising himself up and scratching his torso. 'This bed's hosting more foreign friggin' life forms than Area 51!'

'I'm amazed it's not the *bugs* doing the complaining,' retorted Chad. 'And you needn't worry about spending any more time in it. I've just been speaking to command on the radio. They're calling us home.'

'*Home*...? I thought we'd been given a free hand on this one.'

'We had... until you decided to use it to pick up the phone last night!'

Bob sank back into his pillow. 'So that's what this is about. I thought we'd exhausted our differences on the subject.'

'No... You just refused to accept the fact that breaking all the rules of procedure was the stupidest of all the stupid things you've ever done.' A loud knocking reverberated around the walls as the pipes argued as to whether to give up their water. 'Well... now you'll get the chance to hear it from someone else.

249

'Yes... we know. And it was your conscience that recognised the difference. That is why you were chosen. You can do what you like with the cheques, Norman. They are meaningless to us. All we care is that you achieve the task we have set you.'

Do what you like with the cheques! Norman felt his head begging to party. *A blank chequebook... with no less a guarantor than the Archangel Gabriel! That'd impress them at the nearest Ferrari garage! They were bound to be devout Catholics. This meant riches beyond his wildest...... Ah...... wait a minute...... Shit... there it was... ... The catch.* He'd thought it too good to be true. An uninvited guest had just gate crashed his celebrations and switched on the lights. It looked suspiciously like his conscience.

With all of Heaven watching, how could he spend the money on anything but that for which it had been intended? If it was now impossible to deny the existence of Heaven, he could hardly deny the existence of its oppugnant neighbour. Hell was no longer a mild expletive. And if he wanted to avoid its warmer climes, perhaps he'd be wise not to let greed get the better of him. He'd have to save mankind without the aid of a sports car.

But all was not lost... At least he'd be able to build the computer system of his dreams, boasting a size and power limited only by his expertise, imagination and the strength of downstairs' ceiling joists.

'I'm going to need a crowbar to get the crates open properly,' he announced delicately, deciding to test the water as far as peripheral extras were concerned. It would be a cruel irony indeed if his soul were to be cast into eternal damnation for the purchase of ironmongery.

'Then you'll be able to buy the best,' said Gabriel.

Norman wasn't sure if there was such a thing as a deluxe crowbar. 'And a hammer,' he added. 'I had a real job fixing the end back on the crate this morning using my plimsolls.'

'I suggest you get another pair whilst you're out shopping for the hammer,' said Gabriel, gazing down at Norman's battered footwear.

Okay, thought Norman. *It wasn't quite a Ferrari... but it was a* that. I take it you haven't received your mail this morning?'

'You mean… other than this crate…? No.'

'When you do, you will find it contains a chequebook, every cheque of which has been signed. All you have to do is fill in the details. I take it this will solve your problem?'

Norman looked at him in astonishment. 'But… what amount should I make each one out for?'

Gabriel shrugged. 'That's entirely up to you.'

Norman wasn't sure he could believe his ears… which didn't much matter, seeing as they were being bypassed anyway. 'You trust me *that* much?'

'We've put our faith in you to save the Universe. We're hardly likely to worry about your abuse of an illusionary distraction like money. Besides… there's something I haven't told you. When searching for a mortal to undertake the task, you weren't the *only* one considered. But something occurred that singled you out from the rest. Cast your mind back to an evening you spent in this room twenty-seven of your days ago.'

This was as pointless as asking Norman to remember the last time he'd used a plate without having to wash it up first.

'You accessed the records of your bank via your computer,' Gabriel reminded him.

Norman's demeanour changed to that of a puppy caught missing its litter tray. 'It rings a *vague* bell,' he admitted sheepishly.

That bell had tolled inside his head like Big Ben on New Year's Eve. The word *accessed* Gabriel had so diplomatically used could equally well have been substituted by the word *hacked.*

'Then… you might *vaguely* remember using your skills to erase your overdraft, confident in the knowledge that such an action would be totally undetectable.'

By now, the ringing in Norman's head resembled a campanological masterclass.

'We thought at that point we'd lost you. But then we watched you reverse your actions and reinstate your balance.'

'It wasn't about the money,' explained Norman hastily. 'It was the *challenge*.'

'*More* of them? What do you mean *more*… and for what possible reason?'

'So that you can begin working on the next stage of your mission,' explained Gabriel. 'Why do you think we asked you to write the program in the first place? You're going to have to encode many other images and sounds before your work is done.'

'But what on earth has this to do with saving the Universe?' protested Norman. 'If it's in such danger, shouldn't I be getting on with the more important stuff?'

'This *is* the important stuff,' said Gabriel.

Norman's neck jerked forward. 'What…? Storing music and pictures on a computer?'

'Just because you can't see a connection, doesn't mean there isn't one. It's a simple enough truth, but one you may do well to remember.'

'But… how many of these encodings am I going to have to undertake?'

Gabriel thought awhile. 'At a rough estimate… I'd say a couple of thousand.'

'A couple of *thousand!*' blurted Norman. 'Are you serious…? Do you know what that would take?'

'I'm aware of the time involved,' said Gabriel. 'Even if I don't recognise the concept myself. Which is why you must start right away.'

'I wasn't talking about *time*. I was referring to *memory!*'

'Memory? What is there to forget?'

'*Computer* memory! The amount of space my program needed to store those test samples was enormous, given they're now in the form of raw, binary code! I doubt I've got enough room left on my hard drive to store the artwork for a postage stamp!'

'Then you must get more of this *memory*,' said Gabriel. 'I take it this can be achieved?'

'Well… er… yes,' stuttered Norman. 'But it'll be extremely expensive!'

'Cost is not a problem,' said Gabriel. 'I was about to come to

'Don't stare Timmy,' pleaded Mummy. 'It's rude.'

'But Mummy... he thinks there's someone there!'

Mummy felt herself being sucked into a whirling vortex... the other passengers sympathising with her predicament via the backs of their heads.

'The nice man's only talking to himself, darling.' She thought use of the word *nice* to be a sensible strategy.

There was a momentary promise of silence.

'Then why's he shouting, Mummy?' Timmy's synaptic connections had come of age. 'He wouldn't have to shout if he was talking to himself, would he, Mummy? He wouldn't have to shout!'

Mummy felt her heartbeat warming her cheeks. 'He's shouting because... he's deaf,' she tried desperately.

This seemed to work. She could just make out Timmy's reflection in the glass – head bent to one side – standing directly beside the man and staring hard at him.

Then what had been working broke.

'Phewww...! He stinks, Mummy!'

Don't hold your nose, thought Mummy. *Please don't hold your nose!*

Timmy held his nose.

'Timmy. You mustn't say such things! It's very rude!'

'It's alright, Mummy... He can't hear me... He's DEAF!' shouted Timmy, as loud as he could in Donald's ear.

Timmy felt the floor of the bus jerk from beneath his feet as his head found itself firmly clamped to a warm, palpitating bosom.

* * *

'I thought we'd proved my program works,' said Norman, pointing at the newly delivered crate dwarfing his sofa.

'Precisely,' agreed Gabriel. 'Which is why you must put it to use right away. You'll be receiving many more of these deliveries over the coming weeks.'

'Whoa... just a second,' objected Norman, raising a hand.

SPIES, BUT IN BATTALIONS!'

Such words – when delivered aloud by an angst-ridden thespian assuming the mask of King Claudius in Hamlet – strike out at the audience with a richness undiminished by time.

When delivered aloud on the number 19 bus to Charing Cross Road by an unshaven man with suspect trousers, they strike fear.

The silence – in so confined a space – was palpable.

Such fear was not of the sentiment itself... nor of a threat to the physical well-being of any of the bus's passengers. It was simply a fear of becoming... *involved.*

The view through the windows suddenly took on extra interest to those who'd just found themselves to be on the wrong side of the glass. Personal spaces were fortified, drawbridges raised and all castle lights extinguished. Following his outburst, Donald found himself amidst a bus-load of people who were suddenly *not at home.*

Except for one.

'Mummy... That man just shouted!'

Mummy did her best to pretend the child wasn't hers, forcing out a barely audible 'Mmm... dear.'

'He did, Mummy... I heard him...! He shouted at that empty seat next to him!'

'Oh, look, Timmy,' said Mummy quickly. 'Look at all those pretty shops!'

'But there's no one in that seat... is there Mummy...? There's no one sitting there!'

It was every mother's nightmare... her flesh and blood, innocently standing on the other side of the moat... waving at the enemy.

She kept her face towards the window. 'Shall we count the shops, Timmy?' she tried, brightly. 'Look... One... Two...'

'But there isn't... Mummy... is there?'

Situations involving fat people were bad enough... dwarves, people in wheelchairs and those suffering facial disfigurements harder still. Men with long hair could usually be placated with a smile... But etiquette-immune *vagrants!*

'Good morning, gentlemen!'

Oppenheimer jumped as Gabriel passed him. 'Oh… and good morning to you, Madam,' returned the landlord brightly, leering at the Archangel's behind.

'Did you know there's blood on the hallway carpet?' whispered Gabriel as he glided by Norman and into the room.

'There's been a slight accident,' returned Norman. 'But, more importantly… there's something I need to ask you about before we go any further.'

'Right now?' Gabriel looked about himself in surprise.

Norman lowered his voice. 'Mister Oppenheimer says his father's name was Thomas.'

'Yes?'

'But, in attempting to prove your existence to me, you said it was Helmut.'

'That's right.'

'Well… apparently, that's the name of his uncle!'

'I know… it's a sad case… but it happens,' said Gabriel philosophically.

'Oh… I see.' Norman turned to his landlord and smiled weakly. 'I have to go now, Mister Oppenheimer. Perhaps we could talk later about the damage downstairs?'

'You can bet the dollar on your bottom,' said Oppenheimer. He gave Gabriel a wink and chanced an admiring glance at the Archangel's legs.

'It's a shame your father's brother wasn't still around today,' added Norman as a diplomatic parting shot. 'We could have got him to repair the hat stand himself.'

'You jump to the wrong conclusion,' said Oppenheimer casually. 'Uncle Helmut wasn't my father's brother… he was my *mother's*.'

'A *very* sad case,' whispered Gabriel, as Norman gingerly closed the door.

*   *   *

'WHEN SORROWS COME, THEY COME NOT SINGLE

255

father would often say, "Gertie, you think more of that hat stand than you do of me"... to which she would reply, "Thomas... you have no idea!"... But now it can't hold hats... and it doesn't even *stand!*'

To Norman, this wasn't a bad thing. He'd often wondered why such an inordinately huge object had been allowed to clutter the hallway... its elephantine base made all the more grotesque by the hotchpotch of badly carved forest animals frolicking their way around it. Rabbits seem to have been Uncle Helmut's favourites... though they might well have been otters... or elephants... it was hard to tell. Either way, it was now considerably less offensive than it had been half an hour earlier.

However... having solved the mystery of why it had been there in the first place, the hat stand now produced an even greater conundrum.

'Your parents were Gertie and *Thomas?*' enquired Norman, confused.

'Yah, that is right... Though mother's full name was Gertrude.'

'Not Gertrude and *Helmut?*'

'I've just told you... Helmut was my *uncle.*' Oppenheimer's eyes glazed and a rare smile bent his lips. 'He was such a part of my early life... I cannot recall a time when he wasn't always visiting us.' The smile collapsed. 'Why are you asking me this?'

'No reason,' said Norman quickly. 'Look... Mister Oppenheimer. I'm sorry about your hat stand. I'll see it gets repaired... As for this second crate... I wasn't expecting it. They've obviously made a mistake. I'll sort it out right away.'

This seemed to soothe Oppenheimer. But Norman's readiness to please had also sharpened the landlord's curiosity.

'Tell me... what is it that comes in these crates?'

Norman suddenly felt a desperate urge to slam the door and escape back to the safety of his inner-sanctum. Mister Oppenheimer's foot – skilfully placed against the door frame – advised against it.

Norman prayed for a miracle.

'Same time tomorrow, then,' said Flowers, without looking back.

Norman glanced at Oppenheimer. 'Apparently.'

'Be careful of my stairs,' warned Oppenheimer, as the crate began its descent.

'Don't worry, sir,' strained a voice. 'It's always easier going down than it is coming up... Everything's under control.'

The next sound was that of a large object crashing to the hallway... followed by two grown men whimpering in agony.

'Excuse me, Mister Penkridge,' came a voice apologetically from below. 'Any chance of you calling for an ambulance?'

The siren had barely faded as Oppenheimer began his inquisition.

'Norman... for the last eighteen months you have been the model tenant. Never do I have a problem with you. But suddenly everything changes. First you have late night guests who keep me awake... then there are these crates delivered by men who wear crash helmets for protection... apparently against *themselves...!* What is going on?'

'Nothing, Mister Oppenheimer. Look... I thought we'd sorted the misunderstanding about my visitor... and as for these deliveries... I wasn't aware receiving post was forbidden.'

'*Post?*' exclaimed the landlord incredulously. 'Are you *serious?* Post is something that drops *onto* the hall floor... not *through* it...! What kind of *post* can flatten a hat stand?'

This last remark was in reference to a hideous piece of furniture that had just lost its ability to scare first-time visitors. To be fair... it had been *Nobby* who'd flattened it... the ensuing weight of the crate merely guaranteeing he'd done a thorough job.

'I'll have you know, that was a family heirloom. As a young boy, I watched my Uncle Helmut carve it with his own hands.'

Given the standard of craftsmanship involved, Norman found it hard to believe Uncle Helmut hadn't used his *feet*.

'It was my mother's pride and joy... God rest her soul. She would spend hour upon hour polishing it until it shone. My

257

In an uncanny display of timekeeping, the knock announcing Nobby and Flower's ten o'clock arrival coincided perfectly with the chime from the wall clock in the hall downstairs.

The crate they had just wrestled to the top of the landing was even larger than the one they had come to collect. Norman was surprised to see it. He hadn't been expecting a replacement.

The sounds of two delivery men attempting the world's first synchronised double hernia had also brought Oppenheimer out of his room... and he was now standing behind them, trying to figure out if the delivery of large wooden boxes was permitted under the tenancy agreement.

'Morning, Mister Penkridge,' said Flowers, fighting for breath. 'One crate to pick up and one to stay. If you could just sign the docket as before, we'll bring this one in and take the other... strength permitting... off yer hands.'

Given they seemed to know a lot more about what was going on than he did, Norman did as he was asked... watching as they manoeuvred the crate by means of an uncoordinated shuffle.

Both couriers were wearing helmets, the insignia of two overlapping *Vs* just visible above their raised visors. It was the same as that stitched onto the front of their navy-blue tunics. The helmets boasted a leather neck protector. Though why anyone would need to use force against *these* two individuals eluded Norman. It would be like mugging Laurel and Hardy, he thought.

Flowers – the larger of the two – signalled for Nobby to put his end down by means of a grimaced nod. 'Is the other one ready for collection, sir?' he wheezed, turning his pained expression towards Norman.

'Er... yes... I've repackaged it as best I could.'

The two men performed a cursory examination of the crate in question and – having satisfied themselves it wouldn't disintegrate mid-lift – hoisted it up and shuffled back out through the door.

You're obviously even more stupid than I thought!'

'Was it my accent?' asked Bob innocently .

'It was every word you uttered! Even if it'd been *remotely* convincing, did it not occur to that excuse of a brain of yours that if the Amish we ran into refused to travel in anything more modern than a horse and cart, they sure as hell ain't gonna be using a telephone to communicate!'

'As a matter of fact, that's *exactly* what occurred to me,' said Bob, a grin breaking out across his face.

His reaction fuelled Chad's incredulity. 'What is this...? What's the big idea?'

Bob's grin widened.

'All you've done is poke a stick into a hornets' nest!' shouted Chad. 'How the hell's that gonna help us?'

'Never look a gift horse in the mouth,' said Bob calmly. 'Except when it's presented by someone with Greek ancestry.'

'What the *hell* are you on about?'

'Because it may well turn out to be a very useful *Trojan* horse.'

Chad looked at him in bewilderment. 'What are you on about...? What's any of that got to do with acting like an asshole and compromising our mission?'

'Compromising... no. Contributing to... yes. And for asshole, you can substitute artful. You know the trouble with you, Chad? You're so concerned with thinking in straight lines, you've forgotten the advantage of throwing a curved ball once in a while.'

Chad stared at him blankly.

'You see... I just couldn't face the thought of spending all that time in a library. But now that the proverbial's about to hit the fan back at Mennonite headquarters... all we've gotta do is get hold of their call log for the following hours and check out who's on it. I guarantee you – given the incredible secrecy surrounding this whole charade – whoever's responsible for arranging things in the first place will definitely be receiving a call around about now!'

phone again. 'Britain...? No...! I told you... it's in The United States... A...mer...ica... You know... that place whose flag everyone loves to burn...... Oh... *bitten...!* Have I been *bitten...*? No... why d'ya ask...? ... *Bats...*? What the friggin' hell have *bats* to do with anything...? ... Oh, I *see...* a *joke*.' Bob held the bridge of his nose. 'No... No... I think you'll find that's *Transylvania...* Mine's about four thousand miles west and has slightly fewer castles... That's right... *Pennsylvania*.' He looked at Chad despairingly then let out a heavy sigh. 'No... the number's not six five thousand and I don't want to speak to a Mister Miller.'

Chad eyed him warily as Bob struggled to get the operator to forget about a career in stand-up comedy and simply do as he was told.

'About friggin' time,' he announced, after considerable effort. 'It's ringing.' After a few seconds his expression brightened. 'Oh... Yah, hello... Am I through to the headquarters of the Mennonite community...? ... I am... Goot... My name is Jakob Johannson.'

Chad made a panicked lunge for the receiver, but was thwarted by Bob deftly rolling to one side. 'What the hell are you playing at?' he hissed, his eyes dancing in horror.

'Yah, I know... it's a bad line,' continued Bob, thrusting out a hand to ensure his partner remained at arm's length. 'I'm calling from the Middle East... ... Yah... I'm out here representing the Amish community at the gathering of faiths at Arwan El Kahab. I understand you had representatives here yourselves.' There was a short silence. 'Unfortunately... my colleagues and I had an accident on the way and were unable to attend the meeting. I was hoping – given our historic and cultural links – you might be able to put me in touch with someone who can fill us in on what it was all about.' Another silence. 'Yah... that is correct... Jakob Johannson.' Bob's features hung expectantly, then dropped in disgust as he jerked the receiver away from his ear. 'They've hung up!'

'There's a surprise!' exclaimed Chad, exploding in anger and snatching the receiver from Bob's hands. 'Did you honestly think they'd fall for such a cheap trick? What are you... nuts?

own private oasis of insalubrity.

The light switch in the room actually worked... though perhaps it would have been better if it hadn't. The walls of the room suggested it had once been rented out to the local firing squad... and a lethally dilapidated ceiling fan hovered menacingly above two hygienically challenged, single bedspreads. The beds themselves hadn't so much been made as *approximated*... and the cracked sink in the corner of the room had long forgotten it used to be white. A badly painted picture of an Arabian girl, with eyes resembling balls of molasses, had fallen from its mounting and was propped against an inebriated wardrobe, the tilting door of which refused to shut.

'It's not just this that needs hanging!' said Bob, examining the picture and visualising the hotel's proprietor enthusiastically counting their money. 'Unlimited expenses and we end up in this friggin' dump!' He ran his finger contemptuously through a layer of grime that had taken up permanent residence on the frame.

'We were hardly likely to find an *en suite* Jacuzzi out here in the middle of nowhere,' said Chad wearily. 'If you're not happy with the accommodation, you could always spend another night in the van.' He threw his bag and himself onto one of the beds.

'The prospect of *that* suddenly appears extremely attractive,' said Bob, collapsing onto the other. 'But then I wouldn't have the use of one of these!' He reached for the Bakelite telephone atop a reading table separating the two beds.

Its mouthpiece seemed to double as a menu card for room service, its eye-watering aroma hinting at previous occupants' culinary preferences.

'Hello...? Hello?' he bellowed into it. 'Yeah...! I wanna make an International call... Can you put me through to the operator?' He gave Chad a wink and waited for a connection. 'Hello...? Yeah... The United States... ... That's right... I'm calling Pennsylvania... ... Penn...syl...vania.'

'What are you up to?' said Chad uneasily, raising himself from his bed.

'Just saddling up,' grinned Bob, turning his attention to the

Gabriel looked mortified. 'You mean...'

Norman nodded.

'Fishnets and everything?'

Norman nodded again.

There was an embarrassing silence.

'The things we do for humanity,' muttered Gabriel as he moved towards the door. He waited for Norman to open it. 'Goodnight,' he said timidly... and delicately descended the stairs.

* * *

The only reason the *Hotel Bedouin* had a plaque on the wall boasting three stars was because the proprietor had stolen it from a rival one down the road.

The reception area was pleasant enough... the white, tiled floor, ornate ceiling fan and collection of native flora in relatively clean, terracotta pots giving it an atmosphere of small Middle-Eastern town decadence.

Unfortunately, any pretence of refinement was dropped the minute you climbed the stairs. At the precise point where one's line of sight had ended when stood at the entrance deciding on whether to part with one's money, the walls ran out of paint; the staircase, its carpet; and first time guests, their faith in human nature. It also happened to be the point where the smell of inadequate plumbing first assaulted the nostrils. The only saving grace was that the hotel's decor would have appeared far worse than it did had there been any bulbs in the light sockets with which to illuminate the filth.

The numbers on the doors were displayed in cheap, self-adhesive metal labelling. Had they been of the slightly more expensive, raised variety, Chad and Bob might at least have been able to *read* their way along the darkened corridors as one might use Braille.

The unfeasibly large key fob – which had been presented to them on payment upfront – was covered in more paint than the door itself... the rusted key at the end of it, a passport to their

'I beg your pardon?'

'The painting by Mondrian...propped against your sofa...Is that how you encoded it...exactly as you're seeing it now?'

Norman stared at the canvas. 'Mondrian?...Er...yes!'

'It's upside down,' said Gabriel. 'Little wonder it didn't match.'

Norman tilted his head. *No wonder it had seemed familiar,* he thought. *But how could a work by Mondrian correspond to a piece of music by Schoenberg? That made even less sense. What was going on? And what on earth had this to do with saving the Universe?*

'All in good time,' said Gabriel. 'Now...perhaps you could rectify the problem.'

Norman shrugged. 'Piece of cake for a computer.' He called the picture up on his screen and flipped it, the process taking a fraction of a second.

Its re-encoding took a little longer.

When the computer had finally finished its task, Norman instructed it to compare the two files again. He closed his eyes and prepared himself for the agony of another *clang*.

Ting.

'It's worked!' he squealed, as *"FILES COMPATIBLE"* winked at him from the screen. 'Don't ask me how...but we've done it!'

Gabriel showed no emotion, causing Norman's excitement to trip over itself. 'Not quite...Now we get to the serious part. Get as much sleep as you can, Norman. It's going to be in even shorter supply during the coming weeks. There is much to be done. I shall return tomorrow and give you your next instructions.' He started to fade.

'No! Wait!' yelled Norman, in panic.

'You must learn to be patient,' came Gabriel's voice. 'Tomorrow will come soon enough.'

'It's not tomorrow I'm worried about!' shouted Norman. 'It's *today*. You can't go like that!'

The lights in the flat flickered as Gabriel re-emerged. *'Can't?'*

'Not that way...Please...It's Mister Oppenheimer. He's got to see you leave...otherwise he'll think you stayed the night and revoke my tenancy!'

263

'But then… I mean… *how?*' Norman's brain was struggling to keep up. 'How can a painted canvas possibly be an exact binary clone of something a composer had pulled from his imagination?'

Gabriel looked at Norman the way a loving parent might an inquisitive child. 'You ask too many questions, Norman. You will just have to accept that it is so.'

Norman was about to raise an objection when the computer gave a discordant *clang*.

He'd rather been hoping for a pleasant *ting*, along with the words *"FILES COMPATIBLE"* appearing on the screen.

"FILES INCOMPATIBLE" flashed mockingly at him.

'Is there a problem?' asked Gabriel, the vibrations from Norman's despondency hitting him like a tsunami.

'You could say that,' replied Norman. 'The files don't match.'

'*Ah…*' said Gabriel heavily.

'But I did everything *exactly* as you asked me to.'

'Including the calibration?'

'To the letter.'

'And you've pressed the right buttons?'

Norman looked at him disdainfully.

'Then… the error must be in your programming.'

Norman felt the hackles on the back of his neck begin to stir. He might be a complete and utter failure when it came to… well… almost everything really. But when it came to computer programming…

'I don't make mistakes,' he scowled, examining the lines of code on an adjacent screen.

'Norman?'

'In fact, it's far more likely the problem lies with your samples.'

'Norman.'

'I *thought* the chances of matching the two would be imposs_'

'NORMAN!'

His name vibrated through his body and terminated in his testicles.

'The Mondrian…' said Gabriel softly. 'Is that how you see it?'

now comes the crucial bit. I've devised a second program that'll check the binary files to see if they're identical.'

'Then, you'd better get on and use it. Time is of the essence and we have very little of it.'

Norman sat himself at the computer again. 'You do realise just how accurate these files would need to be to register as interchangeable?' he ventured.

Gabriel nodded.

'And that the odds of a painting's binary code corresponding *exactly* to that of an audio sample are fantastically astronomical?'

'A miracle, by your earthly standards,' agreed Gabriel.

Norman blew out his cheeks and instructed the computer to compare the two files.

There was an awkward silence whilst it made up its mind.

'I must say... I was surprised by the audio sample,' said Norman, circumnavigating the tension. 'I thought it might consist of mathematically generated sine waves... or something like that.'

Gabriel took a moment to reflect on the comment. 'I don't think it'd be very interesting for the listener if it did.'

'Interesting?' Norman looked perplexed. 'Surely that wasn't a consideration?'

'I think Mister Schoenberg might take issue with you there,' said Gabriel nonchalantly.

'Schoenberg?'

'Arnold.'

Norman looked at him blankly.

'The *composer*,' prompted Gabriel, his voice rising on the last syllable.

Norman still looked at him blankly

'It's one of his piano pieces.'

'But... I don't understand. I thought this was a scientific test. A matter of mathematics. I assumed the two samples had been generated from the same computer source and that all I'd be doing is reversing them!'

'From the same source, yes,' confirmed Gabriel. 'But who said anything about it being a computer?'

convert the assembled image into a binary code.

The sun, which had been marking time across an arc of faded carpet, had long been replaced by the artificial glow of a halogen street lamp by the time the words *file conversion complete* appeared on the screen again.

'Norman!'

Startled, Norman's eyes ricocheted around the room... ending up where they had started.

'Norman! It's me!'

The voice was Gabriel's, as clear as if he were standing just a few feet away.

But he wasn't.

'I can't see you!' shouted Norman. 'Where are you?'

'Where do you think? I'm outside on the landing. Let me in!'

Norman bolted towards the door and yanked it open.

'Remember what I said, Norman,' came Oppenheimer's voice from the hallway below. 'Your lady friend can't stay!'

'If I were capable of feelings, I'd be experiencing humiliation right now,' said Gabriel, floating past indignantly.

'Oppenheimer *saw* you?'

'I don't think he could really *miss* me!' exclaimed Gabriel. 'For some reason, he's chosen to visualise me wearing fishnet tights and an inappropriately-short, leather skirt. I wouldn't mind... but I wasn't even colour coordinated!'

'He thinks you're a woma_'

'Yes... thank you, Norman,' interjected Gabriel hastily. 'I was rather hoping he did. The alternative doesn't bear thinking about!'

Norman quickly closed the door. 'I'm sorry for any embarrassment. But look on the bright side... It's solved the problem of the electrical interference. I didn't get so much as a flicker.'

'Which is more than can be said for your landlord,' said Gabriel impassively. 'Now... I take it you've made use of what you were sent this morning.'

'The samples? Yes. I've just finished converting them. But

Deciding that random to the eye was acceptable, but random to the ear was painful, he settled himself in front of his computer and instructed it to convert the audio sample using his program. It immediately obliged and whirred into action, its hard drive fluttering dispassionately.

This was its beauty. No *ifs* and *buts*. It did as it was told. Without so much as a sniff of attitude, it began converting the sample into a single string of binary digits... a procession of noughts and ones that, in themselves, made up the immutable foundations of its universe.

The true miracle of computers is not that they can be used to send men into space, create virtual worlds or shrink the real one to the distance it takes a finger to confirm the sending of an e-mail... but that all these things can be achieved from a language consisting of just A and B... a condition of on or off... a question of yes or no... a state of *to be or not to be*.

Occasionally they got confused and had a minor breakdown... but then, mused Norman, didn't everybody?

He remained in his chair, mesmerised by the ceaseless flickering of the hard drive's LED. Eventually, it stopped its private chatter and the words *file conversion complete* appeared on the screen.

Now came the harder part.

Norman had rather hoped to be able to input the visual image into the computer using an ordinary flatbed scanner. But the scale of the canvas put paid to that.

It took a rummage through a box of redundant computer peripherals to provide the solution. It came in the form of his very first scanner, a hand-held affair that enabled the capture of an image in a series of separate strips which were then stitched together.

With no margin for error, the next couple of hours were spent painstakingly ensuring that each scanned strip perfectly matched its neighbour... pixel by pixel. By the time he'd finished, his brain felt as if it had been put through the full load cycle of a washing machine.

It was with relief that he finally instructed the program to objects didn't get delivered to your front door by a figment of your imagination.

The small package contained a compact disc, unbranded and unmarked. He placed it in the CD drive of his computer and waited for what he expected would be a series of orderly, computer-generated tones. But what leapt out from the speakers was anything but. His ears were assaulted by an amorphous barrage of notes recklessly lobbed from a piano, seemingly chosen at random and delivered without any regard to rhythm, form or melody. It was as if a cat, walking across a keyboard, had been frightened into a self-perpetuating dance by the performance of its paws.

Appreciating he only had to *convert* the sound, not *listen* to it, he switched it off and turned his attention to the crate. It would contain the audio sample's visual twin, he assumed.

Curiosity bursting, he examined the crate for an access point. The process took all of five seconds, the words *open here* clearly stencilled in red at one end.

What *hadn't* been stencilled was the fact you needed a crowbar to do so... and that it would take the best part of an hour should you have to resort to using a knife and fork, plastic spaghetti ladle and the cleaner end of a wooden toilet brush.

The best part of an hour later, Norman finally prised the side from the crate and got his first peek inside. Expertly encased between layers of packaging material was an artist's canvas, somewhat dwarfed by the crate itself.

Removing it carefully, he propped it against the sofa and attached the remains of a bacon sandwich to his heel as he stood back to get a better view.

The canvas was approximately two and a half feet square and had a number of straight, black lines horizontally and vertically traversing its white background. Some of the squares formed by the lines' intersections and the edges of the canvas had been filled with bright, simple colours. As a random pattern, Norman found it quite pleasing to the eye... something he considered might look nice on a duvet cover. It had a vaguely familiar look to it which he couldn't quite place.

'That'll do fine. Thanks.'

The crate was gently lowered to the ground… then backs straightened with professional caution.

Norman handed back the clipboard. He wasn't sure whether he was meant to tip for such a service. He thought he'd wait and see if the two men hovered expectantly.

'So… we'll see you tomorrow, then,' said the first courier, cheerily.

'At ten,' added the second.

Norman was confused. Did a loitered farewell count as a hover and, furthermore, why were they coming back?

'*Ten?*' he probed.

'To pick it up. At least, that's what it says 'ere.' The courier checked his clipboard. 'Were you expecting differently, sir?'

'Er… no… That's… exactly what I thought… So… see you tomorrow evening then.'

'Morning, sir.'

'Yes… Good morning to you too.' Norman attempted something resembling a polite bow.

'No… Morning, as in *tomorrow morning*, sir. That's what time we'll be back.'

'At ten,' chimed his partner, with a less than intelligent grin.

'Yes… I got that bit… thank you.' Norman felt a desperate need to close the door. He definitely wasn't a people person. Idiots came even further down his list.

The couriers turned as if to leave… then had a change of heart.

This was *serious* hovering, thought Norman.

'By the way… I'm Flowers… and this 'ere is Nobby.'

Nobby nodded.

Norman nodded back.

The acknowledgment over, the two men saw themselves out… tip-less.

Norman shut the door and took a few calming breaths. He was obviously now in possession of the audio and visual samples Gabriel had told him would test his program.

They were also irrefutable proof he wasn't going mad. Solid

269

commotion on the stairs in which the voices of two men parenthesised the sliding of a large object up them.

There was a knock on the door.

Norman drew a deep breath and prepared himself for contact with the outside world.

It turned out to be two heavily sweating, helmeted couriers... each one struggling with his end of a large, narrow wooden crate.

They seemed as surprised to see him as he was to see them... which struck Norman as very odd, given it was *they* who'd knocked on *his* door.

'Mister Penkridge?' said one, telegraphing his surprise with a backward jerk of the head.

'Yes?' said Norman cautiously.

'Mister *Norman* Penkridge?' asked the other, reading Norman's name from a clipboard with supporting disbelief.

'Yes?'

'And this is definitely 66c Armageddon Terrace?'

Norman couldn't help feeling it was a pretty stupid question. If it was his name on the clipboard, it'd be one hell of a coincidence to have encountered him at the *wrong* address. He nodded.

The courier with the clipboard slapped the top of the crate. 'In that case... this is for you.' He handed Norman his clipboard and pen. 'Just put yer cross on there, sir and print yer name below.' He pointed to a space on the delivery document which indicated that the crate had been sent from a company calling itself *Templar Resources*. 'It's two packages you're signing for.'

The second courier handed over a small, padded envelope. 'You may want us to bring this larger one in for you, sir. It's a bit on the 'eavy side.'

Norman gave a panicked glance back into his bedsit. 'Er... yes... just a second... I'll make some space.' He effected a stooped, half-turned retreat... doing his best to clear a path through the mess on the floor as he went.

'Will 'ere do, sir?' grunted the lead courier, as they reached the end of his trail and found themselves thwarted by the sofa.

radio. I need a contact number for the Mennonites in Pennsylvania.'

'What are you up to?'

'Let's just say... if we need to get past a wall of silence, perhaps we should employ a Trojan horse!'

As the four Amish gentlemen watched the van melt into the heat haze, one of them turned toward the others. 'Such a shame they felt it necessary to lie about their names.'

'That's not all they lied about,' said another. 'Did you see that surveillance paraphernalia in the back of their van?'

'Perhaps that's why they didn't take the easy option and offer us a lift,' said a third, brushing the dust from his broadfall trousers.

'Yes... very strange men,' added Jakob, replacing his hat.

* * *

Twenty-four hours had elapsed since Norman's last celestial visit... most of them spent refining and checking the code for his new program.

The only interruption – other than a few hours sleep – had been a second visit from Oppenheimer, who'd been sitting in his living room, the door into the hall wide open, waiting for Norman's *guest* to leave. When it had gotten to the early part of the evening without so much as a creak of a stair, his patience had finally snapped. He'd stormed up to Norman's room, cursing in his native tongue, demanding to be let inside. Norman had dutifully obliged, watching with amusement as his increasingly confused landlord searched every possible hiding place until, scarlet-faced, he'd been forced to concede that he must've been mistaken. But he'd left, warning Norman he wouldn't tolerate any future "abuse of his hospitality".

It was now ten o'clock the morning after, and Norman could hear voices in the hall downstairs. One of them sounded like Oppenheimer's... though the others were unfamiliar to him.

The muffled conversation was followed by a brief

colleague's eye.

'You can assist us with our more immediate problem, if you like,' said another of the Amish gentlemen, stepping in to change the conversation and giving Jakob a look of admonishment. 'We have the skills to rebuild our wheel, but they are worthless without tools and some fresh spokes.'

'Tools we have a plenty,' chirped Bob.

'But there isn't a tree for miles from which to cut the wood,' observed Jakob.

'Spokes we're a little short on,' admitted Bob.

'These gentlemen have enough already,' interjected Chad. 'All you need to do is remove two spokes from each of the remaining wheels, then use them to rebuild the broken one. As long as you take it easy, it should get you to the nearest town.'

There were unanimous nods of admiration.

'Simple, but effective!' exclaimed Jakob.

'He is, isn't he?' said Bob. 'I'll fetch the toolbox.'

The sun had passed its zenith by the time the repaired wheel was triumphantly slid onto its axle. The men embraced each other and shook Chad and Bob warmly by the hand.

'Now we must look at getting back,' said Jakob, unhooking his black, lapel-less jacket from the front of the buggy.

'Just remember to take it easy,' said Chad. 'There are only so many times you can pull this trick!'

'Daniel Dare and Quentin Mekon!' frowned Chad, as the van moved off. 'You were sailing a bit close to the wind with that one!'

'Like they're gonna know,' said Bob, giving a parting wave to the men outside.

'And so much for being covert. You should've told them we were scientists or something. I saw one of them taking an unhealthy interest in our equipment.'

'Relax,' said Bob confidently. 'You were right. They're living in another age. They wouldn't have a clue as to what this stuff was for. Talking of which… see if you can get command on the

272

it.'

Chad's facial expression was now so contorted, he was in danger of asphyxiating himself.

'Allow me to introduce myself,' Bob continued. 'I'm Daniel Dare and this is my partner Quentin Mekon.'

Chad managed a tortured smile in acknowledgement.

'We're the tail end of the security precautions for your meeting,' explained Bob. 'It was our job to ensure nobody eavesdropped on it. You've got to be so careful these days... haven't you Quentin?'

Quentin gave an embarrassed nod.

The Amish gentlemen dropped their guard. 'Then, you'll know we're a little late,' said one.

'It's all very awkward and rather embarrassing,' added Jakob. 'As representatives of our community, we thought it inappropriate to accept the transportation provided and elected to get ourselves to Arwan El Kahab by traditional means. Unfortunately... Herman isn't as young as he used to be and we had to keep stopping.'

'And which one of you is Herman?' enquired Chad, scouring their faces.

'The nearside horse,' replied Jakob. 'And then this happened!' He pointed to the wheel lying on the ground. 'We'd been continuing on in the hope that the meeting would last several days, given its immense importance. But seeing as you two gentlemen are making your way from it, I assume our efforts were in vain.'

"fraid so,' confirmed Chad.

'Though not entirely wasted,' chipped in Bob, a glint in his eye. 'We could put you in touch with some of those who attended the meeting, to discuss what occurred during your absence. Is there any particular group you'd feel more comfortable doing that with?'

'Maybe one from the wider Mennonite community,' replied Jakob keenly. 'Our histories are intertwined and they hail from our part of the country.'

'Then we'll assist you with that,' said Bob, catching his

273

answered our prayers for help... He has sent us our fellow countrymen!'

The assumption that the Lord should be praised for anything to do with the situation irritated Chad immensely. In his opinion... if you were foolish enough to assume that chance had played no part in it whatsoever, you were even more so not to think a benevolent God wouldn't have put you in this situation in the first place... and if he had, that the help he'd send would be a local wheelwright with appurtenant skills as opposed to two fellow Americans with absolutely none.

The four Amish gentlemen didn't seem bothered by such theological inconsistencies. They were already competing to shake the hand of Bob, who had gotten out of the van and was now standing by the remains of a shattered wheel pretending he dealt with this sort of emergency every day.

The problem was clear. One of the buggy's four wheels had struck a large rock, breaking eight of its twelve spokes. The men, though unhurt, were clearly going nowhere.

'You gentlemen seem to be a long way from home,' said Chad politely, joining his colleague. 'My partner thinks you might be missionaries... but I'd hazard a guess the congregation would be pretty sparse if you recruited them from these parts.'

The men looked at each other warily.

'We're on our way to a gathering,' said the oldest of the four, stepping forward and extending his hand in greeting. 'Or, more accurately, we *were*. I'm Jakob Johansson and these good men and I are representatives of the Old Order Amish Community.'

The remaining three gentlemen touched the brims of their straw hats in salutation.

'Then you must've been on your way to the gathering at Arwan El Kahab,' said Bob matter-of-factly.

He might as well have told them what each had eaten for breakfast that morning. Their look of surprise was only eclipsed by the look of anxiety that quickly replaced it... though it paled into insignificance compared to the one on Chad's face.

'You have knowledge of it?' said the elder awkwardly.

'More than that,' replied Bob brightly. 'We've just come from

'What's that... only half armed?'

'AMISH, idiot. You know... the religious sect from Pennsylvania the tourists gawp at... wide brimmed hats and Abraham Lincoln beards... don't believe in modern technology.'

'That's handy,' said Bob.

'Why?'

'They won't have guns.'

Chad shook his head. 'I didn't think they had communities out here.'

'Perhaps they're missionaries?'

'Who knows. Let's not get involved.'

Bob could now clearly see for himself four men standing around a large, circular object that was lying on the ground. As they drew nearer, one took off his hat and stepped into the road, waving it so as to flag them down.

'Too late,' said Bob. 'Looks like they need some help.'

As the van rolled to a halt, the hat-waver approached the driver's window with a mixed expression of desperation and relief. He smiled awkwardly. 'We,' he announced loudly in a tourist-abroad manner and thumping his chest vigorously, 'have big problem!'

'You sure do,' muttered Bob under his breath. '*We* have the guns.'

The stranger then began cavorting about as if holding the imaginary reins of an imaginary horse. The imaginary horse then appeared to have an imaginary heart attack, which – it transpired – was bad mime for a non-imaginary wheel coming off a non-imaginary cart. 'No go! No go!' he shouted fervently... then stared and awaited a reaction.

Bob's was surprise that a man whose religious beliefs forbade him from watching television should be so bad at a parlour game like *charades*. 'And which part of Pennsylvania are you from?' he enquired. 'I recognise the accent, but the syntax is a little more difficult to place.'

The Amish gentleman looked stunned. 'You're American?' he asked incredulously, then turned towards his companions with raised hands. 'Praise the Lord!' he exulted. 'He has not only

275

possible – with odds of only three hundred and sixty-five to one – the date for that meeting was chosen by chance and the location because it was remote, secret and neutral. We can't discount *anything*. However... in the absence of anything better to go on, I suggest we tiptoe along the assumption it *is* important and see where it leads. Perhaps we should start by examining the history of this area and its archaeology. Whoever had the knowledge and skill to fashion those crystals the way they did must've caused ripples around here. Someone, somewhere must've left a record of what they were up to.'

Bob gave the steering wheel a slap. 'Great! We get unlimited expenses and you wanna spend them rooting around some dusty library?'

'A bit of culture might do you good.'

'A few weeks on a beach would do me better.'

'Find one with a library next to it and I'll consider it.'

'Perhaps I'll find a way to crack the wall of silence first,' said Bob. 'Sounds like it might be more exciting.'

They had been travelling in silence for about half an hour when Bob suddenly lifted his foot from the accelerator.

'Problem?' enquired Chad, looking up from a map.

'Not sure,' said Bob, squinting hard through the windscreen as the van began to slow. 'It's difficult to make out through this heat haze... but it looks like there's something stationary blocking the road ahead.'

Chad instinctively checked the holster beneath his trouser leg... then jumped into the back of the van. 'Don't stop,' he said, making a grab for the binoculars. 'Just take it nice and slow.'

'Could be a mule and cart,' said Bob, shielding his eyes from the sun's glare.

'They're horses,' announced Chad from behind. 'And it's a buggy. There are some guys standing by it... they've spotted us... they're pointing.'

'Can you make out if they're armed?' asked Bob, slowing the vehicle to a crawl.

'Armed, no,' replied Chad calmly. 'Amish, yes.'

victim of an horrific shooting – wasted no time in reacting with maximum force.

*   *   *

The road from the temple at Arwan El Kahab was not an easy one. Getting on it was simple enough... *Staying* on it required a little more effort. If the wheels of your vehicle were not being drawn into the spine-wrenching potholes that littered its route, the chances are they were being forced over the residue that should've been in them in the first place.

Even if you managed to avoid these unforgiving obstacles, you still had to cope with the sheer monotony of the terrain through which it ran.

Ask any shepherd.

Chad and Bob tried to keep their minds occupied by reviewing the options for their next move. The problem was... there didn't appear to be many.

It was accepted that, short of Bob taking holy orders and infiltrating the Church as a fifth columnist – in which case, his constant use of the word *friggin'* might present a problem – there was little that could be done against a total wall of silence.

'We need to find a way to break it,' insisted Bob.

'In the meantime... let's work on what we've got,' suggested Chad. 'April twenty-third. Whoever built that temple went to an awful lotta trouble to mark that date. If it meant so much to them, it could be our next clue.'

'*Could?*' exclaimed Bob. 'You've got the Supreme Being's entire sales team turning up to celebrate the friggin' thing and you think there's a possibility for *doubt?*'

'There's always a possibility for *anything*... including coincidence. Let's not run away with ourselves. We've worked together long enough for you to know my golden rule.'

'I know, I know,' groaned Bob wearily. '*Find the connection beyond coincidence.*'

'Precisely... It's the only guarantee we don't get blown off-course by a quirk of fate posing as something grander. It's just

Lambert's cherry pie in the day room for the Monsignor. But be as quick as you can because he's got to run.'

There was a silence.

'Are you there, Miss Gusset?'

'Yes, sir.'

'Did you hear what I said?'

'I'm not sure, sir.'

'Which bit are you not sure about?'

There was another silence.

'All of it.'

'Right... Listen carefully, Miss Gusset... I said... Piece... of... pie... please... in... the... day... room.'

There was the sound of heavy breathing from the intercom.

'Did you get that Miss Gusset?'

'Oh, yes...! I certainly did, sir!'

'And Miss Gusset?'

'Sir?'

'Be as quick as you can. The Monsignor's got to run.'

There was a yelp from the intercom before it went dead.

'Strange woman!' said Snogden-Lambert, sitting back in his chair. 'I'm sure she's not all there.'

It was approximately five minutes later when a team of specialist armed police officers smashed their way through the office door and wrestled a shocked Monsignor Hoff violently to the ground. Peter Snogden-Lambert looked on in frozen horror as his protesting visitor was sat upon, handcuffed and ordered to be silent by a number of highly-strung men from behind fully-loaded guns. Miss Gusset viewed proceedings from the doorway – safe in the considerable arms of Brian the security guard – her white blouse stained red. To her dying day, she would swear she heard Peter Snogden-Lambert utter the words "*Peter Piper's in the grey room*" and then tell her to be as quick as she could because "*the Monsignor's got a gun*". In her panic to alert security, she'd grabbed for the phone and inadvertently tipped Mrs Snogden-Lambert's cherry pie over the front of her blouse. On their arrival, the police – assuming she'd been the

The two men looked at each other.

'Look... before you go, Monsignor Hoff... About earlier...
I...'

'Is that the time?' said the Monsignor hastily, glancing at his
wristwatch. 'I'd better get a move on. I'm supposed to be in Paris
this afternoon to discuss the loan of some French paintings
from the Louvre.'

'Yes... of course. Feel free to use one of our telephones if
you'd rather call your office before you leave. There's one in the
staff day room. I'll make sure you're not disturbed.'

'That *would* be useful.'

Had Snogden-Lambert left it at that, he might eventually
have retired a happy and contented man... the memory of the
day's unfortunate misunderstanding comfortably faded by the
passage of time. But fate can be exceptionally cruel... no more so
than when it demonstrates it has a sense of humour.

'I would have thought you must be getting hungry by now,
Monsignor Hoff? Perhaps I could organise some lunch before
you go?'

'That's very kind... but I'll grab something on the way to the
airport.'

'I'll hear of no such thing! My wife sent me off to work this
morning with one of her delicious homemade cherry pies and I
insist you avail yourself of a slice or two! She'd be most
disappointed if you didn't!'

'I really must be going.'

'Nonsense... I'll get my secretary to put some in the day
room. You can enjoy it whilst you're making your call. It won't
take a minute.'

The Monsignor looked apprehensive. 'Perhaps just a small
slice, then.'

Snogden-Lambert flashed an exaggerated smile and pressed
the button on his intercom. 'Miss Gusset?'

'Sir?'

'Can you hear me?'

'Pardon?'

'Listen... I'd like you to put a piece of Mrs Snogden-

279

into a passing black hole.

The two men attempted to iron out the minutiae of their deal, whilst doing their best to avoid making eye contact with each other. The floor had never felt so popular.

For Snogden-Lambert, there was only one thing worse than totally humiliating yourself in front of a complete stranger and then having to continue discussions alone with them in a room for a couple of hours... and that was totally humiliating yourself in front of a complete stranger and then having to continue discussions alone with them in a room for a couple of hours whilst pretending nothing had happened.

The tea-break had been the worst... there ensuing tortured minutes of biscuit dunking in excruciating silence... a silence broken only by the occasional slurp and chink of teaspoons upon best china.

But what could the gallery director have done? That brief window of opportunity when a grovelled apology might have had some effect had passed in the blinking of a non-contactable eye.

Would things have been any better had he explained to the Monsignor that he had simply mistaken him for the accomplice of a lunatic, urine-stained tramp?

He somehow didn't think so.

To say the two men negotiated the rest of the agreement would be something of a kindness to Snogden-Lambert. The Monsignor let it be known on what terms he would like things to be done and Snogden-Lambert sycophantically acquiesced. The gallery director had made enough waves to sink his career and – whilst attempting to appear composed above surface – was paddling like mad below to reach calmer waters.

The two men battled on through an air of strained cordiality until everything that needed to be discussed had been.

'I think we've covered all the relevant points, Mister Snogden-Lambert. I'll now make contact with my office and inform them of the details.'

'Right you are... Well... splendid... I'll put things into motion my end and see it all runs smoothly.'

PHONE!'

There was a period of silence, interspersed with some distorted snivelling and nose blowing.

'Line one, sir.'

Snogden-Lambert picked up his phone. 'Yes... hello. This is Peter Snogden-Lam... ... Yes, that's right... I'm phoning regarding your representative who I'm expecting to meet today.' He eyed his visitor contemptuously. 'We've been having a slight problem with the local fruit-cake community and I was wondering if you were now in a position to furnish me with the name of your man and what time we could be expecting him to call...?' There was a pause, followed by a look of surprise on Snogden-Lambert's face. He glanced at his wristwatch. 'Then he should be here by now... No... No, he hasn't... Are you sure about that...? Yes... His name...? Oh...!' The colour drained from Snogden-Lambert's cheeks as blood deserted them the way rats might a sinking ship. It also deserted the rest of his head, brain, legs and anything else that might stand accused of being associated with him. He glanced at his visitor who was glaring incandescently back at him. 'I see...' he continued, his voice beginning to falter. 'Yes... Monsignor Hoff... Of course... Dick Hoff... And the reason for the exhibition... Saint Pedalo... Yes, I've heard of him. Patron saint of beach entertainment, I believe... That's correct... Yes... I bet they will... make a change from renting deckchairs... well thank you... you've been most helpful... Goodbye.'

Snogden-Lambert carefully replaced the receiver on its cradle.

'Miss Gusset,' he said sweetly into the intercom. 'How's that tea coming along?'

The next two hours were the hardest and longest of Peter Snogden-Lambert's entire life... not that they exactly skipped by for his visitor either.

The pendulum attached to the clock of life swung as if made of some super-heavyweight element yet to be discovered in a far off galaxy... an element so heavy it could refuse to be drawn cheek, à la Shirley Temple. 'And will they be turning up with their heads wrapped in tin foil...? Or will you be the one adopting that particular mode of attire, *Monsignor* Hoff? Might brighten up that dreary cassock you're wearing... Not exactly this year's fashion, is it...? Get it in a fancy dress shop, did we?'

The Monsignor looked at him, horrified. 'I beg your pardon!' he exclaimed, rising to his feet.

'SIT DOWN AND DON'T MOVE!' bellowed Snogden-Lambert, aggressively stabbing his finger at the chair.

The Monsignor instinctively did as he was told.

Snogden-Lambert calmly placed his other finger on the intercom button. 'Miss Gusset. Would you kindly get the Vatican on the phone, please.'

'Pardon?'

'Get... the... Vatican... on... the... phone.'

'Too much pie!'

Snogden-Lambert gave the intercom another thump.

'Say that again, Miss Gusset. It sounded like "*too much pie*".'

'That's right.'

'What is?'

'Too much pie.'

'WHAT?'

'That's what I said, sir... Too much pie.'

'PIE?'

'Yes, sir... Pie as in the cherry pie you brought in with you this morning.'

Snogden-Lambert felt his nerves trembling as one might feel the earth vibrating shortly before a colossal earthquake.

'I KNOW WHAT A BLOODY PIE IS, MISS GUSSET! I WAS SLIGHTLY CURIOUS AS TO WHY YOU MENTIONED ONE!'

An unusual sound emanated from the intercom. If it hadn't been hurled across the room the previous day, it would have been recognisable as Miss Gusset crying.

'You said you were getting fat again on your own,' she blubbed.

'I SAID... GET... THE... VATICAN... ON... THE...

282

The Monsignor appeared to take a mental deep breath. 'Beach entertainment.'

Snogden-Lambert looked at him askance. 'Beach entertainment?' Not only did the gallery director smell a rat, he was sure he could detect a fart from the very Pied Piper himself. Did this man take him for a complete imbecile, he wondered? Firstly... his name shortened to an obscenity. Secondly... he was asking him to believe that the Vatican intended organising a major exhibition at only a week's notice. And thirdly... it was to celebrate a saint who had about as much to do with the world of art as Mister Snogden-Lambert had to do with Mrs Snogden-Lambert these days. Was this the latest craze... impersonating Vatican officials? Mind you... at least this one had bothered to dress the part.

'Is he really?' said Snogden-Lambert sarcastically. 'So... I suppose you'll be holding this exhibition at the end of a pier, then... will you?'

The Monsignor looked puzzled. 'Actually... we were thinking of a central London location.'

'Oh... what a good idea!' gushed Snogden-Lambert derisively. 'You could cover the floor with sand and hang a volleyball net between the Gainsborough and the Hockney.'

There was yet another awkward silence whilst the Monsignor considered how best to react to the gallery director's strange outbursts.

'Did I tell you we've managed to secure a sponsor?' he asked brightly, deciding it better to soothe a savage beast than prod it with a stick.

'Really?' said Snogden-Lambert, stretching out the word with as much cynicism as possible. 'And who might that be?'

Snogden-Lambert's demeanour was now so extraordinary, the Monsignor felt reluctant to continue the conversation. 'The National Association of Deckchair Attendants,' he said slowly.

Snogden-Lambert closed his eyes in wearied disgust. *Was there no depth at which this man would stop digging?* 'Of course! Silly me!' he cooed in a voice better suited to attracting the attention of a baby in a pram. He placed a single finger to his

283

'No… Not lunatics.'

'Then surely we must be talking about Saint Angelico.'

'We must? Why?'

'Patron saint of artists?'

'As a matter of fact, we're not.'

Snogden-Lambert marshalled his enthusiasm again. 'In that case… it must be Saint Bernward, the patron saint of painters?'

The Monsignor shook his head.

'Saint Anthony the Abbott… patron saint of *brush makers?*' He was getting desperate.

'I'm afraid it isn't.'

Snogden-Lambert considered the dwindling possibilities.

'I take it they have *some* connection with the art world, though?'

The Monsignor thought awhile. 'Not that I can think of.'

'An association with the subjects in the paintings, perhaps?'

The Monsignor thought again. 'Highly unlikely.'

Snogden-Lambert found his enthusiasm running down like a clockwork toy in the last throes of an unwound spring.

'The patron saint of exhibitions, maybe?'

'Is there one?'

Snogden-Lambert shrugged.

The Monsignor looked at him awkwardly.

'Perhaps it would be best if you put me out of my misery,' suggested Snogden-Lambert gently.

'It's…' The Monsignor appeared to give the answer some consideration before parting with it. '…Saint Pedalo.'

'Saint *Pedalo?*' said Snogden-Lambert warily. 'I don't believe I've heard of him.'

'No… erm… not a lot of people have. That's one of the reasons we're holding the exhibition. To bring attention to his great work.'

'And what's he the patron saint of?'

There was another silence.

The Monsignor looked uncomfortable.

Snogden-Lambert beckoned him with expectant eyes to share some of that discomfort.

remarkably soothing effect upon Snogden-Lambert's heavily furrowed brow.

'Far be it for me to criticise your method of operation, Monsignor Hoff,' he said, raising his hands in submission and visualising the amount he would be expecting for such obsequiousness. 'I'm sure if God can build the entire world in six days, seven should be enough for His Church to hang a few works of art on the wall.'

'You must understand, Mister Snogden-Lambert, that being an anniversary, we cannot simply move the date to a later one. Having decided to run with this project, we must do exactly that… run!'

'And who exactly are we running *for?*'

'I'm sorry?'

'This saint whose canonisation you're celebrating? I assume he must be one of the big boys?'

'Big boys?'

'Yes… I mean… he must be one of the more important saints for you to go to all this trouble.'

'There's no such thing as an *unimportant* saint,' said the Monsignor stiffly. 'And I don't think Saint Margaret of Antioch would have liked to have heard herself described as "one of the big boys".'

'Feminist, was she?'

'The patron saint of women, actually.'

'So this exhibition is to celebrate *her?*'

'I was making a point… that not all our saints are male. As with the case of Saint Christina the Astonishing.'

'*Astonishing*, eh?… And is she the patron saint of anything?'

'Lunatics,' replied the Monsignor coldly, with an emphasis on the word that made the gallery director rather uncomfortable.

'Ah…' said Snogden-Lambert, raising a solitary finger. 'Then would I be right in thinking that the saint you're honouring is the patron saint of something or other?'

'You would.'

'*Lunatics?*' enquired Snogden-Lambert delicately.

fact Snogden-Lambert found curious.

'Well... we haven't really considered that there should be a theme, as such... More...' The Monsignor gazed upwards as if he might find the words he was looking for floating in the air. 'More... a general celebration of art.'

Snogden-Lambert scrutinised his notes.

'But it says here that the exhibition is to mark an anniversary.'

The Monsignor shifted uncomfortably in his seat.

'Yes...' he replied slowly, drawing the word out as if to give himself time to think. 'I suppose it could be considered both a celebration of art... and an anniversary.'

Snogden-Lambert's eyes narrowed to slits again. 'An anniversary of *what*, exactly?'

'The... anniversary of... the canonisation of one of our saints,' replied the Monsignor diffidently, adding swiftly, 'Now, perhaps we should discuss delivery dates.'

'Very well,' said Snogden-Lambert guardedly, his eyes scrutinising the Monsignor's comportment. 'When do you intend holding this exhibition?'

The Monsignor started fiddling with a large silver cross that was hanging from his neck. 'Actually... we were thinking of next week.'

Snogden-Lambert's head twitched in disbelief. For a moment he thought he was suffering from *buggered intercom syndrome* again. 'Next week?' he spluttered in a pitch a full octave above his normal. 'Did I hear you correctly, Monsignor Hoff?'

'Well... yes... if that's not a problem for you. We're looking to get started as soon as we can.'

'I should think you are! We allow at *least* six *months* to organise one of our exhibitions. It usually takes a week to decide on the price of the brochure!'

'I appreciate it's all a little bit last minute,' said the Monsignor quickly. 'But we were hoping that our financial contribution would take into account any inconvenience such a short timescale may cause you and your gallery.'

The words "financial contribution" seemed to have a

quickly but quietly charged at her like a tip-toeing rhinoceros.

'*Don't you dare use the mugs,*' he hissed through clenched teeth, then swung around, teeth still clenched, a broad smile on his face.

Miss Gusset made her escape.

'To business,' said Snogden-Lambert brightly, settling himself in his chair. 'Now... It's my understanding, Monsignor Hoff, that your Church is interested in borrowing a number of our paintings for an exhibition you intend holding... and that these would be required for a period of... let me see...' He glanced at some scribbled notes in front of him. 'Three weeks.'

'That is correct. And in return, we would be happy to loan your gallery a comparable number of paintings from the Vatican's private collection.'

Snogden-Lambert coughed awkwardly.

'Along with a sizeable monetary donation,' added the Monsignor.

Snogden-Lambert doodled a large, thick *tick* on the paper and sat back in his chair. 'Then I think we have the basis of a deal beneficial to both parties,' he announced smugly. 'Now... before we discuss delivery dates, insurance issues, security concerns, etcetera, etcetera, there is one question I've been dying to ask you.' He peered at his notes again. 'Given the rather... shall we say... *disparate* selection of paintings you've requested, I was wondering as to the theme of your exhibition.'

The Monsignor looked at him blankly. 'I'm sorry?'

Snogden-Lambert ran the question back in his mind to check it was as straightforward as he had initially assumed it to be.

'The theme, Monsignor Hoff... The concept behind the project? After all... you'll be exhibiting works of art that range from the old masters to the modernists... and whilst ours are mostly those of British painters, I was given the impression by your office that they are to be displayed alongside paintings from the Church's own collection, as well as those from many of our foreign counterparts. I was wondering, therefore, what could possibly tie all of these paintings together?'

The Monsignor seemed to be struggling with the question, a

administer absolution. Having satisfied himself that these fingers had never had to rummage about in a litter bin for breakfast, he continued his inspection along his visitor's arm, shooting up briefly to a rather puzzled face and then all the way down to a well-polished pair of shoes. Everything seemed in order. Very neat and tidy, with the added reassurance of a slight smell of soap. Snogden-Lambert relaxed his hunched shoulders and offered his own hand in return.

'Dick Hoff,' said his visitor.

'I beg your pardon?' exclaimed Snogden-Lambert, snatching it back.

His visitor looked at him uneasily.

'Monsignor Richard Hoff... Senior Exhibitions Adviser to the Church of Rome... I was under the impression you were expecting me.'

Snogden-Lambert tilted his head to one side and viewed his visitor through narrowed eyes.

'You're not Italian,' he said suspiciously.

The Monsignor smiled diplomatically. 'No, I'm not. And neither is the Pope! It's a large church, Mister Snogden-Lambert. We get about a bit!'

Snogden-Lambert glanced across at Miss Gusset, who was trying her best to look detached from the proceedings rather than embarrassed by them. He suddenly felt foolish. The Monsignor was clearly who he said he was... and given the opportunity this meeting afforded the gallery, he needed to pull himself together.

'You must pardon my inquisitorial nature, Monsignor Hoff. Only, we had a rather unfortunate... *incident*... here yesterday.'

He flashed a daggered stare at Miss Gusset, who flashed hers towards a large hole that Donald Tucker-Jenkins had kicked in the decorative latticework surround that used to hide the radiator.

'Please take a seat. I'll get my secretary to bring us some tea.' He nodded at Miss Gusset to do just that, discreetly mouthing the words "*best china*" at her. She, in turn, mouthed back the word "*pardon?*" then recoiled in fear as Snogden-Lambert not Watt and he's definitely never been knighted.'

Snogden-Lambert continued lowering his head until his brow was a few inches above the desktop.

'Miss Gusset?' he whimpered.

'Sir?'

'Would you ask him if he's from the Vatican.'

'Sorry, sir... that last bit again?'

'Is... he... from... the... Vatican?'

'No, sir... it's not that prat again. I think it might be the real person this time.'

Snogden-Lambert began banging his head repeatedly on the desk.

'Excuse me, sir? I think there's something wrong with my intercom. It seems to be making a knocking noise.'

'Send him in, would you please, Miss Gusset,' muttered Snogden-Lambert under his breath.

There was another silence.

'I'll send him in then, shall I?'

Snogden-Lambert stopped hurting himself and sat upright. He shook another two pills from the container and swallowed them quickly. Having patted what little hair he had into place, he adjusted his collar and tie... then placed both hands, palms down, on his desk.

The door opened to reveal Miss Gusset alongside a gentleman in his late fifties, ecclesiastically attired in a black cassock.

'The gentleman from the Vatican to see you, sir.' she announced, showing him in.

Snogden-Lambert smiled painfully and rose to greet his visitor.

'Ah... Mister Snogden-Lambert!' said the Vatican's representative warmly, extending his hand. 'It's so kind of you to see me at such short notice.'

Snogden-Lambert nodded in acknowledgement, but kept *his* hand firmly by his side. He examined his visitor's fingernails. They were clean and well-manicured, and attached to the fingers of a hand that looked like its only daily toil was to

'CHECK HIS NAME, MISS GUSSET! JUST CHECK HIS BLOODY NAME!'

Snogden-Lambert reached into the central drawer of his desk and grabbed a small, white container. He prised off the top and shook out one of the pills inside. His nerves had never been his strong point and yesterday's episode with Tucker-Jenkins had left them considerably weakened. Even the phantom conducting of a full performance of Mozart's Clarinet Concerto had failed to soothe them completely. Mrs Snogden-Lambert had tried to do her best, sending him to work that morning with a freshly-baked cherry pie, his favourite comfort food. It was currently sat on Miss Gusset's desk, away from early morning temptation. His nerves hadn't been helped by another telephone call from the Vatican informing him that a representative would call that day to discuss the loan of paintings. Unfortunately, the caller wasn't in a position to tell him the name of their representative or, indeed, the time he would be arriving. Snogden-Lambert had instructed Miss Gusset to put a large line through his diary for that day and to keep it free of appointments. This would be an important meeting. There was a lot at stake for the gallery, both in prestige and monetary considerations. He couldn't afford any mistakes. This time he'd make sure he was conversing with the real thing. If his visitor had so much as a hint of dandruff...

The intercom crackled and what sounded like "*I've chucked his gnome*" came out.

'I take it you've checked his name,' said Snogden-Lambert brusquely.

There was a brief silence.

'That's what I've just said, sir.'

'What is it?'

'Er... no... it's not.'

'Not what?'

'No, sir.'

Snogden-Lambert's head dropped.

'No, sir... what?' he said slowly.

'Just a second.' There was another pause. 'He says his name's

'*And* a totally free hand.'

'Then let's use it to get outta here!' Bob opened the driver's door and hoisted himself into the cab. 'Another night spent in this friggin' van together and I'll be able to claim palimony!'

'Another night spent in this van together and I'll be able to claim psychological abuse,' countered Chad, clambering into the passenger seat.

The entomological life forms, for whom the temple was home, scuttled for cover as the van exited the courtyard at speed, a plume of dust trailing behind. By the time the last speck had settled, all that could be heard was the sound of cicadas breaking through the heat.

Had the two men bothered to glance back, they might just have made out the figure of an old man, dressed from head to toe in white, watching them leave from the shadows of the courtyard wall.

* * *

Peter Snogden-Lambert gave the intercom a thump with the side of his fist.

'Could you say that again, Miss Gusset. Only it sounded like *"your fist is in my ear"!*'

'I said... your visitor's here.'

The intercom sounded like a provincial train station's public address system at the best of times. But since having been sent flying across the room by a recalcitrant Donald Tucker-Jenkins – prior to Brian the security guard engaging him in a headlock – it was all but useless.

'Right... Before you send him in, could you make sure he is who he says he is.'

'Sorry, sir...What was that last bit?'

'THAT HE IS WHO HE SAYS HE IS.'

'Thirty years to be sexiest?'

'Pardon?'

'You want me to make sure he's got thirty years to be sexiest?'

other an eminent physician. Career choice… anything that didn't run the risk of working in their considerable shadows. Determined to prove he made the right decision and win their approval and admiration… How am I doing?'

'I prefer it when you're being funny.'

'Okay… Try this. How come I've got overactive sweat glands on every part of my friggin' body except the roof of my mouth? I've got so much sand in my underpants, my balls feel like they're on vacation. My armpits smell like the inside of a Turkish wrestler's jockstrap and you're about to suggest we hang around here until we discover why nothing whatsoever happened. Curious thing is… I know I should be, but I ain't laughing.' Bob strode off forcefully towards the front of the van.

'Who said anything about staying?' shouted Chad after him. 'We've done all we can here. We can go wherever we like on this one, just so long as we come up with some answers at the end of it.'

Bob – who'd been about to reach for the driver's door – froze.

'That's right,' said Chad. 'I was on the radio whilst you were taking a dump. They've given us total *carte blanche* to get to the bottom of this matter and discover what's going on. It's up to us how we go about it. But this is the best bit…' Chad's face erupted into an uncontrollable grin. 'They've sanctioned unlimited expenses!'

Bob's eyebrows shot up his forehead as far as they could without detaching themselves. 'Are you serious?'

'Absolutely!'

'No friggin' way!'

'Friggin' way, Bob! This one must be rattling the powers that be even more than we thought! Seems they're prepared to throw everything at it.'

'But that don't make sense… The last I heard, there was more slashing going on around departmental budgets than Jack the Ripper in a brothel. What's with the sudden change of heart?'

'Someone at the top's obviously pulling strings,' said Chad.

Bob let out a low whistle. 'Unlimited expenses, you say?'

With that, Gabriel faded… leaving Norman to wonder who *the* untidiest had belonged to.

*　　*　　*

'Are you serious?' asked Bob, slamming shut the largest of the van's external lockers.

'Absolutely,' replied Chad, stuffing the remains of a US Government issue chocolate ration into his mouth.

The two men had spent yet another night within the confines of the temple walls, having deemed it prudent to wait until daylight before tackling the difficult road back to civilisation. The aircrew from the helicopter had taken pity on them and donated their emergency food rations, along with a few extra blankets.

Bob shook his head irritably. 'But what else is there to investigate? I thought we'd solved the mystery of the goddam lights.'

'The lights, maybe. But we're still no nearer knowing what those guys intended discussing before they got themselves spooked.'

'Let me see,' said Bob with telegraphed sarcasm. 'Could that be because clairvoyance ain't included in our job description?'

'Not good enough for those back home, Bob. Why d'ya think they put *us* on this case in the first place?'

'Because we sweat less than anyone else?'

'Not true in your case. Try… because we're the best team they've got. Pure and simple. And I don't intend letting that change.'

'Or letting anyone down,' added Bob.

'Precisely. We've got a reputation within the department to maintain.'

'I wasn't talking about the department. I was talking about *you*… and your family.'

'What's my family got to do with anything?'

'Everything! After all… Chad Cheadle… only child… needing to prove something to his folks… one a hotshot attorney… the what Gabriel had just told him, the reason for him standing in it in the first place – he was understandably perturbed. 'But how can you be so sure we'll destroy ourselves?' he exclaimed.

'Because you've been stubbornly working at it for thousands of years,' replied Gabriel matter-of-factly.

'But we could stop!' insisted Norman.

'Which is where you come in. Now… how have you gotten on with the task I set?'

Norman's expression brightened as his own ego got the better of him, oblivious of the irony. 'I've almost finished! It took me a while to work out the best way to ensure the correct correlation of light to sound, but I think I've found the solution. It was simply a question of…'

'I'm pleased to hear it,' Gabriel interrupted him. 'Once the program is completed, you'll need to test it.'

'Test?' The enthusiasm fell from Norman's face. In his excitement to achieve what had been asked of him, he'd failed to consider how such a thing could be done.

'Of course!' said Gabriel. 'The mathematics must be infallible. Just one frequency out of place with your correlation and our entire mission will come to nothing.'

'But… how…'

'Don't worry. We have prepared everything. Tomorrow you will take delivery of two packages. The first will contain an audio recording, the second a picture. Both must be encoded using your program. If it has been compiled correctly in accordance with my instructions, you will find both codes to be identical. Do you think you'll be ready by tomorrow?'

Norman tried to visualise when tomorrow might be. He had completely lost track of time. 'I'll do my best.'

'We know,' said Gabriel. 'That is why we chose you. Now… I should leave you to finish your work. Oh… and Norman… one final thing.'

'Yes?'

'When you have… perhaps you might like to think about cleaning your flat. It almost wins the prize for the untidiest abode I've ever encountered!'

will. For the true essence of that soul is love, and it is love's nature to give... to create light where there is darkness and bring things into being.' Gabriel took a cursory look at his wings. 'Given your upbringing, you'd be best to think of that love as God and the oneness of soul as Heaven.' His countenance darkened. 'But that gift has been abused. For, in experiencing the materialisation of spirit, those points of soul have indulged that illusion of individuality and created the concept of ego. It has caused them to forget their true nature, so wrapped up have they become in material distractions and flattered by a false sense of power. In believing themselves to be separate from their true source, they have inadvertently allowed a dangerous element to come into being. Evil.'

At this point, the heavenly choir was brought to an abrupt halt by the banging of a broom handle on the ceiling below.

Norman winced sympathetically.

'Where was I?' muttered Gabriel, momentarily distracted. 'Ah, yes... evil.' The music started up again, a little quieter than before. 'That negative force has become the expression of the most distant of those souls... those that have fallen the furthest from grace. Through your history, more advanced souls have been sent to walk amongst the wayward ones and enlighten them as to their true state. But it can take many life lessons for a corrupted soul to regain its purity. You call it reincarnation. Though the entire process requires aeons to complete, time was not considered a problem, as it is only a concept of your own making. What *is* a problem is that, due to man's selfish nature, your planet's now running out of it, and if those life lessons aren't completed before it's destroyed, Heaven will remain forever fragmented and the infallibility of love will no longer be law. The infallibility of Evil will take its place and bring about the destruction of all things. Given the Universal truth will be an *untruth*... God will cease to exist.'

Whilst God had ceased to exist for Norman many years earlier, he still believed in love... even if he'd experienced little of it in his life. Furthermore... given the destruction of all things meant the bedsit in which he was standing – and, from

295

Norman seemed to question every word he uttered without accepting! 'There you go again with your *either or* logic.' He gave a patient sigh. 'Look, Norman... When your door is open, what do you see?'

Norman deliberated for some time. To him, it had the hallmarks of a trick question. But unable to think of an alternative answer, he offered the obvious one.

'The landing?'

'Correct. Because the rays of light reflected from its surface tell you it's there. But what do you see when the door is closed?'

.... Nope. He'd have to go with the obvious again.

'The door?'

'Precisely... You can't see the landing through the door because its molecules – vibrating at a different frequency – are stopping the rays of light from passing through. But those blocked light frequencies are no more capable of making a noise as they strike it than I am. I'm as bound by the laws of nature as everything else. In order to knock, I'd have to raise my frequency to such a level as to become totally immersed in your Earth plane. And that wouldn't do... for it was just such an occurrence that got us into this mess in the first place!'

'Knocking on a door?'

'You can forget the door now, Norman,' said Gabriel, a slight irritation creeping into his voice. 'I'm referring to tasting the sins of the flesh.'

Norman scratched the tip of his ear. Doors he could cope with. He'd grasped the analogy and had felt comfortable. Sins of the flesh... now that was something else. He'd actually experienced *doors*. 'Sorry... I'm afraid you've lost me.'

'Then I'll explain. After all... it's the reason we're having this conversation in the first place.'

Despite an absence of cherubs, a heavenly choir sounded forth with all its majesty.

'In truth, Norman Penkridge, you are no more solid than I am. You are the imagination of a greater soul experiencing itself subjectively from a myriad of vantage points. Your sense of self is merely one such point given the gift of free spiritual beings vibrate at a different frequency. In order to communicate with you, we have to raise it until it's within a range your brains can perceive. It's as we're stepping up through the Earth plane's lower frequencies that the problems occur. There's no way around it, I'm afraid... short of materialising outside in the street and walking up the stairs.'

Norman looked at him expectantly.

'What?' exclaimed Gabriel.

'Not that I'm advocating you go as far as the pavement, of course,' hastened Norman. 'Perhaps you could try the hallway or something?'

Gabriel held his stare of disapproval. 'It's *highly* irregular,' he glowered. 'I mean...'

Norman shrugged and tried his best to look sympathetic. It was enough to direct the Archangel's protestations into a *cul-de-sac*.

'Well... so is the situation, I suppose. If it means an end to your problem, I'll have to give it a go. Just one thing, though... When I get to your door, I won't be able to knock. It's the old problem with solids, you see.'

'Can't you just sort of... float through?'

'Norman! I'm a heavenly messenger, not a ghost!'

'Isn't it all the same sort of thing.'

'It most definitely is not!' Gabriel ruffled his wings. 'I'm very much a living entity, thank you, albeit in a different energy form to the ones you're used to dealing with. A ghost is just a fleeting memory of energy its former self once had. Memory passes through a door as easy as water seeps through a cloth. But if *I* wanted to pass through it, I'd have to alter my vibration to that of its molecules... and then we'd be back to square one when I changed back.'

'But I don't understand,' said Norman. 'Surely if you're too solid too pass through something, you can't be *not-solid-enough* to knock on it!'

Gabriel recalled with fondness the days when his appearance would cause Kings to fall prostrate in front of him in total submission, accepting every word he uttered without question.

and quickly slammed the door shut.

'I know you've got someone in there, Norman!' yelled a muffled voice. 'Don't think you can pull the wool over my nose. I'll be waiting downstairs. They can't stay in there forever!'

There was the muffled sound of disappearing footsteps.

'Having problems, Norman?'

Norman spun half-circle to see the Archangel leaning casually against his desk. His wings appeared to be folded behind him and the usual trappings of trumpet-blowing cherubs and choral accompaniment were conspicuous by their absence.

'Oh... hello there!' He wasn't quite sure how you greeted an Archangel once you'd got past the looking horrified and passing out stage. 'Problems...? You could say that. But nothing I can't handle. It's just my landlord, Mister Oppenheimer.'

'You mean Helmut and Gertrude's son,' said Gabriel, with a twinkle in his eye.

Norman shifted uncomfortably.

'What is it, Norman? You have something on your mind. I'm trying hard to respect your privacy, so you'll have to tell me what it is.'

'Well,' said Norman uncomfortably, 'I don't wish to be disrespectful, what with you being an Archangel and all that. But perhaps you wouldn't mind keeping your voice down. Otherwise things could get awkward.'

'We don't do volume,' said Gabriel. 'That's your end... remember? We just do vibrations.'

'Then, could you vibrate a little less?'

'Very well,' said Gabriel softly.

'And whilst we're on the subject... you're arrival seems to be having an effect on the electronic items in my flat. That includes my computer. If I hadn't saved my work a few moments earlier, I reckon I'd have lost it!'

'Ah, yes,' said Gabriel, nodding his head. 'It's something we're encountering more and more of as your time passes. It used to be the odd barking dog or startled horse. Now it's car alarms and anything with a computer chip inside. You see... we

'*HE?*' Oppenheimer looked bewildered. '*He…?* Norman… is there more to this than I thought? When I said I didn't have you down as a ladies' man, I never imagined…'

This was all getting too much for Norman's sleep-starved brain. He decided to let Oppenheimer have his pound of flesh so that he could get to bed.

'Okay… I meant *she! She* didn't stay.'

'But you said *he!*'

'I said *he*, but meant *she!*'

'Norman! What wrong end of the stick am I getting hold of?'

'Look, Mister Oppenheimer… I had a guest last night, but they didn't stay… We talked – as you rightly pointed out – and then they left. That's the truth… I promise!'

His landlord gazed inquisitorially. 'Did they jump from the window?' he said slowly.

'I beg your pardon?'

'The question is simple enough. I asked you if they jumped from the window.'

Flown could have been a possibility, thought Norman.

'Because, you see… that is the only way they could have left your room without using the stairs and having to pass by *my* door… which I left open all night.'

'If you didn't see them go, you must have fallen asleep,' suggested Norman. 'Look… why don't you come in and see for yourself? There's no one in here!' He started to close the door in order to release the security chain. It had suddenly occurred to him that he had nothing to fear from Oppenheimer searching the flat.

Boing. Boing.

'Spikey?… Oh no!'

'Norman?'

'Not the microwave!'

Ping.

'NORMAN!'

'I've got to go, Mister Oppenheimer. I'll explain another time!'

Norman heard the video recorder place itself into rewind

'But wait!' The landlord's eyes widened as if auditioning for the role in a cheap horror movie. 'I hear another voice... and then I tell myself, "Norman is not alone. He has someone up there with him".'

Norman felt reality flex its muscles. Had Oppenheimer also heard the Archangel? Even though Norman had convinced himself the experience had been real, it felt extremely strange having someone else confirm it... not least when that *someone* was as odious and unspiritual as the man whose face was currently impersonating a door jam.

'Are you *sure* you heard another voice?' ventured Norman, his thoughts racing to construct a plausible excuse.

'Of course! You are not suggesting it was in my head?'

Norman thought it best not to go into that one. In fact... he'd rather not be going into *anything* with Oppenheimer on this particular subject. His mind began to wander through the consequences of his conversation having been overheard.

'There is no mistaking what I hear,' Oppenheimer persisted. 'You had company. She was definitely not a figment of my imagination!'

The landlord's unshaven face rudely snapped back into focus.

'*SHE?*'

'What of it?'

'You said *she!*'

'Don't try and deny it, Norman. I never had you down as a ladies' man... but I know what I am hearing.'

Norman figured that Oppenheimer's suspicious mind was interpreting Gabriel's vibrations the only way it could.

'You know the rules, Norman. Guests are not allowed to stay overnight. This puts you in serious breach of your tenancy agreement.'

The phrase *breach of your tenancy agreement* sent a chill through Norman. It was Oppenheimer's favourite weapon. He presented it like a black-hatted gunslinger pulling back the side of his coat to reveal a holstered gun.

'No... You don't understand,' explained Norman hurriedly. 'You've got the wrong end of the stick! He didn't stay!'

cloaked in a heavy European accent.

'Just a second!' Norman hit the save button on his screen and glanced around the flat. The prospect of a visitor of the terrestrial kind suddenly gave it an extremely untidy appearance. There was the usual assortment of used cups and plates scattered across the floor... a stack of books, magazines and junk mail suitably interspersed, along with some half-eaten toast, the wrapper of a large chocolate bar and the entire contents of a non-existent laundry basket.

'I'm coming!' he yelled, tip-toeing his way through the minefield of obstacles and wishing he'd pretended to be out. He slid the security chain into position and opened the door the few inches it permitted.

A stubbled, weaselly-featured face pushed itself into the narrow gap. 'Good morning to you, Norman.'

'Good morning, Mister Oppenheimer. And to what do I owe this pleasure?'

The beady eyes of his landlord darted straight past him.

'You owe it to the fact I have trouble sleeping last night,' he replied, raising himself onto the balls of his feet so as to get a better view of his tenant's inner sanctum.

'That's funny... me too,' replied Norman, doing the same and nonchalantly raising an arm so as to thwart him.

'This, I can believe,' said Oppenheimer, quickly switching his gaze to under Norman's armpit. 'Because all night I hear you tap tapping on your machine.'

'Computer.'

'Yah... Whatever.'

'I'm sorry if it kept you awake, Mister Oppenheimer. I had some very important work to do.'

'It wasn't your working that bothered me,' said Oppenheimer, making eye contact for the first time.

'Oh?'

'No... you see, I hear you talking in your room last night. At first I think you are talking to yourself because I know you have no friends.'

Norman's raised arm sagged a little.

Fine, if it's the lyrics of a good song. But good news is no news. People want to be frightened. They *expect* to feel insecure. Feeling insecure gives them security. What's more… capitalism thrives on competition. Take that away from the human psyche and we're finished. God help us, Mister Prometheus, if he ever manages to persuade his followers that they're all meant to be on the same side!'

There was a collective murmur of agreement.

Mister Zeus's countenance darkened. 'Now understand this. Something is afoot. Something bigger than centuries of division. Something bigger than the individual religions themselves. They are talking and coordinating with each other. Furthermore… they seem to be in a hurry to do whatever it is they have in mind to do. It is your job, Mister Prometheus, to get inside that mind and report back to us. We don't care what it takes or how you go about it. We want results!'

'You'll have them,' promised Mister Prometheus, chastened.

'We'd better,' replied Mister Zeus coldly. 'Otherwise the consequences don't bear thinking about… especially for *you!*'

There was a collective sharp intake of breath.

*　　*　　*

A knock on the door jolted Norman from the problems of a binary world. The clock in the bottom right-hand corner of his computer screen showed nine forty-five in the morning… the lines of programmer's code sprawling across the rest of it that he had not slept. He reached for a mug of tea and attached the stone cold skin that had been floating on its surface to his upper lip.

Taking advantage of a break in concentration, his eyes did their best to remind him that they were tired. If forty winks were out of the question, just one would be appreciated. He rubbed them vigorously as if doing so might appease them.

It didn't.

There was another rap on the door.

'Norman? Are you at home?' The muffled words were

There was a collective titter.

Mister Prometheus rode the wave of ridicule. Surely sarcasm, he thought, was not a weapon the true ancient Gods of Greece would have availed themselves of. After all... could you imagine the *real* Zeus swapping his thunderbolts for a little bit of verbal irony?

'The men who made that discovery are two of my finest agents,' said Mister Prometheus defensively. 'The point behind the lighting illusion is that it obviously produced some form of mass hysteria, causing those in the temple to believe that they were witnessing something spiritual. Their period of inactivity in the dark was, no doubt, a direct result of this. Perhaps they were praying. Perhaps it was fear. Whatever it was, it had a profound enough effect on everyone to cause them to adjourn their meeting. We may never know what was to be discussed. All we can say is that nothing was and, in that, we should have nothing to be concerned about.'

Had Mister Zeus been the genuine article, he would have thrown his heaviest and most jagged thunderbolt. As it was, he had to make do with another well-aimed shot of trenchant sarcasm. He offered a look of pretend enlightenment. 'Of course not... How foolish of us to think otherwise.' His countenance suddenly changed. 'Are you *mad*, Mister Prometheus?' he bellowed. 'Have you taken leave of your senses and expect us to follow? Have you and your Government remotely bothered to think this one through? For the first time in the history of our Universe, there's a danger of reconciliation between the faiths – promising the devastating consequence of world peace – and you say we have nothing to be concerned about!'

Mister Prometheus tried to stop his eyebrows fusing together in a look of absolute incredulity... unsuccessfully.

'Religions have one purpose, Mister Prometheus... to divide those who put their faith in God. Division means distrust and distrust means defence. Defence means armaments, and armaments mean massive profits. Are you getting the bigger picture, Mister Prometheus? If not... consider our media empires. Since when did peace, love and harmony ever sell!

303

body fluids were making their escape... leaving him to it.

He effected a loud cough which had a very small swallow attached to the end of it. You didn't get to be a senior member of the CIA's directorate of operations without developing a mastery of subterfuge. 'Are we not in danger of shooting the messenger, here?' he said uncomfortably.

'You would be best advised not to put ideas into our head,' replied Mister Zeus coldly.

Of this, Mister Prometheus had no doubt. The twenty-three individuals behind the collective stare were amongst the richest and most powerful on Earth. Between them, they headed the majority of the world's multi-national corporations. If a Government could be likened to the conductor of an orchestra, these were the instrument makers and suppliers. Without them there would be no music. Their power and influence transcended national borders. They were above individual governments. They were *the* government, elected by everyone who had ever purchased their products... from deodorant to detonators, dog food to debt. They, in turn, bought media empires, small countries, politicians and, of course... Mister Prometheus.

Flattered by power and believing themselves to be invincible, they had styled themselves on the gods of Ancient Greece, adopting the names of their mythical counterparts to add gravitas to their meetings. Sadly, Mister Dionysus had taken it a stage further, choosing to turn up in a white, off-the-shoulder robe with tightly permed hair and beard. His behaviour would have been better tolerated by the others, were it not for his constant insistence that he and Mister Atlas wrestle each other... naked.

'It seems to me, Mister Prometheus, that all your men on the ground have discovered is an ancient lighting illusion. Would they have us believe that the temple at Arwan El Kahab was an early form of discotheque? Should they also have us believe that the world's religious leaders went there for a good night out, only to return when they discovered the original occupants had forgotten to install a matching sound system?'

'And might we remind you, Mister Prometheus, that you are more than adequately recompensed for that danger. And given that you have proved yourself willing to compromise your professional position for a handful of silver, talk of your integrity is infelicitous.'

Mister Prometheus's jutting jaw suddenly felt rather foolish. It had pushed out boldly to attack, but had been forced to freeze mid-rant, as the canvas on which his brain had been preparing to spar was abruptly pulled from under it. Unpalatable as Mister Apollo's remarks had been, they were extremely accurate.

The smallest bead of sweat squeezed its way through the epidermis just above his right temple, then sank a thin, salted trail down the side of his face. Knowing his next move was being collectively scrutinised, Mister Prometheus prayed it had gone unnoticed.

It had.

The collective stare had far bigger things on its collective mind. It sensed blood. Sweat and tears were not enough. It was moving its way towards his tormented mandible.

Mister Prometheus's *mandibula* remained jutted. Relaxation now would signal defeat. But... what was this...? The collective stare wasn't stopping. It was continuing... heading straight for his Adam's apple.

These were ruthless individuals indeed, without soul or mercy... like a crowd at the coliseum baying for the lions to be released, they were awaiting the ultimate sign of mental capitulation... the discrediting gulp. The collective stare had morphed into a collective smirk.

Mister Prometheus desperately tried to fight it, but his throat was rapidly filling up. Why was it that when humiliated in public, even your own saliva turned against you?

He attempted to bluff it out, as if having adopted a pose he struck every day. Another bead of sweat followed the previous one... only this time it was bigger and its descent more rapid.

His saliva level had reached critical.

Shit... Spillage was imminent.

Now his eyes were beginning to water. It seemed his entire

myriad of final, fragmented, multi-coloured beams converged upon a gigantic crystal hanging above it and were reflected downwards in a single, awesome, shimmering column of light.

* * *

Twenty-three pairs of eyes drilled their collective steely gaze through the tension around a massive, marble table and into those of a twenty-fourth.

'Are you seriously suggesting to this meeting, Mister Prometheus, that having assembled themselves from the four corners of the globe at unfeasibly short notice, the greatest coming together of religious leaders in the history of this planet simply sat there in the dark for fifteen minutes without saying a word... then got up and went home?'

Mister Prometheus felt the ice-chilled hand of pressure grip the back of his neck. Why did people refer to the four corners of the globe, he mused? Globes didn't have corners. And if it was a throwback to when the world was considered flat and envisaged as a two-dimensional map, surely when the world was discovered to be round, two sets of those corners came together and became exactly the same place. Wouldn't it therefore be more accurate to refer to the *two* corners of the globe... if you were going to bother referring to them at all?

He raised his hands in exasperation. 'As illogical as it sounds, Mister Zeus... that is *precisely* what my operatives on the ground assured me happened.'

The collective stare hardened.

'You wouldn't be holding something back from us, would you, Mister Prometheus?' voiced another. 'Something your Government would rather keep to themselves, perhaps? Something you might not wish to share with this council?'

Mister Prometheus felt the chill on the back of his neck assuaged by a warm flush of anger. 'Are you questioning my integrity, Mister Apollo? If so... might I remind you of the danger I constantly place myself in by regularly attending this council! If it were to be discovered that I...'

crystal. 'Now, Bob!' he shouted, his arms shaking with the strain. 'Connect the terminals!'

After a few seconds of silence, the crystal exploded in light… razor-sharp rays shooting out in every direction and sending a roosting flock of birds scurrying for the open window. The rays were magnificent, cutting through the temple's half-light with energy and purpose, striking hard at opposing surfaces which, themselves, burst forth into yet more explosions of light. From these secondary illuminations, finer still beams shot out and repeated the process until the whole temple appeared to twinkle.

'There are hundreds of these things!' shouted Chad. 'They're magnifying and splitting the beam into thousands of smaller ones! Look at 'em go!'

The temple's interior was awash with lines of multi-coloured light streaming from wall to wall. It was as if the night sky had decided to join up its dots. Only the absence of total darkness seemed to prevent the last of those lines reaching their intended targets.

'So much for miracles!' yelled Chad. 'I told you we'd find the answer!'

'It's pretty impressive… I'll give you that!' shouted Bob. 'But… and not that I'm splitting hairs here… we've still not got any light above our central plinth!'

'No problem! You're looking at the effect of a portable searchlight. They had the power of the sun. All we need is a stronger source of light.'

'And where the hell are we gonna get one of those?'

It was early evening when the sound of Yankee Zero Three's rotor blades announced themselves against the gully walls. With some skilful manoeuvring and a little bit of guidance from below, its powerful searchlight cut through the temple's darkness and triggered an even more spectacular *son et lumière*.

Except there was no *son*.

At least, there wasn't if you discounted the whoops of delight from the two men dancing around the large central plinth as the feet... but eventually it came hurtling up through the gloom and towards his body. He snatched out and caught hold of it. 'Now... tie the searchlight to your end,' he instructed. 'Make sure it's switched on, but disconnected from the terminals.'

There was some unintelligible muttering below.

Chad unclipped his flashlight and shone it at the reason for his climb. Attached to the front of the spur was the biggest crystal he'd ever seen... roughly cut, with a number of finger-like crystalline structures projecting from its surface. It was colourless with its transparency, but its multifaceted surface sparkled with rainbow hues as every edge refracted the flashlight's beam like a prism. 'You gotta see this thing, Bob!' he shouted down. 'It's beautiful!'

'Beauty is a solid floor beneath my feet,' came back the reply.

Chad flicked the beam of his flashlight backwards and forwards like a hesitant painter practising the first few strokes of a masterpiece. The rainbows danced obediently, the shards of light he'd witnessed earlier spinning off into the darkness, less evident under such a weak light.

There was a tug on the rope.

'Searchlight's secured. Pull her up!'

A few minutes later the searchlight was nestling in Chad's lap as he delicately inched himself forward, his body working its way along the narrow spur in a series of short jolts. He did his best to imagine he was just a few feet from the ground, but his colleague's quips about the poor standard of ancient mortar and the stress coefficient of unsupported masonry made it all but impossible.

'A small piece of advice,' continued the tireless stream of comments from below. 'When you get to the end... don't forget to stop!'

Having manoeuvred himself to within a few feet of the crystal, Chad heeded the advice. He took a deep breath, grasped the searchlight firmly with both hands, raised it above his head and – with a final check to make sure he'd got his distances right – allowed himself to drop forward onto his stomach. The head of the searchlight came to rest perfectly against the front of the observing the dancing shadows of yet more recesses cut into the stone. They were the same as he'd seen from atop the window ledge, and had unwittingly buried a surveillance device inside one the previous afternoon. They stretched from where he was standing right up to the spur itself, conveniently – though maybe not coincidentally, he thought – at intervals suggesting their use as hand and footholds.

'Bob! I'm gonna try and take a closer look! I need you and the rope down here! I'm also gonna need the searchlight! D'ya reckon the cables will reach this far?'

'Are you kiddin'?' came a faint voice. 'They're stretched tighter than your humour muscle! But don't fret… I'll think of something.'

Chad was already spread-eagled a third of the way up the wall when Bob arrived and deposited something heavy on the ground below him.

'The van's engine battery,' explained Bob. 'If you fall… try and avoid landing on it. The van won't start if it's flat!'

'Almost funny… How about doing something useful like shining some light on these footholds above me.'

Bob duly obliged.

With the effort of hauling his bodyweight up to such a height for the second time that day, it was with relief that the spur finally loomed within touching distance. Chad raised himself the final few feet and clambered across onto it… thankful for the rest it afforded his tired arms and legs.

'Now what?' shouted Bob, picking his colleague out with the light.

Carefully twisting himself around, Chad sat with his back against the wall, his legs dangling either side of the spur. 'Now it's your turn to exert yourself,' he answered, breathing deeply. 'I need you to throw that rope up to me.'

'I'd climb up with it,' came the retort. 'But that ledge you're sitting on doesn't look like it's capable of taking *your* weight, let alone *both* of ours!'

Chad waited patiently whilst a series of failed attempts took place beneath him. A couple of times he felt the rope strike his

The lamp was twisted gently.

'There!'

'I see it!'

Something glistened brightly at the far end of the temple.

'What is it?'

'Dunno. But I'll stake everything I've got it's not been placed in that particular spot by accident. Can we focus the beam on this thing, Bob? The light's spreading too much'

'Nope. That's as good as it gets.'

'What about making it brighter?'

'No can do.'

'Shit!'

The object continued to play with the light being thrown on it, twinkling star-like against the illuminated area of stonework caught in the beam's diffusion.

Chad could just make out a series of small, square recesses cut into the surrounding slabs of masonry. 'We're gonna have to take a closer look,' he said. 'I'll need you to keep shining the light while I go down and mark out exactly where that thing is.'

'Don't be long,' grimaced Bob. 'This thing's melting my ear!'

'Don't understand that,' said Chad, attaching himself to the rope. 'There's a big enough draught blowing through from the other one!' He launched himself from the ledge and abseiled into the gloom.

Chad stood at the foot of the far wall and gazed upwards. He could see the object clearly now, the beam from Bob's searchlight hitting it front on and illuminating its dome-shaped surface. A number of small angular protrusions refracted faint shards of light which quickly evaporated as they struck out into the gloom. Approximately two feet in diameter, it was attached to a thin spur of masonry projecting roughly four feet out from the wall.

He unclipped the flashlight from his belt and shone its puny beam over the wall's surface. Dark squares appeared at regular intervals, and as he moved his own light backwards and forwards – watching them flicker to and fro – he realised he was

Piper?'

'It's Peter Piper as in picked a bloody pickled pepper, Miss Gusset! Now do something about it!'

'I'll go and find the grey room, sir!'

'SOD THE FUCKING GREY ROOM! GO AND GET SECURITY! I'VE GOT A NUTTER IN HERE!'

* * *

'I hardly think this thing's gonna recreate your shaft of sunlight,' said Bob, awkwardly balancing a huge, portable searchlight on his shoulder and taking care not to pull its connecting leads from the van's battery below.

'I wasn't aware we had a choice,' countered Chad, carefully manoeuvring himself behind his colleague, the narrow window ledge offering little room for mistakes. 'Not unless you wanna hang around another three hundred and sixty-four days to prove my theory.' He glanced over his shoulder and aligned the searchlight as best he could with the angle of the channel in the gully walls. 'I reckon that's about it. Now, whatever you do, don't move. It's perfectly centred.'

'Forget about me. You just concentrate on your precious angle.'

'Okay. Here we go. Switch her on!'

Bob fumbled with the back of the lamp and a beam of light shot out into the gloom of the temple's interior, the two men watching as it struck the far wall.

'Ooh… more masonry,' cooed Bob. 'There's a surprise!'

'Keep still!' Chad took another glance over his shoulder and readjusted the light's angle.

'Yep… more masonry… a little higher up this time.'

Chad continued his adjustments.

'Wait a minute! What was that?'

Chad looked around.

'No… you've lost it now.'

'Which way?'

'A little to your left.'

about the experience?'

'Being thrown out for pissing myself.'

'Ah...' Snogden-Lambert glanced at his watch. They should have been here by now. They had a pass key. What was keeping them? He lent forward and pressed the button on the intercom again.

'Miss Gusset?'

'Yes, sir?'

'Will anyone be visiting me soon?'

'No, sir.'

There was a pause.

'Why not, Miss Gusset?'

'Because you asked not to be disturbed, sir.'

'Yes... but Miss Gusset... that was then and this is now. Will... *ahem*... Peter Piper be visiting me soon?'

'I shouldn't think so, sir.'

'Why not?'

'He hasn't booked an appointment.'

'He doesn't need an appointment, Miss Gusset.' Snogden-Lambert's voice was climbing steadily in pitch as well as gaining in vibrato. 'You tell him to come *straight* in!'

'But he's not here, sir.'

'Then where is he, Miss Gusset?'

'Who? Mr Piper?'

'Yes... Peter Piper... Where is he Miss Gusset?'

'He's in the grey room, sir.'

'What grey room?'

'The grey room you told me he was in!'

The underarms of Snogden-Lambert's shirt began to glisten. 'Miss Gusset... I think we're at cross purposes here. Listen carefully... Peter Piper is in the *grey* room. Do you understand Miss Gusset?'

Another silence.

'That's what I've just said,' replied Miss Gusset.

'No, Miss Gusset... listen... *Peter Piper* is in the grey room...! P...e...t...e...r P...i...p...e...r... *Now* do you understand?'

'Oh, I *see!* Is that Mr Peter Piper as in hyphenated Peter-

312

Piper was in the grey room as meaning Peter Snogden-Lambert was being held against his will in his office. A possible hostage scenario had always been considered, given the desire of certain members of the criminal fraternity to get their hands on anything worth hanging on a wall and putting a red rope in front of. Unfortunately for Peter Snogden-Lambert, Mrs Fanshawe-Whittingham was, at that very moment, enjoying a cream tea in Ventnor and oblivious to the fact that her temporary replacement had not been instructed in the use of security codes.

'Pardon?' said Miss Gusset.

'I said... Peter Piper is in the grey room.' Snogden-Lambert smiled feebly at Donald and hoped he wouldn't notice the beads of perspiration beginning to collect on his brow.

'Would you like to open another window?' asked Donald, noticing the beads of perspiration beginning to collect on Snogden-Lambert's brow.

There was a deafening silence.

'Is he?' came Miss Gusset's voice from the intercom.

'Yes... he is,' sung Snogden-Lambert anxiously.

There was another silence.

'Righty ho!' said Miss Gusset.

Peter Snogden-Lambert sat down and flashed yet another inane smile at his visitor.

Donald flashed one back.

It would just be a question of playing for time and waiting now. They'd rehearsed this scenario many times before with perfectly choreographed results. Little did Snogden-Lambert think it would ever be enacted for real. He drummed his fingers on his leg. 'Tell me,' he said politely, his ears straining to hear the sound of security assembling outside the door. 'Have you actually visited our gallery before, Mr Tucker-Jenkins?'

'Oh yes.'

'And did you enjoy yourself?'

'Can't say that I did.'

'Oh, that's a shame.' Snogden-Lambert gave a worried glance towards the door. He could hear nothing. 'What didn't you like

313

one's head don't always make perfect sense, do they? But I'm slowly piecing it all together... though *why* it's going to happen is still a mystery to me. I tried to ignore the messages at first... but they're getting louder and more persistent. I've tried going to sleep with my head wrapped in tin foil to keep the noise down, but started picking up mobile phone conversations. I've never known such heavy psychic traffic before!'

Snogden-Lambert forced a smile onto his face and slowly rose from his chair, his eyes fixed on his visitor whilst his peripheral vision searched for the door.

'You're not from the Vatican, are you?' he said in a measured tone.

'The Vatican? *Me?*' exclaimed Donald. 'Good God, man! Haven't you been listening to a thing I've been telling you?'

Snogden-Lambert backed himself over to the door and fumbled behind his back for the handle.

'OF COURSE I LOCKED IT!' shouted Donald over his left shoulder.

'Who are you talking to?' asked Snogden-Lambert weakly.

'They're at it again,' replied Donald. 'Always telling me what to do as if I'm a complete idiot. YES I'VE GOT THE KEY! WHAT DO YOU TAKE ME FOR? Now, perhaps we should work out how we're going to alert the other galleries.'

'Alert?' Snogden-Lambert mentally caressed the word. 'Yes... we must alert others, mustn't we!' He cautiously made his way over to the desk. 'Will you excuse me a moment, Mr Tucker-Jenkins?' He leant forward and nervously pressed a button on his intercom.

'Ahem... Miss Gusset. Peter Piper is in the grey room!'

Now, it is a fact that if you are ever sat in a certain London concert hall and an announcement comes across the public address system that a Mr Sands is in the green room, make sure you leave the building as fast as your legs will carry you. It's a coded warning to the staff that a fire has been discovered and that they must evacuate the public without causing mass hysteria. Had Mrs Fanshawe-Whittingham been on the end of the intercom, she would have interpreted the fact that Peter taken. All you can tell me is that they *will* be taken. Am I understanding you correctly, Mr Tucker-Jenkins?'

'Absolutely!' said Donald, with a look of triumph.

'Then, Mr Tucker-Jenkins... why are you here?'

Donald's smugness evaporated. 'I've just told you!'

'Told me what?'

'That some of your paintings are going to be taken!'

'But I knew that already!'

'You did?'

'Yes! They told me this morning!'

'You've been receiving messages too?' Donald's eyes widened with excitement.

'Of course! And they said you'd be coming to see me to discuss the matter further. But if you know so little about the whole thing, what precisely can we discuss?'

'Well... there's the question of security, isn't there?'

Snogden-Lambert's countenance transformed with an explosion of relief. 'Oh... I see!' he exclaimed. 'You're here to discuss *security*! Of course! Now I understand! Well... I'm more than happy to entrust the Vatican with that responsibility. I'm sure their arrangements will be of the highest standard.'

'No... you don't understand,' said Donald gravely. 'From what I've been told... if you go ahead and lend your paintings to the Vatican, it's *them* who'll be doing the stealing!'

Snogden-Lambert looked at him blankly. 'I beg your pardon!'

'Oh yes!' asserted Donald. 'After all... you didn't think they would go to all the trouble of borrowing your paintings only to get someone else to steal them, did you?'

'*Steal* them?' exclaimed Snogden-Lambert, unable to believe what he was hearing. 'You're telling me the Holy Church of Rome intends to *steal* our paintings... and blatantly doing so in my own office before we've even sent them!'

'Well... there's no point in telling you *after* you've sent them, is there?' said Donald incredulously.

'Mr Tucker-Jenkins! Is this some sort of joke?'

'I assure you, sir... it's deadly serious. At first, I wasn't sure how the paintings were going to be removed. The voices in in hand, if it's all the same to you.'

'Then… would you excuse me if I opened a window. Only, it's a little…' Snogden-Lambert searched diplomatically for the right word, '*stuffy*… in here.'

He did just that and took a deep breath of exhaust-polluted air as it wafted in and countered the sickly stench of body odour garnished with a soupçon of stale urine. He was about to suggest he get Miss Gusset to find a temporary home for Donald's bags, but turned to find them clutched firmly to the chest of their owner, now comfortably reposed in *his* deluxe, leather, executive's chair with matching vinyl trim. This wasn't quite the emissary from Rome he'd envisaged.

'I'll sit here then, shall I?' he said awkwardly, settling himself into a plain, chrome-framed chair facing the front of his own desk. He lent forward and reversed his jotter and pen set. 'Now… perhaps we could start by discussing dates and then go on to the actual paintings in question.'

'Ah… now that's where things get a little complicated,' said Donald stiffly. 'You see… I haven't been given any dates or, indeed, told which paintings are involved.'

'Oh!' said Snogden-Lambert, with a look of polite surprise. 'I see… so… I'll be informed of those later on will I?'

'I'm sure you'll be the first to know!' said Donald, with equal surprise.

Snogden-Lambert looked at him blankly… then gave a forced laugh, presuming a joke to have been made.

'Well, I suppose we should talk logistics then. Now, Mr Tucker-Jenkins… in the interest of…'

'I'm afraid I can't tell you how it's going to be done either,' Donald interrupted him. 'Suffice to say… it's *definitely* going to happen.'

Snogden-Lambert's eyebrows knitted themselves into an expression of confusion. He placed his pen on the jotter with contained precision.

'Right… now let me see if I've got this straight. You don't have any information as to what paintings will need to be taken, when they will need to be taken or, indeed, *how* they will be scribbled entry.

'But this is the one you've just made!' he exclaimed.

'Perhaps I should explain,' interjected Donald hastily, Miss Gusset's quivering bottom lip about to embarrass all three of them. 'I am here on a matter of extreme urgency, hence my rather unfortunate appearance. Home is a stranger to me at the moment, sir, so you must take me as you find me. As the good book says, "*judge not, that ye be not judged*". But I digress. To the point... I'm here to discuss the removal from this gallery of some of your paintings and offer you whatever assistance I can regarding this matter.'

Snogden-Lambert's earlier telephone conversation flashed across his mind and a penny – albeit of the wrong currency – dropped.

'Oh I see!' he exclaimed. 'You're here regarding the Vatican's request to borrow some of our paintings for their exhibition!'

Donald nodded to himself. 'So, *that's* what it's all about!'

'Yes... I understand,' misinterpreted Snogden-Lambert. 'My goodness, that was quick! You don't waste time, do you?'

'Not with something as consequential as this,' said Donald. 'There's obviously much to consider.'

'Indeed there is! Indeed there is! Miss Gusset... Mr Tucker-Jenkins and I have some extremely important business to attend to. Kindly hold my calls and note that we are not to be disturbed under *any* circumstances whatsoever. Is that understood Miss Gusset? *Whatsoever!*'

The last word was delivered with such finality that Miss Gusset was left in no doubt as to its relevance regarding her career prospects. Nothing and no one would enter that office whilst she had a breath left in her body... not to mention a job. She nodded vigorously and left the two men to continue their business.

'Perhaps you'd like to freshen up before we start?' suggested Snogden-Lambert, as the door closed behind them. Rome obviously kept this man very busy to warrant such an *unusual* appearance, he mused.

'That is very kind... but I'd rather get straight to the matter

A red-cheeked Miss Gusset entered cautiously and scribbled something into a large diary lying on the desk.

'And what are we doing now, Miss Gusset?'

'We're making an appointment for the gentleman outside to see you, sir,'

'Excellent, Miss Gusset! Excellent!' He raised his hands and instructed an invisible string section to bow forth. No sooner had they done so than a loud voice bellowed out above the music.

'Aha...! Bach's Brandenburg Concerto in D Major. One of the finest examples of contrapuntal invention ever written! The mathematics of Heaven expressed in temporal form! Did you know he fathered twenty children? It's a wonder he ever had the energy to compose!'

Peter Snogden-Lambert left the string section to cope as best they could without him and stared at the dishevelled gentleman, who was clutching a number of carrier bags and standing in his office.

'And who the hell are you?' he said curtly.

'Allow me to introduce myself, sir,' said the carrier bag-wielding gentleman, with a smile that revealed the more stubborn parts of that morning's breakfast. 'My name is Donald Tucker-Jenkins.'

Miss Gusset's eyes shot skyward.

Snogden-Lambert looked his visitor up and down with disdain. The *up* bit was bad enough... the *down* bit didn't bear thinking about. He'd never seen such stains in public.

'Are you an artist?' he enquired.

'Oh... that I wish the good Lord had gifted me so!'

'Then what are you doing bringing yourself and your dirt into my office?'

Donald Tucker-Jenkins returned the gaze of contempt. 'I have an appointment with you, sir... dirt and all.'

Snogden-Lambert flashed a look at Miss Gusset.

'It's in the book, sir,' she said, sheepishly nodding towards the diary on the desk.

Snogden-Lambert flicked it open for that day and studied the

'If they haven't, perhaps they'd like to make one. And if they have... perhaps you'd like to pay a little more attention to keeping my diary up-to-date.'

She felt the cheeks of her face begin to tingle and beat a hasty retreat... returning a few moments later.

'He says his appointment is with Des Tinny, sir.'

'Des Tinny? There's no one here of that name... There used to be a Desmond Tillingbrooke-Thornton down in Admin, but I've never heard the name Tinny used before... Ask him if he's got the right building.'

'Yes, sir.'

She scuttled out and scuttled back. 'My mistake, sir. Apparently his appointment is with *destiny*... and it's of vital importance that he speaks to you.'

Snogden-Lambert blinked heavily, as if doing so might awaken him from a dream and have Mrs Fanshawe-Whittingham standing reassuringly in front of him.

'Miss Gusset!' There was a pause for effect. 'I am in charge of one of the largest national art collections in Europe. If someone wants to see me, they can bloody well book an appointment in advance. Is that clear?'

Miss Gusset managed an almost inaudible 'yes, sir' and exited before the tears came.

Snogden-Lambert sat back in his deluxe, leather, executive's chair with matching vinyl trim and rued the day he'd allowed Mrs Fanshawe-Whittingham to take two weeks off to visit her sister on the Isle of Wight. He needed her now more than ever. Five minutes earlier he'd received a telephone call from the Vatican in Rome requesting the loan of some of the gallery's most important paintings for an exhibition they intended holding to mark some ecclesiastical anniversary or other. In return, they were prepared to loan him a number of Italian Masters the following summer, as well as make a sizeable donation towards the gallery's upkeep. Having agreed in principle, he'd been informed that someone would be contacting him in the near future to take the matter further. It would need careful arranging.

suggesting they most certainly did not.

His secretary hesitated. It was her first week as a temp at the gallery and she was already feeling totally and humiliatingly inadequate. She'd been sent by the agency to fill in for a Mrs Fanshawe-Whittingham, the director's PA and a woman who – according to her boss – could make a Swiss timepiece look inefficient. This was probably just as well, as from what she could ascertain, *his* entire day seemed to be solely spent conducting a large, invisible orchestra – classical accompaniment courtesy of a hi-fi system in his office – whilst sonorously *pomming* over the best bits. Personally, she couldn't stand that kind of music... and herein lay the root of her problem. She felt like a fish out of water in such a cultured environment and figured everyone else thought it of her too. The disconnected smiles had begun on her first day, after Mr Snogden-Lambert had asked her to fetch him a cappuccino. How was she to know it wasn't the name of an Italian artist? She'd spent the next two hours scouring the walls of the gallery trying to find one of his paintings and wondering how on earth she was going to get it up the stairs when she did.

She was even inadequately short on surnames. Everyone seemed to have at least two. Even the night watchman was a Carter-Smith. And how did that particular genealogical sleight-of-hand originate? Obviously not the proud alliance of two notable families at some point in their history, but rather a couple trying to pretend they weren't from two very ordinary ones. Anyone with more than two names, in her book, had to be a snob. Perhaps if she'd stuck her mother's maiden name in front of her own and thrown in a hyphen she might have felt more at home. Then again... given her mother's maiden name was Brown, it might have made things worse.

'You're daydreaming again, Miss Gusset. I asked you if they have an appointment.'

'What, sir? Oh... yes... sorry... I'll go and see.' She turned to leave.

'And Miss Gusset!'

'Sir?'

alarm clock that makes Stonehenge look like a pile of stones.'

'Stonehenge *is* a pile of stones!' said Bob.

'I'm looking at a man-made, pinhole view out into the valley which would send a solitary shaft of light bang into the centre of this window at sunset. Taking into account its precision and the sun's movement between the equinoxes, I'd say it's been designed to do so on a particular day of the year.'

'And on what day of the year would I need to be holding your hand to see it?'

'Are you serious? It's gotta be yesterday. I'll get the eggheads back at command to check the math, but I think we've found the source of our illuminations. It's why we lost the light early last night. The gully walls screened it out before the horizon could. Then – for a brief period of time – it was allowed to squeeze through a channel and hit a designated spot!'

'But why go to all that trouble?'

'The ancients were always at it. You've got temples and monuments around the world aligned to mark important astronomical and calendrical events.'

'Only one problem, Einstein. Since when did April twenty-third mark an important event? We ain't exactly talking summer solstice.'

'Find that out, Bob, and we may be closer to wrapping this whole mystery up.'

'Correction,' said Bob. 'Find the way your single ray of light managed to transform itself into the awesome display we witnessed last night and I might be more impressed.'

'I'm still working on that.'

'Does that mean you're coming down?'

'No, Bob... It means you're coming up!'

* * *

'Excuse me, sir! There's someone out here to see you.'

Peter Snogden-Lambert stopped waving his arms and looked up from his desk.

'Do they have an appointment?' he asked, in a tone

321

lines. He lent against the upright stanchion of the window to steady his arm and zoomed in on the rock. Carved into the linear edge, with incredible geometric precision, was a semi-circular trough horizontally following the line of the gully. Where it stopped, another outcropping from the opposite wall blocked his line of sight. But carved into that section too – identical but for it being in reverse – was another trough running in precisely the same direction. With the advantage of his distant perspective, the two opposing semi-circles almost appeared to touch and form a single, perfect circle.

He straightened himself up and slowly moved his body until they did. As soon as the circle was formed, the bright blue of the valley sky flashed into view through the man-made channel and struck his binoculars. From a distance – and so long as your field of vision was aligned as precisely as his – it gave the illusion of looking through a pipe, so straight in construction that an arrow could have been fired through it without touching the sides. But move a little to the left or right, or alter your perspective vertically, and the effect instantly disappeared.

Chad's heartbeat quickened. He lowered his binoculars and noted the position of his head in relationship to the window. It couldn't have been more central had he tried. A rush of adrenalin shot through his body. 'Bob!' he shouted down. 'Which way did we think this gully was aligned?'

'No *think* and *was* about it,' came the response. 'It is and always will be running East to West, from here out into the valley.'

'Perfect!'

'For what?'

'An interesting sunset!'

'Now you really *have* gone soft on me,' said Bob. 'Shall I climb up so that we can watch it together... maybe even hold hands?'

'You think I wanna hold your hand with all that scratching you do? Besides... if my reckoning is correct, we won't be seeing one from up here tonight.'

'You mean, we're going home?' said Bob enthusiastically.

'I mean... I believe I've discovered a sophisticated, ancient

'If I fall, I'll make sure it's on you!' Chad promised, hoisting himself off the ground.

With alternate use of the ascenders, he skilfully inched himself up until he'd reached a height that threatened serious injury.

'How's the lactic acid in those arms, Spiderman? Beginning to realise it's easier barking orders from the ground than doing the real work?' Bob taunted.

'Actually… I was thinking how pleasant it was getting away from all that sweating you've been doing these past few days. The air's considerably fresher up here.' Gritting his teeth, Chad hauled himself ever higher, finally reaching a point where the rope lay too tight to the wall to raise the ascenders any further. Reaching up, he fumbled for the lip of the window. Mustering what strength he had left, he grabbed hold of the masonry and hoisted himself up onto the ledge.

A slow series of handclaps emanated from below.

'Can we establish it's a window now, Chad? When you look through one end, can you see through to the other? How did those ancients do it, I ask myself?'

Chad was more interested in *why* they'd done it. Why just the one small opening? He looked out at the courtyard bathed in the early morning shadow of the temple and towards the gorge in front of him. From his precarious vantage point, he should've had the perfect view along its length. But certain outcroppings at various points along its walls conspired to prevent him seeing directly through into the open valley beyond. From a defensive point of view, this would have been an advantage. For it meant anyone passing by and casually glancing into the gorge wouldn't be able to see the building at its far end.

Something about the outcroppings bothered him. A couple seemed unnatural in their shape. It was as if parts of them had been hewn away by human hand rather than gently weathered over the millennia. Unclipping the binoculars from his belt, he used them to focus in on one of the suspect outcroppings at a point where its soft, natural contours gave way to a perfectly vertical section of a few feet or more. Nature didn't do straight window. 'We're gonna need a rope, climbing harness, binoculars and a flashlight.'

Bob gave a pained stare. 'Oh... come on!' he groaned. 'Monkey Man doesn't wanna play today! Not in *this* heat.'

Monkey Man was Chad's pet name for Bob whenever the need arose to secrete surveillance equipment in some inaccessible and lofty place. It would invariably be Bob who ended up precariously suspended from a rope.

'Monkey Man doesn't have to. It's *me* who'll be doing the climbing this time,' Chad surprised him.

'What's this? You going soft on me? Finally feeling guilty about it being the good-looking one who risks his neck every time?'

'That face will always say Monkey Man to me,' said Chad. 'It's far better suited to dangling from ridiculous places than mine. That's not praise, Bob... but acknowledgement of the fact you're closer to your simian ancestry. But this time I need someone with brains at the end of the rope.'

'I'll get the equipment from the van,' said Bob, shaking off the insults. 'This'll be worth watching!'

Having securely tightened the straps of his harness, Chad clipped a large flashlight and binoculars to his belt.

After many attempts and much cursing, Bob had succeeded in throwing one end of a long rope through the window, having tied the other to a huge, metal handle attached to the doors beneath the portico.

Chad slipped its free end through the ascenders connected to his harness... slid the devices as high as they would go... then placed his foot into one of the stirrups. 'You sure you got this thing attached securely?' he asked, pulling on the rope to check its tension.

Bob scratched his head. 'Well, it's hard to say,' he frowned, 'what with my simian-like brain. I'm not sure whether they taught me that a simple granny knot would comfortably hold the weight of a fully-grown man... or that it wouldn't. I guess you'll just have to climb up and find out.'

illuminations, culminating in a shower of light directly above this stone.' He peered up into the gloom enveloping the ceiling.

'Correct,' affirmed Bob.

'We know the light was real as all four cameras registered it.'

'Correct.'

'Lights don't materialise out of thin air... which means there has to be a power source of some kind.'

'Correct.'

'We can discount anything supernatural... as one of us, at least, is not stupid.'

'Incorrect... We're *both* spending another day here.'

Chad frowned. 'Where was I?'

'Ruling out it being a miracle.'

'You betcha. Miracles are just that one in a billion chance whose time has finally come. You'll always find science behind them, no matter how long the odds.'

'So where's your science in this place?' Bob smirked. 'I can see a helluva lotta stone... and precious little else.'

'Agreed. Which means we can rule out an *artificial* light source.'

'Not unless one of those priests had a generator hidden under his cassock.'

'Not large on the probability scale, Bob... Leaving us only one option. The light source *had* to be natural.'

'Brilliant deduction, Sherlock. But aren't you forgetting one thing? We'd lost the daylight *before* the fireworks appeared.'

'Precisely! So maybe that's our first clue, given there was a discrepancy over the time the sun should've set. I've gone through the calculation a million times. There were *definitely* a few minutes of daylight missing. Could it be significant that the light display occurred during that period and didn't extend beyond it?'

'Interesting point,' acknowledged Bob. He gazed up at the area of stonework towering above the main doors. 'Well... if it's a natural light source you're searching for, the builders of this place have made it about as easy as it gets!'

'Exactly what I was thinking,' said Chad, studying the solitary envisaged when first briefed about the mission. An ancient temple to him was either a pile of rubble that an overpriced guidebook convinced you would have been worth visiting had you turned up a couple of thousand years earlier, or an awe-inspiring testament to the ingenuity and tenacity of earlier civilisations that embarrassed the hell out of your twenty-first century smugness.

The temple at Arwan El Kahab was neither.

Practical is a word sometimes used to politely describe decor which demonstrates a complete lack of imagination. The temple at Arwan El Kahab *aspired* to be practical... and even failed at that.

The fact there was only one solitary window to illuminate its entire interior meant that when the large entrance doors were closed, the inside became unfeasibly gloomy. The situation wasn't helped by the temple itself being shielded from the bulk of the day's sunlight by the steep sides of the gorge in which it lay hidden. A number of stone protuberances jutting from the interior walls suggested – from the sooted masonry surrounding them – that they'd once been used to accommodate artificial illumination. But it all seemed so unnecessary. It would have been far simpler, Chad reasoned, if the temple's architects had included a few more windows in their original design. After all... holes cost nothing and were extremely easy to draw.

Then again, nothing surprised him when it came to religious minds. They were anathema to him. Being religious, he argued, was like being a junkie. You got to view the world through exceptionally rose-tinted glasses... occasionally spoke to someone who wasn't there... became a pontificating bore when conversing with others about your fixation... and for the promise of something better to come, traded the ability to think rationally for a life based on guilt and a paranoia that has you believing someone is watching your every move.

'Let's go through this methodically and see what we've got.' Chad ran his hand over the smooth surface of the plinth above which the spectacular column of light had danced the previous evening. 'Last night we witnessed a short series of unexplained already witnessed their interference, though it is presently more from curiosity than maliciousness. But their inquisitiveness, if allowed to grow, could present a serious problem. We must act quickly and without delay. So, listen carefully... It is vital you do *exactly* as asked.'

Norman leant forward eagerly.

'Your first task is to devise a computer program that can break down images and sound into a binary code and store the information digitally.' Gabriel paused, in order the point be understood.

'Is that it?' exclaimed Norman. 'That's all you want me to do?' He turned towards his computer. 'No problem!'

'Norman.'

'It's a piece of cake! All I have to do is configure the...'

'NORMAN!'

His fillings rattled again.

'Listen...! *Carefully!*'

He nodded sheepishly.

'The binary code for both images and sound must relate in *exact* mathematical proportion to one another as they coexist in the real world. In other words... you must be able to store their constituent wavelengths and frequencies in a precise ratio, enabling a direct numerical comparison between these individual expressions of creative energy. For our purposes, you will assume the visible spectrum of light to range from a wavelength of three hundred and ninety nanometres to one of seven hundred and forty nanometres, correlating directly with an audible range between twenty and twenty thousand hertz. Furthermore... you must be able to replay these separate codes simultaneously and in such a way as to produce a physical expression of their binary nature. Is that clear?'

Norman stared at the Archangel. 'I think I'll need to write it down.'

*   *   *

Chad surveyed the temple's interior. It wasn't at all what he'd not succeed. Time will be your enemy as it will be their ally. Our coalition of helpers is in danger of being unravelled by it. We must achieve our task before this happens... You alone, Norman, will know the true importance of this mission... and you alone must bear that burden.'

Norman was used to bearing burdens. There was his personality, for one.

He struggled for the right words to utter at such a portentous moment, groping around in what seemed a pathetically inadequate vocabulary. 'Why me?' he eventually blurted out, the words sounding like an echo from his childhood.

'Because you have the skills and temperament to achieve the task,' came the answer.

Norman felt a flush of pride.

'And absolutely no friends to distract you,' added Gabriel bluntly.

A flush of despondency followed.

'And you have the vision.'

'I *do?*'

'Of course. I'm standing right here in front of you. Now... I expect you'll be wondering what it is we want you to do?'

'I was rather.'

'The answer to that is complex.'

Norman thought it might be. 'It doesn't involve carpentry, does it?' he asked warily. The thought had occurred that he might be expected to build an ark. After all... he wasn't *that* far from London Zoo. Obtaining the timber might present a headache, mind... not to mention the excessive amount of hammering involved.

Gabriel shook his head. 'We need your programming skills.'

'To save the *Universe?*'

'Precisely. Your task will be broken down into a number of assignments. You will be informed of each assignment only as you have need to undertake it. That way you will be protected for as long as possible.'

'*Protected.* Protected from *what?*'

'From those who may misinterpret our mission. We have

328

In an attempt to survive, he'd embarked on writing a computer game that would set the world alight. But despite numerous attempts, he hadn't even got it to smoulder. Not for want of expertise. His genius for programming meant he could easily produce on screen what he had in his mind. The trouble was... what he had in his mind seemed to be in everybody else's. His games – though technically brilliant – lacked originality. It was no good getting a metal aardvark to bounce if the *reason* for him bouncing was short on creative flair.

If computers had failed to provide an answer to his future, they'd also been unable to provide him with an answer for his past. Despite their vast powers of calculation, they were incapable of resolving the one question that had haunted him for so long... *Why him?*

Why had fate singled him out that day in class? Why couldn't it have been one of the *other* children who'd unintentionally disgraced themselves? What had been so special about *his* bowels?

'Norman! Are you listening to what I'm saying?' asked Gabriel sharply. 'It is you we have chosen to be our instrument here on Earth.'

Norman's thoughts found themselves yanked back inside the walls of his bedsit.

The heavenly choir performed fortissimo.

'You mean... you want me to become the next... *Saviour?*' he stuttered.

The music crashed to an ungainly halt.

'Good grief, no!' winced Gabriel. 'We'll need someone with personality for *that.*'

It started up again.

'No, Norman... yours will be the pivotal role in a plan as complex as it is vital. There are others who will help you. They will act because of their faith and because they have been commanded so to do. But they will not know the true meaning of their participation and must never come to know yours. This last point is crucial. For there are others who will threaten our mission through greed and ignorance. It is imperative they do needles and stifling smell of father's pipe smoke into the invigorating, no-nonsense world of binary logic.

It was a world blissfully free from all the products of muddled human thinking that had caused him so much pain... cruelty, prejudice, injustice, ignorance and indifference. It was a world without judgement, exciting and new, with clearly defined rules... whose interface did exactly what it was told and never let him down. He could *trust* a computer. It was a kindred spirit... an empathetic silicon soul.

To be or not to be... and nothing in-between.

Quickly realising that he who mastered its technology would be mastering the technology of the future, he'd devoted every moment of his spare time to doing just that; finally coming to understand computers better than he understood the outside world... and certainly better than the outside world would ever understand him.

But perhaps their greatest blessing had been that he could indulge his passion without having to venture beyond the comfort zone of his four bedroom walls... his only voluntary attempt at assimilation into the maelstrom beyond them being a three-year university course in *advanced computer studies*. Even then, he'd merely dipped a toe in it. Social interaction was deemed an unnecessary interruption to his quest for further knowledge... as was sleeping, eating, personal hygiene and members of the opposite sex. In fact, he'd managed to complete his course a virgin... thus achieving a first for students worldwide, as well as in his degree.

Graduating with ridiculous ease, he regarded this period as a complete and utter waste of time. Not only had he ended up teaching the lecturers more than they'd taught him, his degree had failed to secure him a job.

An astute human resources manager might spot that this was due to one glaring fault in his interview technique... He failed to turn up for them. Freed from the ordeal of education, he'd retreated back behind the safety of his four walls; the only thing now standing between him and a glowing career being his front door.

mother made her way out of the school gates, a large plastic bag held out stiffly in front of her as if containing some deadly radioactive isotope. The scene would have been comic enough – to anyone but himself – without the embarrassment of one final detail. It was engineered, he swore, by forces beyond him in order he provide the punch line to some grand cosmic joke. The bag had come from his mother's bakery. The picture left forever scarred upon his brain, was that of the one on the bag itself... a large, brown chocolate éclair.

He was never allowed to forget it. From that day on, he became Pooey Penkridge... victim, social outcast and butt of everyone's jokes. The fact his name lent itself to such alliteration was only further proof the Universe was out to get him.

In such a warped Universe, missing the toilet by sixty seconds or twenty-seven feet and four inches not only ruined your chances of being picked anywhere but last for team events, it also gave you a flea infestation. It became common knowledge that if any of his classmates touched him, they too would suffer the same affliction... though, curiously enough, only temporarily. When such contact *did* occur, the victim would thoughtfully warn others in the vicinity by screaming '*fleas*' at the top of their voice whilst waving the infected limb about hysterically.

Understandably, he couldn't expect to be invited to birthday parties. After all... he might've infected the cake.

Without the prospect of peer-bonding during *pin the tail on the donkey* or *pass the parcel,* he'd been forced to look elsewhere for companionship.

And that's when he found it... the answer to his loneliness... an outlet for his rapidly developing intellect... a reciprocating intelligence that didn't care *who* it got touched by.

His first *computer.*

It entered into his life one Christmas morning with the force of a religion. Ensconced between a plate of mince pies and a pile of hastily discarded wrapping paper, he found himself transported from the mind-numbing *clack* of mother's knitting

331

national treasures?'

'Something's going to happen to you in a minute!' said the paper's editor, brandishing a ruler.

'Aha!' said Donald cheerfully. 'You see... you *are* capable of reporting something before the event!'

He felt himself tumbling backwards as a searing pain flashed across his buttocks.

'I TOLD YOU WE SHOULD'VE GONE TO THE TABLOIDS!' he yelped.

* * *

If Norman had considered having an audience with the Archangel Gabriel as suffering delusions of grandeur, where did being chosen from the whole of humanity to help save the Universe rank?

Then again, perhaps he shouldn't have been surprised. He'd always known he was different... ever since fate cruelly singled him out in his first year at school.

It had been an unfortunate incident – or, more accurately, *accident* – resulting from a combination of misplaced optimism and an equally misplaced bowel movement.

The school had called his mother away from her job at the local baker's, to bring clean underwear and a fresh pair of shorts... whilst *he* had been forced to stand awkwardly at the back of the classroom, suffering the taunts and stares of his peers. The teacher wasn't being cruel. She just didn't think it a good idea if he sat down. He'd sobbed until his throat was raw. But the final ignominy was having pretty Julie Swanson – the focus of his young, unrequited love – chosen to be the one to open the windows and let in some fresh air. He could just about have lived with that. It was the fact she'd felt it necessary to hold her nose whilst doing so that finally crushed what little self-esteem he'd had left.

Children could be cruel, he'd learnt... though not as cruel as life. For having been cleaned up and returned to the classroom, he was forced to sit with his jeering classmates and watch as his single particle of sunlight to the combined mass of all matter... It's all on the brink of ceasing to exist. And the responsibility for its salvation has been placed upon *your* shoulders.'

The choir *hallelujahed* with such intensity, the fillings of Norman's teeth rattled. 'I... I... don't understand!' he stuttered.

'Put another way...' said Gabriel. 'The lights are about to go out.'

'Then I *did* hear correctly,' gasped Norman. 'It's true what I heard!'

'Technically... *felt vibrated*,' Gabriel corrected him. 'But, yes... it is.'

Norman took a moment to dwell on the implications of what he'd just been told, then looked at the Archangel, ashen faced. 'Can I raise a practical point?' he asked.

Gabriel nodded.

'Whatever happened to "fear not!"?'

* * *

Donald Tucker-Jenkins was gripping the edge of the desk so tightly, his fingers were turning white. 'But you're a newspaper editor!' he yelled, as a handful of journalists tried to prise them off. 'You're supposed to report the news!'

'Unlike some of our competitors, we don't print fiction!' responded the owner of the desk, handing one of his employees a sharpened pencil. 'And any news we do print is done *after* it's happened, not before!'

Donald felt a stabbing pain in the back of his hand. 'That's not true!' he howled. 'What about your horoscope?'

'Get him out of here!' said the desk owner angrily.

'If not the actual broadsheet... how about the Sunday supplement?' pleaded Donald stubbornly.

'I'll put you in hospital!' squealed one of the journalists, examining an imprint of Donald's teeth on their arm.

'I was rather hoping for the art pages,' said Donald, wrapping his legs around the base of a photocopier. 'Doesn't anybody care that something's going to happen to some of our greatest

Norman shook with anticipation.

'Not bad,' said Gabriel.

'Thanks.'

'For a mortal. But before you go, Norman,' said Gabriel gently, 'there's just one thing.'

'Mmm?'

'How will you know that the answer your landlord gives you is the correct one?'

Norman looked at him blankly.

'I'll put it another way... What if his parents are not who he believes them to be? That, after all, is a possibility... is it not?'

'A *slight* possibility,' conceded Norman.

'Most unlike you, Norman. I'll take that as a yes. And, if that's the case, it's possible that our answers will not tally... and you'll *still* not have proof that I do not exist. For only if the answers are the same will you know that I exist outside of your imagination. So seeing as you can only prove my *existence* – not my *non-existence* – by going downstairs, bothering to do so would mean you accept the possibility of my existence in the first place. So why not just accept it now and save yourself the journey?'

Norman felt his King wobble.

'Besides,' added Gabriel. 'Who's to say that your landlord isn't a figment of your imagination as well... along with this bedsit and everything in your entire life?'

Norman's king crashed to the floor. 'I suppose a small miracle's out of the question?' he whined.

'You have it in my patience,' retorted Gabriel. 'So... now that we accept I exist... let us proceed.' He expanded his wings, cuing the heavenly choir to increase its volume and flooding 66c Armageddon Terrace, once more, with musical gorgeousness.

'You have been chosen, Norman Penkridge, from the entire ocean of Humankind, to assist the powers of Heaven in this, its greatest moment of peril. For its very existence is in jeopardy, threatening the extinction of all life and matter in your Universe... and everybody else's. From the humblest blade of grass to the complex gravitational pattern of the stars... from a opponent a question he *himself* didn't know the answer to? If the answer, when verified, was correct, he'd have demonstrated that his visitation existed independently of himself.

He broke from his tactical stare and brought his Queen's Knight out into the open. 'Can I ask you something?'

Gabriel bowed his head and stared at the floor. 'Helmut and Gertrude.'

'Pardon?'

'Helmut and Gertrude,' repeated Gabriel.

'Helmut and Gertrude what?'

'Sorry... Oppenheimer. Helmut and Gertrude Oppenheimer. You were going to ask me the name of your landlord's parents.'

'I was?' This was news to Norman. He hadn't yet thought of his question... though had to confess – if he had – that would probably have been it.

'Yes,' replied Gabriel. 'And I'm as surprised as you. I thought you were going to ask for proof of God's existence or that I perform some kind of miracle.'

Norman's castle slid into place. 'Would you mind if I just popped downstairs for a minute?' he asked.

'What... right now?'

'Yes.'

'Well... it's highly irregular. In fact... it's something of a first. Most people are content to fall on their knees or prostrate themselves before me. You really are unusual to say the least, Norman Penkridge!'

'I'll be as quick as I can.'

'Where are you going?'

'I want to ask my landlord something.'

'What?'

Norman placed his castle boldly in front of his opponent's queen. 'The name of his parents.' He waited for a reaction.

'But I've just told you!' exclaimed Gabriel. 'Helmut and Gertrude Oppenh...'

There was an awkward silence.

A knowing smile crept into Gabriel's countenance.

His King had been exposed.

Damn! Norman flinched again. It was getting embarrassing. How could he win against an opponent who was himself... only better informed? If he was going to succeed, he needed to think in a way that would lure himself into a trap.

'You see,' continued Gabriel, 'not *everything* can be explained in black and white.'

Black and white! The phrase gifted Norman an idea. *That's it!*

'A mental game of *chess?*' queried Gabriel.

'Stop cheating!' protested Norman. 'Reading my mind isn't fair!'

'I thought you thought I *was* your mind?' countered Gabriel.

Norman's shoulders drooped. *Good point! Opponent's King's Pawn two squares forward. This isn't going to be easy.*

'I'd have thought it would be slightly harder than *not easy*,' suggested Gabriel. 'Try *impossible*.'

He's at it again!

Norman realised he'd have to find a way of stopping his opponent knowing what he was thinking. He concentrated on the image of an everyday object so as to block his deeper thoughts.

'A dustbin?' winced Gabriel.

At last! Queen's Pawn two squares forward.

'Move noted,' acknowledged Gabriel. 'Though if *I'm* unable to focus on anything other than the object you're now concentrating so hard on... how can *you?*'

Norman telepathically received an image of his opponent's bishop sliding out from the pack to take his dustbin.

He's right.

'Thank you.'

Norman quickly switched his attention to the poster of Xanthia on his wall and its two stand-out features, hoping they might provide a more challenging distraction for the Archangel.

'*Norman?*' said Gabriel uneasily.

It seemed to be working.

Perhaps, he privately mused as he seized the advantage, it wasn't a case of proving he was smarter than his opponent. Perhaps it was a case of proving he *wasn't*. What if he asked his

The Archangel looked at him blankly.

'Because you'll always know what it is I'm about to think... Isn't that so?'

Gabriel said nothing.

'Well... isn't it?'

'Are you asking me as a figment of your imagination or as a representative of the Supreme Being who is all-knowing?' replied Gabriel calmly. 'Either way, the answer to your question is *yes*.'

Norman flinched. *He's good*, he thought. *Though maybe that should be... I'm good?*

'I can see you're still having trouble coming to terms with all this,' sighed Gabriel. 'It seems that very quality which attracted us to you in the first place is what's making it hard for you to accept the situation.'

'And what quality is that?' challenged Norman.

'The ability to condense complex situations into a simple logical understanding,' replied Gabriel.

'Well, I'm certainly having trouble with this particular one!' Norman agreed.

'That's because great strengths become great weaknesses if they narrow the mind. You're trying too hard to reduce everything to a simple state of yes or no. True?'

'No.'

The Archangel coughed politely.

'That's not fair!'

'It's why you're so good at programming computers,' said Gabriel. 'You think like one.'

'That doesn't mean I'm not open-minded!'

'Have you ever considered that I might be here and not here at exactly the same moment in time?' asked Gabriel.

'Of course not!'

Gabriel smiled.

'Wait a minute!' objected Norman. 'That's nothing to do with not being open-minded. It's just an impossible situation!'

'Is it? Then how come you acknowledge my being here by talking to me, then continue to insist to yourself that I'm not!'

337

And the more he endeavoured to do so, the more difficult it became.

'Don't worry,' advised Gabriel. 'Your brain's trying too hard. Just accept what you see and it'll get easier.'

Norman removed his hands. 'It's accepting what I'm seeing that's the *difficult* bit!' he exclaimed.

'It's all down to you,' said Gabriel. 'You put the wings on me, so their feathers feel reassuringly familiar to you. That's why you're seeing them so clearly. But the rest will come in time. Just have faith and relax.'

Norman grudgingly released the claw-like grip his toes had applied to the end of his socks. But his doubts refused to stand down. *There had to be a logical explanation for all this.*

'I would have given you more time to get over our first meeting,' said Gabriel, glancing at the computer screen, 'but you've rather forced my hand.'

Norman followed his gaze. 'I'm not sure I understand.'

'Your letter. It's only natural you're feeling confused and disorientated. But whilst we appreciate your desire to share this experience with another, this cannot be, for reasons that will make themselves obvious. This is very important, Norman. Do you understand?'

Having just convinced himself the Archangel didn't exist, Norman felt himself to be in an extremely awkward position.

If what he was seeing and hearing was nothing more than the product of his own psychosis, then the command not to tell anybody about it was being given by the very hallucination for which he required help.

Should he feel proud, he pondered, or deeply embarrassed to have been outwitted by his own imagination? Furthermore... if his hallucination had proved itself to be cleverer than he, shouldn't he be following its advice?

'I think that's a good idea,' suggested Gabriel, reading his mind.

'Just a second!' said Norman, engrossed in his own line of thought. 'If you're the product of my imagination, I should *expect* you to be one step ahead of me!'

338

serotonin levels. She'll recommend a good night's sleep... that I simply laugh the whole thing off. As easy as that... Problem solved. God... she's brilliant!'

He leant back contentedly and pondered whether cherubs should begin with a capital C.

Boing. Boing.

Spikey?

The little Aardvark had materialised in the guise of a bouncing screensaver. At least... the computer's screen had gone blank and Spikey was bouncing all over it.

Norman felt the blood chill in his veins. He didn't *have* a Spikey screensaver.

He shot a quick glance towards the microwave.

Ping.

As the image of a video player flitted across his mind, the real one switched itself on and spat out the tape.

He groaned.

An orange-sized ball of light appeared exactly where it had the night before.

After a few seconds of nonchalant hovering, it pulsated... then exploded, leaving the room bathed in an aura of light. Once more, cherubs appeared with their trumpets, the heavenly choir giving forth in full voice. And in the midst of it all... Gabriel... the tips of his wings lightly dusting the polystyrene coving that nestled pointlessly between the walls and ceiling.

'Don't look so surprised,' he announced. 'I told you I'd be back.'

'Oh, God,' whimpered Norman, covering his eyes with his hands.

'Not quite,' said Gabriel, still clearly visible.

At least... *some* parts were. Others seemed less so.

The wings were magnificent, their detail clearer than anything Norman had ever seen before. He could make out the barbs of each feather as if viewing them through a magnifying glass. But when it came to recognising what the Archangel was wearing or the finer details of his face, he found the opposite applied. He seemed unable to focus on what was before him.

Xanthia would know *exactly* what to do!

It never ceased to amaze Norman how one so young and beautiful – without any formal training or higher education – managed to impart such mature words of wisdom to the predominantly male readers of her tabloid agony column, *Ask Xanthia*. True, the problems she dealt with always seemed to be of an overtly sexual nature; and true, the only evidence she actually wrote the replies herself lay in the semi-naked picture of her which graced the top of the column... just above the words *Guys... wanna offload on Xanthia?* But this was good enough for him. She wouldn't lend her name to anything sordid or underhand. Not his Xanthia.

He started to type.

He pictured her collagen-injected lips reading his words.

She appeared to be reading them incredibly slowly. Probably because she was deliberating on every word, he reasoned. She wouldn't want to make a hasty judgement. She would take her time... try to understand his inner turmoil. Perhaps she'd want to meet him face to face to talk the matter over. After all... she'd need to delve deeply into his psychological make-up before delivering her judgement. She'd want to connect with him.

He pictured her connecting with him.

His pulse rate quickened.

He put it down to nerves and wiped the dribble from his chin.

He thought it best to omit the bit about him passing out. He also thought it best to omit the fact his attempt at capturing a moving image of the visitation had merely resulted in him capturing a still image of her breasts... heavenly though they may be.

As he typed, he felt a large weight being lifted from his shoulders. Just *sharing* his experience with her was having a cathartic effect.

'She'll be thinking *hallucination*,' he told himself. 'Probably due to the lateness of the hour... or perhaps an imbalance in my

A pencil-thin shaft of sunlight squeezed its way between a fissure in the gully and filtered its way through the driver's window to the chrome surround of the van's cigarette lighter. Then – carefully observing the rules of refracted light as defined by *Sod's Law* – struck Chad squarely in the eyes with laser precision. He flinched from the intrusion. It would have woken him had he ever managed to sleep, wedged – as he was – across the front seats. Instead... it came as a welcome relief, marking the end of an excruciatingly long night spent trying to ignore the freezing temperature, his cramped surroundings and the staggering array of weird and wonderful noises emanating from both ends of his colleague.

On cue, Bob let out the kind of snort usually associated with a zoo or some remote and inaccessible cave. Chad fumbled between the driver's pedals for one of his shoes and aimed it at the slumbering mass in the back of the van.

'Time to rise and shine, Sleeping Beauty.'

'Don't you have to kiss me first?' came the mumbled reply.

'I'd rather kiss the spectre of Death,' responded Chad.

'I bet he's not as coquettish,' pouted Bob.

Chad raised himself up on one elbow, carefully extricating himself from the confines of the overhanging steering column. 'Any more coffee in the flask?' he yawned.

'There's sweet f-all, Wonder Boy. Operations didn't know you intended turning our one day assignment into a full-blown vacation.'

'How's the water situation?'

'Slightly worse than the coffee one.'

Chad delicately lowered himself onto his back and stared at the beads of condensation gathering on the cab roof and threatening to attack. 'Then I guess we'd better not waste time getting started. Let's see what caused the fireworks last night and get ourselves outta here.'

'Sounds good in principle,' said Bob. 'Just don't think it's going to be so easy in practice.'

A matching shoe struck him on the head.

It was a bit like when you meet a stranger at a party and they deftly slip the topic of reincarnation into the conversation. At first, things appear balanced and reasonable. Then you're informed that... yes... they've been regressed and... would you believe it... were once an Egyptian princess... or – better still – Merlin at the court of King Arthur.

If you've had a few drinks, you might be impressed. If you haven't... you'll wish you had.

They never turn out to be humble Joseph Soap – lifelong farm worker and liver of a perfectly normal, humdrum existence – who died peacefully in his sleep of old age... without ever having had his throat cut or been chased across fields by the King's men.

Was the fact his brain had produced the Archangel Gabriel a sign of mental delusion stemming from repressed feelings of superiority, he wondered?

Prior to his research, he would have reasoned that a celestial entity couldn't get much grander. But having just found out that they could get *seven levels* grander, he comforted himself with the fact that at least his subconscious hadn't deemed it necessary to conjure up the divine embodiment of death.

And if he finally needed convincing that it was all in his mind, there was Gabriel's parting comment. He swore he'd heard him say something about helping to save the Universe. Things couldn't be more absurd than that. It *had* to be a mental aberration.

Which brought him full circle.

It was all too confusing.

He looked across to the spot where he'd experienced the Archangel standing the previous evening and wondered who in the entire – hopefully *not* endangered – Universe, would be able to offer him sensible counsel?

And then it hit him.

Of course! Why didn't he think of it before?

His answer was looking straight back at him... with a pout.

* * *

342

either-he-goes-or-I-do ultimatum, and Norman found himself quickly promoted to second alter boy's assistant, a position he endured until the lure of university furnished him with an excuse to stop going through the motions... and his parents a chance to emigrate to Canada.

In all that time, he never actually found God... and the nearest he'd come to a miracle was witnessing first-time visitors to the congregation succeeding in singing along to the more *progressive* hymns on offer... those whose melodies put Spikey's jumping abilities to shame.

In recent years, he'd taken to writing *ATHEIST* on forms, next to the box requesting his religion. [For the record... next to the one marked *SEX*, he'd taken to writing *CHANCE WOULD BE A FINE THING*].

Now – having dismissed Heaven as a fairytale – a part of it had ended up floating above his living room carpet... suggesting that if there *was* a God, it certainly *did* move in mysterious ways.

So... back to his problem.

He saw the image of an angel because that, according to Gabriel, was what his indoctrinated subconscious expected he should in such circumstances. But what if he'd been schooled in a different faith? Gabriel would presumably have appeared in an alternative guise and with a completely different name.

In that case... which form would be the *real* heavenly messenger?

If Gabriel were to be believed... it didn't matter. Therefore, were bejewelled elephants and bizarre, multi-limbed figures – even creatures resembling half a monkey and half a crocodile – as valid a part of Heaven's hierarchy as Cherubim and Seraphim? And more perplexingly... wouldn't this mean that all things and everything were possible at the same time?

And then there was the matter of the Top Banana.

It was one thing to accept he'd actually had an encounter with an angel in the first place. But the *Archangel Gabriel?*

Even Joan of Arc only claimed to communicate with a few dead Saints... and look what happened to *her!*

result of advantageous cell mutations over a frighteningly long period of time had been trumped by religious indoctrination over an incomparably shorter one.

It started with excruciating attempts at *All Things Bright and Beautiful*... aged five... inflicting pain on his fellow peers in equal measures of tone deafness and stubborn determination.

But it was the words, not the butchered notes, that mattered... *The Lord God made them all.*

Aged five... who were you to argue? Not only were you struggling to come to terms with having to tie your own shoe laces... should you be of the mind to advance Darwinism to its logical conclusion, whilst mucking about on the swings, and bring the matter up in assembly, you were at a height preordained by natural selection for receiving a clip around the head for insubordination and cheek.

Had he hoped to escape further indoctrination with a few crucified melodies and the occasional mumbled *Amen*, he was to be disappointed.

Heaven – to Norman's parents – was having him out of the house for as long as possible. So, at the earliest opportunity, they'd enlisted him in Sunday school, a hotbed of religious activity which taught him, via large, colourful picture books, that Jesus... judging by his long, golden, ringletted hair and pale, kindly countenance... was obviously a western European... as were his disciples... excepting Judas, of course... and that God had a beard.

When he'd outgrown the pictures and started questioning Miss Primm – his teacher and vicar's fiancée – as to what *adultery* involved and what exactly a *sodomite* did, he'd been hastily moved up into the church choir.

There was, of course, one glaringly obvious problem.

It was recognised by Gavin Thebston, choir master and campest ever winner of *The Doris Picklehorn Musical Scholarship*, fifteen seconds into *Mein Gott Ist Meine Liebe,* when Norman's descending tenor line didn't... it flat-lined.

Gavin – accompanied by an unnecessary amount of hand waving and hair tossing – offered Miss Primm's fiancé a hissed governing body, answering directly to He-who-knew-all-the-answers-anyway.

These were followed by Virtues. Responsible for miracles, they apparently emitted beams of divine energy and worked on a *the-more-you-put-in-the-more-you-get-out* basis. The more attuned and cooperative mortals became with them, the more spiritual muscle at their disposal and better it was for everyone... a bit like the Mafia, but with a slightly different ethical slant.

Further still down the pecking-order came Powers... *Bearers of the conscience of all Humanity*. Clearly not a nine to five occupation. Given they boasted amongst their ranks the Angel of Birth, one might initially be excited at the prospect of bumping into one. But given they also boasted the Angel of Death... then again, perhaps not.

Finally, you had the lowest sphere, whose beings acted as heavenly messengers, the highest of which were Principalities... responsible for guarding over entire countries, but who would gladly consider the odd city if needs must.

It was the level below these that Archangels occupied... above your ordinary Angel and responsible for keeping an eye on what mankind got up to as a collective whole. Gabriel was one of only a handful named in the Bible and it was he who had been chosen to impart the news to the Virgin Mary that she was in for a bit of a shock and had better dust off the knitting needles.

And that's how it was... unless, of course, you were one of the countless millions of other souls on the planet who believed something entirely different altogether... which is where Norman's fierce sense of logic encountered its first dilemma... if you didn't include believing in a God in the first place.

His own belief system – or lack of one – had developed in tandem with his pubic hair.

Having never volunteered to be religious, the concept of a supreme being was programmed into him from an early age, before he'd had time to do some programming of his own. In balder times, the notion that he was nothing more than the time...? When next time?'

The phrase 'what about the message?' was the last thing to be heard... if you didn't count the spluttered gurgle of an Armitage & Shanks self-fill, overhead toilet cistern, circa 1930, from above 66d's bathroom floorboards.

It was now second number forty-seven thousand, eight hundred and twenty-eight and things hadn't gotten any clearer.

Norman had, however, become more knowledgeable.

In an attempt to reconcile what had happened to him, he'd spent the best part of those seconds surfing the internet. At first he'd explored *delusional disorders*, thinking it better if he could put his encounter down to something that could be scientifically explained. But the thought of not being able to trust his own senses upset him so much, he'd hedged his bets and studied *celestial beings and the workings of Heaven*, hoping to discover exactly what an Archangel was and the likelihood of you coming across one in your bedsit.

According to his research, the odds were pretty slim.

There were seven ranks of celestial beings if you believed the Old Testament... nine if you considered the New. They comprised Angels, Archangels, Principalities, Powers, Virtues, Dominions, and Thrones, with The New Testament throwing in Cherubim and Seraphim for good measure. Together, these made up the nine choirs of Angels.

He'd sung about Cherubim and Seraphim in school assemblies, assuming them to be something akin to frankincense and myrrh. But Cherubim were God's throne bearers and Seraphim, its Guardians. They were placed at numbers two and one respectively in the hierarchy of celestial entities... assuming the Supreme Being to be beyond a digit, of course.

At number three in this heavenly hit parade sat Thrones... 'Buddy Angels' for the planets. As each planet had one, there was, it followed, an Earth Angel who – in Norman's humble opinion – had drawn the short straw.

Next came Dominions... bureaucrats of the divine realm, in charge of the lower orders; a kind of unelected, celestial known it was because of Chad's insistence that this was so, he would have admired him even more.

Chad awaited a reaction.

'You're such a sanctimonious asshole!' Bob obliged.

* * *

The last twenty-four hours had not been the easiest for Norman Penkridge. The day had started ordinarily enough. At least... the first fifteen seconds of it had.

It was the sixteenth where things had gotten a little sticky. This was the second in which thoughts of reaching for his slippers had been rudely interrupted by the recollection of an angelic encounter the previous night.

Seconds seventeen to forty-nine were a bit of a blur... and those from fifty onwards, complete confusion, as thoughts ricocheted around his head like the metal ball in a pinball machine, his mind trying to come to terms with exactly what *had* happened.

It was a dream, it had suggested weakly.

No it wasn't, it had countered strongly. Dreams didn't involve writing the words *whatever I think in the morning, I certainly wasn't dreaming* on a desktop jotter.

And then there was his attempt at capturing the event on his computer.

He'd played the footage over and over again before going to bed that night and a hundred times more in the morning. But the scenario remained unchanged. There was the picture of Xanthia on the wall... and the only voice that could be heard was his own saying, 'Maybe it would be better if we started right from the beginning. Perhaps a formal introduction would help. I realise you're an angel ... but do you have a name?'

A brief period of silence followed before the exhalation of a long, low whistle and then the words 'Oh boy... Top banana!'... more silence... a failed attempt to pass out... some profuse apologising... an even longer silence and then his frantic pleading of 'Whoa...! Where are you going...? Wait...! Next the General demanded.

Bob awaited the answer with interest.

'We've a little more work to do,' Chad replied.

'And what *exactly* might that be?' enquired the General.

Bob looked to his partner. 'Classified?' he ventured.

Chad nodded.

The van door slammed shut.

'So,' said Bob, as the General's disgruntled voice was heard barking orders to his Lieutenant. 'Why d'ya wanna spend another day in this friggin' sweat hole? You suddenly become a tourist?'

Chad stared at him incredulously. 'You saw what I saw. The lights... the electrical disturbances... everyone sitting in total darkness and not saying a word... their coming all the way here to say and do absolutely nothing of importance whatsoever. Any of that make sense to you?'

Bob shook his head. 'Nope... not a bit of it.'

'Precisely! And you wanna pack up and go without attempting to discover some answers? There's gotta be a reason for what just happened. And we're gonna find it!'

Of this, his partner had no doubt. For all Bob's constant taunting, there was no one he admired more than the man sat in front of him, determination etched into his face. He was one of those rare individuals who could demonstrate the same relaxed pulse rate and clarity of thought under fire as he might whilst sunning himself on a beach. Nothing phased him and nothing got the better of him. But his greatest asset was his ability to think rationally and logically... to mentally compartmentalise, applying a considerable intellect objectively and unfettered to any problems that got in his way. He was the department's golden boy; Eliot Ness and Sherlock Holmes rolled into one. If they'd given him a blue cape and red underpants, Bob swore the man would be able to fly. That's why they'd picked him for this particular mission and why he wasn't going to let them down. There was only one thing that mystified him, and that was how he – Bob – had been lucky enough to remain paired to the best of the bunch over all these years. If he'd stout cigar.

'So, come on boys… what's the story?'

Chad and Bob looked at each other and then at their visitor.

'Sorry, General,' said Chad calmly. 'That's classified information.'

'Wait a second!' said the General assertively. 'Don't give me that operational crap! I've damn near busted my butt getting this lot out here without having them tear each other apart. And now, after less than twenty minutes in some goddam disused Santa's Grotto, they wanna go home. So… I'd at least like to know what all this bullshit's been about!'

'It's classified bullshit,' said Bob sweetly. 'Besides… you wouldn't believe us if we told you.'

'Try me!' said the General, an even wider grin wrapped around his cigar.

'No can do,' said Chad.

The General's demeanour changed. 'Okay… Then I hope you have yourselves a safe journey tonight… because don't think of calling on my boys for assistance if you lose that poor excuse of a road in the dark and find yourselves belly up in some goddam wadi!'

'Thanks for your concern,' said Chad, 'but we're staying here.'

Bob – having just helped himself to a large mouthful of water – saw most of it re-emerge as he tried to prevent himself from becoming the first person to drown in the middle of a desert. Wiping the spillage from his chin, he shot a pained, *now what?* expression at Chad.

'You can't drive this van outta here in broad daylight tomorrow!' protested the General. 'You guys ain't supposed to be here. Someone could be checking on *us*.'

'Not a problem,' said Chad coolly. 'We're sticking here for at least another twenty-four hours. The dust will have well and truly settled by then.'

This time he received the full *are-you-friggin'-serious* stare from his partner.

'And what *possible* reason is there for you guys staying on?'

Four heads? That bush didn't even have one! insisted the Jews... adding as an afterthought, *albeit it did talk before it combusted.*

Bush? gasped the Druids. *Do you not know a sacred oak tree when you see one?*

Perhaps it was both but in different incarnations, suggested the Buddhists diplomatically.

Don't start that again! groaned the Gnostics.

Who are you to tell us what to do? weighed in the Protestants. *We'll start whatever we want!*

People! People! appealed the Bahá'ís. *Are we not one?*

That depends, mused the Taoists.

By the way, interjected the Mennonites politely. *Anybody seen the Amish?*

And so the conversation continued... degenerating into personal insults about each other's mode of attire and a hotly contested dispute as to which day of the week – if any – the Sabbath should be held on.

Chad and Bob tried to make sense of it all as the clamour of voices increased, but were finally forced to give up when the resulting surge in volume caused the microphones to distort.

It reached a peak when the Protestants threatened to thump everyone... the Jains pointing out that they considered the threat unfair, given they weren't allowed to thump back.

As battle fatigue finally dulled the vigour of theological argument, the idea slowly dawned that perhaps a command from the almighty should take precedent over whether a monk's scapular was more appropriate to execute it in than a costume better suited to the wardrobe of a touring theatrical company.

A sense of importance and gravitas returned.

Whatever our differences, we must return forthwith and implement our instructions, said the Catholics solemnly.

There they go again! exclaimed the Muslims. *Why is it they always have to take charge?*

There was a mad rush for the temple door before anyone else could answer.

The van door slid open to reveal a grinning face attached to a

'But it's going to be on a huge scale!' said Donald. 'It's going to affect the whole world!'

'And all you can be definite about is that it starts with the theft of some paintings?'

Donald gave the matter some thought. '*Possibly.*'

'That's what I thought. Now, if you'll excuse me, sir, I've got to deal with the line of people behind you who will, no doubt, have more pressing crimes to report... such as missing pets, unfair traffic wardens and failure to realise their MOT had expired three years ago. Good day.'

'I KNOW HE'S BEING IRONIC!' yelled Donald to himself.

The desk sergeant snorted and lifted the desk flap.

Donald turned and ran.

*　　*　　*

After quarter of an hour, the silence in the temple ended as abruptly as it had begun, an eruption of frenzied voices swamping Chad's headphones. It was as if a spell had been broken, instantly releasing its victims from a deep paralysis.

The cardinals were the first to rise, signalling for calm. Unaware that each religion had interpreted their own visitation, they sought to exploit what they believed to be their good fortune. *We give praise to God that His heavenly representative has appeared before us all, confirming the Christian doctrine to be the one true way!*

What are they on about? objected the Muslims.

'Fair question,' murmured Bob, shaking his head.

The appearance of the Archangel Gabriel, returned the Catholics confidently.

Since when? frowned the Shintoists.

'Another fair question,' mumbled Chad.

Surely you mean the Guru Nanak, voiced the Sikhs.

We think you'll find his name is Moroni, the Mormons challenged them.

Not according to the Hindus. *With four heads and four arms, it was most definitely Brahma.*

'We should open a window?'

'The audio's working perfectly!'

Bob looked at him blankly.

'Don't you see, Bob? It's been picking up all the time. They're just not saying anything! They're sitting in total silence!'

As the penny dropped, Bob jerked his body into action. 'And darkness! Shit! I was so distracted by those friggin' lights, I forgot to switch over to night vision! Give me a second.'

It took seven before the ghostly images of men sitting quietly and staring at an empty space in front of them filled the screens, the bright white of their widened eyes contrasting eerily with the background of nondescript green.

'What the hell's going on?' said Bob, holding his head.

'Search me,' responded Chad. 'Are the machines still recording?'

'Affirmative,' shouted Bob loudly.

The two men sat and observed the sight in front of them without further comment.

Those in the temple did the same... though what they were watching was *far* more interesting.

*　　*　　*

'Go away!' said the policeman forcefully.

'At least take my name!' insisted Donald Tucker-Jenkins, stabbing the counter with his finger.

The desk sergeant looked at him dispassionately. 'And for what possible purpose?'

'Well... you may need to talk to me again when things start to happen. I could have valuable information.'

'Then it's a shame you can't give it to us now... isn't it, sir?' said the desk sergeant, dryly. 'Whilst we applaud members of the public coming in to inform us of crimes about to be committed, it does help if they're able to furnish us with useful facts such as what, when, where and even why. Unfortunately – in your case – you're unable to furnish us with *any* of the aforementioned.'

'Negative.'

'Camera two?'

'Negative.'

'Camera three?'

'Chad! It's all as dead as a friggin' dodo. This is pointless!'

'I'll take that as a negative, shall I?'

Bob shook his head and slumped back in his chair. 'I hope they give us a decent pension.' Sighing heavily, he tapped out a cigarette from its packet. 'It's just a question of whether we bother to mention the lights or not in our report. I'd much rather face early retirement than men in white coats.'

'Audio one... negative,' muttered Chad quietly to himself.

In the temple, it was a different story.

At the precise moment the individually interpreted visitations appealed for silence, the column of light had spectacularly dissolved. For the two men in the surveillance van, the show was over. For those in the temple, it had only just begun.

The multitude sat in silent rapture, heeding their visitations' instructions. You could have heard a pin drop.

Which is why a sudden yelp of intense pain from a corner of the chamber – in which the shaman from Papua New Guinea had just encountered a scavenging scorpion – caused a few of the seated mass to jump with shock and a member of the Seventh Day Adventists to break wind.

'Audio five... a yelp!'

'Pardon?'

'I heard a yelp on five!'

'Hearing voices? Now, that's definitely the first sign of mad...'

Chad raised his hand for silence.

'And a fart!' he exclaimed. 'My audio check just produced a fart!'

'I usually blame the dog.' Bob took a long draw on his cigarette and slowly released the smoke into the air.

'You know what this means?' said Chad excitedly.

353

'Earthquake?' Bob nervously gripped the side of his chair.

Before Chad could answer, the disturbances abruptly ceased.

A huge column of rainbow-flecked light now stood upright upon the large, central pedestal.

Those inside the temple were in total disarray, many having fallen to their knees in prayer. Others were crossing themselves wildly, whilst some seemed at a loss as to what to do next.

The *real* reason for their hysteria, however, was not being seen by the two men in the van. At the precise moment the refracted rays had converged upon the central pedestal, a brilliant orange ball of light had appeared in the middle of it and exploded. At that point, each onlooker had received their own personal heavenly visitation. Angels, Gods, spirits and the occasional burning bush had appeared in accordance with the beholder's faith. In the midst of it all, a shaman from Papua New Guinea ran screaming to the rear of the building, diving into the nearest corner and cowering in terror.

'We've gotta get the machines recording again,' yelled Chad, replacing his headphones, despite the cacophony of tongues now spewing out of them. 'If we don't get proof of this, we're looking at an earlier than anticipated retirement!'

'Or a forced trip to an asylum!' said Bob, furiously attacking the console in front of him.

'How we doin'?'

'Give me a few seconds!'

The screens suddenly went dark and the clamour from Chad's headphones came to an abrupt halt.

'What've you done?'

'Don't blame me!' said Bob, quickly raising his hands in the air. 'We've lost total transmission!'

'Impossible!'

'Power failure?'

'No way. Everything's on independent batteries. It's a failsafe system. It can't happen!'

'Well *something* friggin' has!'

'We need to do an emergency check,' said Chad, composing himself. 'Camera one?'

'What's happening?' demanded Chad, rising from his seat.

'Must be a technical glitch,' said Bob, fiddling with the controls.

'Can't be! It's being picked up by all four cameras.'

'Interference?'

'From *what*? We're in the middle of nowhere!'

The two men watched in silence as the shimmering light continued flickering back and forth... in bemusement as it consolidated its brightness into a single, intense beam... then, in utter bewilderment as the solitary shaft of light splintered into a myriad of iridescent rays, each one striking out in a separate direction and cutting angled swathes through the gloom.

A buzz of excitement filled Chad's headphones. 'I can tell you one thing... It's not our equipment. Those guys are seeing what we are!'

'You're not kiddin'!' said Bob, studying the monitors so intently his nose hair was being wooed by static. 'You should see the expressions on their faces! But what the hell is it?'

'I Dunno!'

'Maybe we should inform the General. They may need assistance in there.'

'No way!' Chad cut him short. 'We're under strict orders not to intervene, remember?'

'Whoa!' whooped Bob, like a child at a funfair. 'Look at it now...! It's forming itself into a friggin' *shape!*'

The random shards of light were fusing into a coherent pattern, directly above the temple's central plinth.

A burst of white noise shot through Chad's headphones.

'Shit!' he howled, wrenching them from his head.

'The picture's going!' shouted Bob, the screens in front of him striped with interference. 'We're losing them!'

'We're losing *everything!* Look at the audio meters! They've gone crazy!'

The two men watched helplessly as the banks of racked equipment went into overdrive. Machines were thrown out of record and meter needles clattered violently as a tremor, increasing in frequency, began to rock the van.

Bob squinted at the screens. 'Mister Chaos, from the look of things. The big guns are grabbing the front seats and leaving the less pacifist religions to play musical chairs for the remainder. How about your end?'

'Sounds like they're in a hurry.'

'I'm not surprised. I just hope they've brought candles with 'em. It's getting friggin' dark in there!'

'That's the curious thing,' said Chad, scratching his chin. 'The timing's of their own choosing. Not that an earlier start would've made much difference, given there's only one window in the entire building!'

'Not that *we* need worry. I just have to switch to night vision and if one of those guys so much as picks his nose and sticks the booger on his plinth, I'll know about it!'

'You can put that to the test in...' Chad glanced at his wristwatch, 'four minutes and twenty seconds from... now.'

Bob shook his head and sniggered.

Chad raised his middle finger.

'Very nice,' said Bob. 'But I think you'll be needing that to wind your watch. I reckon it's running slow.'

The inside of the temple had just been plunged into darkness.

Chad turned and anxiously studied the screens. 'I don't understand,' he muttered, checking his watch against the van's clock. 'That's impossible. I triple-checked my calculations. It's April, twenty-third and I used the correct GPS coordinates. We should *definitely* have a few minutes of daylight left!'

'Then how come it's as dark as a camel's rectum in there?'

Chad fidgeted uncomfortably.

Bob was about to ask him if he had the correct GPS coordinates for the person who'd sold him his watch, when any sarcasm was instantly guillotined. 'I'll be damned!' He dropped his feet to the floor and blinked heavily, his eyes transfixed on the monitors in front of him. 'What the hell...'

They were showing the temple's interior awash with glistening light, its rapid shimmering to and fro causing the four screens to phosphoresce.

'A...friggin'...firmative, then.'

'Camera three?'

'Ditto'

Chad paused and swallowed his annoyance. 'Camera four?'

'Ditto to that ditto.'

There was silence.

'Well?'

'Well, what?'

'Aren't you gonna check me on my audio?'

'Okay, sure...... Chad?'

'Yeah?'

'How's your audio since we last checked it for the fuckteenth time a couple of minutes ago?'

'Properly, Bob! There's no point in having a procedure if you're not gonna follow it!'

'Jeez, Chad! Can't you remove the rule book from your ass just *once* in your friggin' life? You're the one with the headphones. You can either hear them coming in or you can't!'

'Throw away the method, Bob, and you throw away the certainty of success.'

Bob lifted a leg and gave his reply.

Chad bit his lip and muttered 'Audio one... affirmative... Audio two... affirmative...' quietly to himself... until he'd completed the procedure. This was the big one. He knew from the reaction coming out of Washington that it didn't get much bigger. When you had the leaders of every conceivable religion on Earth meeting at short notice and not letting on what it's about, you could be sure the red phones were ringing hot. Now wasn't the time to mess up. He pressed his headphones against his head as the chaotic babble of voices increased in them. 'You got anything interesting your end?'

Bob puffed out his cheeks. 'Looks like they're arguing over the seating arrangements. Told you they should've booked a conference room. Could've had printed name plaques on every chair... and I'd have a nice seating plan in front of me telling me who was friggin' who.'

'Anyone appear to be in charge?'

examined the reddening sky, the last shafts of sunlight squeezing their way through the gorge and striking the area around a small, solitary window, high in the temple's façade.

A sudden urgency overtook them.

'Thank you for your help, General,' said the Cardinal briskly. 'We'll manage ourselves from here.'

'You're welcome. We'll leave you to it and... well... good luck.'

'Sir... I really must insist!' interjected the Lieutenant pressingly from behind the General's shoulder.

'Goddamit, man! What is it *now?*'

The Lieutenant nodded towards a vehicle resembling a cross between an ice-cream van and a fish tank. The lone and rather distressed occupant was in the process of sliding down the inside of one of the glass panels, a splayed nose doing its best to slow his descent.

'Oh shit!' cried the Cardinal, picking up the hem of his cassock and racing over towards it.

'As I said,' the General shouted after him. 'You people just do what you gotta do. You have my word, and that of my Government, that you'll be afforded complete and utter privacy!'

'Okay, Bob... This is it. They're coming in!' Chad sat up and smartly adjusted his headphones.

His partner, by contrast, leisurely flicked a row of switches beneath a wall of video monitors and kept his feet on the console.

'Better run a final check,' said Chad, his back to him. 'Camera one?'

'Oh, come on. You've had us run through this a hundred times already,' groaned Bob. 'Relax... It's all working perfectly.'

'Camera one?' repeated Chad tersely.

'Affirmative,' Bob mumbled.

'Camera two?'

'That as well.'

'The word's "affirmative", Bob.'

358

could you possibly mistake God's meaning? His words were there in black and white! They'd be saying next that Dinosaurs really existed!

There was an awkward silence.

Or that Jesus wasn't the Son of God!

Ahem, coughed the Jews.

Excuse us, interjected the Hindus. *In this argument, you cannot simply dismiss the Vedas. After all... four hundred million of our followers cannot be wrong.*

Over nine hundred million of ours say they can! countered the Protestants aggressively.

Such Western imperial arrogance! shouted the Muslims. *Your numbers are meaningless, given the weakness of your daily observance!*

'Whoa there, people ... Whoa there!' shouted the General, raising his hands aloft and signalling for calm. 'Let's not start World War Three here, folks. At least, not over the death of a goddam fly... no matter *whom* the critter might've been in a previous life.'

The fly had in fact been another fly in a previous life, but that was neither here nor there. It had come as quite a shock to his circling comrades to see him lying on the ground, much wider and flatter than in his most recent incarnation. This was a new experience for them. The sudden swish of a donkey's tail was the greatest hazard normally faced. The shepherds just let them be, a symbiotic relationship having developed to benefit both species. To flies, the advantage of being able to land without being rudely greeted by a giant, pink appendage was obvious. To shepherds, the flies were something exciting to observe... and, on the dullest days, gossip about.

But now temptation had entered the valley in the guise of something new. The grass had appeared less brown and, as a result, countless future generations of flies would never be... and that was an awful lot of flies.

'Maybe we should be thinking of getting you people inside,' suggested the General smartly. 'Time's pressing on and it looks as if we're beginning to lose the light.'

The religious leaders stopped their bickering and anxiously

rather modest, four-column portico, drawing the observer's eyes away from an otherwise bland façade. In front of this lay the simple, walled courtyard into which it now seemed a host of carnival floats had gotten lost and shed their entire occupants.

Some of the assembled throng had chosen to kiss the ground on which they had been deposited; others to kneel or stand in prayer; others still to search for misplaced crosiers, prayer wheels, censers and all manner of religious paraphernalia to which they felt compelled to be attached. The place had never experienced such colour and gratuitous gilding. Had Father Christmas walked by, he might only have been noticed by the fact that he was unsuitably attired for the weather.

Given the temple courtyard now contained representatives of the biggest reason for conflict in the history of the world, the atmosphere appeared good-natured...

...until an Archbishop from the Greek Orthodox Church swatted a fly that landed on his cheek.

His action prompted a strong rebuke from the Jains, who reminded him that *every living thing was sacred*.

The Buddhists further increased the tension by suggesting *the fly could well have been a significant soul in a previous incarnation*.

The Taoists took issue. *Weren't all souls significant?*

The Catholics raised their eyes derisively. *There was a hierarchy when it came to such matters. Someone ultimately had to be in charge and, therefore, deemed closer to God.*

Why? the Quakers challenged.

And deemed by whom? added the Wesleyans.

Ever heard of the Apostolic Succession?

That was just a contrivance for seizing the reins of power, offered the Gnostics.

No it wasn't. It was God's will.

Says who?

God!

Not according to the Bible.

That depends on how you interpret it.

Interpret it? shrieked the Christian Fundamentalists. *How*

360

escorted inside, Lieutenant. Give you a chance to put all that excellent drill training to good use.'

'But... sir!'

'Do as you're told, laddie,' hissed the General through clenched teeth. 'We don't want this lot mixing any more than is necessary, now do we?' He smiled warmly at the group of Cardinals like a demented ventriloquist.

The courtyard was now abuzz with men of every race and religion... and even the occasional female, if you looked hard enough... seemingly competing with each other through their attire. This was also true of their facial hair... *most* of the women excepted. This was an historic meeting of leaders. Not of the political variety, but of the myriad of religions spanning the globe. There was not a religion known to man that had not sent a representative to the temple... though not *all* had made it.

The absent exception to this total representation of faith on Earth was a delegation from the Amish. Although invited, they'd insisted on using a horse-drawn carriage to attend the meeting in accordance with their strict religious practices and were nowhere to be seen.

As the last bus threw open its doors, a plume of heavily scented smoke wafted out, gently caressing the nostrils of those who were within inhaling distance. It was followed by a group of swaying Calvinists, a Coptic priest who appeared to have rediscovered the meaning of the Universe and, finally, a band of grinning Rastafarians, complete with oversized hats... and oversized cigarettes.

The drab temple walls of Arwan El Kahab stood at odds with the multi-coloured crowd now assembling in front of them.

The Sons of the Shaken Spear had chosen the location for their holy place with considered care. It was extremely well concealed, the stone walls abutting a sudden end to a narrow gorge that ran perfectly West to East from the valley into the mountains.

The temple itself had been built with functionality in mind, rather than an eye to increasing the sale of souvenir postcards. The only nod and a wink towards its significant heritage was a against the tight chin strap of his helmet.

'Jeez, man,' the officer drawled. 'You look like someone's just pushed a gun up your ass. It's too hot for all that West Point crap. You're about to witness history being made, so try to relax a little and enjoy it.'

'Yes, sir!' shouted the Lieutenant stiffly.

'And Lieutenant.'

'Sir!'

'May I remind you this is a sacred site. Show some fuckin' respect and quit with the goddam shouting. Besides, it's so quiet I could hear a grasshopper fart.'

'Yes... sir,' answered the Lieutenant awkwardly.

The senior officer turned his head and squinted at the procession of cars and buses beginning to enter through the stone arch, a phalanx of motorcycle outriders peeling away and pulling smartly over to the far side of the courtyard.

'Here we go,' he muttered. 'The international God squad... This could get interesting!' He threw his cigar to the ground, grinding it with the heel of his boot, and strolled over to where a number of men were attempting to extricate themselves – along with a mass of white and purple robes – from a stretched Mercedes.

The Lieutenant followed clumsily behind, his stuttering West Point stride at odds with his superior's casual amble.

'Ah... your eminences.' said the officer, extending his hand in greeting to the nearest of the emerging luminaries. 'I trust your journey's been bearable.'

'Apparently a little more so than yours, General,' replied the addressee, observing the officer's other hand inelegantly reorganising his underwear.

'Not exactly built for comfort!' said the General, with a broad smile.

'You or the Jeep?' said the luminary, with a thinner one.

'I meant my pants,' replied the General civilly.

'Sir?' interjected the Lieutenant. 'May I interrupt?'

'No you may not,' said the General, without bothering to look at him. 'I'm sure the Cardinals here would like to be respect. It was an integral part of their training to recognise that should conflict arise between a thin piece of rotating steel and a rather large static piece of mountainside, the former would come off the worst every time, along with those it was keeping in the air. This wasn't a situation they wanted to hang around in for longer than was necessary.

'Team Leader... this is Yankee Zero Three... No sign of bandits... Target appears clear... Repeat... target appears clear.'

'Affirmative, Yankee Zero Three,' came the crackled reply. 'Convoy closing in on target. Make yourselves scarce.'

The swirls of dust began to dance to a more chaotic tune as the pilots wasted no time in removing themselves from their precarious airspace.

Eventually, the drone of their engines faded and the dust settled.

But peace was short-lived.

The first vehicle to pass under the stone-shouldered arch and into the large courtyard was one of many troop-carrying trucks spearheading the string of vehicles now snaking their way along the gorge. Its wheels had barely stopped turning when dozens of heavily armed soldiers leapt from beneath its canopy and dispersed themselves to various corners of the courtyard in a well-rehearsed manoeuvre. Other trucks followed, their occupants employing the same procedure.

It wasn't until a jeep swerved dramatically to a halt behind the last of them, and its passenger dismounted, that the first words were spoken.

They consisted of a profanity, followed by a crude reference to the said profaner's chafed buttocks and belonged to an overweight, cigar-chewing officer who stood, hands on over-ample hips, surveying the stone edifice in front of him like a reluctant tourist.

'Men deployed, sir!' barked a younger and much fitter looking officer type who had run to join him.

The senior officer turned to his Lieutenant and studied him for a while. The soldier remained frozen, awaiting his orders, the only perceptible movement a slight grinding of his jaw good reason why I shouldn't be allowed to wander about these fine works of art as I please. This is, after all, a *public* gallery.'

'Certainly, sir,' said the guard calmly. 'Would the fact you appear to have relieved yourself whilst you were asleep be a good place to start?'

Donald looked down at a large, dark stain on the front of his trousers. 'Ah....' he said quietly.

He was still trying to think of a reason why urinating in a public place should not be grounds for removal as he was physically manhandled through the gallery's doors by the security guard's larger partner, Brian.

Brian was one of those security guards who did not see the necessity in spending hours developing the art of detached sarcasm. He spent them instead developing his biceps, triceps and a neck wider than his head.

A line of queuing school children watched in amusement as a sodden-trousered vagrant was roughly deposited on the steps outside.

* * *

The dust swirled manically around the temple's courtyard, whipped into an unwelcome frenzy by the downforce from the helicopters' blades. It had been quite happy to sit there for decade upon decade, quietly minding its own business and doing nothing in particular. Occasionally, it would find itself stirred into action by the odd, disorientated gust of wind that happened to chance upon the narrow gorge in which the temple of Arwan El Kahab lay hidden. But now the twenty-first century had decided to pay it a visit, the heavy droning *phut, phut* of the rotaries ricocheting from the valley walls, desecrating the very sanctity of the temple's stones and rudely trampling upon generations of calm.

The various life forms that managed to eke out an existence within the temple's perimeter scuttled to the nearest nook or cranny and burrowed a little deeper than was usual.

The pilots eyed the steep walls of the gorge with professional beginning to redden. 'This is an art gallery, sir, not a hostel for the homeless. If you don't remove yourself and your baggage immediately, I'll have you and it physically thrown out!'

'How dare you!' said the man indignantly, following his chastisement with another outburst. 'OF COURSE I'LL TELL HIM!' He calmed himself. 'I'll have you know I possess a very nice home, thank you.'

'Then perhaps you'd kindly go to it, sir!'

'Aha!' said the man, as if he'd just played checkmate. 'That's just what they want me to do!'

The security guard looked at him wearily, his shoulders dropping as he concluded that a few minutes of humouring was preferable to an embarrassing scuffle in public. 'And who are *they?*'

'That's the problem. I don't rightly know. You see... I'm getting messages, but they're all rather confused. Something big's about to happen, but I can't work out what. It involves works of art and massive underhandedness. Apart from that, it's not making much sense.'

'*Really?*' muttered the guard. 'Look, sir, I...'

'Donald!' A hand shot out in greeting. 'Donald Tucker-Jenkins.'

By instinct, the guard made as if to return the gesture, then thought better of it as he viewed the state of the hand he'd be making contact with. He gave a half-hearted salute instead, along with a Freudian click of his heels. 'Look, Donald...'

'Mr Tucker-Jenkins to you,' said Donald firmly. 'And I'm here to keep an eye on the paintings.'

The guard looked at him exasperatingly. 'Ditto.'

'Ah...' said Donald, with yet another checkmate expression. 'But they know that *you* are.'

'Would this be the *they* of whom you have no idea who *they* are?' asked the guard, reemploying his powers of sarcasm.

'Precisely!'

'Then I'll keep an eye out for them, sir. Now... Thank you for your assistance. And if I can just escort you to the entrance...'

'Just one second!' interjected Donald feistily. 'Give me *one* on a bench designated for members of the public.'

This retort was delivered in the detached, matter-of-fact mode of sarcasm security guards secretly delight in using. It is something they work hard at... usually whilst sat for interminable lengths of time in the human equivalent of broom cupboards or whilst standing at supermarket entrances, pretending not to have noticed that their hat is the wrong size for their head. Like their idols – traffic policeman – they perfect this art in order to give the illusion that they are addressing you from a parallel Universe; one where the concept of *getting personal* does not exist... along with its associated consequence, *getting thumped*. It is the aural equivalent of not making eye contact.

'I *am* a member of the public,' grinned the gentleman.

'For members of the public... to... sit... upon,' responded the guard tersely.

The gentleman roused himself from his prone position and rubbed his face vigorously with the palm of an extremely filthy hand. 'You obviously have no idea who I am,' he said grandly. His voice was deep and rich; his accent suggesting his clothes had once seen better times, not to mention washing powder. He moved his hand to a shock of unkempt, hair. 'IT'S ALRIGHT!' he yelled at the top of his voice, addressing the empty space to his left and nearly causing the security guard to have a heart attack. 'LEAVE IT TO ME! I'LL HANDLE IT!'

The guard looked at him uneasily, the penny having dropped that the safety bubble around his parallel Universe had just been popped.

'Now, now... No need for that, sir,' he said cautiously, bending down to pick up some carrier bags that had been propped against the end of the bench. 'Let's just help you up with your things and get you on your way.'

'Don't you *dare* touch those!' bellowed the man, grabbing hold of the bags and clutching them tightly to his chest. 'IT'S OK!' he shouted. 'EQUIPMENT SECURED! NO NEED TO PANIC!'

'Right, that's it!' The guard straightened up, his face

the same roof.'

'Talkin' of roofs...' Bob scowled at the vaulted stonework above him. 'You'd think they'd have picked a Hyatt Regency or somewhere with a bit of friggin' air conditioning. But this ancient dump? What's that all about? It don't even have any goddam electricity!' He lashed out with his foot at one of many small, mushroom-shaped stone plinths radiating out concentrically from a far larger one in the centre. 'And as for the prehistoric seating arrangements... They're gonna end up with piles the size of pomegranates sat on these friggin' relics!' He shook his head. 'I tell you, Chad... it don't add up. Our boys didn't even have this freak-hole on a map. They had to route a spy satellite over to check it actually *existed*. So how the hell did *that* lot know about it?'

Chad picked up a large holdall. 'Our boys don't have the location for *God* on their maps, but our expected guests will quite happily tell you how to find him!'

'And the secrecy?' Bob frowned. 'They call up out of the blue requesting a military escort. Then... when asked what in hell they're up to, conveniently turn Trappist.'

'Well... if you can bear to drag that sodden butt crack of yours back to the van, we'll get everything switched on and wait to find out the answer.'

* * *

'Excuse me, sir!' The security guard rocked backwards and forwards on the balls of his feet, so as to fill in time whilst waiting for a response. 'Sir!' he said a little louder. 'You can't sleep here! You'll have to move on.'

'Mmm?' The dishevelled figure whom he was addressing began to stir.

'That's a gentleman. Let's be having you now.'

The *gentleman* in question opened his eyes and viewed the guard with distain. 'It's alright, officer,' he whispered loudly. 'I'm on a *very* important mission.'

'No you're not, sir,' replied the guard dispassionately. 'You're

His request bounced its way around the cavernous walls.

'You'll have to make this the last one, Chad. Command have been on the radio. The convoy's getting close.'

Chad took the small object from his colleague's hand and carefully placed it inside the hole. 'No problem. This one gives us a total of six audio and four visual. That's more than enough surveillance for a place this size. I just gotta place this and we're outta here.'

'Not a moment too soon,' whinged his colleague, tugging at the rear of his trousers. 'I've got so much sweat running down my butt crack, I ain't sure whether I'm wearing my pants or swimming in 'em!'

'TMI,' groaned Chad 'Besides... with a surname like Papadopoulos, I'd have thought you'd be genetically engineered to cope with such heat.'

'Listen... Just because my old man sweats his *arxidia* off in the kitchen of a Greek restaurant whilst yours plays with his in some air-conditioned attorney's office, it don't mean my butt crack is any less prone to a drenching than yours!'

'I was referring to what is probably a very fine lineage stretching back to the Helladic or Mycenaean civilisations, Bob. But, as always... you've managed to steer the conversation back to the rear end of the human anatomy.'

Bob passed wind in protest.

'There... perfect!' Chad leant back to admire his handiwork. 'They'll need divine intervention to spot those!'

'Given some of 'em claim to receive it, you'd better pray it ain't forthcoming,' said Bob, wiping an uncomfortable mixture of sweat and dust from his brow. 'I've never known Command so spooked. The top brass have been running around like someone's rammed chilli-coated suppositories up their a...'

Chad raised his eyebrows expectantly.

'Yeah, yeah,' acknowledged Bob, 'But you've gotta admit... this meeting's really got 'em shitting shrapnel.'

Chad lowered himself to the floor and brushed the dirt from his clothes. 'Hardly surprising. It's a miracle these guys are acknowledging one another, let alone agreeing to meet under

'I could switch it off,' suggested Norman feebly.

'It is of no consequence now,' said Gabriel, flexing his wings as if preparing to take flight. 'It is obvious you are not ready.' The aura around him began to flicker.

'Whoa!' shouted Norman, as a chill flowed into the room. 'Where are you going?'

'Goodbye Norman. You must be given time to dwell on your experience. I *will* visit you again... and maybe without scaring you next time.'

'Wait!' shouted Norman. 'Next time...? *When* next time?'

The vision of Gabriel and his ethereal entourage began to fade. The heavenly choir performed a diminuendo, leaving the hum of late-night traffic to take its place. After a few seconds, all traces of the light had extinguished.

The flat seemed cramped and dirty.

'What about the message?' shouted Norman, his voice suddenly sounding ridiculous in the emptiness.

There was a short silence.

'Oh... that?' came a faint voice from the ether. 'The entire fabric of the Universe is in danger of total and utter annihilation... and we've chosen you to help us save it.'

A toilet flushed on the floor above.

*　　　*　　　*

Chad Cheadle blew into the recess, removing centuries of dust from the ancient stonework. He felt tentatively about inside the small alcove, trying hard to recollect whether scorpions inhabited that god-forsaken part of the world. It was probably not the best way to find out. But when you've been raised in the privileged, well-manicured suburbs of Boston, Massachusetts, the concept of *death by venomous bite* doesn't seriously enter your psyche.

Fortunately for him, the scorpions for whom the recess was home were preoccupied with scavenging for food in a corner at the rear of the temple.

'OK. Pass it up.'

Norman would have let out an even longer, lower whistle...
were it not for the fact he'd forgotten to breathe in since the last
one.

'Oh boy,' he wheezed. 'Top banana!'

'Not quite,' said Gabriel. 'But certainly not an everyday
occurrence.'

'I got *that* bit prior to my first blacking out,' confirmed
Norman weakly.

'First?'

'Yes... I'm off for another... Goodbye.' Norman's eyes rolled
towards the top of his head.

'NORMAN!' The room and everything in it, everything that
had ever been in it and everything that would ever be in it,
reverberated with his name. 'You *must* hear what it is I have
come to say!'

Norman's eyes sheepishly backtracked.

'You must fully absorb what I am about to impart.'

Norman nodded lamely.

'It is of the utmost importance your mind records every
detail.'

As soon as Norman's stumbling thoughts registered the word
"*records*", they tripped over the image of his webcam.

There was an instant change of hue in the room. The
cherubs began gravitating towards the spot where his mind had
landed.

Norman desperately tried to erase the device from his
thoughts. But as soon as he focused on doing so, it caused his
neuropile to light up like a neon-illuminated Christmas tree.

'Norman!' bellowed Gabriel, shaking his head in
admonishment. 'I'm very disappointed in you. For one so
bright, you have proved to be extremely foolish.'

Norman's thoughts scrambled for an excuse. 'Don't take it
personally. I'm just having trouble with your existing. I thought
a bit of concrete evidence might...'

'Faith!' Gabriel interrupted him. 'That's all that was required.
It's what links us all to the ultimate power behind the Universe.
Faith is trust... Trust is love.'

'Of course! You don't think I've gone to all this trouble just to scare you?'

'To be quite honest,' sighed Norman, 'I'm not sure *what* to think anymore.'

This wasn't strictly true. His logical thought process – in an attempt to rescue itself from total redundancy – had seized upon an idea.

Fumbling behind his back, he surreptitiously located his webcam. It was normally used for sending pictures of himself over the internet... usually to allegedly attractive girls who turned out – after some rather lengthy and steamy correspondence – to be not only singularly unattractive, but of a different sex altogether.

Moving it to one side, so that the angel was within its scope, he orientated the fingers of his other hand on a keyboard and secretly triggered its recording.

'Maybe it would be better if we started right from the beginning,' he suggested, desperate to prevent his guest from spotting the direction in which his mind was travelling. 'Perhaps a formal introduction would help. I realise you're an angel ... but do you have a name?'

No sooner had the question left his lips, than the light in the room increased in brilliance and the cherubs, who had hitherto been content to float idly about, stirred themselves into action. Once again, the sound of a heavenly choir issued forth.

'Given the perspective from which you've chosen to interpret me, I am not just *any* angel,' announced Norman's visitor above it, puffing out his wings with sudden authority. 'I am...'

The heavenly choir swelled majestically.

'...an *Archangel*.'

Norman let out a long, low whistle.

There was something akin to a heavenly timpani roll.

'And you shall know me as...'

A stirring fanfare shook the light fittings.

'Gabriel.'

A crescendo of gorgeousness embraced the room.

crowded into his halls of residence kitchen.

The reason why it had been done with such ritualistic reverence eluded him until about ten minutes after he'd imbibed the foul tasting offering. As a yellow tea-towel gently morphed itself into a grinning teddy bear and enquired as to his well-being, the thought occurred to him that all was not quite as it should be. *Alice Through the Looking Glass* began to appear a sane and creditable read. A spaghetti stain on the wall had kept him entertained for more time than the cooker clock was capable of showing, whilst music from a nearby set of stereo speakers flew at him as a stream of three-dimensional notes, swirling above his head until they exploded like fireworks, raining down on him as confetti.

His thoughts had waltzed their way through the rest of the evening, giddily observing everything as if for the very first time until, just as he was convincing himself that the meaning of life had something to do with a stunning new shade of purple he'd just discovered, he found himself jettisoned down a mental drain of despair and self-loathing, causing him to throw up over an open bread bin and the last communal packet of cream crackers.

He was never invited to partake again.

But this time it was different. Reality's walls had bent so much on the first occasion, he'd even believed himself attractive to women... his confidence buoyed by the knowledge he could fly. But if the angel was an hallucination, everything else was exactly as it should be. Stains were stains, tea-towels tea-towels and – rather than a member of the opposite sex – the only thing he was likely to make an impression on, should he choose to leap out of the window, was the pavement.

It was all too confusing.

'Not really,' opined the angel.

'Oh God...' groaned Norman... then added politely, 'Mind if I pass out again?'

'Well... as a matter of fact, I do. I haven't delivered my message yet.'

'Message?'

appearing as everyone from Buddha to Shiva, Mohammed to Brahma, Nanak to Lakshmi. And as for Vishnu... you can pick any one of ten possible manifestations with *that* guy.'

'And atheists?' asked Norman cautiously. 'What if I told you I don't believe in the workings of Heaven?'

'It's a bit late for that, wouldn't you say?' The angel acknowledged the host of cherubs floating lazily about the room. 'I'm just grateful you didn't give me a harp. They're so passé. And you've certainly done me proud with these wings!' He ruffled them as if trying them out for the first time. 'Very impressive... though totally unnecessary. They're a testament to your logical thinking. People envisage us floating in the air and assume we must have something to keep us there. It's the same thing with fairies.'

'*Fairies?*'

'Another incarnation we're occasionally forced to adopt. You see... everyone believes in something. I've been envisaged as everything from a dead relative to a water sprite. Curiously, a four foot high, silver-skinned creature with almond-shaped eyes seems to be the current favourite. Most extraordinary!' The angel allowed himself a half-smile. 'Though there's a tribe in Papua New Guinea who beat even *that*. They scare themselves witless imagining us as this multi-tusked creature, the top half of which resembles a monkey... the bottom half, a crocodile. Trouble is, they never hang around long enough to hear what it is we've come to say!'

Norman didn't blame them. He wished *he'd* run away instead of engaging an apparition in philosophical conversation. His senses were feeling like *nonsenses*... which was most uncomfortable for someone who prided themselves in their ability to understand the world in black and white. Shades of grey could be tolerated... colours were for dreamers... but hovering angels in the small hours of the morning?

This wasn't the first time reality and he had begged to differ. He'd had a slight *contretemps* with it once before. It had occurred at university, on an occasion when a large saucepan of mushroom broth had been passed around the eager students

373

primitive level.' The angel glanced at his chest. '*Very* primitive, in some cases.'

Norman's bleached tripe pallor became suffused with pink.

'Don't worry,' said the angel. 'I've had far worse. You'd be surprised what you encounter when you drop in on people unannounced during the dead of night.'

'Perhaps you should give them a warning,' suggested Norman. 'Slip a note under their door. Something along the lines of "You're about to receive a heavenly visitation... Put the kettle on".'

'I'm afraid that's out of the question,' smiled the angel. 'We have a problem with a certain aspect of your dimension. We don't do *solid*.'

Seeking to verify the claim, Norman reached out so as to touch the edge of the angel's shimmering aura. His hand passed straight through, a mild, tingling sensation the only thing to greet it, along with a slight drop in temperature.

'See what I mean? I wouldn't be able to hold the pen... let alone a cup and saucer. That's why I try the "fear not" approach. It's traditional... if a little optimistic.'

Transfixed, Norman continued waving his hand through the angel, not bothering to consider whether this might be unpleasant for his illuminated guest or, indeed, extremely rude.

'I wouldn't concern yourself too much with the appearance side of things, if I were you. It's all in your head. You're merely seeing what you *think* you should under the circumstances.'

'So, let me get this right...' said Norman, struggling to get to grips with a concept that, if possessing handles, would not only be hypothetical ones, but through which his hands would pass even if they weren't. 'I'm only seeing you as an angel... because I *think* you're one?'

'Oh, I'm an angel alright. But angels take many forms. True... most in the Western world see us as you are doing now... romantically ethereal... gorgeous set of wings... that sort of thing. But some opt for an image of the Madonna... or even the Nazarene himself. But find yourself in the East and it's a completely different story. We're kept well on our toes...

Norman would stop concentrating on the area above his midriff.

'But that's just it!' stuttered Norman. 'I *didn't* expect to see you. In fact, you're the *last* thing I expected to see!'

'I was referring to the *way* you're seeing me,' clarified the angel. 'The image your subconscious has chosen to project me as.'

'My *subconscious?*' Norman's stare turned inward. 'Then... I'm *imagining* all this...! You're not real...! Oh, thank God...! For one awful minute I thought I *wasn't* going mad!'

'I hate to disappoint you,' said the angel, 'but you're perfectly sane... and I, in an existential sense, at least, am perfectly real.'

'Excuse me?'

'Real is relative... I'm real in the sense that I exist, but not in a dimension your senses could recognise. So I've bypassed them and gone direct. What you're witnessing is your brain's interpretation of my vibration.'

Norman tried to corral his scattering thoughts and apply some logical reasoning. He shut his eyes to catch the angel out, but to his amazement, could still see the shimmering outline of his visitor standing in front of him.

'You shouldn't be so surprised,' said the angel. 'It happens all the time. Like when you dream. Whole worlds created without the presence of matter.'

'But that's different,' insisted Norman.

'Is it?'

Norman considered the idea. *Bollocks!* he thought, after he had.

'Not a word I can say I've heard uttered in my presence before!' flinched the angel.

For Norman, things had just taken a turn for the worst. 'I didn't utter it,' he ventured slowly. 'I *thought* it!'

'Same thing where I come from,' shrugged the angel.

'You can read my mind?' Norman groaned and desperately tried to ignore the sight of Xanthia's magnificent breasts uncannily positioned beyond his visitor.

'Let's just say... I can *feel* it. It vibrates too, though on a very

Norman spun and found himself face to face with his inquisitor, a host of cherubs circling patiently in attendance. He opened his mouth to scream but nothing came out.

'Only... you look a little pale.'

Such a statement would have been appropriate at any ordinary moment in Norman's life. His skin's failure to embrace the sun – or any daylight, come to that – meant it had the permanent pallor of trench foot. But at such an *extra*ordinary moment as this, it was doing an excellent impersonation of bleached tripe.

'And *you* look...' Norman fished for the appropriate word... hoping that whilst doing so, he might be rescued by yet another blackout, sparing him the few niggling problems *being conscious* seemed to be causing at that particular moment in time.

It didn't happen.

The angel raised his eyebrows expectantly.

'Translucent!' blurted Norman finally.

Although looking at the perfectly formed vision of a three-dimensional heavenly messenger, he could see the poster of the love of his life, Xanthia, through its chest... which seemed even more bizarre, given it wasn't just her *face* he could see.

The circling cherubs were doing their best not to smirk.

Xanthia had entered Norman's life via page three of a tabloid newspaper, and from that moment on had taken over his nocturnal fantasies as well as his bedsit wall. Whilst realising she might not be his intellectual equal, Norman had convinced himself that – should they ever meet – she would see past his nerdish appearance, recognise a kindred spirit and fall madly in love... the two living happily ever after.

In reality, the following would apply:

$$likelihood\ of\ event \ x \ \frac{positive\ thinking}{scale\ of\ unattractiveness} = in\ your\ dreams$$

'I look as you expect to see me,' said the angel, wishing

Its abilities are limited. It's either there or it isn't... a state of being or not being. To be or not to be.

On its own, it would marvel in wonder at the power required to produce even the smallest tic on the face of the village idiot. But connected to its neighbours, as part of a fabulously intricate network and working for the good of the whole, it has become the force behind our history, the exploration of our present and the hope for our future.

Connection is king. The better your neural network, the higher your intellect. The more advanced your synaptic interrelations, the greater your chance of being able to stand in public without dribbling.

Ask any troll.

For an aspiring brain cell... it's not *what* you know, but *who* you know.

Thus the neurologically well-connected pass through life able to think beyond the normal confines of structured thought; some finding answers to questions where no one thought of looking... or understood the questions in the first place; some achieving levels of skill that push back the boundaries of art and science; and some occasionally developing a strange propensity for wearing odd socks and stained kipper ties.

Norman Penkridge belonged to the latter.

Norman slowly opened his eyes and waited for his brain to engage. His head was throbbing and he was trying to work out why he was staring up at the ceiling whilst not wearing pyjamas. Gingerly pulling himself to his feet, his memory came trickling back.

Something to do with an angel... and a ball of light.

He stopped to consider his position. Zorgan was frozen in time on the computer screen, patiently awaiting the player's next command, whilst Spikey was nowhere to be seen.

'Oh... thank God!' he sighed. 'It was a dream! A bloody *dream!*'

'Are you alright?' enquired the seven-foot angel standing directly behind him.

Then came the buses. Not the rusty, open-windowed sort that people hang from or carry chickens in... but the air-conditioned, darkened-windows type that suggested none of its occupants had been required to have their ticket punched.

The convoy was rounded off by a string of military jeeps and yet more trucks carrying soldiers.

The shepherds watched in awed silence as it passed, heading in the direction of the abandoned temple. Not a syllable was uttered until the last speck of dust had settled, the convoy had faded out of sight and a familiar nothing, once more, filled the air.

'Erm... did you see what I just saw?' enquired Shepherd One cautiously.

Shepherd Two and Shepherd Three nodded slowly.

'In that case... I think I've got a headache.'

Shepherds Two and Three nodded again.

The flies had disappeared.

* * *

Becoming a genius is not that difficult. At least not for the genius, who – let's face it – has very little say in the matter.

Depending on your doctrine, intelligence is either a gift from the Gods or the triumph of three thousand, seven hundred million years of evolution... give or take the odd million and depending on which day you started counting.

At first sight, they are such opposing camps that the myopia of dogma usually prevents us from seeing a third possibility... that *both* the above are true.

If we were to break intelligence down into its lowest common denominator, we would find ourselves squinting at the humble brain cell.

As an individual, this microscopic fellow could be forgiven for having a sense of worthlessness... not to mention a height complex. As just one of a trillion such cells within the cerebral cortex, it could also be forgiven for having something of an identity crisis.

And then monotony stood on its head.

At first, it took the form of a lazy hum, building imperceptibly from the silence of the horizon and accompanied by a small cloud of dust that appeared to trace the line of the old road.

By the time the cloud had grown so large it obscured the hills behind and its accompanying hum was shaking the air, shepherds Two and Three, along with a rudely awoken Shepherd One, had become too transfixed to turn tail and run.

The first thing they saw break from the cover of the cloud was a large, wingless creature, with refulgent talons and bared teeth. It moved its vast bulk in a series of fits and starts, hovering in the air for a while as if waiting for the cloud below to catch up... then moving off again to repeat the procedure a little further along the road, like a dragonfly dancing above the surface of a pond.

At least... that's what the shepherds saw. Anyone else would probably have recognised it as a helicopter... and if they subscribed to *Military Enthusiast Monthly*... a Cobra V250 attack module, with heat-seeking missiles and rapid-fire capability, performing advanced scouting manoeuvres requisite for a following convoy. In fact... they would have eventually seen four such machines, upon the front of which had been painted a row of shark-like teeth... presumably to strike fear into the hearts of the enemy below... along with any non-combative shepherds in the vicinity.

The Cobra's *raison d'être* became obvious as it passed directly below the shepherds' vantage point. At the head of a vast convoy sped a number of military trucks, rows of armed soldiers visible beneath their flapping canopies. These were followed by a swarm of motorbike outriders, their charges a hotchpotch of civilian vehicles, mostly of the stretched limousine variety. Though there was one curious conveyance that looked like a glass tank on wheels, whose passenger – an old man dressed from head to toe in white – kept crossing himself every time it bounced over a pothole.

The two had snake-eyed each other for the best part of an hour.

Shepherd Three had then cautioned Shepherd One against the dangers of over-trimming... hoping his intervention might break the impasse.

Shepherd One, stunned by Shepherd Three's radical viewpoint, had dropped his eyes.

Shepherd Two had continued to eye Shepherd One suspiciously... until realising his opponent had fallen asleep.

'Tumbleweed!' shouted Shepherd Three excitedly, his outstretched finger straining to a point somewhere in the distance.

Shepherd Two hurriedly clambered to his knees, placing himself behind Shepherd Three so as to use his colleague's arm as a positioning sight.

'It's a huge bit!'

Shepherd One, startled from his slumber, shielded his eyes from the glare of the sun and measured their gaze. 'Would you be referring to that over there?' he asked, nodding in the same direction.

An hour of circling flies passed.

'Y...e...s,' replied Shepherd Three, drawing the word out with measured caution.

'Bush,' said Shepherd One nonchalantly, closing his eyes again.

'Ah...' Shepherd Three sheepishly let his finger drop.

Shepherd Two administered the mother of all admonishing stares and resumed his position. 'That's the seventh time in three years!' he moaned. 'I wouldn't mind, but it's always the same bloody bush!'

Shepherd One shook his head in disbelief for at least the next two hours, whilst Shepherd Three attempted to discover whether it was actually possible to observe his toenails growing.

been any to watch.

Across the floor of the valley ran a road. At least, it had *once* been a road. And it didn't so much run now as limp. The abandonment of the ancient temple of Arwan El Kahab, to which it had once conveyed travellers, had sealed its fate. The temple's occupants, a highly secretive sect calling themselves *The Sons of the Shaken Spear,* had claimed to have received messages from Heaven that a final, all-powerful Saviour would appear sometime towards the end of the sixteenth century and deliver the world from an impending catastrophe. But the sect disappeared into history when the date for the new Saviour's arrival came and went without so much as a postcard from him. The riveting distraction of a pilgrim's sandals in full, pious motion had long since been replaced by swirls of dust... and they weren't nearly half as interesting.

Flies circled the shepherds for the same reason their ancestors had circled the shepherds' ancestors... There was nothing better to do. How they longed to circle a pilgrim for a change... just like the old days. Had one appeared on the road, you would not have seen them for dust.

Literally.

Even the sky had little to do. It hung where it always had, impeccably blue, with not even the merest wisp of a cloud to tempt the imagination.

But there *was* an atmosphere. Not the one of severe, oppressive heat that was part of a weather spell the region had been experiencing for the last ten thousand years... but the kind that has three men shifting uncomfortably from one buttock to the other whilst trying hard to ignore each other's gaze. They hadn't spoken for a while.

When they had, Shepherd One had decided to break the previous hour's silence by announcing that he'd trimmed the wick of his oil lamp the night before.

Shepherd Two had looked at him incredulously for twenty minutes... then accused him of showing off. Was it not true Shepherd One had also claimed to have trimmed the wick of his oil lamp not more than a week ago?

not the brash fanfare one might expect, but a sound like a huge choir singing nothing in particular but very nicely thank you. It was the kind of music designed to calm the listener.

It wasn't working.

It was also the kind of music that usually heralds the appearance of something grand and mind-blowing.

That bit was.

As a circle of trumpet-blowing cherubs began to rotate slowly around the light's centre, there appeared in the midst of it all a magnificent, seven-foot angel… resplendent in heavenly robes and with a wingspan reaching from the corner bookshelf to the bathroom door.

66c Armageddon Terrace had just become the equivalent of a three-dimensional Botticelli painting.

Norman's jaw was now hanging so low, it was in danger of getting carpet burn.

The angel appeared to observe Norman for a short time then – to the accompaniment of the heavenly choir – spoke.

'Fear not,' it said, proffering a kindly smile.

Norman's power of speech had deserted him. His whole body would have followed, were it not for the fact his legs could no longer function. All he could manage was a barely audible gasp, which, if amplified, would have sounded remarkably like *'No shit!'*

There is one final option the logical brain can adopt when confronted by an apparent miracle, in order to prevent insanity… and that is shutdown, causing a total blackout.

Norman's brain adopted it.

*   *   *

The shepherds sat on their hill, observing the parched and barren valley below. It was the same sight their ancestors had observed for millennia before them, and *their* ancestors for millennia before that. Such was the mind-stupefying boredom provoked by this landscape, watching the grass grow would have been considered an indescribable pleasure… had there

Armageddon Terrace, Paddington, London. In fact... not the kind of occurrence you would expect *anywhere* in the known Universe.

A small ball of light, the size of an orange, appeared in front of a poster of page three stunner Xanthia. It did nothing for a few seconds... then, in an apparent change of heart, pulsated in time with the computer code. Not that Norman spotted the connection. His jaw had dropped to the level of imbecile, his eyes transfixed on the quivering globe.

The good thing about having an extremely logical mind is that, when encountering the unexplained, you attempt to explain it... well... er... logically. The bad thing is that when you fail – as will happen when observing any floating ball of light in your room – your brain has nowhere else to go... unlike that of a less logical person, who can at least avoid impending insanity by clinging to the concept of a miracle.

If, on a biologically linked scale of miracles, a floating ball of light ranked as your common or garden dust mite, what happened next would have to be marked down as an extremely overweight and pregnant blue whale.

The light ball exploded – like a supernova but on a bedsit scale – emitting a sudden burst of blinding light which then imploded, leaving the room bathed in a warm and shimmering glow. At the same time, all the usual external sounds of a room at night – late-night traffic hum, the rattle of a distant train, bouncing aardvarks etc. – became muffled and as one.

Norman felt his heart beating at the back of his throat.

He'd heard of light being described as harsh, gentle, cold or warm... but this one seemed... *friendly?*

He peered into its centre.

The 'overweight and pregnant blue whale' scale of miracle analogy was about to become pathetically inadequate. No animal large enough has ever existed that could be analogous to the host of trumpet blowing cherubs that began to emerge from it.

Had Norman been capable of clear and rational thought, he would have thought it curious that their trumpets gave forth places elsewhere. Some young men put grease on their hair to be fashionable. Norman didn't need to bother.

He moved the offending layer about a bit using the outside of a crumpled t-shirt, then replaced his glasses on an equally oiled nose.

The code continued to pulsate.

'Surely not a virus?' he mumbled, frantically attacking the keyboard in front of him, his eyes darting to and fro across the screen as if umpiring an extremely manic game of tennis.

Boing.

Ping.

Boing.

'Ping? Where the hell did *that* come from?'

He spun around and quizzed the pizza-encrusted microwave that had just announced dinner was ready. The problem was... it was two fifteen in the morning and – despite the noisy protestations of his stomach – he'd had nothing to put inside it for the last twenty-four hours.

Boing. Boing.

The lights in the bedsit flickered violently.

Voltage spikes! That had to be it.

The bedsit's wiring was appalling. You could turn the bathroom light off and on simply by having your upstairs neighbour stamp his feet. God help you if you were in the middle of a nice, relaxing, hot bath and he decided to put on his flamenco records.

Ping.

Phrrrrrrr.

'*Now* what?'

The video machine had switched itself on and was rewinding its tape.

Norman felt a strange tingle run up his spine... register with his brain... then escape back down through his underpants... along his legs... and earth itself in a worn, 1960's paisley carpet via a pair of supermarket's own-brand plimsolls.

And then it happened.

Not the kind of occurrence you would expect at 66c

jaws... appeared to draw breath... then let forth...

Spikey... the metal aardvark?

'What the fu_!'

Norman Penkridge slouched back in his chair – interlocked hands resting exasperatingly on his head – and watched as Spikey bounced around the screen in front of him to the accompaniment of a series of cartoon-like *boings*.

Such a sight would not have been out of place in *Spikey's Grand Day Out*, Norman's first serious foray into the world of computer games programming. But the little metal aardvark – loveable though he was – appeared a poor substitute for a hail of deadly, green acid-mucus... and had most definitely never been offered a cameo role in *Zorgan and the Perils of the Universe*.

Boing.

'This can't be!' Norman hastily examined the lines of computer code displayed on an adjacent screen. 'It's just not possible!'

There was only one thing more *just-not-possible* than a computer-generated aardvark – renowned as he might be for his fantastic jumping abilities – having jumped from one folder on the computer's hard drive into another... and that was that Norman Penkridge – when it came to programming – could have made a mistake.

Boing.

It just didn't happen.

Boing. Boing.

He understood computers because his mind functioned like one. He had the kind of IQ that frightened people... much the same way people frightened him.

As if Spikey's unwarranted trampolining wasn't alarming enough for such a logical mind, the lines of code began to pulsate and blur.

Norman removed a pair of thick, black-rimmed glasses, drew them to within squinting distance and examined their lenses. Perhaps, he reasoned, the aberration was due to the layer of grease that had been allowed to build up on them... much like it had on his cooker... kitchenette worktop... and quite a few

Princess Aihtnax cowered behind Zorgan, her protector's muscular frame shielding her from the approaching troll.

It stopped... a sense of victory in its stance, certain its opponent had used the last of his energy dispatching its fellow warriors. Raising a corner of its mouth, it let fall a slow, cascade of saliva. This, for a troll, was the equivalent of a smile... and is why you don't see many of them sitting in comedy clubs.

It drew its sword.

Zorgan dropped to one knee, head bowed, the sobbing princess helplessly clutching at his heaving, sweat-covered shoulders.

The troll seemed momentarily surprised that victory could be so easy... then raised its weapon in a little-too-prematurely-relaxed manner.

Cocksure in combat is fine. Cocksure can even unsettle your opponent and give you that vital edge. But cocksureness can also blind you to the possibility of that opponent rolling to one side, pulling his double-bladed titanium axe from the chest of a nearby corpse and sending it hurtling towards your Adam's apple – shards of glistening light emanating from its razor-sharp edges – all before you've had a chance to readjust an inappropriately supercilious grin.

For the record... cocksure is quickly replaced by acute embarrassment as you realise it's not the wind whistling past your ears you can feel, but your ears whistling past the wind.

head – body = deep shit

Victorious, Zorgan turned to comfort the princess. But their embrace was short lived. Above them came the sound of giant wings dissecting the air, a colossal shadow enveloping the ground below. Zorgan instinctively turned his gaze skyward to meet the threat, but time had surely outrun him. He was weapon-less... and what little energy he had possessed was now spent. The hideous form above opened its stinking, razor-sharp

386

much as the faintest impression of their buttocks on the bar-stool of existence.

Others – more sanguine – see the slaking of their thirst as the purpose; the glass gloriously half full and a gift from some higher power, draining the last drop with a religious zeal that comes from believing that when they're done, the brewery awaits.

But then there are those exquisite exceptions... a rare few who – having drunk their fill – bid *adieu*, yet place a full glass back on the table. They have achieved immortality... though not through the cheating of death, but by the realisation that death is a cheat.

For – as sure as you are reading this – it will appear one day... ghoulishly cowled, scythe in hand, silently beckoning... demanding the removal of your presence from time's journey... its skeletal finger summoning the cessation of your thoughts, feelings and everything you've fondly come to think of as *you*.

If the maths helps...

$$death = 0$$

Resistance is futile. After all... the shock will have been enough to kill you.

But what Death will fail to inform you – in all its melodramatic muteness – is that you are allowed to leave a part of that *you* behind.

Those who realised this and prepared in advance, now stand for all time in history, their psyches still burning bright, expressing themselves perdurably and inspiring others. These are the great artists of genius: painters, sculptors, writers and composers who reached into their souls for answers to their three score years and ten, and found a way to encode in their art what they discovered, in order that others might one day discover it too.

*   *   *

To be or not to be? That is not only the question... it also happens to be the answer.

When *Homo erectus* first brushed the dirt from his fingers, noticed they came in convenient bunches of ten and inadvertently discovered arithmetic, little did he realise the psychological burden this would heap upon mankind. For, in doing so, those who followed would be able to calculate just how stupefyingly puny their allocation of three score years and ten was when matched against the gargantuan age of the Universe.

$$13,820,000,000 - 70 = unfair$$

Worse still, they would also come to appreciate just how disturbingly finite three score years and ten appears within the greater scheme of things.

[the ability to reason anything at all] –
([the ability to reason anything at all] x [time in which to do it] x
[unfair]) = death

From *Homo erectus* to *Homo permanently horizontalus* in the blink of the cosmological eye.

Ever since these epiphanies, man has quested for not only the reason behind such injustice, but more to the point... the point itself.

Many conclude there isn't one. Fatalistically supping from life's half empty glass until time is called, they depart without so

We are all in this together.

There is no such thing as separateness...

Everything is connected to everything else...

Dedicated to Sarah Jane Nye for love and encouragement in this world…

and Daphne Isobel Nye for love and encouragement in another.